A HEART
MOST CERTAIN

Books by Melissa Jagears

*Love by the Letter**
A Bride for Keeps
A Bride in Store
A Bride at Last

TEAVILLE MORAL SOCIETY

*Engaging the Competition***
A Heart Most Certain

*e-novella. Also included in the *With All My Heart* novella collection.
**e-novella. Also included in the *With This Ring?* novella collection.

TEAVILLE
MORAL SOCIETY

A Heart
Most Certain

Melissa Jagears

BethanyHouse

a division of Baker Publishing Group
Minneapolis, Minnesota

Published by Bethany House Publishers
11400 Hampshire Avenue South
Bloomington, Minnesota 55438
www.bethanyhouse.com

Bethany House Publishers is a division of
Baker Publishing Group, Grand Rapids, Michigan

Printed in the United States of America

ISBN 978-0-7642-1751-7

Library of Congress Control Number: 2016931075

Unless otherwise indicated, Scripture quotations are from the King James Version
of the Bible.

Scripture quotations labeled NASB are from the New American Standard Bible®, copy-
right © 1960, 1962, 1963, 1968, 1971, 1972, 1973, 1975, 1977, 1995 by The Lockman
Foundation. Used by permission. (www.Lockman.org)

This is a work of fiction. Names, characters, incidents, and dialogues are products
of the author's imagination and are not to be construed as real. Any resemblance to
actual events or persons, living or dead, is entirely coincidental.

Cover design by Koechel Peterson & Associates / Jon Godfredson
Cover mansion photo by Cindy Price

Author represented by Natasha Kern Literary Agency

16   17   18   19   20   21   22   7   6   5   4   3   2   1

To Karen Riekeman,
who saved Nicholas from being named Friedrich, listened
to me babble about this story for hours, read a draft of
this despite difficult circumstances, and is one of the main
reasons I'll miss living in the middle of nowhere.

1

Lydia King took a tentative step into Mr. Lowe's hazy office, feeling like Bob Cratchit approaching Scrooge. Had Cratchit's heart pitter-pattered as fast as hers? Except his heartbeat wouldn't have had anything to do with Scrooge's looks—thin blue lips, pointed nose, and red eyes, per Dickens.

Scrooge wasn't a fraction as handsome as Mr. Lowe. His dark sideswept hair, strong jaw shadowed with stubble, and piercing hazel eyes made him one of the best-looking men in Teaville.

"Are you coming in any farther?" Mr. Lowe raised his right eyebrow and tipped his head toward an ornate green leather chair, giving her a tilted smile. "Have a seat."

She squared her shoulders and glided over to the fancy chair—a strange piece of furniture to be positioned in the middle of a lumber office otherwise bare of anything but plain wood walls, a massive desk, and a man as good-looking as the sawdust in the office was thick. A layer of powdery dust covered every nook and cranny—despite the fact Mr. Lowe likely did no manual labor at the sawmill—and flighty bits danced to the sawmill's whine in the sunlight streaming through the unadorned windows.

Above Mr. Lowe's amused brow, a few feathery wood flakes rested on his wavy dark hair. He couldn't be as terrible as the ladies from the moral society insisted. Not with that smile.

She grinned back and took a deep breath. "You may not know my name, Mr. Lowe, but perhaps you recognize me from church. I'm Lydia King." She trailed her slender fingers through the silty dust covering the brass tacks on the end of the chair's arm. "On behalf of the Teaville Ladies Moral Society, I've been tasked to present you with the opportunity to support our—"

"No."

She blinked. "I haven't finished asking yet."

He tucked his pencil behind his ear and crossed his arms. "The answer will still be no."

"But you don't even know what worthy cause we've decided to undertake this year." She squeezed the armrests. Dickens had gotten Scrooge all wrong—he definitely did not have red eyes or thin blue lips. They were hazel and a manly pink, respectively.

"Perhaps it's like last year's?" The show of white teeth against dark stubble made him decidedly handsomer, even if his smile was more of a sneer. He looked toward the ceiling. "I believe you ladies decided our church needed a new bell."

"The old system was dangerous. Why, with each pull, the bell could have crashed down on any one of the children."

"Then forgo ringing the bell."

Well, didn't he have all the answers. But the cold glint in his eye wouldn't silence her. Throwing back her shoulders, she locked onto his stare. Money was needed if they were to increase production and help more families this winter. And not only would his money do more good for the poor outside of his pockets than in them, but Mrs. Little seemed to believe that her getting a donation from Mr. Lowe would prove whether or not Lydia was worthy of marrying her son. "I'm sure this year's project will meet your approval, if you'd let me share."

He shrugged. "I was trying to save you breath."

"I haven't a shortage of breath."

His lips twitched as he leaned back in his chair. He pulled the pencil from behind his ear and rolled it between his fingers. "Then do share, Miss King."

"We ladies quilt at our weekly meetings, but cutting out the blocks by hand takes a lot of time. With machines, we could do more. We'd like to—"

"I'm sorry to interrupt, sir." Mr. Lowe's secretary poked his head through the door, his bulbous nose out of place on his rail-thin body. "There's been an accident. Nothing terrible, but it needs your immediate attention."

Mr. Lowe crossed the room and glanced out the window. "I should've noticed it'd gone quiet." He pulled a frock coat off a hook and shrugged into it.

Lydia folded her hands demurely. She'd wait for him to return; she wasn't about to tell Sebastian's mother she'd left without a dime. What was simply pocket change to Mr. Lowe could decide her future. She needed to marry Sebastian Little before her father put them into so much debt that Sebastian changed his mind about her suitability.

If she didn't marry before long, she'd soon be poor enough to need one of the moral-society quilts. However, a warm blanket would do little to ease Mama's suffering.

Mr. Lowe stopped in front of her as he made quick work of his buttons. "I'm afraid my answer is still no." He flashed a smile and bobbed his head. "Good day, Miss King."

Lydia turned the page and hooked her foot around the leg of Mr. Lowe's big green chair.

"Goodness, Miss King!"

She jumped at Mr. Lowe's secretary's surprised voice and fumbled the book.

The cloth-bound volume slid down her white ruffled skirt and landed pages down on the floor.

"You startled me, miss." The secretary's large Adam's apple descended with his noisy swallow. "I didn't expect you in here."

"I apologize." Lydia leaned over, grabbed the book, and winced. The center pages had folded back upon themselves. Considering its tight binding, Mr. Lowe hadn't yet read his brand-new copy of Mark Twain's *Roughing It*. She brushed the clingy sawdust off the page edges. "I was waiting for Mr. Lowe, and I couldn't resist." She held out the book limply and then shook her head. "I shouldn't have taken it off his desk, but it looked . . ." *Neglected.* Sitting under a thin covering of sawdust, the title she'd been eyeing in *Harper's Bazar* for several weeks had called to her. "Anyway, I thought I'd bide my time until he returned."

"Mr. Lowe isn't returning."

"The accident?" She bit her lip. Before she'd started reading, she'd fumed over Mr. Lowe's rude departure, but if someone had been hurt, she'd need to repent every bit of that anger.

"A stack of lumber fell and knocked out a fence. Mr. Borror received a nasty bump to the head, so Mr. Lowe sent him home two hours ago."

"Two hours?" Lydia turned to the clock at the back of the office and her heart sank. Two hours and fifteen minutes to be exact. She rubbed her hand down her face. "You say he isn't coming back?" If only he'd returned and donated a few dollars toward the quilting project, the moral society might excuse her for missing half their meeting. She didn't relish telling Sebastian's mother that not only had she failed but she'd also lost herself in a book she wasn't supposed to be reading.

"Yes, ma'am. On Monday afternoons, he goes to his office at the Mining and Gas Company."

All the way down Maple Street—in the opposite direction of the church.

"I'm afraid we didn't realize you had other business or he'd have returned."

Her shoulders slumped. "No other business. I hadn't finished my proposal."

"I thought I heard him decline."

"Without fully knowing what he rejected. He'll change his mind when he hears the rest of what I have to say."

The secretary's mouth twitched, an apparition of a smile on his thread-thin lips. "Mr. Lowe never changes his mind."

"There's a first time for everything." Lydia picked her embroidered reticule off the floor and swatted at the wood curls clinging to its tassels. "I'll bid you good day. I'm afraid I'm late." She inclined her head, swept past him, and raced toward Teaville's Freewill Church as fast as she could without breaking into an unladylike stride.

Thankful for uncrowded sidewalks, she rushed across the alleyways, where the strong north wind whipped through and spiraled up her cloak. She eyed the bicycle shop window as she clipped along, wishing she had enough money for one of those contraptions. But she never would. Unless she married Sebastian, and then she'd have no need of one. She'd have a personal vehicle.

She wiggled her slightly cold toes as she waited for traffic to clear and imagined fur blankets and coal heat in a cozy black buggy for the upcoming winter. She crossed the brick street, then raced past the line of hardware stores. Turning north onto Walnut, she kept her focus on Freewill Church's stone bell tower while strong gusts sent newly fallen leaves pirouetting about her ankles.

The heavy front doors of the massive sandstone church slammed behind her, and she scurried down to an out-of-the-way room in the dank basement. About a dozen women sat around the room's large quilting frame. Half of them were the matriarchs of the church, the other half their daughters or young women without children.

She slipped onto the bench behind the quilting frame next to Evelyn Wisely, the dark-headed woman closest to her in age. Lydia ignored the pointed stares of the women who'd stopped chatting.

She took the needle Evelyn handed her. "I'm afraid Mr. Lowe kept me waiting."

"You've procured a donation, then?" Rebecca Little narrowed her eyes, turning the wrinkles in her brow into deep rivulets. This woman could very well be her future mother-in-law. Unfortunately, they'd never gotten along, and not at all since her son, Sebastian, had begun courting her.

"No, he didn't allow me more than a dozen words."

Mrs. Little harrumphed and returned to her stitching.

Bernadette Wisely, the pastor's wife and Evelyn's mother, pulled her thread through a blue-sprigged calico quilt block. "Ah well, we didn't expect anything."

"So why bother with him?" Lydia stabbed her needle into her block. "I've never once seen the man give an offering."

"For shame, Lydia," Evelyn said softly, then dropped her gaze. "We should only answer to the Lord for our giving."

Criticism from gentle Evelyn bit. Lydia swallowed to wet her dry throat. "But that's just it. I've never seen him give."

Evelyn pulled a loose thread from a frayed block. "At one time or another, I'm sure all of us have done something that everyone in this room would denounce if we opened ourselves up to criticism."

If Evelyn had done anything worse than swat a fly, she'd be surprised.

"Like watching who puts what in the bag, perhaps?" Mrs. Little snapped her thread, her dark eyes intense.

Lydia glanced around the room at the handful of ladies who'd found other places to look—all except Charlotte Gray, who went by Charlie. She looked ready to hogtie their group leader, and if not for her mother sitting beside her she likely would have. Dressed as Charlie was, in a man's Stetson, split skirt, and thick boots, it wouldn't have been surprising if she had a rope hidden amid the folds of her skirt.

Lydia shook her head slightly so Charlie wouldn't come to her defense. "I just meant I don't think it matters who talks to him."

12

Lydia dropped her gaze to her stitches. "Why not have me petition someone else? Mr. Johansen, the police officers, perhaps the men at—"

"I gave you one person with whom to prove yourself." Mrs. Little shook her head. "Do you give up that easily?"

Lydia forced herself not to sink lower in her chair.

"I've spent years convincing people to give to my husband's and son's campaigns." Mrs. Little's face grew sterner. "Raising funds is necessary if we want politicians in power who'll eradicate the red-light districts blighting Kansas and flouting state law."

The ladies' murmuring in assent hummed around the room.

Lydia stared at the swirls in the fabric pattern. If she didn't succeed in obtaining at least a small amount of money from the wealthiest man in the county, Mrs. Little might convince her son she wasn't qualified to be his wife. As a state representative, he'd want a wife who'd collect handfuls of votes—like his mother did.

Charlie's foot stomped. "I could hogtie Lowe till his fingers fell asleep and he couldn't pinch pennies anymore."

"Exactly why we're not sending you, Charlotte Gray." Mrs. Little glared.

Charlie's mother elbowed her, and with a huff, her feisty friend surrendered to her mother's silent plea. Charlie found her needle again, the one she'd been failing to thread since Lydia's arrival.

Poor Charlie. If she hated anything more than sewing, Lydia had no idea what it could be.

Lydia didn't particularly enjoy coming to this quilting group either with the way Mrs. Little ran things. But how else could she help others? Being poor, all she had to give was time and sewing skills.

"Dearest . . . " Bernadette gripped Lydia's shoulder and sneaked a glance at Mrs. Little. "Perhaps you should try again."

"I have faith in you." Evelyn flashed her an encouraging smile, but its brightness paled under the encompassing shadow of Mrs. Little's scowl.

Well, she had about as much faith in herself as Mrs. Little did, so it was time to trust God. Surely He had blessed her with tenacity and Mr. Lowe with a huge bank account so people poorer than herself could get what they needed for the winter.

2

"You have such beautiful hair. It's a shame to put it up." Mama glided into Lydia's bedroom like a ghost, though the scent of her homemade rose soap proved she still lived. Sarah King's slow smile transformed her haggard face a tiny bit—but not enough. She took Lydia's comb and a handful of her daughter's hair and threaded her fingers through the dark waves. "So like mine used to be."

Lydia's gaze drifted from Mama's pallid features to her thinning hair. She would rather imagine Mama as she'd once been, but Lydia suspected she only had a few more years, maybe only a handful of months, to look into those eyes, a pale blue like her own. Hopefully Mama would make it to Lydia's twenty-third birthday, for twenty-two years with her mother was simply not enough.

Lydia took the comb back before Mama could turn her wavy locks into a massive cloud.

"Did you have a restful nap?" Lydia warmed some hair gloss in her palms to weigh down her subtle spirals and pushed her hair forward, making a pleasant puff above her forehead.

Mama didn't answer. Her eyes were duller than usual.

Lydia stopped pinning up her curls. "Mama, what is it?"

"Did Papa tell you Dr. Lindon came today?"

"Again?" Lydia's breath caught. "Why?"

She wouldn't meet her daughter's eyes. "Have you seen your father since you've been home?"

"No, but I thought nothing of it. It's payday."

Mama's shoulders slumped, and Lydia squeezed her canister of hair gloss but refrained from crushing it. Why couldn't she keep from speaking ill of Papa when it only upset her mother? He was a ne'er-do-well, and nothing would change that. Mama knew it, she knew it, the whole town knew it. Venting her frustration over his gambling when medical bills needed to be paid wouldn't make her mother feel better.

Mama grabbed hold of the bed's steel-pipe footboard and lowered herself onto the mattress. "Dr. Lindon believes my time to leave this Earth may be sooner than later."

Lydia's throat clogged. Moisture pressed against her eyes, hot and thick. "How long?" Her raspy voice tattled on her threatening tears.

"Now remember, according to his prediction last year, I should've been frolicking with our Maker eight months ago."

Lydia moved over to the mattress and snatched up her mother's hand.

"I'd rather not voice his newest prophecy."

"Oh, Mama."

She squeezed Lydia's hand pitifully.

"Does Papa know?"

"Yes, he was here."

A stab of guilt pervaded her chest. She'd so quickly jumped to the usual conclusion of his whereabouts. For all his ill-fated business schemes and lackluster fathering skills, he did love Mama. Well, as much as he could love anything that didn't involve a wager.

"Don't judge him too harshly, my dear."

How could she not? If he didn't constantly put them in a lurch, her mother wouldn't need to excuse his behavior. Lydia nodded but didn't look Mama in the eye. "I should stay in tonight. You shouldn't be alone."

"No, you should go, now more than ever."

"But—"

"I can't have you hovering over me for the rest of my life." She looked away. "I won't tether you to a sickroom."

"But a watched pot never boils. If I stare at you all day, every day, I might get to keep you forever."

A tiny smile perked Mama's grayish lips. "You look lovely. Sebastian will be enchanted with how you've done your hair."

Tears pricked her eyes again at the change of subject. If it wasn't for Mama's wish for her to marry, she wouldn't bother going. "Let us hope."

If she could marry before Mama took to her deathbed, perhaps her mother's last days would be easier. She rose and kissed her mother's temple. "Wish me luck. I'm stopping by Mr. Lowe's gas company before dinner. Mrs. Little thinks procuring a donation from him will prove whether or not I'm capable of raising campaign finances and garnering votes." Could she really win Sebastian's admiration by proving she could raise funds? But what else did she have besides a pretty face and a petite figure to entice him into a commitment? "Though I'm certain I'd have an easier time convincing a turkey to crawl onto our table and stuff itself for Thanksgiving than getting Mr. Lowe to hand me a penny."

Mama laughed, but her chuckles turned into deep, throaty coughs. Lydia exchanged Mama's blood-spotted handkerchief for a fresh one. She shouldn't have made her laugh. She put her arm around Mama's frail, trembling body, seized so hard with spasms she feared her mother's bones would crack.

After the coughing fit ended, Lydia brewed the doctor's special tea, thankful the fit had subsided enough that she felt comfortable leaving.

"Go and have a merry time, Lydia dear. After you pluck Mr. Lowe's feathers, of course." She smiled wanly as she pulled the sewing basket closer and pulled out the dress the neighbor's wife had ordered. "I shall be fine."

"I'll return home the moment dinner is over." She frowned at the garment her mother would insist on working on instead of resting like she ought. "Though I expect you to be in bed long before then."

"Of course, my dear. Do not fret."

Then why did God give her so many trials? The Almighty seemed bent on testing her lately. She retrieved her secondhand evening coat and leaned over to plant a kiss on Mama's moist forehead. "I shall try."

As she stepped out of doors, a buggy clattered past on the brick street of her run-down little neighborhood, and the autumn wind played in her hair. She hugged herself against the cool breeze, but the second she descended the first stair, her father appeared from behind the bushes separating their dismal yard from the road, his gaze pinned to his feet. Then he about-faced and stomped the other way.

"What are you doing, Papa?"

He glanced at her, then returned to pacing.

She wanted to huff and walk past, but what if he was worried about Mama? If so, how short a time had the doctor given her? She looked over her shoulder. Should she leave the house if any minute could be her mother's last? She gripped the porch balustrade. "Papa?"

"What, Lydia?" His unkempt eyebrows twitched above his glassy eyes.

"Is Mama all right?"

"She won't be when she gets wind of what I've done." He moaned, not with sadness but deprecation.

Worried about himself, not Mama.

Lydia gripped the railing to keep from lunging at him and flailing her fists like she had as a little girl whenever he'd made Mama cry.

He paced in a short, choppy path twice more before stopping in front of her and pulling the hair at the nape of his neck. "How much money do you have?"

Of course. She'd been a fool to believe he'd have done anything else on payday besides creep into an illegal saloon and gamble. She turned her head away, trying to find a way to answer without lying. "How much did you lose?"

"All of it."

What did he mean *all of it*?

Lydia wrung her hands. What if Sebastian broke things off because of her utter poverty rather than her inability to campaign and influence? She might be able to do something about the latter, but her gambling father held the trump in regards to the former. "You can't have lost everything."

"I was only trying to pay the doctor's exorbitant fee." He raised his fist and shook it at the sky. "God surely should have blessed my hand."

He dropped onto the bottom step, tucked his elbows between his knees, and slumped. "Dr. Lindon won't wait."

Unable to sit next to him on the tiny stoop, she slid past him onto the sidewalk. "Of course he'll wait. Just like all the others." What other choice did the doctor have?

Papa looked up at her, then down, and slowly back up.

She swallowed, his eyes too assessing.

"You seeing Sebastian tonight?"

"He invited me to dinner with his parents again."

Papa stood and tucked an errant curl behind her left ear. She worked to keep herself still and her eyes on the ground.

He lifted her chin. "Do you have any rouge? Coal? You could pretty yourself up more."

She pressed her lips together. The fact that she'd pinched her cheeks and bit her lips a few dozen times made her wish she hadn't even done that. "I'll not paint myself like some lady of the evening."

"Keeping his interest is crucial." His eyes suddenly lit and he let out a relieved laugh. "Why, things aren't as bad as I thought. By Jove, you're good for something!" A stupid grin brightened his face, and he chucked her chin. "You make certain Roger's son is happy, and we've no worries."

What was he talking about? She licked her lips. "How's that?"

"Nothing to worry your pretty head over." He turned her around, and with a hand to the small of her back, pushed her out of the yard. "You save your Papa by charming that windbag's son before he changes his mind."

She wrapped her arms about herself and nodded. Marrying Sebastian would make both her parents happy. If that wasn't a direct sign from God to ignore her misgivings, she didn't know what was.

3

To squeeze away the chill her father sent her away with, Lydia tucked her arms under her cloak and dropped her gaze to the sidewalk whenever men passed her on her way to Lowe's gas company office. How many of them sneaked over to The Line at night like Papa and threw away the money their families needed on watered-down moonshine and a fling with the queen of spades?

Mrs. Little shouldn't worry about her dedication to raising funds for Sebastian's campaigns. If Lydia married her son, she was all too glad to join their family's crusade to close down the dens of iniquity that robbed so many wives of their husbands' attention and little girls of their fathers' promises.

But how did Papa expect Sebastian to save her family from ruin? Sebastian would take care of her if they wed, but what did Papa expect to get out of the deal? Would he constantly beg them for money after she married?

She rubbed the callus on her finger. How much loathsome mending had she been forced to take on to pay off Papa's accumulating debts? She'd once dreamed of attending college, but now all she hoped to afford was fabric for a wedding-worthy dress and a headstone for Mama.

The *tink* of a bell pulled her gaze off her feet. Mr. Lowe—tall and overly handsome—backed out of his office half a block away, turned over a placard, and pocketed his key.

With a huff, she blew away the fine hair tickling her forehead and raced down the storefront-lined road to catch him, but her ladylike pace was no match for his purposeful stride. She sped up so she wouldn't have to call out for him to stop.

He tipped his hat as he passed people on the sidewalk and to someone down the alley next to Minnie's Hotel.

Lydia glanced down the narrow street.

An old lady in a torn black dress stood in the shadows shaking slop from a clay pot. The woman looked up and scowled.

Lydia sidestepped to the sidewalk's edge and hurried after Mr. Lowe.

He stopped, his hands tense at his side.

Immediately she slowed and touched a gloved hand to her face. Was she flushed? That might be good. Pink cheeks would heighten her charm. Now if she could manage to keep from sounding winded when she spoke.

He pivoted, pushed his felt hat off his forehead, and stiffened. "Ah, Miss King."

She fluttered her hands down to her waist and clasped them together. Innocuous small talk should disarm him. "Good afternoon. It's a rather pleasant day for walking."

He looked to the sky and frowned. A gray frothy haze hung low in the steel-colored sky. "Hadn't noticed."

She could have pinched herself. Looking dull-witted wouldn't help her cause. "I mean . . . I am pleased that it isn't raining yet."

"I hope you get where you're going before it does." He looked ready to turn and dart away.

She sidled forward, cutting him off from the direction he'd been headed. "I think walking does wonders for the lungs, don't you? I take it you believe in exercise since you often walk about town."

"Hmmm, that's the nicest assumption I've heard so far. Usually I hear I'm too stingy to pay the livery man or no one can stand me long enough to drive me home."

She winced inwardly at how she'd thought so herself. "Well, it truly is unhealthy to sit all day. Mind if I join you?"

"Are you giving me a choice?" His eyes narrowed.

"I won't be any trouble." She batted her eyes and hoped her smile didn't look fake, since her teeth were dry from prolonged exposure.

He pulled the brim of his hat down to his eyebrows. "I can't stop you from walking where you please."

She smiled as if that were the greatest invitation she could ever receive. "Great."

He turned and headed toward the railroad tracks, his mansion not far past them on the southern outskirts, where the town disappeared and the gentle roll of the southeast Kansas hills could be seen for miles.

He took one long stride for her every two steps. Didn't the man know he shouldn't force a lady to gallop?

When she caught up, she replastered the pleasantness onto her face. "My, you walk uncommonly quick."

"And you are uncommonly tenacious." His eyes held no sparkle.

Was that good or bad? "I don't understand your meaning."

"My secretary told me you waited for me earlier today—and I apologize you were left alone so long—but I can only assume you are currently walking beside me to try again to needle money out of me."

"I accept your apology." Her lips tightened with the effort to keep them in a pleasing curve. "No harm done. As for needling—"

"Ah, and so the puncturing begins." He walked even faster.

The warmth in her face seeped out, turning her cheeks cold and brittle. She wouldn't take it anymore. "How can you be so rude to me yet tip your hat to a woman tossing slop in the alley? I don't believe anyone's ever treated me as poorly as you."

He halted.

Her arm brushed his as she blew past. Three steps later, she'd slowed enough to turn without falling on her backside. "I'm only asking for Christian charity and to be heard. There's nothing wrong with that." She glared, waiting for his excuses. Then, realizing her scowl couldn't be attractive, she exhaled sharply and forced her facial muscles to relax.

He could affront her, rail at her, spit at her feet. But she could endure his rudeness for a donation. "If you would just listen, we'll never have to see each other again."

His eyes rolled toward the dark heavens, as if he were pleading for the ten thousand angels who hadn't rescued Christ to condescend to rescue him.

But then his shoulders sagged. "I apologize for not giving you the same courtesy I gave Mrs. Willis."

"Who?"

"The lady with the pot in the alley."

He knew the chambermaid's name? "Apology accepted." She let her fists slip off her hips. "I know you're every bit of a gentleman, a man of good fortune, and are as concerned for the poor Mrs. Williamses of this town as I am."

"Willis."

"Yes, women like her who often don't have enough money to buy essentials. With winter only weeks away, the moral society wants to provide blankets for the needy. But sewing a quilt by hand takes a long time. With machines, we could produce more. A Burdick sewing machine is less than sixteen dollars."

Mr. Lowe stood silently, his gaze pinned to hers. He was listening!

She plowed on. "We'd like to purchase two for the church. Whereas I could only finish about one block a day, I could potentially finish five in the same amount of time. With two machines being employed while the other women quilt, we could potentially finish about eight more quilts a year. Though I suppose we could do more if we tied them. And our other donations would be used to purchase enough material and notions to keep up with our increased production."

His face hadn't moved, and yet it somehow turned harder. Maybe his listening wasn't a good thing.

"I'd hoped you'd be kind enough to pay for the two sewing machines since you're a well-off member of our church and care about the Mrs. Williamses of the world."

He lifted an eyebrow.

She cleared her throat. "I mean Mrs. Willistons." At the almost imperceptible shaking of his head, she backpedaled. "Well, whatever their names . . . those who need blankets."

Sunrays escaped from behind a storm cloud, and light flickered across his immobile face. He must know he was being stubborn for no good reason. For him, thirty dollars was nothing.

She tilted her head to the side and exercised her eyelids.

"Is that the end of your spiel, Miss King?"

"Yes." She quit batting her eyelashes and tucked in her lips.

"Wonderful." He steepled his hands in front of him. "Now that I've heard your argument in its entirety, I stand by my initial decision. I wish you luck getting money from someone else."

Her lungs deflated. "But—"

"The day's almost over. Surely you don't want to vex yourself by arguing. I wouldn't want to ruin your walk on such a fine day." He shook his head, then rubbed the back of his neck. "I need to be on my way."

She strangled her skirt with shaky hands. Mrs. Little expected her to give up, which meant she wouldn't, no matter how appealing the idea. Maybe if she tried to befriend him . . . goodness knows the man couldn't have any real friends. He never hosted dinners or held a dance, despite the fact it was well-known his entire third floor was a ballroom. "All right, but might I continue walking with you?"

"Seems I can't stop you." He took off like the lightning bolts dancing amid the far-off clouds.

After walking two blocks in silence, she chose a neutral topic.

"Have you enjoyed church this past month? I've learned much from the sermons in James. It's my favorite book."

"They've been good."

Not much of an answer, but at least he hadn't ignored her. "Will you attend the Bible study starting Wednesday? I hear Mr. Taylor has chosen the topic of Christian Virtues."

His jaw grew tight. "I believe I'll stay home and read."

"What will you read?" The question flew out of her mouth before she'd thought.

If he actually did read, how tedious would this conversation be? He probably read engineering manuals or—

He shrugged. "I don't know. Aquinas, Augustine, Donne, Bunyan, Edwards. Someone I trust to teach me about virtue, if that's what I desire to learn."

"You have all those?" She bit her lip to keep from begging to borrow the whole stack. "I love the few Donne poems I've been lucky enough to read."

"Yes, they're quite good." He tucked his hands in his pockets and charged toward the small hill where his mansion sat. He stopped at his iron entry gate attached to stone pillars, an unnecessary structure since there was no fencing, though it was lovely draped with trumpet flower vines during the summer.

She stopped, saddened she'd just found a topic with which she might have engaged him. But when he opened his gate and stood waiting, she nearly did a cartwheel. Chitchatting had gotten her further than she'd hoped.

However . . .

She looked behind her to see if anyone was watching. Even though this road out of town was never busy and only a few buildings lined it, what might people think if they saw her walking alone with him up to his mansion?

Though if Mrs. Little found out she'd been given such an invitation and not used it to squeeze out three thousand pennies from him . . .

Lydia stepped inside. "I was thinking—"

Without waiting, he quickly turned to eat up the ground with long-legged strides. His driveway snaked along the thick curves of the landscape, but she hadn't the time to take in the terrain. The pace he set up the incline was grueling, and she'd already started huffing before they'd reached the gate.

At the crest of the hill, he slowed, making her want to break into the Hallelujah Chorus despite being too winded to sing.

He put his hands in his pockets and stared off at the delicate cloud-to-cloud lightning, too far away to be heard.

"The way Donne explores the contradictions in life makes reading his poetry similar to . . . I don't know." Mr. Lowe broke off from his hesitant speech and stood silent for a moment. "It's like the feeling you get when you find something in a Bible passage that gives you insight into yourself or the world. A gem worthy of meditating on, savoring . . ." He reached up to play with his collar. "I'm sorry. That probably made little sense."

Lydia barely kept herself from clapping. He actually read, really read! Surely he'd listen to her requests with a more sympathetic ear if he discovered she had the same interests. "Do you have a favorite poet?"

"Byron, Coleridge, Poe . . ." He broke off with a huffed chuckle. "The dark ones apparently."

"I love Byron. Which is your favorite piece?"

"'When We Two Parted,' perhaps."

"I don't remember that one." She frowned. Hopefully she could find something they'd both read before he dismissed her.

"I'll lend you my Byron, if you wish." He resumed walking and took the massive porch stairs two at a time.

She raced eagerly after him despite her tight lungs. If only he weren't half a foot taller than her, her legs might not have been burning to keep up.

He spun in front of his towering double doors and held out his hand. "But, ah . . . remain here if you would."

The heavily stained door slammed, leaving her alone in the moist cold. She stopped short of kicking his door in frustration. He could have at least let her into his entry hall. But he was a thoughtless man, so she shouldn't be surprised.

But did thoughtless men read Augustine and Donne?

The house was gargantuan, so his library had to be of remarkable size. She'd already borrowed all the books her old high school teacher, Charlie's husband, owned thrice over, and she hadn't enough money to buy more than one a month—if that.

She eased toward the door's glass but stopped shy of hooding her eyes against the glare. Female voices sounded inside, and Mr. Lowe's quick baritone barked a one-word reply. She scurried back from the door.

Instead of Mr. Lowe, a woman with soft dark curls framing sharp, serious eyes opened the door. She was likely in her early thirties, like Mr. Lowe, but her black dress and dirty white apron bespoke her position as a servant. The woman stepped onto the porch and held out two books.

"I'm sorry, but Mr. Lowe had a pressing matter arise. He said to give you these and bid you good day."

Lydia blinked hard. Maybe she shouldn't take the books. If he wasn't willing to help poor people with blankets, should she take his books for her own entertainment? Yet her feet moved toward them as if they had free will. The temptation to borrow something she hadn't read a dozen times over was too much. She took the stack: a small leather-bound volume of Byron sat atop Mark Twain's *Roughing It*.

She forced her eyes off the beautiful poetry cover. "I hope the matter detaining him isn't serious."

"He's always serious." The woman took a step back, a grim set to her mouth.

"I see." But she didn't, not really.

The servant ducked her head dismissively. "Good day, miss." And the door shut with a resounding *thud*.

4

Nicholas stood far enough behind his mansion's Tiffany glass front door that if Miss King turned, she'd not see his silhouette. She was already at the bottom of his driveway, the books he'd lent her hugged to her chest.

His housekeeper, Caroline O'Conner, returned from a quick trip to the basement. "You could've seen her off personally."

"I was talking too much."

"Oh?" Caroline moved to the window. "She had the most arresting eyes. So light blue they were almost colorless. Quite the contrast with all that dark hair."

Yes. Though her excessive eyelash batting had made it difficult to take her seriously, the constant movement had pulled his gaze back to those navy-rimmed, pale blue irises countless times.

"I couldn't give her what she wanted. If I give to one beggar, I'll have a line of them at my door."

"She doesn't look the beggarly type."

No. Even worse. Her expressions—shifting from self-abasement to entreaty and back—had been hard enough to resist, but when they'd discussed literature, her eyes downright sparkled. He'd almost given in to her inane charity request just to see what she'd do when truly excited.

But it was the principle of the thing.

He wouldn't compromise his integrity to see a pretty woman give him a real smile. He sighed and shrugged out of his frock coat. Miss King must think him the most ill-mannered man in Kansas. Not that he'd argue that. Hopefully this was the last time he'd see her near his offices. None of the other ladies from that moral-society group had pestered him more than once. A quick and rude refusal kept people from hoping for things they'd never get—usually. And yet Miss King stuck around, even after he'd shut the door in her face.

"I should have invited her in and forced you to be sociable." Caroline's face looked amused.

"She can't come in." He lowered his voice. "Not with the maids here."

Caroline glanced through the archway into the music room, where Effie and Violet waxed the hardwood floor. "You know as well as I do the chance of her recognizing them is minimal."

"We can't take that chance. When I entertain guests, the maids best stay in the kitchen or the basement."

"And when do you plan on entertaining?"

"Never. For how am I supposed to entertain without servants serving?" People complicated things. Complicated everything. And that woman . . . He peeked out the window again, but she'd already disappeared.

Caroline crossed her arms and winked. "She's quite pretty. I can't think of any reason why she wouldn't take a shine to you. Invite her family over, and I'll make sure the maids are busy elsewhere."

No, he couldn't. Not even if he wanted to. Which he didn't. Attractive features suckered men into things they didn't think through. He knew that firsthand. "Don't get your matchmaking hopes up. Rumor has it she's about to be engaged to the mayor's son."

"Oh." Her face wrinkled like a scolded puppy. "Pity."

Yes, it was. If Miss King was involved with Sebastian Little, she was likely untrustworthy or naïve. A minx might lay in wait behind those beguiling eyes.

"If you aren't setting your cap for her, then there's no reason to keep looking out the window." Caroline raised her eyebrows. "Or is there?"

He tried to make a menacing face, but the woman only smiled. He walked over to his ivory-topped table and snatched cards and letters off the silver tray. On top was a fine linen envelope with Mr. Tiffany's business address in the upper left corner. "Ah, finally."

He opened the missive and scanned its contents before handing it to Caroline. "Mr. Tiffany will arrive in five weeks to personally install the gasolier in the dining room. Make sure the dining set is covered."

This last fixture would complete construction. But living in a three-story mansion as a bachelor was absurd. And yet, he'd built it anyway. How else could he assuage the guilt over his late wife's death? Not that anything he'd done so far had made him feel better.

Maybe his cousin Roxie could help him figure out what to do with the house. "Tell Roxie I need to talk with her." He shuffled through the other envelopes—bills and more bills and a letter from Henri Beauchamp. He turned it over and ripped off the flap.

Caroline cleared her throat and wrung her hands.

"Yes?" He discarded the envelope.

"I'm afraid she's leaving." His housekeeper wouldn't meet his eyes, her voice barely a whisper.

His heart jumped hard against his chest. Each and every woman who'd come to work for him in an attempt to leave her past behind had left within months, but his cousin had been with him for more than two years. She wouldn't leave him. Surely Caroline meant someone else.

Anyone but Roxie, Lord.

"Why didn't you inform me the moment I walked in?" His hands fisted involuntarily, crumpling Henri's letter.

Caroline shook her head. "She intends to leave at the end of the week, sir."

He let out a rickety breath, and his heartbeat slowed. Every girl who'd left had slipped away in the middle of the night, but Roxie was family.

At least he had time to talk sense into her, or at minimum, persuade her to leave her son behind. "Where is she?"

Caroline shrugged. "She's playing with Francis right now, but she asked me to watch him after supper so you two could talk."

He gave a sharp nod. He'd wait instead of upsetting his cousin and her son by interrupting their game. "Good. I'll convince her to stay then."

"I hope you will."

"I'll let you return to your work."

Just when he thought things couldn't get worse. . . . He shuffled into the dining room though he had an hour to wait until supper. Slumping in his chair at the head of the table, he stared at the hole in the ceiling that had been prepared for his custom-made Tiffany lamp, the final touch for his empty, showy house—the kind of house he never wanted.

By summer, his six years of bartering, diverting business funds, and doing some construction himself would be over. One hundred twenty-five thousand dollars sitting on top of a hill. A steal of a deal completed.

And Roxie was leaving, throwing away everything he'd given her.

He slammed his fist on the table.

He should just burn the whole thing to the ground.

5

Lydia cut her ham gently so as not to clink her silverware against Mrs. Little's fine china. The older woman was glowering at her enough as it was. She didn't want to give her any more reason to frost her with those ice-cold eyes.

Sebastian's father, Teaville's newly appointed mayor, speared a baby potato with his fork and pointed the utensil at his wife. "You need to stop visiting Mrs. Johansen." The mayor was the mirror image of his son, though the elder was thicker in stature and had a ruddier face and gray streaks at his temples. "Vargis and Athenasmear don't like her husband, so the sooner we cut ties with them the better."

Mrs. Little lifted her hand as if she were about to cut him off.

"You will not risk it." Mayor Little smacked the table.

"She doesn't matter anyway." Mrs. Little lifted her palm in surrender, but the gleam in her eye didn't look submissive. "And if we aren't going to risk anything, then you'll have to give James Furp the boot."

Mayor Little ground his teeth, glaring at his wife.

Every scrape of Lydia's fork seemed ten times louder in the awkward silence. Polite people would engage their guest in conversation, not bicker as if she weren't there.

What was wrong with them? At the fall festival last week, they'd acted like a pair of lovebirds. Tonight, they seemed ready to peck each other's eyes out.

Sebastian leaned back in the seat across from her; his tall, lanky frame made the chair look child-sized. "That was excellent fare, Mother."

Lydia eyed his clean plate. No doubt he'd perfected the art of shoveling food to stay out of his parents' dinner conversations.

Mrs. Little flicked her eyes to Sebastian and shrugged. "That's the only reason I keep the cook. She's so slovenly. All that flour behind the stove and in the corners . . ."

Lydia accidently swallowed a chunk of meat whole. Her eyes watered, and she took a sip of tea, hoping it would clear the obstruction. She raised her napkin to her mouth and coughed a little, desperate to keep her composure. If a little flour in the kitchen was too messy for Mrs. Little, how would she react to her guest choking at the table with tea spurting from her nose?

She'd rather die of asphyxiation than disgrace herself in such a manner.

"Are you all right, Miss King?" Mayor Little's question forced her to focus through tear-glazed eyes.

She tried a quick inhale, glad to discover she could breathe. "Yes, sir." A cough escaped, and she fought the urge to give in to more. At least her distress had distracted the mayor from his wife for the moment.

"This port is exceedingly fine." Sebastian swirled his glass of wine. He slanted his eyes at her, his hair feathering out wildly at his receding hairline. "How did you like the pork loin?"

"It was delicious." Even if she had choked on it.

"Did you taste a hint of cinnamon? I detected something unusual."

"I'm not sure." And this was exactly why one should read books. To avoid having to talk about the weather, the food, and the neighbor's curtains. If she were in love she probably wouldn't care, but she wasn't, and his conversation topics grew more tedious with each dinner date.

She needed to distract him from telling her how crisp the potatoes had been and keep his parents from restarting their feud. "Have any of you read a good book lately?"

Mrs. Little cocked a brow.

Silence.

"Well, I've been reading Twain—"

"Did the high school assign Twain?" Mayor Little hung an arm over the back of his chair.

"Well, no. There I read Cicero, Virgil—"

"I still have no idea why parents allow their girls to take the collegiate course." The mayor held out his hand as if he were addressing a crowd. "What good is a woman who can quote Cicero?" The mayor's hot glare settled on his son as if Sebastian needed to answer for her choice of classes. "All a woman needs is a pretty smile."

She forced herself to loosen her grip before she cracked her goblet's stem. "No learning is wasted, Mayor Little, even on a woman. It sharpens the mind. And since I understand rhetoric, I'll be better able to help Sebastian than if I only knew how to sing arias and coordinate dinner linens." Lydia kept her gaze off Mrs. Little, afraid the woman would take what she said as an insult.

"Darling, he only meant you'd be pleasing to look at on the campaign trail." Sebastian looked at her as if she were standing on her head. "And there's something to be said for a woman whose speech isn't . . . so combative." His sentence hung in the air.

Did he direct that comment just to her or to his mother as well? She wasn't the only one at this table needing lessons on social niceties.

Mrs. Little harrumphed.

Lydia averted her gaze, sure her unchristian thoughts could be seen in her eyes.

"Perhaps some of your learning might prove helpful, but I still worry about your father." Mayor Little swiveled toward his son again. "He's a liability."

35

Lydia's shoulders fell. If only she could slide down in a puddle of pleats under the dining room table. Would her father's choices haunt the rest of her life? And why hadn't the mayor waited to grill his son on his choice of a wife in private?

"I don't intend to give him money, Father." Sebastian glanced at her, and she gave him a conceding look. Since she went to great lengths to hide her nickels from the man, she could hardly fault Sebastian for the same.

Sebastian turned to her. "How's your mother doing?"

His look of concern made her relax. "Poorly, I'm afraid."

"Perhaps I ought to take her soup." Mrs. Little signaled for her dishes to be cleared. "I'm sure her care consumes your time." She narrowed her eyes ever so slightly. "Will it keep you from petitioning Mr. Lowe again anytime soon?"

Why was Mrs. Little fixated on her squeezing money out of the man? "I intend to try again as soon as I can." But she'd have to think of a new tactic.

Mrs. Little's mouth twitched in displeasure.

"What is this about Lowe?" Mayor Little waved a servant over and grabbed the port from the man's hands. He tipped himself a glass and thunked the bottle on the table.

"We're raising funds for our quilt project, so I challenged Miss King to fish something out of Mr. Lowe's pockets." Mrs. Little glared at her husband. "Instead of riling her up over things she can't change, I'm teaching her how to woo the citizenry. She needs some real skills to help Sebastian."

"Mother . . ." Sebastian finally set down his ever-swirling wine glass. "Don't make her jump through ridiculous hoops."

Lydia focused on her lap. She should've stayed quiet.

"Nonsense. I don't sit around reading all day. I work long hours for you both. If I didn't contribute to your political ambitions by schmoozing and prodding, you wouldn't be where you are today."

"That's enough, Rebecca." Mayor Little's voice boomed, and the manservant clearing his place setting jumped, dropping a sauce-laden spoon onto the pristine tablecloth. The man hung his head like an oft-beaten dog and apologized profusely as he wiped up the mess.

Lydia pushed away from the table. Her napkin tumbled off her lap, but she didn't rescue it. "I'm afraid I need . . . some air. Excuse me, please."

As she made her way to the back of the house, Mayor Little's grouchy voice followed. "Why are you thinking of marrying her again?"

Her hand froze on the doorknob. Should she wait to hear Sebastian's answer? He'd never said more about his intentions than believing they could be of service to one another—he'd provide for her financially and she'd support him during campaigns. But she had a suspicion Papa had foisted her on Sebastian in an attempt to make good on a losing poker hand.

"She's beautiful and young." Sebastian's voice sounded smooth, disinterested.

Her hand tightened on the glass knob. Was that all? The world was silent, as if the earth held its breath with her.

". . . and smart."

A tug of a smile pulled at the corner of her mouth. Despite his disdain for her novels, perhaps he knew her schooling and reading were beneficial.

Mayor Little grunted. "Too smart. She won't take your word for things, will question every little thing you . . ."

Lydia slipped outside and quietly closed the door before slogging over to the back porch bench. Perhaps a minute or two of night air would relieve the pounding in her temples. The threatening storm seemed to have decided against visiting Teaville, but it had left the air smelling fresh, regardless.

Should she marry a man whose parents seemed set against her? Who gave her a headache with their seemingly never-ending private bickering?

She needed this to work. If Papa bankrupted her family, Sebastian could make sure her mother had medical care.

But was keeping her mother healthy for a few more months

worth enduring a marriage like that of their parents'? Of course, once Mama was gone, Papa would probably go even deeper into debt, and then where would she be?

The door opened, then clicked shut.

"I hope I'm not disturbing you." Sebastian walked over and sat beside her, balancing his wine glass on his knee. "I wanted to apologize for Mother. She's not feeling well."

"I'm sorry to hear that." Though his mother had seemed well enough to argue with her husband for fifteen solid minutes.

"What does she want you to get out of Lowe?"

She repressed a sigh. She didn't want to talk about Mr. Lowe. At the moment, she disliked him for making her life an extra bit harder. "About thirty dollars."

Thirty dollars. Sebastian's kingdom for thirty dollars. Maybe she'd extract the sum from her meager savings account, claim Mr. Lowe had succumbed, and be done with it. Even though they weren't yet engaged, surely Sebastian would give her money in an emergency. "Enough for the sewing machines your mother wants for the moral society."

Sebastian's grunt sounded unimpressed. "That can't be so hard. The man's made of money."

His long fingers laced through hers, and she tried to relax but couldn't look at him or their entwined hands. Lydia stared at a large tree dancing in the sudden turn of the wind, its browning leaves crinkling against each other. "Your parents don't seem to think we'd be a good match."

"I wouldn't listen to their relationship advice." He huffed. "Your parents married for love, as did mine. None of them ended up happy. The decision to marry shouldn't be based upon a whirlwind of nonsensical feelings."

"No," she whispered. "We can't be nonsensical." A beggar woman who hoped a handsome prince would fall in love with her was clearly irrational.

She didn't need a fairy-tale ending anyway.

"I don't see why our plan wouldn't work. All you need to do is help me campaign during election years, and in the interims, you'll be a woman of means." He caressed the rough patch on her thumb.

Yes, like Charlotte Lucas in *Pride and Prejudice*, she'd been offered a comfortable home and protection—and there was no earthly reason she couldn't be as happy with him as with any other.

"You'd have nothing to worry about except pleasing me." Sebastian turned her face toward him, the thick scent of wine warming his breath. She forced herself not to back away as his mouth approached hers.

What was wrong with her? She'd always wanted to be kissed. Why be scared?

Her eyes went wide as he pressed his mouth against hers. Shouldn't his lips be soft? Or sweet and tantalizing? Instead he tasted like the beet soup she'd gagged down at dinner. And what a ridiculous thing to think of during her first kiss. She should be focusing on the kiss itself.

Forcing herself to relax, she found the kissing sensations oddly pleasant, even if tainted by dinner's overabundance of garlic.

How long was he going to kiss her? His parents might come outside at any moment. Her cheeks flamed, and she tipped her head forward and broke away. They weren't properly engaged yet. His mother surely wouldn't approve of them kissing until then.

She scooted away. He moved closer.

She had to get his mind off kissing her again. "If I don't get a donation from Mr. Lowe for the moral society, will you be concerned that I won't be able to help with your campaigns?"

He licked his lips, staring at hers for a few seconds before turning to take another sip of his wine. "Sometimes you need to present people with the chance to give to a good cause numerous times before they succumb. Lowe's supposedly holier-than-thou, though, so he should come around. Shouldn't be too hard to convince him to support my campaign either. He'd agree that the riffraff in this town needs to be cleaned up." He smiled. "After you get Mother her thirty dollars, why don't you work on getting somewhere between five hundred to a thousand for me?"

"Of course, why not?" As if one thousand dollars wasn't extravagant.

Granted, if anybody in town could afford to donate such a sum, it'd be Mr. Lowe . . . but she'd likely have more luck squeezing one thousand thirty dollars out of a brick.

6

Nicholas paced his study waiting for his cousin Roxie to appear. A surge of wind hit the side of the house, smacking a loose shutter hard against the window behind him and flickering the gas lanterns on the wall. Maybe that storm was coming after all.

If God added rain and thunder to the violent wind, then everything around him would be an echo of his mood—like in *The Fall of the House of Usher*. Had Miss King read that story? He ambled to his bookshelf to peruse his collection of Poe but stopped himself. She already had his Byron and Twain. If he lent her anything else she might misread his generosity for . . . generosity.

And she mustn't believe he possessed such a trait.

A tap on the study door sounded, light and hesitant.

He blew out a breath. "Come in."

The door opened, and Roxie's golden head poked in. "Is this a good time?"

"Of course." An hour ago would have been better for his nerves. He gestured for her to take a seat.

"I would've come sooner, but Francis went missing." She stepped through the door and onto his green-and-gold Persian rug. "I finally found him in a closet upstairs playing pirate." Her face radiated a happiness he hadn't seen since he'd left South Carolina fifteen years ago.

Roxie dropped onto the sofa, leaned back, and closed her eyes as if she were enjoying a dip in a hot spring.

He rubbed his jaw. He'd expected her to come in hesitant, worried about his impending lecture. "Did Miss O'Conner not find you?" Surely Roxie knew Miss O'Conner wouldn't keep the news of her planned departure from him.

"She took Francis downstairs for a game before bed. He's going to miss that bowling alley." She winced and shot a glance at him.

His heart sunk. "Francis loves it here, Roxie." As much as he opposed separating a boy from his mother, he should've adopted Francis when she'd offered.

"And he'll find things to love about Montana."

"Montana?" He sucked air through his teeth. Was she headed to Butte and that awful Dumas place he'd heard about? He walked over to the couch and sat on the arm. "I can't force you to stay . . . but Francis is well-adjusted. I know I said you shouldn't give him up, but if you insist on leaving, then let him live with me. He needs—"

"Hush, Nicholas. It isn't what you're thinking." She took his fisted hand between her two dainty ones. "My faith will keep me from straying down that path again."

"You might plan to make it on your own, but if people find out—"

She shook her head. "I'm going to a place no one knows me."

"I trust your intentions, but what if you can't find work? With Francis to take care of . . . if he got sick or was in need, the lure of—"

"I won't go near a red-light district again, Nicholas. Besides, I doubt there's such a place near the Flathead Reservation."

Roxie released his hand and pulled a letter from her pocket. "I've been writing a man." Her whisper was barely intelligible. "And he wants to marry me."

Nicholas swallowed down the emotion in his throat. Why must he be the one to dash her hopes? "Every woman dreams of being a bride, and you expected to marry Francis's father, but a man willing to marry a prostitute—a former prostitute even . . ." He couldn't look at the fragile expression on her face any longer and turned to stare at the darkened window.

This past year, he'd thought he could help some of the women back into good society through marriage. But he'd found out what most men willing to marry soiled doves expected from their wives . . . "How can we be sure he wouldn't expect you to supplement his income working the only trade he figures you're good at?"

She dipped her head and stared at the letter she caressed. "When I first arrived here, I was lonely. You worked all day, and Francis was so little. And . . . you hadn't any maids I felt I could talk to until this past year. So I amused myself by answering personal ads—pretending I was a lady again. I never intended to string men along, but Larry was so . . . so fascinating. The way he talked about the Jocko River teeming with trout. It was like corresponding with a poet."

The lump in Nicholas's throat ached. She looked so hopeful and innocent. He'd always thought she was level-headed, but dreams were just dreams. She had to know this wouldn't work. "So you haven't told him, then?"

"I told each man as soon as he offered to marry me. The other ten—"

"Ten," he sputtered.

She giggled and ducked her head. "Yes. Ten. I really shouldn't have done it, but most proposed by the third letter, so they hadn't got their hopes up long." She looked at him, her eyes suddenly heavy with guilt. "And yes, two of them wrote back offering me a position as a working wife. But I promise you, I'll never do it again. Not even if I have to live in your basement for the rest of my life."

She unfolded her letter and smoothed it against her lap. "But Larry's different."

"Or he might intend to lead you astray once you arrive." He

stared at the paper, willing it to contain words that would convince him. "He'd have to possess a rare character to accept . . . to believe—"

"He'd have to be a man like you." She poked him in the knee. "You can't be the only one."

"Sometimes I feel like it." He captured her hand. "How can you be certain Larry is honorable?"

"Here, read it. I don't mind." She held out the letter, the paper doing a jittery dance in front of her.

The return address read Reverend Larry Stipps.

"A preacher?" His foot slipped off the hassock with a thud, and he caught himself before he fell on Roxie. No reverend would marry a woman like his cousin.

"I know. How dumb could I be, wooing a preacher man. . . . Well, he's more a self-proclaimed evangelist to the Indians." She gestured to the note he held, a silent command for him to read.

Nicholas unfolded the missive and turned it toward the gas light.

"Read it aloud." She clutched at her neck. "Please."

He cleared his throat.

"My dearest Roxanna, I received your letter, and I will not lie. Though it contained the answer I'd hoped for in regards to my proposal, I sat in shock for some time over the rest. At first, I felt confused, even cheated. But I've done a lot of praying these last nine months, and I think I've prayed more than I ever have this past week.

Despite what others might think, I can't deny that I love you. What was true last month, is true this very second. Though the details you divulged have given me pause, you're still the woman I love, and your past is part of who you are. I—"

Roxie's gulp of air and stifled sob stopped him from reading further.

"I'm sorry." She took his proffered hanky and caught the tear running down her cheek. "I've read those words at least twenty times a day. But hearing you read them . . . Well, I'd almost believed I'd made them up, that my brain had superimposed my dreams upon his words of rejection." She sucked in a shuddery breath. "Because he should've rejected me."

Nicholas pulled her close and rubbed her arm, then examined the man's firm handwriting. "No, you read his words correctly." And amazing they were. He'd always believed the church should reach out to sinners and offer them hope, as Christ had, but the churches he'd attended seemed quicker to condemn than forgive. Yet this man . . . he offered Roxie more than Nicholas had ever expected for her. "What does Larry do besides preach?"

"He's a trapper, a mountain man."

"Living shut up in a snowy cabin away from civilization isn't an easy life."

She stiffened. "Right now we never leave your property, my parents have disowned me, and if the townspeople learned of my past, they'd call my son names like—"

"Shh, say no more. You're right. I'm not providing any better."

"Don't say that." She blasted the words as if he were her six-year-old. "I only came here hoping you'd take Francis before you tossed me back onto the street. I never expected you to take me in too." She took back her letter. "You're the reason I have this chance."

"And a shaky chance it is, Roxie." He didn't want to hurt her, but he had to be honest. "If this"—he tapped the letter—"turns out to be a sham, get yourself to a boardinghouse and wire me directly. I'll pay whatever it takes to bring you back."

"Thank you." She swallowed and stood. "I already bought our tickets. We leave at the end of the week."

"You should've let me get your tickets."

"I love you, Nicholas, but I want to pay for them myself. You've provided for me so well that I've never had to touch the money I brought with me. Besides, you've given me too much as it is." She wrapped her arms around him and squeezed hard. "Thank you . . . for everything."

The woman in his embrace was so different from the hardened lady of the night who'd appeared on his doorstep two years ago, pleading on her knees for him to adopt the scared little boy she'd pushed across his threshold.

This preacher mountain man better be exactly who he said he was.

He held her tightly for a few more seconds before mussing her hair.

She squeaked and pulled away. "Brat!"

"Worm."

She pursed her lips, her hands firmly planted on her hips. "I hate to admit it, but I'll miss your sorry face."

He swallowed his retort and shook his head. "You wait until you're waving from the train before you tell me good-bye."

"Yes, sir."

He stood and kissed the top of her head through her gauzy cap. "As for Francis . . ." He'd miss that kid. "I'll take off Thursday so I can fish with him one last time."

"He'd like that." She stood on tiptoe to kiss his cheek. "I'd better go tuck him in."

"Would you send Miss O'Conner down?"

"Of course."

He watched her disappear up the stairwell before returning to his armchair. Through the picture window, the light of a carriage lantern in the distance faded behind a line of trees. Would Roxie vanish like that? Her life snuffed out, too far away for him to help. Or would her faith in God, her forgiven past, and Larry's sincerity keep her the rosy-cheeked woman she'd finally become once again?

He must stifle his pessimism. If God couldn't provide his cousin an opportunity to reenter good society, then he couldn't either.

"Miss Lowe said you wanted to see me?"

He turned toward Caroline and grinned. Her hair bun teetered on the side of her head and moisture glistened above her brow. "I see Francis wore you out. Come in."

"He's a handful." She stood planted in the doorway with her hands at her sides.

"It's after hours. You can sit."

Her rigidity melted with a drawn-out sigh. She dragged herself over to the seat Roxie had vacated.

"It seems my cousin will indeed be leaving us."

She worried her lip. "You're all right with this?"

He shrugged. "She appears to have a legitimate way back into the world, and if I don't trust God could provide her that, then what are we doing? It's what we've wanted for them all along."

"Where's she going?"

"Montana. Getting married to a preacher."

Caroline hummed in doubt.

Hopefully Roxie would confide in her about Larry and ease Caroline's misgivings. "Roxie bought her own train tickets, which I'm sure consumed her savings. How is her wardrobe?"

"She has six decent dresses, and the boy is well outfitted."

"Any of those dresses worthy of being married in?"

"They're all simple ones, like she wore today."

"I want you to purchase a nice Sunday dress for her and any-thing else a bride would want on her wedding day. Don't ask her, because she'll refuse." He loosened his money clip and pulled out several bills. "And buy Francis a fishing rod. Seems there's trout to be had in Montana."

She sniffed. "Yes, sir."

Were tears glistening along her lower lashes? "I never took you for a sentimental woman, Caroline." He threw her a devilish grin. "Crying at the mere mention of a wedding, are you?"

"No, sir." She swiped at her eyes. "It's just that if my sister ever wanted a second chance, I hadn't much hope she'd have one. But now that your cousin has . . . Well, a miracle like this makes me want to believe God exists." She clasped his hand instead of taking the money. "Don't you give up on assisting these ladies. You're the only reason I haven't."

7

Lydia stomped into Lowe's lumber office. If Sebastian wanted a thousand dollars in addition to the thirty dollars Mr. Lowe seemed so determined not to part with, she'd get it. Along with a partridge in a pear tree.

She headed straight for Mr. Lowe's secretary's desk and steeled her back for her upcoming appointment. She would not be rescheduled again. He didn't need *another* week to find a fifteen-minute slot for her.

Mr. Black looked up and smiled. "You haven't changed your mind, then?"

"No." She pointed to his open desk calendar. "I've got fifteen minutes before he leaves for lunch, right? Penciled in. Official."

"I admire your persistence, though I doubt it'll do any good." Mr. Black got up, walked to Mr. Lowe's office, and knocked on the door. "Miss King to see you."

"What?"

Had Mr. Black not told him of the appointment? Was that why this one hadn't been canceled?

"Miss King, sir." The secretary pulled a face that barely covered his amusement as he opened the door.

She'd take this appointment however it came. She needed Mr.

Lowe to give—not just to help her and Sebastian, but to help Teaville. He could do more for the poor than anyone else in town.

She gave Mr. Black a nod before charging in.

Mr. Lowe stood behind his desk and gestured toward the big green chair. His eyes were wide and his eyebrows high on his forehead. "Have a seat?"

"Thank you." She sat and arranged her skirts.

"I hope you came to see me today for a reason other than that of our previous conversations." He settled back in his chair and interlaced his fingers atop his chest.

She sucked in a fortifying breath. "I did."

Was there a ghost of a smile on those lips? "Glad to hear it." He gestured for her to speak.

"I'm here to offer you a chance to do your Christian duty to give from your excess."

His eyes shuttered. He leaned forward and folded his arms on the desktop. "I've already said no to your project." Any hint of a smile vanished.

"I realize that." She plunged into her first tactic. "How long have you attended a church?"

His face scrunched in confusion. "All my life."

"And you've not heard a sermon about tithing?" She lifted a brow.

He gave her a look any parent would have slapped clean off his face. "I've listened to countless sermons on tithing."

"Perhaps another might help."

He guffawed—whether from amusement or irritation, she couldn't tell. "Miss King, if it would make you happy, preach your heart out." He leaned back in his seat, a ridiculous smile on his face.

Unsettled by his Cheshire-cat grin, she tore her gaze away so she could recall the list of topics she'd planned to cover. "Well, first, the Bible says true religion is seeing to the needs of orphans and widows."

His upper lip inched up a notch on the right side. "That would be James 1:27."

All right, so he knew his Bible. "Very good. So we ladies are simply trying to provide you an avenue to practice your religion."

"Who says I don't practice my religion?" His eyes narrowed and his face hardened. And yet . . . was that a twinkle in his hazel eyes?

She fidgeted under his glare. "Perhaps I'm wrong, but I don't believe you've given ten percent to our church."

"You're not wrong, but I answer to God, not you."

"Perhaps my request is God's way of showing you that you should."

"So you're here to call out your Christian brother for neglecting his spiritual disciplines?" He now sported that same tight-lipped, obnoxious smile Sebastian wore when he boasted about out-arguing another lawyer in the courtroom.

"Yes." Her voice wavered.

"And like the Bible says, you've come to me first, privately, to point out my faults?"

She worried her lip. He didn't look a bit contrite. "I suppose so. That's in Matthew 18, right?"

He nodded, but he didn't seem impressed. "If you read that verse carefully, you'd see it says you should confront the person who has sinned against *you*, and, Miss King, I fail to see how I've sinned against you. Other than not granting your persistent request, which is not a sin. You don't always get what you want. I think the whole book of Ecclesiastes testifies to that." He started to rise. "There's no need to continue this conversation."

She gripped the armrests, stabbing her nails into the leather. He didn't know everything. And he certainly didn't know her future was affected by her ability to procure his donation. If he really cared about widows and orphans, he'd not be fighting her one whit. "I scheduled fifteen minutes of your time, and I want all fifteen."

"Of course you do." He plunked back in his chair and eyed her. "Have you heard the saying, 'You catch more flies with honey than vinegar'?"

"I tried honey, and you slammed a door in my face."

"Yes then, I . . ." He looked off into space and clicked his tongue. "I agree, you were much more congenial that day. Forgive me."

"Yet being friendly didn't work."

"I didn't say honey always works—it's a proverb, not a law." He threw her a wicked grin. "It so happens I'm a fastidious fly."

"I wish you didn't find this so amusing." She tried not to scowl. Did he relish making people squirm? "Poverty is not funny."

He sighed. "Go on, then."

Lord, give me the right words. "We ladies are trying to make a difference in the lives of the unfortunate—"

"Truly?"

"Of course." She huffed at the interruption.

"I'm sorry, continue." His chair creaked as he readjusted himself into a nonchalant pose. His hands steepled against his mouth as if he planned to listen, but the sudden dullness in his expression indicated her credibility was tumbling in flames.

She had to get on his good side somehow. "Let me start over." She glanced at the clock. Only eight more minutes to convince him. How had she lost so much time?

"This project clearly means a lot to you." He didn't look so inflexible anymore.

"It does." She clasped her hands. "I'm not asking for much."

His posture softened, and so did his eyes. "Look, Miss King, why don't you return next year? Perhaps I'll like your benevolence project then. I'm bound to agree with it one year or another."

She ran her thumb along the seams of her glove. Had he ever given any of the other women this offer? But next year's project wouldn't help her now. And if she couldn't obtain Mrs. Little's thirty dollars, she had no hope of a thousand for Sebastian. She stared at the clock. Five minutes remained. But she couldn't remember any of the other things she'd planned to say.

She was kidding herself; she'd never convince him to give her anything. She probably wasn't fit to raise campaign funds either. "Thank you for your time, Mr. Lowe." She stood, and he did as well.

Crossing his threshold and closing the door behind her, she felt like shaking the sawdust off her feet. Her mother's surviving to be one hundred was more likely than Mr. Lowe spending a penny on a starving baby.

And yet, the back of her neck burned at how easily he'd turned things around on her. Was she wrong? She couldn't be. How could asking a Christian man to help the poor be wrong?

Mr. Black looked up from his desk, his brow furrowed, his teeth worrying his lip—yet was that a sparkle in his eyes?

Was he fighting back a laugh or wondering what she'd do next? Which should be what?

She looked over at the clock, the minute hand still ticks away from the top. "I'm going back in." She tilted her chin, daring Mr. Black to stop her.

"As long as I don't have to join you." He shook his head, an amused curl to his thin lips. "I haven't written my will yet."

"You should come. It's not every day you get to see a miracle."

Mr. Black barked a laugh. "Well, if you succeed, I'll buy you lunch—as long as you bless and multiply it so I don't have to buy a plate for myself."

Leaving Mr. Black chuckling, she marched back toward Mr. Lowe's office, her pulse quickening with each step.

She rapped her knuckles against the door. Mr. Lowe wouldn't notice her heart's sudden erratic rhythm if she held her voice steady, which should be easy since she would only say one word this time.

Just one.

"Come in," Mr. Lowe called.

She yanked her gaze off her feet and swung the door back open.

He groaned and set down a stack of papers. "Miss King . . ."

She held out her hand to stop him from saying more, hoping her face looked sincere, not tempestuous or defiant.

She cleared her throat. "Please?"

A saw's whine filled the silence.

Mr. Lowe shifted in his seat as the saw moaned to a halt. He quirked his eyebrow. "That's all you're going to say?"

She nodded.

"I'm afraid it's still a no."

She refused to look away or reason with him again. The Lord would have to direct Mr. Lowe's heart as He did a river, because the more she talked, the more this man seemed to devalue her and her project.

Mr. Lowe's gaze didn't waver, nor did he say anything else.

Well, evidently God wasn't going to work a miracle in a minute. "I'll return tomorrow, then." She grabbed the glass doorknob behind her.

"You're really coming back?"

She gave him a firm nod. "I am."

He opened his mouth a few times, and finally said, "Why?"

"Maybe I can't soften your heart, but God can do all things. When you change your mind, I'll be here." Actually, only a few days remained until next week's meeting, and hopefully by then the women wouldn't need his donation. But at least she'd prove to Mrs. Little and Sebastian that she wasn't a quitter.

And if she convinced Mr. Lowe to give, the moral society could help more poor people get what they needed.

"You're putting a lot of effort into something so miniscule."

She scrunched her mouth. And he was putting a lot of effort into denying her something financially insignificant to him—she hadn't even asked him for the campaign donation Sebastian wanted yet. "God commands us to love the lowly. I'm willing to do my part, but will you do yours?"

"You didn't come here because of your love for the poor."

"I—"

"The truth, Lydia."

His use of her Christian name startled her. Why did *Lydia* sound more intimate on his lips than Sebastian's?

"God wants charity, but He also wants truth." Nicholas's voice softened. "Are you truly standing in my office because you love the poor so much?"

A swirl of hot and cold whispered across her shoulders, and

she clasped her clammy hands behind her back. It didn't matter whether her motivations were entirely pure or not. Not really. Of course she cared for the poor. She was one of them, for goodness' sake.

"I see I've gotten my answer. Return next year . . . if your project's worthy." He shuffled his papers back into a neat pile.

Did she really have to explain why a Christian should help the poor? "The virtue of the current project is self-explanatory. How can you not—"

"My answer, for this project, shall always be no."

"If Christ himself stood here, pleading on behalf of His lambs, would you say that?" She cringed. Why hadn't she stuck with her one word? Putting herself in Christ's place wouldn't impress Mr. Lowe one bit.

But he only stopped straightening papers and stroked his jaw. The ticking of the clock above her head grew eerily loud.

Meet his eyes. Don't look down. Stop fidgeting. Pray.

Lord, help me to get him to understand how much I need this. Her shoulders slumped. *I need this.*

No need to pray anymore. He was right. The poor were last on her mind, even when they should be first.

"Ah, there—now I see the truth coming." His eyes flashed in triumph.

She averted her gaze. "Perhaps I have other reasons to be insistent, but I do want to help people. Even if my motives aren't the purest, God can still use me, can He not?"

She could feel his gaze intent upon her, but she couldn't look at him. Couldn't bear to see his condescending know-it-all look again. Couldn't let him see how deeply he'd plumbed and how hollow she'd discovered herself to be.

With the heat of defeat rimming her eyes, she gave him a dismissive nod and forced herself to walk out without slumping.

Thankfully Mr. Black was pretending to be busy with his ledger, or else she might not have made it outside before loosing a traitorous sniffle.

8

Nicholas stomped up the train platform stairs and dropped onto a bench to await his friend Henri Beauchamp, who was thankfully nothing like Miss King. Even if the man had his faults, namely talking incessantly, at least he wasn't like the self-important Christians in Teaville. As a non-Christian, Henri cared more for the poor than any of the ladies in that moral society, no matter what they claimed.

How dare she quote the Bible at him!

Miss King had passion, he'd give her that, but she was woefully misdirected. A woman that young and naïve and fervent needed to be protected from and guided through the pitfalls of this world, not be throttled by him in frustration. Yet he'd only kept from doing so this afternoon by grinning like a court jester.

Of course, that temptation hadn't lasted long. She was a woman after all. A young one who believed in what she was doing, which at least counted for something.

But she needed the tutelage of a mature, older woman who knew what righteousness was, not Mrs. Little's group. Not anything dealing with the Littles.

And Sebastian Little was courting her.

Why did her choice of suitor bother him so much?

He rubbed his eyes, trying to erase the image of her pale pink lips puckering up to kiss that weasel.

Mr. Taylor strode past him. "Good afternoon, Lowe."

"Taylor." Nicholas frowned as soon as Mr. Taylor looked the other way. Another *upstanding* member of the community who lived as if Christ only cared what one did while surrounded by church walls. And Taylor planned to teach Christian virtues on Wednesday nights to boot.

But he wouldn't call the man out, not unless he was ready to explain how he knew where Mr. Taylor spent Saturday nights.

Why did he bother going to church with these people? He sighed and tipped his head back, watching a hawk glide in a draft. He didn't fault Henri for scoffing at Christianity because of its hypocrites.

But no matter what anyone did in the name of Jesus, truth didn't change. And that's why he attended Freewill Church— Pastor Wisely preached truth. Too bad a lot of his flock chose to ignore him.

And though Lydia didn't know it, he'd made sure the parsonage's roof had been repaired this year and had occasionally funded Pastor Wisely's specific requests with the tithe he set aside to put to whatever project he felt was worthy. Not that what he did with his money was anyone's concern.

The far-off chug and throb of the train rumbled beneath him, and the sensation shimmied under his skin. Ruminating over Miss King and Mr. Taylor was making him a grumpy companion for his returning friend. He closed his eyes and tried to clear his mind of anything that would tighten his nerves.

The engine stopped, the steam let out a dying hiss, strangers mumbled indistinctly, and dead oak leaves rustled in the tree behind him.

"*Mon ami!*" Henri shouted.

Nicholas took in a fortifying breath, pushed himself off the bench, and waved at Henri on the back of the passenger car's platform. His stout friend disappeared the moment he descended into the crowd.

Breaking through a mass of people and luggage, Henri bowled toward him. The cocky lift to his auburn brow made him almost handsome despite his sallow skin and double chin.

Nicholas gripped him in a quick, hard hug, thumped him on the back, then pushed him to arm's length. "You look older than the last time I saw you."

"Yeah, well, a month and a half will do that to a man, especially when his mother spends most of that time scolding him. Seems every time I go home, I get a year or two's worth of lectures. I believe her rants would age anyone overnight."

"And the bags under your eyes certainly help the look."

Henri took off his spectacles and squeezed the bridge of his nose. "I shared a berth with a man who ought to ask you for a job. He sawed logs with more gusto than any of your fine machinery." Henri replaced his glasses. "I'll have you know, some men do their best woodworking at night."

Nicholas knocked him in the shoulder. "Sounds like a job you'd enjoy." He followed Henri and collected his crate from a porter.

"I take it we're carrying everything ourselves?" Henri's face puckered. "Is your driver's wife keeping him home?"

Nicholas nodded. "Mrs. Parker's dementia gets worse every week."

"What about hiring someone from the livery?"

Nicholas glanced around the platform but didn't see anything else to carry. He had the crate, Henri gripped an attaché case, and an old carpet bag lay at his feet. "Is there more?"

"No." His frown looked more like a pout.

"We can handle this." Nicholas poked Henri's flabby side. "It'll do you good." And it would keep the man from talking so much. Maybe. "Besides, it's too nice of a day to get into a vehicle after you've been on a train all day. Who knows how long this nice weather will last."

"You'll be the death of me."

Nicholas balanced the box on his shoulder. "This is our least dangerous task today."

"We're going out later, then?" Henri grunted as he hefted his bag.

Nicholas started down the road before Henri could hail a cab. "If you have the time."

"I'm sure the mill ran fine without me for almost two months. There's no need to rush back tonight." Henri scuffled behind him. "Anything interesting happen while I've been gone?"

"Roxanna's left." Henri's footsteps stopped behind him, so Nicholas turned to face him. "It's all right. Hopefully a good thing. Left as a mail-order bride on Friday. Took Francis with her."

"And this man knows . . . about . . ."

"Yes, and he doesn't intend to exploit her, if we can believe his letter. She knows she can return, though." Nicholas resumed walking. "The man's a preacher."

"A *preacher*? A preacher took her?" he sputtered.

"I've told you some Christians live what they preach." Nicholas shrugged. "Not that I know many of them."

"You're the only one I respect."

"Pastor Wisely—"

"A nice man, bookish, timid." Henri waved his hand—whether to keep Nicholas from arguing or to indicate he wanted to slow down, Nicholas didn't know. "The man's not done a controversial thing in his life and is too afraid of upsetting his congregation. I'm not saying he's terrible, just not . . . well . . . heroic."

Nicholas didn't like the superiority in his friend's eye. "We're not heroes."

"If people knew what you did—"

"I'm only doing what I should've been doing all along. And I dare say, you wouldn't be so quick to play Robin Hood with me if it caused you hardship."

"No hard . . . ship." Henri's puffing garbled his response.

Nicholas slowed his pace, allowing his friend to catch up.

Just then, Miss King exited Reed's department store and pulled on her gloves.

Nicholas halted. Maybe she wouldn't see them.

Once her gloves were situated, she pivoted toward him, then stopped. Her brow furrowed.

Henri's shuffling feet slowed behind him.

Nicholas suppressed a groan. He couldn't avoid her, couldn't walk past and say nothing. "Good afternoon, Miss King."

She tipped her head as he imagined a queen of England would, regal and dismissive—her gaze fastened on his forehead instead of his eyes. "Mr. Lowe."

Henri took the interlude as an excuse to drop his burdens and swipe at his face. "Must . . . rest."

Nicholas trailed his eyes down the black ribbons on Miss King's pale purple gown. They had the audacity to follow the curves of her body until they reached the black insets of her skirts. Henri was right—he should've hired a cab.

His friend slumped against the lamppost with a moan, so Nicholas reluctantly put down his crate and stuck his hands in his pockets.

Miss King took a step toward him. "Mr. Lowe, I feel compelled to ask—"

"No, please." He held up a hand. "Not again." Could the woman not take no for an answer?

"—for your forgiveness, for attacking you earlier."

What? An apology was the last thing he'd expected. "All right."

The flicker of a smile and the relaxing of her brow made him catch his breath and look to his friend for a distraction—a much uglier distraction. "Have you met my good friend, Mr. Beauchamp?"

"From Beauchamp Mills?"

"One and the same." Henri leaned forward and nodded his head. "Pleased to meet you, Miss King." He glanced between the two of them and smirked.

Nicholas needed to stop the man's assumptions right now. "Miss King attends my church and has lately stopped by on business. I was unfortunately unable to help her."

Her mouth formed a silent word—*unwilling*, perhaps?

She turned to Henri. "I have heard tell Mr. Lowe had no friends, so I'm glad he has you."

He couldn't let himself be ensnared by the beautiful smile she flashed at Henri. He could only handle one high-maintenance friend, and Henri was much safer. Nicholas's mouth didn't dry up at the sight of the thickset Frenchman. "Yes. Henri's a man to be pitied for having to be my friend."

The tweak of her lips indicated her agreement.

Heat crept up his neck with her silence. Even if she didn't call him out on his lack of friendly qualities, the statement was true enough. He wasn't the greatest friend—he probably wasn't even capable of being a good friend to anyone, really.

But Henri was loyal. And loyalty was hard, very hard, to come by. Especially in a wife.

He scowled at the jump in his thoughts and jammed his hands back in his pockets. Even if he wanted to marry again, Lydia was too young to think about. Likely a decade his junior.

Though he was likely closer to her age than Sebastian.

Gritting his teeth, he constrained his brain from wandering further. Any number of foibles might lay hidden under that creamy skin and those pale blue eyes—she was, after all, an active member of that awful moral society.

And he made about as good a husband as he made a friend.

He needed another conversational topic. "I hope your mother's feeling better."

Her face lost every ounce of amusement. "I didn't know you knew about my mother."

"Is she still feeling poorly?"

"Yes." She pressed her lips together and blinked.

Blast. He hadn't intended to make her cry, and the longer teary-eyed females wept, the more he felt like gathering them up and shushing them. How would Lydia feel in his arms, being such a slender thing?

Confound it. He knew better than to think along that vein. Someone needed to slap him.

But Henri was oddly quiet, slouched against the pole, watching with a lazy grin.

Nicholas raked a hand through his hair. "I've been praying she recovers."

She nodded and looked at him—no calculation in her gaze, just sorrow. "I believe that's all we can do."

They stood staring at each other. If she loosed the tears she was holding back, how could he simply hand her a handkerchief? She'd need an embrace, and Henri's wouldn't do.

No. What was he thinking? A woman who'd so easily make him think about gathering her up into his arms needed to be avoided.

Henri cleared his throat.

Nicholas jumped. "I'll see you again, Miss King. At church." *Please, just at church, and only in passing.* How many more times could he turn her down before he caved to her slight pout? Which would get him into hot water with Sebastian Little, and rightly so.

"Good day, Mr. Lowe. Mr. Beauchamp." She bolted, as if electrically shocked from her spot, and walked away at a good clip.

Henri shoved off the lamppost. "What was that?"

Nicholas busied himself with picking up the crate.

"There was something between you two beyond your normal, condescending way of rubbing people wrong."

Nicholas frowned, then wove across the busy street. "That's not particularly nice of you to say."

Henri shrugged and dodged a mule cart. "You know it as well as I do, Mr. High Horse. Not that you don't have reasons to act high and mighty. I wouldn't remain your friend, in light of our philosophical differences, if I hadn't plenty of reasons to respect you." He scurried to catch up. "But you haven't answered my question."

"I told you I disappointed her in matters of business."

Henri huffed. "You like her."

If he lied, Henri would sense it and drill him relentlessly. "She has admirable qualities for someone her age." Perceptive, tenacious, smart—

"Meaning you think she's good-looking." He laughed.

"And you don't think so?"

"She has extremely large mandibles and a pointy chin."

61

"Otherwise known as a heart-shaped face." Nicholas rolled his eyes. "It's an attractive feature."

"She needs more meat on her." Henri stumbled a bit on an uneven paver. "That way, when you take her into your arms, you won't crush her."

Great, now both of them were thinking about his arms wrapped around Miss King. "You can quit your fretting over me crushing her in my arms. She's Sebastian Little's conquest."

Henri stopped in the middle of the sidewalk. "Sebastian? The new mayor's son?"

"Yes."

He made a sad clucking sound. "She'd have been better off with you, scalawag that you are."

It made no difference. "I'm not looking for a wife, never will be." So what if she had everything he'd ever fancied in a woman? Dark hair, blue eyes, a thin figure, determination, intelligence, vivacity. Those qualities led to heartache eventually. He'd married a woman like her once, and he wouldn't repeat that mistake.

"Ah, but with your money, you'd have your choice of respectable women."

Nicholas scowled, and Henri waved his hand at him.

"I know, I know. Your money's exactly why you won't take another, but that girl no doubt would've given you some pretty wee ones . . . if they inherited your jaw."

"Right." His curt reply must have finally warned Henri off. Either that or he was too breathless to speak again. Nicholas continued at a rapid pace, but it wasn't fast enough to keep Henri entirely quiet.

"I wonder how Little reeled her in?" Henri caught his breath and scurried a few more steps. "It's not like the man has a dashing figure . . . and we know where he goes . . ."

Nicholas ignored Henri's breathless listing of Sebastian's widely rumored faults as they entered his friend's yard.

Did Miss King know what the people in the red-light district whispered about the man who courted her? Of course she didn't, and he wouldn't stoop to sharing the accusations with her since all he could share were rumors. Rumors from people whose integrity and uprightness left a lot to be desired.

The rumors flying around about him were just as scandalous and were certainly not true.

He raked a hand through his hair and huffed. He was done thinking of Miss King, especially Miss King and Sebastian Little together.

She was old enough to make her own choices, and her amorous engagements were none of his business.

9

"Caroline?" Nicholas called into the caverns of his gigantic house as he emptied his pockets onto a silver tray on the entry-hall table. It'd been a long week of negotiations, arguments with his supervisors, and a failed attempt at acquiring Wilson's mill. He was ready for a night of putting his feet up and listening to his gramophone or reading a novel if sleep didn't call to him first.

Caroline's hurried steps thumped from near the music room.

He hung up his keys and turned for the stairs to the main part of the house. "Have you seen—*oof!*" He caught Caroline by the arms, yet they both stumbled into the corner table. A green glass vase toppled over the edge and broke against the polished wood floor.

She let out a strangled cry.

"It's all right." He leaned over to pick up the glass shards amid the pink roses and the spreading pool of water. "Far more expensive things could've been broken."

"Oh no, sir. It's Violet." She smashed a lavender-scented handkerchief against her mouth as if she were in danger of adding her stomach's contents to the mess at their feet.

He dropped the broken glass and took her by the arms again. Caroline wasn't a weak woman, but her eyes were glassing over.

"What's wrong?" He jiggled her a little, his heart racing. "What's this about Violet?"

His housekeeper inhaled deeply. "Dead."

"How?" He loosened his grip on Caroline's poor arms.

If Violet's death was anything like that of the last maid's . . . He swallowed against the bile rising in this throat.

"I found her with two laudanum bottles and an empty flask half an hour ago." Caroline wrapped her arms about her middle as if trying to squeeze herself in two. "I don't know where she got them."

"Let's have you sit down." He needed a chair too.

Caroline shook her head furiously. "Yesterday I sent her to Reed's mercantile while the men fixed the elevator pulley." She waved her handkerchief at the offending apparatus. "I'd seen one of the handymen before and thought he might be the sort to recognize the maids, plus I'd caught him in the laundry room, where he had no reason to be. I sent her so I could keep my eye on him."

If only Nicholas could've fixed the contraption himself. "But I saw those men before they left. They didn't seem to be acting peculiar." If they'd recognized Violet . . . were Josephine and Effie in danger?

"No, it wasn't them. Violet returned from Reed's crying. Told me a man cornered her in the store and dragged her out. Told her the other shoppers shouldn't be forced to breathe the same air as her."

"Terrible." But why hadn't Caroline told him this last night? Not that he could have done anything. Hunting the man down and giving him what for would've only ruined Violet's ability to shelter with him—and that of any other woman seeking refuge.

Last night, Violet's smile had had a melancholy twist to it, but he'd seen that smile on her many times. He'd only smiled back and wished her good night.

He'd hoped the maids could one day leave this place—find freedom from their past mistakes and society's judgment—but maybe that would never happen. Twice he'd gotten an out-of-town business connection to hire a maid, only for one of the ladies to be found out and the other to return to prostitution after she'd been fired for not pleasing the housekeeper.

Then there were the women who couldn't reconcile their minds to being worthy of anything but death or abuse, letting their sins haunt them while they scrubbed the mansion's floors, never finding the gumption to reenter good society.

Maybe his mansion was more a prison than a sanctuary.

And the escape Violet had chosen wouldn't release her into a better world, considering she'd refused to believe in the God who warned of heaven and hell.

He rubbed a hand against his suddenly warm eyes.

If only these women's problems were as easy to fix as a poorly tallied ledger.

Caroline blew her nose. "She said the man dragged her into the alley, and when some ladies from the moral society passed by, she screamed out to them. But the drunkard informed them Violet was just a . . . just a . . . well, I can't say it."

She wrung her dainty handkerchief and plopped onto the horse-hair chair beside him. "And I stupidly told Violet she ought to be thankful he didn't do more to her. That she'd have to brace herself to deal with the consequences of her poor choices for the rest of her life." She sputtered, then burst into tears.

Caroline was normally so helpful, so tame-tongued, so nurturing with the women who hid beneath his roof.

"I'd just returned from seeing my sister," she whispered.

Ah. "So I take it your visit wasn't pleasant?"

She dropped her gaze into her lap. Her hands wrung her kerchief so hard her knuckles were turning white.

She glanced up at him for a second before staring blankly at her dirty apron again. "My sister and I had a row, and I took my anger out on Violet." Caroline trembled, despite the house being overly warm. "I killed Violet."

"No you didn't." Nicholas took her hands in his and shushed her. "That's not true."

She pulled away. "Don't try to console me. I should feel the consequences of my actions, as I told Violet she should."

His brass knocker thunked rapidly—Henri's impatient tattoo. Was there a worse time for the man to drop by?

What to do with Caroline? And his poor, departed maid? He ran a hand through his hair. "Where's Violet now?"

Caroline pulled in a rough breath and swiped at her eyes. "Mr. Parker took her body to the coroner about ten minutes ago."

"Nicholas?" The silhouette behind the door pressed against the windowpane. "I can see you." Henri's hot breath fogged the glass.

Nicholas pulled Caroline up and steered her toward the servant's door under the stairwell. "Get yourself together and retire for the night. Your duties for today are over. No argument."

He waited until Caroline's sniffling was out of earshot, braced himself, and then unlocked the door.

"Took you long enough." Henri walked in without so much as a *"May I come in?"* "You really ought to hire yourself a butler again."

That wouldn't happen. The moment Caroline had brought Effie to the mansion several months ago, he'd had to let go of his butler after discovering he occasionally went to the red-light district. Finding servants he could trust would be a monumental task. Thankfully Henri hadn't seen any of the women for more than a few seconds. Roxanna normally served him when he dropped in.

Henri threw his suit coat at the hall tree. "What do you have planned for tonight? I'm up for action, if that's what you've got planned. Work at the mill's been depressing." Rubbing his hands together, he made his way to the study. "And who knows when I'll have time to go prowling about the city with you again."

Nicholas dragged his hand down his face. "I'm not going out tonight."

"All right, then. A night in. It's a shame you have an empty wine cellar. You know the laws have exceptions for personal vineyards."

"I don't want any alcohol in this house." Where had Violet gotten her liquor? He should lock up all medicines tonight to be safe. Did Josephine and Effie feel as desperate as Violet? Maybe he should have Caroline ask them how they're feeling every week or so.

"Don't tell me you're that rigid." Henri tossed a glass paper-weight between his hands. "Jesus drank wine."

Nicholas rolled his eyes. "Next time you're over, bring a barrel of water with you, and pray for a miracle."

Henri leaned forward, a goofy grin lightening his face. "Well then, what shall we do to celebrate?"

Nicholas closed his eyes and prepared himself to smile for what-ever good news Henri was about to spill. He shouldn't ruin Henri's evening with bad tidings—not that he could confide in him about what was going on under his roof.

Henri had known about Roxanna, but not the rest of them. He had once inquired if Roxanna would be open to entertaining his suit. But after Nicholas had explained his cousin's situation, Henri had lost interest—though he'd seemed to accept her presence in the mansion. Roxanna and Caroline had sneaked the ladies in as servants for months now, knowing full well if people discovered his basement was full of ex-prostitutes, no one would believe they were former anything. Would Henri believe ill of him? His friend seemed more accepting of sinners than the Christians in this town, but would he believe everything was upright?

"Well? How do you celebrate without anything good to drink?"

Nicholas rubbed his eyes. "Meat. A steak the size of Texas. But my cook has the day off."

"No wine, no steak . . ."

Nicholas's stomach rumbled. Why not eat? "Let's go to the hotel and celebrate whatever it is you haven't told me."

Henri slapped the desktop. "Mr. Padgett's no longer my com-petitor. We're partners now."

Impressive. If ever a man was more prickly and standoffish than himself, it was Padgett. Not someone he pictured partnering with a man as quirky and carefree as Henri. But perhaps Henri liked collecting taciturn friends. "Padgett's got a lot of connections."

"And I know how to work people. It's perfect."

"Congratulations, buddy."

The door opened, and Caroline walked in with tea.

Nicholas rose. "Miss O'Conner, I gave you orders."

She gave him a wavering smile, her ghastly white face a sure sign she shouldn't be working. "I figured I could do one more thing before I—"

Henri stopped throwing around the paperweight, his gaze landing on the tray of cookies she'd brought in.

Caroline slammed the tray down on the end table, causing the creamer to tumble over, and about-faced. "You're right, I'd best lie down." She rushed out at a pace he'd never seen before.

He set the creamer upright and glanced back to see her disappear around the corner. What had spooked her?

"O'Conner?" Henri stared out the door, rubbing his bristly chin. "Do I know her? Where's she from?"

"I don't know." Nicholas righted the teacups and sopped up the cream. Though he'd been acquainted with her for about a year, she'd only become his housekeeper a few months ago. His last one had quit because of his strange inability to hire any capable maids.

Caroline had never been a prostitute, so he'd never worried about her being seen, but the second she'd glimpsed Henri, she'd grown pale and ran. He thought back. Had she ever served Henri before?

No, that had always been Roxie.

So had Caroline lied to him about her past? Were lies the only way soiled doves could reenter polite society?

He rubbed at the tense knots in his shoulders. No, the story Caroline had told him made sense. But did she know Henri? The man occasionally went to a tavern and played a round of cards, but he'd often derided men foolish enough to flirt with disease and death by visiting sporting women. So he couldn't know Caroline's sister. Where else might she have seen him that would cause such a reaction? He'd have to ask her later. "So how about dinner—in the public eye, behaving like we ought?"

"I shall never behave like I ought. It'd take the fun out of living."
Henri let the chair fall forward. The front legs hit the floor with a
thwack. "Maybe we can swing by Miss King's and bring her along."

Nicholas jerked his head. "Whatever would possess you—"

"A man as glum as you needs a pretty woman on his arm."

"I told you she was taken."

"And I told you it's no fun behaving. Miss King doesn't have a
ring on her finger, does she?"

Nicholas glared at him. He'd not entertain this topic.

"Come now, you'd be less tense if we could get you a woman."
Henri tugged down on his green vest that had wriggled up his
paunch. "And I'd only set you up with the marrying kind." Henri
shoved him on the shoulder as he passed out of the room.

"She'd find me wanting, just as Gracie did."

"You're making excuses." Henri bounded down the small staircase and grabbed their suit coats. "You have money enough to treat
the next one like a queen. Relax."

Nicholas caught the coat Henri threw at him and worked the
buttons through stiff holes. Marriage would solve some of his
problems. If he was married, he and his wife could probably oversee
a house for recovering prostitutes without risking accusations of
impropriety. But what woman of quality would dare be involved?

Caroline would. And she had quite the compelling reason.

Maybe he should consider marrying her. She wasn't bad to
look at with her dark auburn hair and green eyes, a combination
of dark and light—like Lydia.

He shoved away the image of Miss King's pale blues and hustled
after Henri, letting the front door bang shut with the wind. The
thud of Violet's coffin lid would soon sound with the same finality
—and hardly anyone would hear. Would he even be able to get
to her before she was unceremoniously buried? If his late wife's
funeral had attracted no mourners, why would anyone besides the
undertaker bother to witness Violet being lowered into the ground?

How long could he continue this ministry when nothing seemed
to make a difference?

But there was the bright spot of Roxanna's good fortune—she'd written him, and by all accounts, the preacher indeed had told the truth about forgiving her past and had married her right off.

And how else could Nicholas make up for his own past except to continue on?

Quitting was not an option.

And neither was befriending Lydia King.

10

"How's your steak?" Sebastian speared a piece and popped it into his mouth. "I've always said steak should be seasoned with nothing but salt and pepper, but there's something else here. And I find it to be"—he chewed slowly, his eyes studying the ceiling—"interesting."

The men at the table behind Lydia erupted into laughter. She knew they weren't laughing at Sebastian making small talk about meat, since they'd laughed throughout the evening, but Sebastian *was* rather absurdly fixated on parceling out every dish set before him. Which might have been amusing if his fixation on food preparation and presentation didn't seem to portend how dinner conversations would go for the rest of her life.

She needed to steer the conversation away from food. "So, if at some point you decide to stop pursuing elected positions and return to law, what would you expect me to do?"

"Whatever you like."

She played with her fork. "What if I chose to read all day?"

"That would be a waste of time. But if it'd make you happy, I could give you a book allowance. Though I tend to agree with Mother; the Bible is the only reading material a woman needs."

"How much would the allowance be?" She'd never had enough money for books—that's why she had so few and reread so many.

"How many books would you need to waste money on? Too bad we don't have a library in town."

Her passion . . . *a waste*.

She sighed. "Yes, too bad."

"With the population growing, I'm sure the town will build one someday, and then you could borrow to your heart's content." Sebastian used his bread to sop the juices. "Until then, social clubs could occupy you."

"Yes, I'll need to be occupied." If for nothing else but to escape his ramblings about politics and the proper texture of cornbread. "If Teaville ever got one, would you mind if I volunteered there?"

"As long as you don't ignore the children to do so."

Children. She pushed around her steak. How many did he want? No, she wasn't having that discussion right now. "I wouldn't dream of it."

The restaurant's door flew open, and the redheaded man she'd seen with Mr. Lowe several days ago blew in. The stout man waved at a few people, then stopped at a booth beside the door, slapping one of the seated diners on the back with a laugh.

Mr. Lowe came in behind him and handed his hat to a hotel employee. Of course Mr. Lowe would come here to eat; it was his hotel, after all.

She inched toward the wall but then stopped herself. What was she doing, trying to blend in with the wall like she'd used to while reading a novel during science class?

She straightened back up, speared a slice of steak, and took a huge bite. Cold.

"Do you not agree, Lydia?"

"What?" She blinked at Sebastian. What had he said?

"The potatoes?"

She tried not to cringe as she ventured a reply. "Good."

Thankfully he found that response adequate and took the dessert menu from the ledge beside them to peruse.

Mr. Lowe tramped toward an empty table in the back corner. His jaw was tight, his posture slack, and once he sat, his gaze stayed fixed on the rolled silverware he fiddled with. Every few seconds, he pinched the bridge of his nose.

Was he crying?

She squinted against the hazy restaurant lighting. His eyes and cheeks seemed dry.

Perhaps he had a headache. She could sympathize—she'd had one for the last hour.

Mr. Beauchamp sauntered over to their table and knocked Sebastian on the shoulder with a meaty fist. "How are you doing this fine night, Little?"

"You're in fine spirits, Beauchamp, and no wonder. I heard your news about joining up with Padgett."

"Yes, my very good news." Mr. Beauchamp switched his gaze from Sebastian to her, his gaze far too probing, his smile embellished. "I hear you two are to be congratulated as well."

She sucked a breath through clenched teeth.

"Don't rush the lady. We've not declared anything official. Though I'm smitten—how could I not be?" Sebastian winked at her.

Mr. Beauchamp looked at her for a second, his smile looking less authentic by the second, then gave his attention back to Sebastian. "I look forward to working with you now that we have such close partners. One can never have too many connections."

"No." Sebastian glanced toward Mr. Lowe. "Though I don't understand why you'd want some of them."

Mr. Beauchamp looked at his gloomy friend, and his put-on smile faltered. "He's a decent chap."

"A self-righteous chap," Sebastian sneered.

"It pays to have someone on every side, doesn't it, Little?"

Sebastian's gaze twitched toward her for a second and then returned to Mr. Beauchamp. "Of course."

Mr. Beauchamp's green eyes landed on her again, and she dropped her gaze, grabbing the salt shaker.

Once Mr. Beauchamp left their table, Sebastian added more sugar to his tea. "I hope Lowe's not causing you too much trouble." He took a sip, muttered, then added more sugar. "I know Mother says you have to twist a penny out of him to prove your worth, but if you can't get anything from him, I won't fault you."

She exhaled and smiled a little. Would he truly not care if she failed to do as he and his mother wished? She tried to read his countenance, to find the truth behind his eyes.

His facial features were softer than normal as he gazed upon her—until his dinner distracted him again.

She glanced at Mr. Lowe and sighed. Whether or not Sebastian cared if she won over Scrooge, she did. She wanted to convince Mr. Lowe that she wasn't as selfish as he thought her to be, that she did want to help the underprivileged. "I appreciate your concern, but he's not bothering me in the least. I'll get something from him though. Just watch."

"I hope you do." Sebastian sniggered. "That Pharisee needs to be taken down a notch."

Pharisee? Mr. Lowe hadn't sounded Pharisaical in his office a few days ago. Hard-nosed, maybe.

Sebastian's eyes flitted toward the door, where two men she didn't know entered. With a quick dab to his lips, he scooted himself away from the table. "If you don't mind, I need to talk to those gentlemen. Boring business stuff—wouldn't interest you." He set down his napkin and excused himself.

Blowing out a breath, she stared at her barely touched plate but couldn't find the will to figure out for Sebastian what extra spice the cook had put on her now-cold steak.

Mr. Beauchamp slid into a chair across from Mr. Lowe and rumbled a steady stream of chatter as he flipped through his menu. Mr. Lowe smiled when his friend laughed, but the merriment in Mr. Beauchamp's chuckle wasn't mirrored in his friend's eyes.

And then, suddenly, Mr. Beauchamp abandoned their table with a shouted greeting to an older gentleman entering the restaurant. The two of them headed toward the corner where Sebastian was speaking to a man who didn't seem very interested in Sebastian's topic.

How she felt for the poor stranger.

Her eyes flitted back to Mr. Lowe. Sitting alone.

Well, it seemed it had turned into a night of business. How could one more attempt hurt? Swiping crumbs from her lap, she tried to breathe in such a way as to tamp down her heartbeat. She'd have to get used to ignoring her desire to sit in a corner with a book when there were campaigns to finance and donations to obtain.

She walked over to his table and lifted her chin. "Good evening, Mr. Lowe. It seems we've both lost our dinner partners, so I thought I'd come over and ask if you've given any more thought to funding our quilting project?"

"Miss King, please—"

"Or perhaps I could . . ." She wetted her lips and prepared to state the amount of money Sebastian wanted. Even if Mr. Lowe was a man of wealth, it was hard to ask for more money than most would see in three years' time. "I was hoping to get you to consider a campaign donation to Sebastian Little. He's sure that, with your known desire for moral strictness, you'd back his plans to clean up the town and be willing to pledge a generous one thousand dollars to—"

Mr. Lowe snorted, though there was an amused glint in his eyes—a marked improvement from the sour expression he'd worn earlier. "A thousand?"

She put on a smile and attempted to make it look heartfelt. "Or any other sizeable donation you'd like to give to his campaign. Though I'd settle for the thirty dollars for the sewing machines."

He picked up his spoon and twirled it in his hand, watching her intently. "How many times do you plan to ask me for this thirty dollars?"

"As many times as it takes." What was so terrible about providing people with blankets? "You know, if I were you, this wouldn't be such a hard decision. Surely, the cost of our entire project can't be more than what you carry around in your pocket."

"If you were *me*?" Nicholas couldn't believe Lydia had the nerve to invade his dinner to pester him about donations again.

Why she and everyone else thought they could spend his hard-earned cash better than he could was beyond him. People expected generosity from everyone but themselves.

"The cost of two sewing machines won't break your bank." Lydia's voice was contrite, but he still saw hardness in her eyes.

He sighed. Would it hurt him to give her thirty dollars? He'd wasted more than that before. Surely she'd stop pestering him then.

Yet being pestered by her wasn't all that bad.

But if he was going to give her money, he'd do it his way.

"Let's say you were me." He set down his spoon and folded his hands atop the table. "Would your top priority be sewing machines?"

She caught her lip with her teeth, but kept her gaze steady.

He really should stand up in a lady's presence, so he shoved himself out of his chair, maintaining her gaze without blinking. He shouldn't make her squirm too long, even if her expressions were currently entertaining.

The longer she remained silent, the more obvious it became she truly was going to come back to pester him again and again over thirty dollars.

Stubborn.

Confound it all, he liked that. This woman had the kind of personality he could groom. She could help save the world—if she knew what to save it from. "I'll make this easier. If you had excess money, what charities would you choose?"

"The quilting project—"

"Anything besides those infernal machines." If the top of his

77

chair hadn't been made of sturdy wood, it would've splintered in his hands.

She looked toward the ceiling and sighed. "I'd have to think."

"Listen, I agree we're called to help the lowly, but I've seen people do a lot of damage in the name of God's work." He glanced at one of the men in Henri's group. "Paul didn't care why the gospel was preached so long as it was. But why settle?"

"I realize you don't think much of me. But I don't need you to . . . I'll just let you return to your dinner." She pivoted.

"No, wait." He clasped her arm and turned her back. "You have guts. That's worth something. But what I want to know is if you care, truly care, for the unfortunate."

She kept her eyes level with his collarbone. "Of course I do."

"And are you willing to get your hands dirty, or do you expect someone else to do that for you?"

"I don't shy away from difficult things." She crossed her arms. "I'm here fighting for the quilting project though the ladies told me you were hopeless, aren't I?"

Hopeless? He swallowed a growl. Those moral-society ladies. In years past, none had come back once he'd sent them packing—though he'd been nice to Mrs. and Miss Wisely. But he wouldn't fund silly projects just because the people asking for donations were decent.

But the unwavering defiance Lydia possessed in the face of failure was something he couldn't plant inside anyone.

Mrs. Little could never help Lydia harness her talents for God. Maybe he'd volunteer to help the moral society groom one of its members to think their projects through. "All right, Lydia—tell you what I'll do. I want you to write down three things *you* think I should fund. Don't discuss this with the Littles or your ladies' group. Will you agree to that?"

At her nod, he continued. "You said if you were me, these decisions would be easy, so imagine yourself in my position when you choose." He crossed his arms. "If I see *sewing machine* on your list, I'll read no further. Give your wishes to my secretary by eight next Wednesday morning. If they're worthy and sane, I'll grant all three."

She cocked an eyebrow. "Three *wishes*?"

Maybe that wasn't the smartest way to put it, but he didn't care about semantics. "Yes, but please don't come to me again pleading for those quilts. I really do mean no on that."

"I suppose you do."

"No supposing at all."

"Tell Mr. Black he should expect me no later than Wednesday morning at 7:59."

11

Nicholas stopped scribbling. The sawmill's exterior door's hinges whined, followed by footsteps too dainty to be a worker. He leaned to see through the open crack of his office door. A glimpse of pale yellow fabric and raven hair breezed past, then the footfalls stopped. He had to stop himself from smiling.

"I'm glad to see you, Miss King." His secretary's voice was barely audible, but Nicholas still heard the glimmer of merriment in his voice. "Mr. Lowe is eagerly awaiting this."

Nicholas scowled. He'd told Gerald no such thing. His secretary better hold his tongue before he gave her the wrong impression.

"Am I supposed to wait for him?"

"He didn't say so."

"Then I'd best be going. Good day, Mr. Black."

Nicholas doodled to look busy in case she peeked into his office. After the door shut, he strolled into the front office. "Was that Miss King?"

"You know it was." His secretary held out an envelope.

Nicholas took it and forced himself not to look. "Did you get the invoices for Peterson out?"

"Yes, two days ago." Gerald voice was no-nonsense, but his eyes danced. "And yesterday when you asked me, it was one day ago."

He grunted at Gerald, then let himself look at the paper in his hand. Her dark fluid penmanship tempted him to trace the letters in his name. He turned the envelope over so he couldn't see the fine slant of her pen and snatched the letter opener off Gerald's desk. Slicing through the pretty envelope with the dagger-like instrument, he released a fresh burst of floral scent from its confines. Was this what she always smelled like? He'd have to get closer next time—

No. He strangled the handle of the letter opener before stabbing the sharp end into the desktop.

Gerald skewed his eyebrows and yanked the opener from the wood. "Take it easy. Just because Mrs. Greene called you on the carpet doesn't mean you have to kill my desk."

"Mrs. Greene? What're you talking about?"

"You didn't see the editorial this morning?"

Nicholas shook his head, and Gerald winced.

"Guess I have to show it to you now." Gerald pushed a folded newspaper across the desk and sat back. Way back.

The title, "Lowe's Waste and Disregard for the Needs of the Community," admonished him in large letters. He pressed his lips together before something unpleasant escaped, snatched up the periodical, and stomped back to his office.

"Mr. Lowe, if—"

The door's slam cut off his secretary's concerned voice. But at that moment, it was best that he be alone in his office, for who knew what he might be tempted to do with his secretary's letter opener after reading this.

The Ladies' Auxiliary was raising funds for a building and had stopped by last week asking for a donation. He'd offered to sell material to the group wholesale instead, but Mrs. Greene, the president, had expected more. She probably figured he should have financed the whole project.

His quick skim of the editorial made his heart palpitate, though his brain insisted he didn't care. Seemed she'd discovered a surprisingly accurate figure on the cost of building his mansion and couldn't contain her bitterness.

Nicholas trashed the paper and unclenched his jaw. He wouldn't reply, no matter how tempting. God knew why he built the mansion. And Mrs. Greene hadn't bothered to ask—not that he would have explained himself to her.

After Violet's death, and the newest maid giving up and returning to *"where she belonged,"* guilt weighed heavy in his heart. He didn't need any outside chastisement.

Nicholas took a deep breath and blew it out. God had forgiven him his past, and Violet's death wasn't his fault, so he wouldn't let Mrs. Greene's attack mess with his emotions. He picked up Lydia's stationery and rubbed it between his fingers, the silky-smooth paper pleasantly feminine, much like her skin might—

He dropped the letter and made for the window. Shoving up the sash, he inhaled the fresh air, blinking against the image in his mind. How had he gotten so out of control? Anger one minute, desire the next? Fantasizing about a woman he didn't know well had gotten him into trouble before. Big trouble.

And Lydia wasn't even available to court.

He returned to his desk and yanked the letter from its bothersome scented envelope, which he threw in the trash, and unfolded the list. Lydia was a distraction. The faster he was rid of her, the better. He'd look at her requests long enough to turn them down.

No introduction was scrawled at the top of the paper, just a simple list.

1. *Take care of the heating needs of three poor Teaville families this winter.*
2. *Make a donation to the church, preferably ten percent of your income.*
3. *Provide the town with a non-subscription library.*

He sat and reread the list while the wind from the open window licked at his exposed skin. Was his absurd desire to keep her around clouding his judgment, or were these three wishes just right enough that he'd have to honor them?

He chuckled at her first request—an attempt to get him to fund the moral society's blanket project?

Obviously the Bible told him to do number two.

And Lydia would personally benefit from the third wish, but hadn't he often thought the town needed a library? He already lent his personal collection to anyone who asked, and his maid Josephine found solace in the silly novels he ordered for her through *Harper's Bazar*. He had no desire to keep those books, so why not donate them to a library?

Nicholas let his head fall back against his chair. All week he'd dreaded having to deny Lydia her requests. Because if he did, how would he handle her returning to his office at least a dozen more times, complete with her hands on her hips and a sizzling glare, begging him to reconsider her three requests *and* the sewing machines.

But there would be no reason for her to come back and berate him anymore. He was going to grant her wishes. And that sparkle of triumph he'd craved seeing earlier would dance in her light blues.

He got up and closed the window, staring out at his workers carrying lumber from the yard to awaiting wagons. He'd prayed God would direct him to people who could help take over some aspects of his ministry, but maybe God wasn't giving him someone who already cared, but rather someone to mold. Lydia certainly had a passion and concern for others.

Or maybe she wasn't God's answer at all, and his attraction was causing him to lose sight of what was important.

He returned to the desk and reread her list. The wishes were still sane and wise, and his word obligated him.

He crossed the room and opened the door. "Gerald."

"Yes, sir?" Gerald dropped his legs from the top of his desk and had the decency to redden for being caught doing nothing.

"Make an appointment with Miss King to see me at her earliest convenience."

12

Lydia sat in Mr. Lowe's sawdust-free leather chair while he paced behind his desk, not frantically but meditatively. Since she'd not initiated this meeting, she'd let him speak first.

He sighed, his shoulders heaving with melodramatic exaggeration before he pivoted to face her. Legs spread wide, he put his hands behind his back as if he were facing a firing squad.

She tightened the muscles in her face so she wouldn't let loose the tiniest hint of a gloating smile. She'd won!

"Miss King. It seems I can't in good conscience ignore your wishes. All of them are things I'd consider doing myself without your prompting, so we will do them together."

"Together?" She frowned. What did that mean? How on earth was she supposed to help him give money to the church? She could certainly help with the poor families. Maybe he meant he wanted to help with the quilt project! She moved to the edge of her seat and bowed her head to hide her smile.

Forgive me for doubting you'd come through for me.

"Have you spoken to anyone about these wishes?"

At the shake of her head, Nicholas relaxed against his desk. "Wonderful. I will require that you not mention I'm involved with these monetary donations, though I suppose taking credit for the library cannot be helped." He tapped the desktop, where her list sat. "But, beyond secrecy, you will agree to a condition for each wish."

Her heart beat like a tightened drum. What could he possibly want from her? She had nothing. "I'll reserve my agreement until I've heard what they are."

"As to the first wish, you will go with me when I take supplies to the families."

She nodded sharply. "I could be sure you did it, then."

His eyebrows arched, as if surprised. "That shouldn't have been a worry. I told you I would."

She tried to relax her face, blink submissively. If she riled him, he might not follow through. "I didn't mean to question your word."

"As for the library"—he stood and crossed his arms—"you will run it."

Her hand pressed against the flutter in her chest. "Truly?" She'd hoped to have volunteered some hours, but to actually run the library? To buy books without spending a dime of her own money, to decide how they were shelved, to get to read them first! Sebastian could afford a cook and a maid or two, so she could easily spend as many hours as she wanted . . . well . . .

"What about when I have children after I'm married?"

They'd drastically cut down on her availability. Would Mr. Lowe give her a say in running things if she couldn't spend the entire day at the library?

His jaw moved back and forth, and his expression took on an edge.

She fiddled with the buttons on her shirtwaist. Had he forgotten a woman would have to see to such things? "I'm sure I could get someone to work while I'm unable."

"If you so desire, but it's not necessary." He exhaled loudly and dropped onto his desk. "You'll choose the library's operating hours, so you can take time off or cut back if needed. I could always send one of my secretaries over to open it up if someone required something."

She swallowed the giddy giggle swelling inside her and schooled her face into looking as serious as Mr. Lowe's. "All right. So far, I agree."

If she could never become a literature professor, head librarian sounded next to heavenly.

"Good. As for the church donation you requested, I'd like you to be there when I present the money, help me decide what funds should be bolstered."

She gripped the armrests to keep herself from clapping. She wouldn't even have to convince the pastor to use Mr. Lowe's money for the quilting project, she could just tell Pastor Wisely to put money into their account the day Mr. Lowe gave it.

"By the look on your face, it seems you agree to that as well." Mr. Lowe crossed his legs and his arms. "You asked that I give ten percent. I already do so, but I'm willing to give another ten percent this year—paid out in quarters."

He already tithed? No, he couldn't. She played with her gloves to hide the trembling in her fingers. She'd never once seen him put money in the little red velvet offering bags, and if he tithed, why did Pastor Wisely bemoan the church's lack of funding? Surely Mr. Lowe's tithe alone could fund the church. She pressed her jittery fingers against her lips. Maybe he didn't make as much money as she thought.

"Are you having second thoughts?"

She shook her head. He'd chosen to accept her wishes, and he wouldn't destroy his pocketbook to do so. She stood and offered her hand. "I agree, Mr. Lowe. I pledge my secrecy and my aid. Partners?"

He combed his fingers through his hair and stared at her hand. Sealing their deal with a handshake would bind a persnickety man like him.

All of a sudden his hand swallowed hers, and she forced herself not to wince against his strong grip. He looked at her so intently she could hardly breathe. Had she overstepped herself?

She pumped his arm and then tried to let go.

He cleared his throat and released her, then skirted around his desk to again take his chair. "I'll have Mr. Black contact you when I'm ready to start on your list. It will take a bit of planning on my part, but you'll have nothing to do but show up."

None of his conditions put her out, and now he planned to shoulder all the responsibility? She crossed her arms. When things appeared too good to be true . . .

He riffled through his desk drawer and snatched a fountain pen. "Since we'll be working together, you should call me Nicholas."

"Lydia, then." Though he'd used her Christian name twice already.

"And now, I must return to my work." He gave her a dismissive nod and opened a folder on his desk.

"Of course." She smiled at his disguised agitation, most likely already regretting having caved to her wishes. But that handshake would hold him. "A pleasure doing business with you, Nicholas." His name tumbled out too soft, and he quit rolling the pen between his fingers and looked up. A gentle light hit his eye, much like a man enamored. Then he frowned and slumped back against his seat, instantly engrossed with the contents of his folder, chewing on the end of his pen.

She rolled her eyes at herself as she breezed out the door. Nicholas Lowe, enamored? With her? The thrill of getting a donation had addled her brain.

Mr. Black stood, and she couldn't help throwing him a huge smile.

His mouth puckered along with his eyebrows. "So you actually got him to change his mind?"

"Yes." She stopped in front of him and tapped his ledger twice. "I told you I would."

He shook his head, a smile twitching the corners of his thin lips. "I stand corrected." He mock saluted her. "You are my inspiration. I never thought I'd see someone out-stubborn him."

"Well"—she leaned forward and gave a stage whisper—"maybe he's growing soft in his old age."

"Or maybe he's going soft because of you."

Her face muscles went slack, and she could only stare at Mr. Black's merry eyes. He cocked his head as if expecting an answer.

Did Nicholas grant her wishes to win her affection despite his insistence that charity should be done without any underlying motives?

"That can't be right." Her and Mr. Lowe? Ridiculous.

He was too important to feel the need to impress some lowly girl. Lowe's secretary was only teasing. He was a congenial fellow who'd probably rib her more if she protested too much. Mr. Black's words weren't worth pondering.

"Good day, Mr. Black."

"Why are you practically skipping?" Evelyn frowned at Lydia, but an upward curl fought against her friend's downturned lips. Evelyn hadn't a grumpy bone in her body. Though she was half a head taller than most women, she never slumped, always holding her head high, yet never made anyone feel beneath her.

How Lydia wished she could share her victory with her friend! She'd squeezed more out of Nicholas than the moral society had ever dreamed possible. But she wasn't even allowed to whisper her happy news to angelic Evelyn as they tromped behind the other moral-society ladies on Lydia's very first serenade. Not even the sudden temperature drop could dampen her spirits.

"I can't tell you now, but you'll find out soon enough." She tried to shuffle along piously, but since Evelyn kept shaking her head at her, she must be failing.

When the group crossed Eleventh Street, the far-off sound of riotous laughter and music increased, and her high stepping turned molasses slow.

She needed to have her head about her, be serious. Though something in her life had finally gone right by winning over Nicholas, this serenade was an echo of the part that was still wrong.

Lord, please let my father not be here tonight, especially if he'd choose to make a scene because I'm here.

The closer they walked to the blocks between Twelfth and Fourteenth and from Maple to Willow, the harder her heart beat, as if keeping tempo with each pounded note of the out-of-tune piano somewhere ahead of them. When they stepped onto Thirteenth Street, otherwise known as The Line once it hit Maple, Mrs. Little called them to stop in front of an abandoned building.

Lydia shielded her face from the dying rays of the autumn sunset losing its battle against the light spilling out of brothels and saloons—ill disguised as inns and soda fountains to circumvent the law. Only yards away, more people than she'd ever imagined filled the sidewalks. She'd thought people in this section of town would skulk about in the shadows, not laugh and talk merrily, heedless of being seen in such a place.

Mrs. Little cleared her throat, and Lydia threw back her shoulders with the other women, ready to hear their commanding officer's battle plans.

Please Lord, let us do some good. Get my heart right. As Nicholas has shamed me into admitting, I haven't been involved in this group for the right purpose. Let me take our actions seriously, so we can be effective in showing these people their folly.

"Since Lydia and Abbie have never been on one of our serenades, I'll remind everyone of how we should behave." Mrs. Little stopped pacing and clasped her hands behind her. "We'll start at the Red Star. Recently, they've added a lean-to to give them more room for gaming, and it's rumored the owner wants to start a dance hall."

The woman beside Lydia tsked, echoing the others' censuring murmurs.

Mrs. Little paused until they quieted. "We will shame them with the words of righteousness. If you can't read music, beseech God in silent prayer until you've learned the tune. Pray He will use the words of our songs to bring them into repentance. If a drunkard shouts at us, don't flinch. If an owner threatens us, don't stop singing. If a woman of the night glares at us, don't make eye contact. Only speak to those who ask how they can be forgiven and cleansed of their iniquity. If you don't feel ready for such a task, send them to me or Bernadette."

Lydia stood tall. Tonight Mrs. Little would be watching her, sizing her up, and she didn't want to show any signs of weakness.

"With the help of my son and the concerned women of Teaville, we shall eradicate our town's blackest blocks through passing stronger laws and awakening the sinners' guilt."

"Amen," several muttered.

"Let us not grow weary of doing good, but be a light unto the darkness." Mrs. Little shook her fist. "It's time to sing, ladies!"

The women called back with affirmations, but the knot in Lydia's throat kept her from adding a simple *yes* to their chorus.

She swallowed until air found its way into her lungs, then stiffened her limbs until they quit shaking. She'd wrestled with her drunken father many nights throughout her childhood, and she'd won over the tightest miser in Kansas only an hour ago. Singing was nothing to be nervous about.

The women formed a solemn single-file line, and Lydia took the end spot as they marched toward the music that would make a discordant background for their religious hymns and temperance anthems. Would they be heard over the din?

A few doors down from the placard marked *Red Star Inn*, a woman in a bright yellow gown, its neckline revealing cleavage, passed by the line of darkly garbed ladies and seared Lydia with a look of disdain.

A group of men smoking outside The California whistled suggestively as they marched past.

She worked to keep her face expressionless as she tried not to step on Evelyn's heels.

A womanly shape limped out from the shadows of an alleyway, her dress hanging off her shoulder, torn. She stepped under a lamp, revealing stringy hair and prominent cheekbones. The woman took another step, leaving the light and coming closer to the group.

"You want to help me?" The woman's words slurred. "Because I need it."

Lydia tensed. How often had Papa come home, his words smeared together because of too many drinks, and gotten rough with her? Lydia forced her mind off her father. He couldn't poison her against all drunkards. Perhaps some really did want help. She gave the woman a slight nod.

"I need food." A bottle appeared out of nowhere, and the street-walker took a drink. "And laudanum. Something to dull the pain."

Lydia swallowed hard against her constricted throat. "God often lets us experience pain to draw us closer to Him."

"That's all you're going to do for me? Save my soul?" Grabbing a handful of Lydia's wrap, the woman yanked her forward. "I said I was hungry."

"Lydia, walk on!" Mrs. Little stomped back, gripped her arm, and tugged her forward, but the dirty woman had a tight grip on her cloak. Mrs. Little pulled until she'd yanked the fabric from the woman's grasp.

The streetwalker sneered. "You're all the same."

Lydia faced Mrs. Little. "But I thought we were supposed to talk to them if they asked about repent—"

"She was asking you for a handout."

"She mentioned her soul."

"An alley cat is beyond our help. Save your breath."

Mrs. Little pulled her by the arm, dragging her a few feet until they stood in front of the tallest building on Willow. The women gathered in a huddle, and Evelyn sidled close.

"Did you see that lady who talked to me?" Lydia whispered up at her.

Evelyn shook her head, "Did some—"

"Hearken, you destroyers of men's souls." Mrs. Little turned and bellowed to the customers lounging around the front of the saloon. "Cease your drunkenness, your gambling, and your dallying. Listen to what the Lord would have you hear. Ladies, turn to hymn number five-oh-three."

Evelyn gave Lydia a concerned look before flipping open her bookmarked hymnal.

Lydia scrambled to find the right page. A chorus of booing and laughter sounded from the Red Star's windows, but Mrs. Little drowned out the crowd's jeering with a squeeze of her hand organ.

While the rest of the ladies joined the instrument with the first line of the hymn, Lydia glanced back at the streetwalker. The slovenly woman sneered at the assembly, then was overtaken by a violent shiver. She uncorked her little brown bottle, took another glug, and stumbled sideways.

Lydia played with the lapel of her thin wool cloak. Wouldn't God have her give it to the streetwalker who was obviously in need? But before she mustered the courage to ignore Mrs. Little's instructions, the drunk woman threw her empty bottle at their feet. Lydia flinched as glass shards sprinkled the sidewalk and the tops of her boots. Feminine shrieks and male laughter cut off the hymn's melody.

Mrs. Little pressed harder on her accordion. "Last verse, ladies. Then let us sing, 'The Lips that Touch Liquor Shall Never Touch Mine.'"

The street nymph glared straight at Lydia, swore loudly, and disappeared into the alley.

Lydia hugged herself and tried to join in with the song, but it was all she could do not to run home. Mrs. Little was right. She never should have made eye contact.

13

Nicholas walked beside his nag, Buttons, until she stopped to avoid another mud hole. He pulled on the cantankerous horse's halter. "Come on, girl."

Buttons resisted until he couldn't put any more tension on her harness without breaking it, then she lurched forward and plodded on as if she'd been walking at that pace all day.

"You're lucky I need you." He scratched her dirty white neck through her matted yellowed mane, his fingertips poking through his holey gloves. The tiny wagon behind her thumped into a pothole and stopped her progress. He stooped to yank on Buttons's halter to get her moving again.

"Lydia might think we forgot her if you clomp any slower." And he definitely hadn't forgotten her, nor the feel of her hand in his or the light in her eyes when he'd given in to her wishes. Those pale blue irises had turned vibrant in triumph—just as he'd suspected they would.

He rubbed his face, the grit from his hands scouring his cheeks. She was too attractive for her own good. Hopefully God would help him help Lydia discover true charity, otherwise he'd be highly frustrated for the next few weeks, fighting the urge to both caress and wring her beautiful, stubborn neck.

He towed Buttons over the knoll on the outskirts of town and toward the Verdigris River. On the bridge, Lydia sat upon the edge, leaning against a column. Her fitted navy coat contrasted sharply with her light pinstriped skirt, and her cream-colored straw hat called attention to her dark hair. Was that what she'd worn to church earlier? Had his secretary forgotten to tell her to wear work clothes? Good thing he had an old cloak and cap for her or he'd lose another hour taking her back home to change.

He stopped in front of her and grinned at her blank stare. Walking around in disguise was too much fun. "My lady, you're looking too beautiful this afternoon."

"I beg your pardon?" She jutted out her chin. Her fists bunched as if readying to land him a blow if he stepped nearer.

"Begging for more?" He dared to step closer and couldn't help his grin. "Aren't we greedy? I've already given you what you want."

Her eyes widened, and then one eyelid scrunched. Her mouth pursed like a young child who'd been told to go to bed early. "Nicholas?"

His name on her lips only warmed the already mild autumn day. He bowed. "At your service."

She leaned back and pinched her nose. "You smell as if you've lived in those clothes for a year."

"That's because I haven't washed them in about that long."

"You reek of death."

"I don't smell that bad." He'd only smeared his mackintosh and trousers in dirt and splashed them with whiskey last fall.

"I don't know what you're doing—"

"Of course not, or you'd have argued. This saves time."

He offered her his hand, but she turned her nose up and hopped off the bridge's wall herself.

Maybe she thought she was wearing work clothes. After all, a cleverly hidden patch was visible near her knees, but her coat was much too nice. He trailed his hand along Button's dusty side as he ambled back to the wagon and fished out an out-of-fashion cloak. "Exchange your coat with this."

She gave the item a wary look. "Does it smell as bad as you?"

"Worse." He grinned. Hopefully she'd relax. When he disguised himself as Nick, he tried to leave tense Nicholas behind. "It's been in a trunk in the attic for decades." Actually the garment smelled delightful compared to him.

"Why is this necessary?" She took the cloak but held it out as if holding a rat by the tail.

"The people we're visiting won't take charity from high society."

"Charity's charity."

He set the conditions, not her. "I decide how these wishes are meted out, or they don't happen at all. Your pick."

She glanced between the weathered wagon attached to his sorry nag and the ugly cloak in her hand. Several times.

He forced himself not to tap his foot impatiently. Maybe he was asking too much from her too soon. If she went into the Blairs' house looking as if she'd stuffed rotten eggs up her nose, she'd make things worse. "You can do this, Lydia. Remember, you got three wishes out of the stingiest man in town, and he even brought you gifts." He reached back into the wagon and pulled out a limp black bonnet. "Here's another. I promise you, these clothes smell like heaven compared to the places we're going."

"Is that supposed to entice me to put them on?"

"I shouldn't have to entice you to do anything. You wanted me to provide for three poor families, yes?" This was going to be a long day. "Do you think I should've chosen families who bathe in scented water and send out their laundry every week?"

"No." She sighed and dropped the items he'd handed her onto the ground. She wiggled out of her coat and unpinned her hat.

He stooped over to pick up the clothing and handed her each piece. She stuffed her arms into the cloak and jammed the bonnet on her head.

"You need to act as if you aren't wearing a bloody carcass around your neck or a raccoon on your head."

She scowled at him.

"My grandmother always said, *'Be careful or your face will freeze like that.'* So keep that up, it goes well with the ensemble."

"I still don't look as poor as you." She poked out her little leather shoes.

"Today, doesn't matter that much. As long as you don't look so far above me the Blairs wonder why we're together." He pointed over his shoulder. "I have a servant's dress in the wagon that should fit you for next time."

"You mean we aren't doing this all in one day?"

"No, this family lives in the opposite direction of the other two. We need to hurry though—we only have so much time before dark."

"But it's only three o'clock." She looked out over the river valley. "How far must we go?"

He pointed across the water. "A shanty on the other side of that rise."

Her face relaxed. "That won't take more than an hour."

"We're visiting, not just dropping things off and running home."

She stared at the little bump in the landscape, her jaw hard. "For how long?"

"No less than an hour."

"Why?"

"Because it would be rude not to. They have few, if any, visitors. They aren't comfortable with charity to begin with, and they're as valuable in Christ's sight as you are—so we're going to treat them as such." Maybe he was wrong about Lydia. If she couldn't muster up a respectful manner toward these people, she'd ruin the relationship he'd developed with them.

"All right." Her face was still scrunched with repugnance.

He rolled up her coat and crammed it under the wagon's seat. "There isn't enough room up here to ride with you, so I'll walk." Actually, if they sat hip to hip, they could fit. But they shouldn't— for more reasons than him smelling like a wet dog. Plus he'd need to yank on Buttons occasionally.

She put her hand in his, her eyes wide and uneasy.

He placed his other hand atop hers. "Don't worry—you'll be fine. Just stop gnawing off your lower lip. But then again, if you have no lips, they won't notice how awful you smell in that cloak."

14

Lydia struggled to keep her seat as Nicholas fought with the ugly white horse pulling a sorry excuse for a wagon up an incline. He'd probably save time by unhitching Buttons and pulling the cart himself. Was this animal really his? He certainly talked to the nag as if he'd known her his whole life. Once he got Buttons to move again, Nicholas began whistling.

He must have skipped shaving this morning, smeared some dirt across his forehead, and oiled his hair. She wouldn't have given him a second glance if he hadn't stopped and teased her, so good was his disguise. How often did he run around in this getup?

And where had this jovial man come from? Loose and familiar —not cold and hard-nosed.

After cresting the hill, Nicholas pointed at a residence in the valley. "There's the Blairs' house."

Was *house* truly the right word for the structure in front of them? Her grandfather's pig shelter looked sturdier than both the hovel and small barn squatting in a wide circle of mud. The only vegetation in the yard was a cluster of thorn bushes that a black-and-white goat was busily stripping of brown leaves. Broken pottery and jagged tin decorated the grassless lawn.

After three or four more stops and starts, Buttons finally managed to make it down the hill.

"Ho there, Alec?" Nicholas called, a dirty hand cupped against his mouth. "Iona, are you home?"

He knew them by first name? How many times had he visited? She clenched tightly to the seat as Buttons yanked the wagon to the left and nosed at a half-eaten, muck-covered apple.

An older woman in a worn navy dress and a thin purple shawl poked her head out the door, and Nicholas's face brightened. How could he look so comfortable in this dirt yard when he wouldn't condescend to leave his mansion to mingle with the middle class?

When he reached up to help her down, her hands trembled. He winked at her, set her on the ground, then walked straight toward the woman and snatched a dirty urchin out from behind the shabby folds of her skirt.

Spinning the boy around, he tickled his ribs.

The boy's laughter rippled out from deep inside.

"Come now, Errol, if you're laughing"—he dug his fingers into the boy's armpit, causing another round of giggles to escape—"you can't greet Miss King properly."

The little blond boy, four, maybe five years of age, wriggled away and ran back up some kind of ramp to the front door and hid behind what must have been his grandmother's skirts. "Can't catch me!"

Iona harrumphed at the boy, then turned toward Lydia. "Pleased to meet a friend of Nick's."

Nick? So familiar. "Me too."

So he had an overly talkative friend in town and a family of friends poorer than his mansion's mice on the outskirts of town. . . . Somehow she doubted this would be the most surprising thing she'd learn about him today.

"Miss King's a new acquaintance from town."

"Yes. Call me Lydia."

"I'm Iona." She scanned Lydia up and down, frowned, and took a second look. "My son and Theresa are inside. Won't ye come in?"

99

Nicholas tromped up the ramp and ducked to pass under the doorway, which even she had to stoop to enter. The floor was smooth cement—not what she'd expected for a hovel. The smell of must and burnt wood mingled with the scents of the dried herbs and plants hanging from four bare rafters.

A thin woman with large eyes lay propped up in a bed, her long, light brown hair lying loose over her shoulders. Her frayed quilt covered what looked like a wasted lower body.

A strawberry-blond man with dirty, exposed forearms handed the frail woman a steaming mug. He gave her a quick kiss on the hairline before turning to greet them.

Nicholas shook hands with the man, then knelt beside Theresa. "How are you today?"

"Not too bad, now that the rain has stopped." She patted his hand on her shoulder.

Why did these people live in such crude conditions if they were indeed Nicholas's—er, Nick's—friends?

After he briefly introduced her to Errol's parents, Alec and Theresa, Lydia bumped against the unusually low sink table and knocked a glass onto the hard floor. "Sorry."

Iona glared at her but swept up the broken pieces before she could lean over to lend a hand. The incident with last week's streetwalker jumped into her mind. Besides the low-cut neckline of the prostitute's dress, she'd been as pitiful and dirty as these people.

Beside the bed, a cheap oil lamp sat atop a crate nailed to the wall, making a crude shelf for a few books. The fire in the fireplace was stoked, but despite the sulfuric stench of coal smoke in the house, only wood burned there. She scrutinized Alec again. Perhaps he worked a forge, which would explain the dark smudges on his muscular arms and the coal odor.

A long table, two stools, and a straw pallet took up the space against the opposite wall. Lydia folded her hands together, wondering where she should stand—there certainly weren't many places to sit.

Nicholas pulled one of the stools over to Theresa's bedside, snatched Errol onto his lap, and turned to Alec. "Were you able to chink your siding?"

"Aye. Thankfully the cold weather's taking its merry time in getting here." The man's heavy voice boomed with a pleasant musical quality. "Felt a lot like early summer last Lord's day."

Iona took a basket of wadded clothing outside, and the rest of the family hovered around Nicholas, who bantered with them as he had with her on the bridge.

When Alec and Nicholas started discussing Alec's job, which Nicholas had evidently obtained for him, Lydia lowered herself onto the empty stool. The entire family's attention was glued to Nicholas—a man no one in Teaville liked. They'd forgotten all about her.

She closed her eyes and folded her hands. She felt like a little girl in desperate need of a bed to kneel beside. *Lord, you knew his heart all along. How stupid I must have looked to him, insisting he stop shirking his Christian duty and help the poor. Why did he agree to help me since I admitted I had selfish reasons for wanting him to grant my wishes?*

But her hiding in a corner wasn't helping anybody. And these people definitely needed help. Sliding out the door, she picked her way around the refuse in the yard to the wagon and yanked on the crate full of vegetables. The vegetables were mostly wilted, but surely Nicholas had brought them for this family. She *oomph*ed when the crate finally wiggled off the back and dropped into her arms.

"Nah-a-a." The bell around the goat's neck jangled as the beast came over and inspected her cloak. He rubbed his nose against the wool, then chomped and yanked.

She jumped away, but the goat moved with her, nibbling on her pocket. "Go away." She tried to elbow him, but he kept after her. She pushed harder, but the animal's nose stayed buried in her pocket until he pulled out a glove.

After dropping the vegetables, she grabbed for her glove. "Give me that."

Pulling only proved the animal had strong jaw muscles. Wriggling the fabric side to side only made him dig in his feet. "Let go, you wretched thing."

Yanking it loose, she stumbled back. Before she could stuff the glove back in her pocket, the goat snatched a carrot from the vegetable box.

She crammed the glove deep down in her pocket and tossed him another carrot to distract him. She hoisted the vegetables, raced toward the shack, and then slowed.

Iona's guarded gaze followed her as she stirred the washpot near the clothesline.

Her cheeks flamed with the knowledge that this woman had seen her fight with a goat—and lose. To avoid the old woman's disapproving eyes, Lydia dropped her gaze to her feet and pushed through the door.

The crate thumped loud on the table. She cringed, not meaning to have made so much noise.

"Ah, Lydia, we would have gotten that." Nicholas's mouth scrunched to the side, and he turned back to Alec. "Well, I guess we ought to show you what we brought today."

Theresa peered around Errol and frowned. "Thank you, but I hope it wasn't much trouble."

"No trouble." Lydia wiped her forehead with the back of her bare hand instead of fishing out her tatted handkerchief. "There's more outside."

Alec stood. "I'll bring in what's left."

"We'll help. There's a lot to haul." She smiled, but the effort to remain cheery proved difficult when Theresa's and Alec's expressions stiffened.

"Yes." Nicholas stood the boy up. "Errol, we'll need your help too. We—"

"Now hold on." Alec stepped in between her and Nicholas, looking at them both. "We aren't needing no more than that box. I won't say we can't use it, but we didn't ask for it."

"Of course not." Nicholas gripped the man's shoulder. "But

my boss lost a bet—a very long story. He sent a wood stove. The vegetables are from me."

"We've got a fireplace." The man scratched his head and looked back at his wife, who stared blankly.

Surely the man would take what they brought. She glanced over at Errol, who'd gone quiet. They needed so much.

"Theresa got pneumonia twice last winter." Nicholas gestured toward the wall. "And your chinking will be helpful, but an efficient wood stove will—"

"We cannae be taking it."

"Well, I can't take it back." The two men squared off in a silent duel.

Lydia worried her lip. Nicholas could have given wood to anyone, but here he was bullying a man into taking what he irrationally didn't want.

The two men stared at each other for so long she feared she might blurt out something just to break the silence—and she'd certainly say the wrong thing.

"Think of your wife and son." Nicholas turned his eyes to the woman lying stiller than still on the bed. "And your mother, since cooking on a stove would free up some of her time."

Alec's jaw flexed a bit, but when he looked at Theresa his shoulders softened.

"The only charity is the efficient stove. The lumber is just the boss man's trash. We burn the scraps, so why not let you have them? And I'm only to deliver it to you this once. You'll have to collect the wood from now on."

The man pulled on his ear. "I suppose."

Theresa rewarded Alec with a smile, making the big man sigh and smile back.

"There now—thanks for giving in." Nicholas rattled his arm. "I don't know what I'd have done if I had to take it back. Lowe doesn't like being thwarted." He turned and put a hand on Lydia's shoulder. "You and Theresa have a lot in common. Why don't you two talk while we unload?"

She swallowed hard as he steered her toward his vacated seat. Talk? What could she possibly have in common with this woman? The little boy stared at her from his perch near his mother's feet then ran off to join the men.

"Well." Lydia cleared her throat. Her lips twitched, trying to find words.

Theresa canted her body to the side to look her in the eye. "Do you read?"

"Read?" She blinked. Of course she read.

"Books?"

"Yes."

"I suppose that's what Nick meant when he said we had things in common." She lifted an eyebrow. "Unless you're a paraplegic in disguise?"

Lydia blinked. "No." She caught the glimmer in Theresa's eyes and let out a nervous chuckle. "I don't think so anyway."

Theresa rewarded her with a smirk.

Scanning the little library shelf next to the bed, Lydia read the titles. The Bible, a book of Shakespeare's sonnets, *The Invisible Man,* and . . . "Why that's Mr. Gr—" She stopped herself with a cough. She'd almost revealed she recognized her former teacher's copy of *Pride and Prejudice,* though she was supposed to be new to town . . . or was she just supposed to be a new acquaintance? Anyway, that was certainly the same green spine, bent up at the bottom from when she'd dropped it the third, or maybe fourth, time she'd borrowed it from her teacher. "I mean, that's Miss Austen's *Pride and Prejudice,* a favorite of mine." Did Harrison and Charlie Gray already help this family? Why hadn't Charlie or her mother mentioned the Blairs' needs to the women in the moral society? They lived just about a half mile west of here. Lydia would've remembered Charlie talking about a paraplegic neighbor.

"Mine too. I read it a while back and can't wait to read it again." Theresa pushed herself higher on her pillows with a groan. "Charlie Gray loaned it to me. She's a neighbor. She came over last week with a bottle calf for Errol to nurse, just like she did last year." A twinkle brightened Theresa's eye. "Alec knows she only claims to be too busy to take care of it to get him to agree to take half the meat, but Errol's absolute joy over getting to care for another calf kept my husband from turning her away."

Lydia played with her lip. Did Nicholas know Charlie was in the moral society? Seems he might like at least one member of the group.

"So what have you read recently?"

Lydia talked with Theresa, trying to figure out what they'd both read and loved as the men unloaded and then set up the stove using the existing chimney. Iona glared disapprovingly at everyone except Errol as they bustled in and out of the shack, and sporadic goat bleating accompanied the ladies' book discussion. Theresa, forced abed, seemed to have read as much if not more than Lydia, despite having only four books on her makeshift bookshelf.

Too soon, Nicholas, a little out of breath and with pink in his cheeks, lowered himself onto a nearby stump, and Alec dropped one last armful of scrap wood upon the misshapen stack beside the stove.

Theresa reached over and squeezed Nicholas's hand. "Thank you for bringing the stove, and thank your boss for it, if you would."

Nicholas swiped at his forehead with a rag. "I wouldn't bother thanking him. He did it under duress."

"Yes, he's a miserable wretch, from what I've heard." Lydia glanced at Nicholas, expecting him to smirk.

But his frown seemed sincere.

"Well then, I hope to thank him myself one day." Theresa pushed herself up farther on her pillows. "Did you know Lydia has a copy of *Roughing It*?"

"She does?" Nicholas's smile reappeared, though his eyes didn't look as bright. "Maybe she'll lend it to you."

"Oh, well . . . that's not necessary."

Lydia squeezed Theresa's shoulder. "I'll give it to Nick to bring next time he visits."

Errol scooted closer to his mother, and she gathered him up and rubbed her cheek against his dirty hair. Her eyes closed, exhaustion written on every line around her mouth.

Nicholas stood and offered Lydia his arm. "Seems you've lulled her to sleep with all your literature talk."

Theresa's eyes fluttered open. "Of course not. I enjoyed it immensely. I haven't discussed books with anyone for a while—Alec hasn't much time for it with his job and the work around our place." Theresa's lips wriggled slightly. "And Mother refuses to read."

"I got better things tae do," Iona barked from the corner.

"And taking care of me consumes enough time." Theresa leaned over and clasped Lydia's hand. "If you ever have time to stop by again, know you're welcome. Even if all you do is talk about tiresome old books."

Iona grunted.

"I hope to see you again, Theresa." But would she? Lydia exchanged good-byes with the others before leaving. Maybe she could drop by next time she visited Charlie. Then again, if Nicholas didn't bring her, could she show up uninvited?

Nicholas waited for her on the ramp, and she closed the door behind her.

"Don't you feel bad about lying to them?"

He looked as if he'd been waiting to take her arm, but he sort of wilted and then tramped down the rest of the ramp. "I didn't know they were going to become such good friends when I met them." His voice was low, barely above a whisper. "They started out like all the others—just people needing help."

He tilted his head toward her but didn't quite look her in the eyes. "I'm worried that I'll lose their friendship if they find out before I tell them. Though I'm not sure it will matter how or when they find out now—I've misled them for too long."

She'd never imagined herself feeling even a teensy bit sorry for the town's miser, but the gravel in his voice tugged at her heart. She stepped off the ramp. "When do you plan to tell them?"

"Once Alec has this house fixed up so it's worthy of Theresa."

The goat looked up from ripping apart a gunny sack, and Lydia stepped behind Nicholas, hoping the thing hadn't spied her.

"Don't tell me you're afraid of a nanny goat."

A girl was it? "She eats gloves."

Nicholas laughed—though the sound wasn't as joyous as it had been earlier—and helped her up into the wagon. "Besides encountering a vicious goat, this visit wasn't as bad as you expected, was it?"

"You act like you're trying to teach me something."

He crossed his arms, legs spread wide. "Do you still think your quilting project deserves to be funded?"

"Of course."

"Then I'm a terrible teacher."

So he *was* trying to teach her something. "How's that?" Perhaps he was teaching her to be less squeamish of filthiness? One day, if Papa didn't wise up and Sebastian decided against her, they could end up in a shack like this.

Nicholas pulled Buttons until she dragged her feet forward as if slogging through glue. "If I tell you what I'm trying to teach you, you'll say you already know it. And then you'll focus on proving it instead of letting the lesson change your heart."

She crossed her arms. So he had ulterior motives for his acts of charity as well. Of all the high-handed . . . "Then how do you expect me to pass your test?"

He huffed and yanked on Buttons' harness. "Come to the lumberyard next Monday after breakfast. Wear the dress, cloak, and hat with nothing ostentatious. No jewelry, no fancy hairdo, no colors. We won't want to be noticed. Then I'll give you your next lesson."

15

As she scuttled toward the shed behind Lowe's Lumberyard, Lydia clutched his copy of *Roughing It* with her grandmother's gloves, which she'd taken from her mother's trunk. Old and dingy, they went well with the threadbare dress Nicholas had sent home with her. She walked quickly, partially out of fear of being recognized, and partially because her nerves tingled clean down to her toes the closer she got.

Would Nicholas be as jovial as last week, or had he simply been in a good mood because he was visiting friends? Would all these visits be to people with whom Nicholas shared books? But even if not, she'd be less standoffish this time. Nicholas must think she looked down upon the poor or those improperly groomed, and she'd likely reinforced his assumptions with her awkward behavior at the Blairs' house last week—until Theresa mentioned reading. But this time, even if whatever family they visited was entirely illiterate, she'd behave superbly, and he'd realize her previous ill manners were simply because she hadn't known how to act.

A beaten-up post coach was parked behind the lumberyard in an alley. A gray-haired man sat on the box seat. She'd expected a wagon—to haul firewood and a stove again—but maybe things were stuffed in the boot. Neither of the two dappled horses shifting their feet was Buttons, and the driver wasn't Nicholas . . . unless he'd powdered his hair.

Unlike Watson in a few Sherlock Holmes stories, her partner's disguise wouldn't fool her again. Since Thursday, she'd taken a second look at every gentleman who scuffled past her.

Holding her hand against her forehead, she shielded her eyes from the sun and called up, "Are you for hire?"

The man startled on his seat and looked down at her. "Excuse me?"

Unless Nicholas was a magician, that wasn't him.

The battered coach's door swung open. "Get in here before you get us in trouble," Nicholas whispered loudly.

After she'd settled in the seat across from him, he pointed to her face. "I see you've had fun." The tilt of his brow gave away his amusement.

"I thought it would help." She refrained from touching her face despite the itch to rub off the faint wrinkles she'd painted around her eyes with a grease pencil. She'd also applied a little oil into her hair so no one would suspect she'd washed it two days ago. "Who's the old man?"

"My driver."

"I'm glad you're giving him work."

"How's that?"

"Just . . ." She twisted a button at her wrist. Nothing she'd thought about Nicholas was proving true. Her previous assumption that he was too stingy to adequately employ his driver probably wasn't either.

His intense stare made her squirm.

"Well, many assume, with all the walking you do, that he has little opportunity to earn money because you're too tightfisted. Yet you require him to be at your beck and call, taking away his ability to find more work."

He snorted. "I love these stories about me. Don't ever stifle them. They're good for my cover."

So that's why he never defended himself against rumors. "I suppose you pay the driver a handsome salary."

"No." He leaned back in his seat and laced his fingers behind his head. "Only what would be expected for a man in his position, but he can't work most afternoons. His wife has dementia, and the daughter who attends her the most has to return home to cook supper for her family. If they don't keep an eye on Mrs. Parker, she wanders."

"The poor man." One day soon she'd lose her mama to illness, but losing a loved one by loss of mind had to be tougher. "Will we return in time for him to get home?"

"His other daughter can help some evenings, as she will today. I got her a flexible position at Beauchamp's mill so she could assist occasionally without fear of losing her job."

First the Blairs, then the driver and his daughter, plus whomever they were going to visit next. How many more people did Nicholas help that she'd assumed he despised? "You're turning out to be a regular Robin Hood."

He raised a brow. "I do not steal from the rich."

"You're rich, and it seems you distribute more of your wealth to the poor than anyone would've guessed."

"That isn't the same."

"No, but it's more than I gave you credit for." She fiddled with the lint on her sleeve. "More than most do—even Bernadette and Evelyn."

"The Wiselys are good people." Nicholas frowned, the coach's shadows making him look fierce. "I can't believe they'd gossip about such things."

"The only woman in the moral society who defends you is Evelyn. Not because she's certain you deserve it, but because she tries to find the good in everybody."

"And you think Evelyn's naïve for finding good in me?"

"No, she's been right to stick up for you. I'm sorry I haven't joined her, that I assumed the worst, just because . . ." Why had she assumed the worst of him when she'd never even spoken to him? She'd prided herself for abstaining from gossip, but maybe the rumors swayed her more than she'd realized. "I'm sorry I didn't wait to judge what kind of man you were until after I actually met you."

"And what kind of man am I?"

The sharpness in his eyes made her uncomfortable. "I don't know yet, but I'll erase what I thought I knew of you and form my opinion based on our time together."

He hummed affirmatively, but his expression looked unconvinced. When the coach turned, he lifted the leather curtain to look outside.

Lydia caught a glimpse of Beauchamp Mill before he dropped the curtain. Then about a block later, the driver turned west. After a few minutes, she dared to lift the curtain to look herself. "We can't be where I think we are."

He turned toward her. "And where do you think we are?"

"A block away from The Line."

"Correct."

"Why on earth would your driver take us through this part of town?"

"Because we're going to it, not through it."

"I can't go there." She grabbed her collar. "We—"

The carriage clattered and swayed as it crossed the first set of railroad tracks, then another. She tensed her muscles in a hopeless attempt to avoid being sloshed to and fro.

Nicholas seemed to anticipate every jolt and rode out the bumpiness like a sailor swaying confidently on sea legs.

When they clattered over the last set of tracks, Nicholas spoke. "And why can't you go there? I heard you marched down The Line with Mrs. Little's group."

"That was different."

"You're right." He tipped his head forward like a perturbed bull about to charge. "You ladies went to judge, throw stones, and ignore the needs of the people wallowing in sin," he rumbled, his voice filled with exasperation. "But today, I'll require you to actually talk to one instead of throwing condemnation from afar."

"I did talk to one!" Where had this accusation come from? Lydia sat on her hands to keep from crossing her arms and looking like a petulant child. "She threw a glass bottle at me."

He turned his head to the side but kept his gaze on her. His forehead wrinkled. "And she did this after you offered to help her?"

Lydia ground her teeth. She would've helped if not for the others . . . maybe.

But if he was so worried about the needs of that streetwalker, he should be worried about her needs too. She grabbed the front of her worn coat and wriggled it. "I'm in disguise, with a man, inside an enclosed vehicle, in the town's sporting section! Do you have no concern for my reputation?"

"Of course I do. I wouldn't have brought you if the danger was greater than the night you sang 'The Price of a Drink' or 'Come Home, Father' in front of the saloon houses."

Well, she hadn't actually sung, especially not the one about asking Father to come home in case Papa was actually in one of those saloons that night and came out to embarrass her. "So you intend for us to stand on the street outside a saloon and give firewood away?"

"No."

"Don't tell me we're going inside the bar."

He leaned back, his fingers tapping his knees in an agitated staccato. "What would you have us do? Holler the lady's name and drop her firewood in the middle of the str—"

"We're visiting a . . . a—"

"Prostitute?"

She nodded.

"No," he replied.

She sighed in relief.

He leaned back against his seat, his eyes intense. "She isn't anymore."

"That doesn't help." She scowled at him. "Once a prostitute, always—"

"Even one who's turned to God?"

She put her hands against her face and closed her eyes. Had a soiled dove repented? What would the moral-society ladies say to that? They'd be happy of course, but visiting her? "I . . . I'm sure God accepts her, but I can't associate with someone who's been down that path. Do you know what would be said of me?"

"Then what on God's green earth are you women trying to accomplish with your moral society?" He scooted to the edge of his seat as if he wanted to leap over and strangle her.

Lydia pushed herself into the corner. During her father's drunken rages, it was best to keep silent or risk being manhandled. But what had dredged this anger out of Nicholas? It was *her* reputation at stake!

"You moral-society ladies along with the politicians only make things worse. You think kicking prostitutes and gamblers out of town or regulating them to death will solve the problem, but you only drive them underground."

No wonder this Robin Hood had no merry band of followers.

"And once these sinners make their initial mistake, they are never allowed back into your *Christian* society." His voice fogged over and turned scratchy.

No, that wasn't true—at least not in the way he made it sound.

"Do you know how many of them die friendless and humili-ated by the very women they cried out to for comfort in their last days?"

The sound of his holding back unshed tears drained her of any desire to argue.

The coach stopped, but she didn't have to get out. She wouldn't be seen if she stayed inside the vehicle.

After an awkward moment, where he did nothing but stare at the side wall, he jerked himself out of his seat, pushed through the door, and whirled to face her. "Are you coming?"

She pressed a hand to her throat. So he wasn't going to let her out of this? What if she refused? What would happen to the third poor family he was supposed to help, the church donation, the library? "If I don't come, is our wishes agreement canceled?"

The muscles in his neck tensed. His stare made her squirm. "I'll go back to choosing my venues of charity without you." A wicked grin marred, yet at the same time enhanced, his features. "And your precious reputation will remain unblemished by any act of kindness that doesn't meet the approval of those worried only about themselves."

Her heart fluttered in her chest, and her hands shook at his insult. Did that include her? Did he think she cared nothing for anyone but herself? And why did his disapproval hurt so much? "You're being unfair. I do want to help, but if I ruin my reputation, what good am I?"

"Christ didn't worry about his reputation. He associated with those who desperately needed Him. The frowns of the religious leaders didn't stop Him from helping the lowly."

"He was God. He didn't have to care, but I do. My future depends on it. I'm not like you, a man with great wealth." Nicholas hadn't thought this scheme through. At least not how it would affect her. If she did as he suggested, she'd be unmarriageable. With one parent dying and the other squandering every penny they made, how could she possibly recover from a ruined reputation? Did he even care? "If I sully my character to the point no good man would marry me, you'll be adding my name to the list of paupers needing your handouts."

"So marriage to a man who'd fault you for being charitable is more important than the lives of people less fortunate than you?"

How dare he insinuate such a thing? The Bible told people to mind their reputations.

She glanced out the door but couldn't see much, considering Nicholas filled the doorway. Had his raised voice drawn attention? "Choosing to do things your way may doom me to be a penniless spinster."

But not a prostitute. She'd never, ever, let herself go that far.

"If Christ called you to be penniless, would you not become so willingly?"

She worried her lip. How was she supposed to know? Hadn't Christ already called her to poverty given her father's habits and her mother's health? Burning filled the back of her eyes, but she blinked it away and swallowed. This was too much to think about. He shouldn't be pushing her to make a rash decision.

"I see." He stepped back even farther and grabbed the door. "I'll send you home then."

"Wait." She moved to the edge of her seat and peered out. They weren't in the red-light district but in a slum nearby. No one walked the quiet street. "Are you certain I won't be discovered?"

He sighed. "It's very unlikely, but no, I can't promise."

"And you say this woman is Christian."

"Yes, and just as needy as Alec and Theresa. However, as a reformed prostitute, she's more so. Neither side wants her. What kind of life is that? What kind of Christian refuses to help another member of the Body just to maintain one's superior position?" He ran his hands through his hair. "I know society teaches you to ignore soiled doves. I know I'm asking you to get your hands dirty, but—"

"But you're right." Lydia wrung her hands thinking about the streetwalker Mrs. Little had pulled her away from, whose eyes and barbed words had haunted her conscience for a week. "If we claim to want them to know the love of Christ but don't give it, how will they believe?" Her insides quivered at her capitulation. Doing as he asked could destroy her future.

Sebastian wouldn't approve of her stepping out of this carriage.

But Nicholas was the one holding out his hand, a tickle of a smile playing at the corners of his mouth. "Exactly so. And don't forget your third wish—I'm not asking you to serve as the librarian for free. The salary will keep you in a modest home, with all the books you could hope to read in your spinsterhood—if it came to that."

He planned to pay her to do something she would've done for free? How had she missed that detail?

Her hand shook as she placed it in his before stepping down onto the dirt road. She looked up into his softened gaze, the same look his eyes had sported when he'd attended to Theresa and tweaked Errol's nose.

Was she wrong to think he wasn't worried about her? Maybe he just didn't realize that even with a job, a lady's spoiled reputation destroyed more than her pocketbook.

16

Nicholas breathed out the tension that cinched up his every muscle, laced Lydia's arm through his, and pulled her along before she changed her mind and made a scene on the street outside of Queenie's. If they acted normal, as if they were supposed to be here, no one would give them a second look.

Nicholas received a quick, disapproving glance from Mr. Parker before he drove around to the back of the shanty, where he'd unload the scrap lumber stuffed in the fore and hind boots. Queenie wouldn't like the extra charity, but he'd see that she took it.

Apparently he'd misjudged Lydia, just as she had him. Perhaps she really did want to do what God desired, considering she'd stepped out with him. And perhaps God had given him the privilege to help her choose to court God's favor over men's. It was a hard path to follow, though.

Lydia stared at Queenie's little shack as they approached, her eyes blinking back fear.

Was he going about this wrong? No, he'd thought this through. But perhaps he was pushing her too hard, too quickly.

Maybe his disgust with Christian hypocrites was playing more of a role in this "teach Lydia a lesson" notion than it should. She was right. Her future was in his hands right now. He'd talked to her mother's doctor before he'd agreed to these wishes and was told there was no medical procedure he could pay for to slow her inevitable death. And he'd never paid attention to who Lydia's father was. After making inquiries, he knew why he'd never seen him in church. The man was a well-known gambler, and a poor one at that. Her neat appearance had disguised the level of her poverty.

Marrying Sebastian was a financially smart move, but if that was the only reason, he hoped the library salary would free her to do as she pleased. But no matter how badly he wanted her to break away from the man entirely, it wasn't his place to advise her to do so.

She had to decide for herself, not simply kowtow to pressure he might exert. Otherwise he'd be responsible for all repercussions.

He knocked on the door and ran his fingers beneath his scratchy collar. After today, they'd have no need to traipse about this part of town. She'd be fine.

"Who is it?" A woman's suspicious voice called from the other side of a poorly hung door.

"It's Nick."

"Come in."

Lydia shuffle-stepped beside him into the tiny leaning structure.

He needed to let Lydia do as she felt led to do while here; otherwise, anything she did would be his work, not hers.

For some reason, he desperately wanted her to believe in the same things he did, to have the same call to help these people. However, he didn't want to force her into being a hypocrite of another sort. "Queenie, this is Lydia, a friend of mine."

The strong-jawed woman in her early fifties glanced between the two of them with disapproval sparking in her eyes. "I'm not sure this is a good idea, Nick."

Lydia pulled her hand from his grasp.

He hadn't meant to hold on. "She knows who you are and where she is. No one else does."

Queenie's censure was clear by the exaggeratedly slow shake

of her head. "If I can tell she's a lady despite her getup, others will too."

He crossed his arms against his chest. Maybe he'd made a small error in judgment, but this was the best way for Lydia to understand the needs of these people. "She won't be coming again. I only wanted her along on the initial trip, so you could meet."

Queenie stood with her hands on her hips, the wrinkles around her eyes hardening. "Initial trip?"

"Yes. Lydia told me I needed to start spending my money on people other than myself and decided someone like you ought to be a beneficiary."

Lydia's brows shot up.

Maybe he should have told Lydia that Queenie knew his real identity before they entered.

The older woman's eyebrows scrunched together, causing her wrinkles to become more pronounced. "You already pay me more than average to mend and launder your company's uniforms."

"And now I'll be freeing you from using those wages for heating this winter. My driver will deliver wood to you each week so you can spend that money elsewhere."

"I don't need any more help, Nick." She stuck one hand on her bony hip. "You already do more for me than you should."

"It was the lady's idea." He pointed toward Lydia with his thumb.

Queenie looked over at Lydia. The older woman's chin went up a notch, but her shoulders didn't. "I'm sorry that I sounded ungrateful, miss. I thank you for thinking of helping someone like me."

"I'm afraid I'm not as generous as Nicholas wants you to believe." She rubbed her hands together and threw a quick glance at him before taking a hesitant step toward Queenie. "Perhaps you could tell me a little about . . . how you live, being that . . . well, I know very little about you, so how do I know you won't return to—well . . ." Lydia interrupted herself with a cough and clasped her hands together.

"You're right to assume a reformed prostitute rarely remains one." Queenie indicated they should all take a seat.

With only a sofa available besides the rocker Queenie grabbed, Nicholas would have to sit by Lydia or stand.

But the sofa was so short her skirts would likely brush his legs if he sat, and he was already too aware of the scent of her flowery soap mixed with the musty wool cloak he'd given her. He searched for another place to sit, but he ended up leaning against the wall in the corner.

Lydia perched on the edge of her seat as if afraid it would break beneath her. "I've been led to believe that a . . . a woman of your . . . former vocation is led by what's . . ." Her cheeks turned slightly pink. "A deep-seated desire inside you to choose such work. So how do you refrain from returning to living that way if that's true?"

Lord, help this be a good conversation. Let Queenie's testimony turn her heart.

"I can't answer for every woman." Queenie sipped the drink she'd had on a table nearby, her thin hand trembling. "Some do choose this profession, insist they love it. Though I'm not sure that is true, from what I've seen. But even if what they claim is true, they are a minority. Some of the others thought prostitution would answer their problems—lack of work, abusive husbands, the desire to be loved. And others were forced or deceived into the profession. Even the ones who think they'll be adored because they are pretty enough to start in the fancy parlor houses find out soon enough the only direction they can go is down." She set aside her glass and sighed.

"Many wish they could leave, but once you've given up being a lady, life gets harder. Whether one stays or is brave enough to attempt leaving, there's hardships of one kind or another. I won't sully your ears with the suffering working prostitutes face, but a nonworking one often finds herself more alone, more penniless, and more despised than before she was driven into this dark profession."

Queenie looked away but finally turned back to Lydia, whose face wasn't what he'd call encouraging, though she didn't look condemning either.

"If it wasn't for God's love and my love for Him spurring me on, I might have gone back . . ." Her words died off. "I won't lie. If Nick didn't pay me so well—more than I'm worth—I might've been too weak, too poor to keep from returning. Nick's gifts are really God's gifts to me."

He pushed himself out from the shadows. "Queenie ministers to the women here—when they're beaten, when they want out, when no one else will have them."

"I'm rather ineffectual, considering how few try to leave after realizing there's little hope in returning to good society." The woman's hard-edged voice clamped off, and she turned to gaze out the window, blinking her eyes more than necessary. After a long, slow exhale, she pulled up her shoulders. "I appreciate your desire to help me, but Nick provides me with enough. I shouldn't receive more than he already gives. Others need help."

That was true. "However, though I may be delivering scrap lumber to you, I'm not forcing you to keep it. If I delivered to everyone who has a need, I'd call undue attention to myself."

Queenie relaxed. "Understood."

"I'm afraid we better leave before time gets away from us. We have another stop."

Queenie nodded and moved to open her front door. "Thank you both."

"Please don't thank me," Lydia said, her voice raspy. She muttered a good-bye and slipped outside.

Nicholas gave Queenie's shoulder a squeeze before following Lydia to the coach.

Parker stared down at him with a narrow-eyed glare. The man had disliked the idea of bringing Lydia here just as much as Lydia had—and liked the idea of taking her to the next stop even less.

Nicholas looked up at Parker. "Things went better than you expected."

The older man grunted. "You're still wanting me to drive to Thick Lip Annie's?"

"Yes." He would never again be ashamed of helping others because of people's disapproval. "But if you don't want to, I can drive myself." He wouldn't force either Parker or Lydia to do anything.

His driver shook his head and made a gesture for Nicholas to get in.

He grabbed onto the coach door and yanked himself inside.

"Thick Lip Annie's?" Lydia's face was as pale as moonlight inside the dark interior.

"Yes."

"This Annie woman doesn't happen to be retired too?"

He shook his head. He would not feel bad for doing what he knew was right, no matter the censure in her eyes. "You can trust me or not. I promise I'll do nothing to hurt you. But as with Parker, I won't force you. However, if you don't go, this is the end of us working together."

"How can you ask this of me?" She wrung her skirts in her hands. "I've already done more than I ought."

"For the same reason I ask this of myself. When I stand before God, what could I possibly say to explain why I ignored the least of these? Are they not worthy of being helped?"

"Of course they are, but . . . by someone other than me. No one would approve."

"Who else will do it if you and I don't?"

She looked outside the window, her hands tightly clasped in her lap.

"Exactly. Nobody."

She turned to stare at him, and he held her gaze until she looked down at her hands clenched in her lap.

"To Annie's, then," she whispered.

17

In front of Annie's run-down alleyway home, Nicholas exited the carriage and held out his hand to Lydia. Her hand trembled, yet she stepped out onto the buckling brick street, her eyes as big as a frightened fawn's.

Did she really think simply being here would sully her reputation? Just recently she'd high-stepped through the red-light district, singing songs of condemnation with her moral-society ladies.

He'd have to hold his tongue or he'd lose control again as he had on the way to Queenie's.

He should probably apologize for that outburst. He'd not meant to let his emotions take over. "I'm sorry for my tirade earlier. If it makes you feel better, I once believed as you do."

Her eyes narrowed.

He rubbed the back of his neck. How much could he tell her? "I once knew someone who fell rather low, from my own family, even. Two . . . actually." He swallowed against the lump in his throat. Hopefully she'd never ask who. "I hated one of them for it. Left to myself, I don't believe I would've ever changed my opinion of her. But God showed me He cared about her, and if I wanted to follow Him, I had to care too. Summoning up sympathy for her was the hardest thing I've ever done." He pinned his gaze on the crumbling orange brick at their feet.

"If I hadn't been forced to help her, I'd never have wanted to help these people either. But they aren't always as hopeless as polite society claims." Compressing his lips, he looked at her, hoping she was listening—he wasn't pushing her to play with fire just for the thrill of it. She needed to meet these people so they'd ignite compassion within her. "Was Queenie the kind of woman you'd envisioned?"

"No," she whispered.

He wet his lips. "Well, Thick Lips Annie might be closer to what you'd expect."

Lydia stiffened.

"But not everything about her is. She needs help too . . . for other reasons."

"She . . . she won't be in there . . ." Lydia pointed to the run-down building beside them. "With, uh, with a—"

"No. Not this time of day. She's probably only been awake for a few hours."

Lydia looked up and down the alley, no living thing visible besides a tabby perched on a pile of boxes. "Will you be taking me anywhere else in the red-light district?"

"No. And you never have to come again. But I needed you to see who you're helping." Though he hoped she would come again. If so, she might be willing to help with the ladies at the mansion.

But perhaps he aspired too high.

Why did it seem the only people driven to change things were those who'd been personally affected? Yet he wouldn't wish his past experiences on anyone. "From now on, Parker or Henri and I will deliver the firewood. I can't deliver too much at a time or it would be stolen. But per your request, I'll supply them through the winter. After the winter is over, I'll decide whether or not to continue, but you don't have to be involved again—unless you want to be."

A door hinge whined, and Lydia stepped behind him. He turned to see the filthy, tousled head of a toddler peek from the side door of the dilapidated building.

He squatted and held open his arms, palms out. "Hello, Robbie."

The boy hesitantly stepped into the alley and slid toward him.

He'd only succeeded in holding the boy two or three times, and not once had Robbie relaxed in his embrace. But at least the little guy was no longer hiding in a corner. "How've you been?"

The boy stared at him from a few feet away, blinking his doleful eyes.

He'd never heard Robbie speak, so Nicholas tried to read the words chained up behind those rich brown eyes. The toddler was definitely frightened, but considering he was inching closer, it wasn't because of him. "Come now, let's find your mommy."

Robbie took a few more steps forward, then laid his head on Nicholas's shoulder. His body sagged against him and he clung to a fistful of Nicholas's shabby jacket.

The boy's trust made his heart flutter strangely, but the way Robbie held himself told him this wasn't an entirely good thing. He ran his hand along the boy's bony back and ducked his head to look at him. "What's the matter, child?"

Robbie didn't blink.

Nicholas turned to Lydia and shook his head. "He rarely lets me touch him."

She stepped back and looked around the alley again, wringing her hands. "If something's wrong, should I return to the coach?"

He hesitated. "Robbie, is there a man in the house?"

The little boy's head slid against his shoulder negatively.

"I think it's all right, just stay close until we find out what's bothering him."

Lydia slipped her hand in his, and he swallowed against the knot in his throat. Holding a woman's hand, walking in step together, carrying a snuggling child . . . If someone walked past, they'd easily be mistaken for a loving family. He'd given up on ever having one, and this little boy would most likely never get one. He hugged Robbie tighter, saddened for the youngster more than for himself.

He peered down at Lydia. His quest to change her opinion today could ruin her chance at ever having a family as well. Maybe this hadn't been such a good idea.

But he couldn't leave now, not until he knew Robbie would be all right. He shifted the little boy in his arms to knock on the opened door.

No one answered.

He forged in. Little light passed through the covered windows into the sparsely furnished, unoccupied room.

"Annie? Pepper? Angel?"

"Three women work here?" Lydia's whisper was rough.

"No. Annie's got two girls." He tugged her farther inside. "Robbie, where are your sisters?"

The little boy pointed down the hallway.

Nicholas had never entered the back rooms—he'd never before had any reason to. "Annie? Girls?"

He heard scurrying and muttering behind the door to his right. And then a whimper. His heart raced, and he smacked the door open.

Pepper, a girl of thirteen, sat in front of a cracked mirror propped on a low chest of drawers, a mess of face paints in front of her. Angel, nine, sat on the bed, her arms wrapped tight about her knees, tears making wet trails upon her artificially pink cheeks.

His throat clogged over the girls' painted faces. "Where's your mother?"

Angel's head sunk to her bent knees.

"Gone." Pepper thunked a red-colored jar onto the dresser and picked up a brush. "Forever."

"Dead?" Lydia whispered, her free hand at her throat.

"No, but I wish she woulda been."

Nicholas gave her a look. "Now, Pepper."

"I don't want her to die." Angel's voice turned shrill.

"Hush up, Angel." Pepper shot her sister a glare and snarled, "Your hissy fits won't do no good. We have to care for ourselves now, like I done told you." She looked back at him. "What do you want, mister?"

She'd seen him before and knew he meant no harm, and yet her glare was overly hostile.

"I came to speak with your mother."

"She got married to Aces MacGuire last month."

Lydia let go of his hand and frowned at Pepper. "I'm sure your stepfather won't be happy with you painting your faces, nor your mother."

"They ain't here." Pepper loaded her brush with dark powder and leaned toward the mirror. "And they won't be coming back for us. Mother left us with Dirty Emma."

"Dirty Emma . . ." Lydia's expression turned aghast.

"But when Dirty Emma ain't working, she's drinking. And she calls Robbie names, so we ain't staying with her, no matter what Mother said."

Robbie clung to him so hard his little nails dug into his neck. Nicholas wanted to sit to take the weight off his arm, but there was nowhere to do so except next to Angel on the bed.

He sidled to the other side of the vanity and perched on its edge. "Why are you putting on makeup?" Did he dare hope she was playing dress-up? Mischievously amusing herself with things previously denied her?

"Somebody has to work."

Lydia crept closer and picked up a pot of some bright pink stuff. "What kind of work requires you to use—" Her eyes went wide, and she snatched the brush from Pepper's hand. "No." Her guttural whisper ripped through the room.

Yanking the brush back from Lydia, Pepper sneered at her, looking her up and down. "What? Are you going to take us in? How do I know you ain't going to beat us, or run off on us, or drink so much I have to clean you up every night?"

"Why, I'd never—"

"Doesn't matter. You ain't going to be takin' no alley cat's babies home with you. Why you here, anyway?"

Nicholas laid a hand on Pepper. She tried to shrug it off, but he held firm. "Lydia came to help you and your mother. We intend to bring you a wood stove and fuel to burn through the winter."

She eyed Lydia suspiciously, then turned back to him. "Well, we won't be here much longer, so we don't need it."

"Are you going back to Dir—" Lydia's voice shook, and she audibly swallowed. "To Emma's?"

"No, she needs more tending than Robbie. I ain't slaving for her when she don't do nothing but let us sleep under a roof. The landlord don't know Mother's gone yet, so we can stay here another two days."

"Why did your mother leave?" Nicholas watched Lydia look at each of the children, likely struggling with the fact that prostitutes even had children. He'd expected that. Polite society vilified these people to the point most never thought of them as human.

"She and Aces thought they'd go have her work in Clear Springs. With the mining camps up there, she could pull in a lot more money."

"Her husband? Her husband is taking her to work . . ."

Nicholas frowned as the color drained from Lydia's face. He'd wanted her to see this, hadn't he? Now he wished he could sweep her up, along with these three children, and hide them in his home, keeping them from ever facing the harshness of life again.

Maybe he could hide them away—the children at least. But who would raise them? How would he explain their presence to others? He needed to speak with Caroline. "Pepper—"

"Who's bringing you food?" Lydia walked over and sat on the bed, hand extended toward Angel. She must have expected the child to scoot closer and weep in her arms, but instead the girl scooted away, gaping at her as if snakes hung from her nose.

Lydia smiled and put her hand on the girl's shoulder anyway, but then her smile died. She ran her hand down the girl's arm, which Angel yanked from her grip. The little girl scooted farther toward the wall.

"Don't touch Angel." Pepper marched over to the bed, her hands on her hips.

Lydia glanced between the siblings. "How much have you eaten since your mother's been gone?"

Pepper only narrowed her eyes.

Standing, Lydia mirrored the younger woman's antagonistic posture. "You said you could take better care of your siblings than Emma, yet your sister's stomach is rumbling and her arms—"

"Our stomachs are always rumbling. If Momma never had enough for us, then why would Dirty Emma? She told me to get a job and so I am. Madam Careless wants both me and Angel to start work next week."

"Angel?" Lydia drooped onto the bed and stared at the nine-year-old still curled against the wall.

"Pepper, you can't." Nicholas's heart was about to implode. If he couldn't make her change direction . . . *Lord, help me stop these children from going where they cannot return. Surely you sent me and Lydia here this day for this reason. Help me convince Pepper.* "Who will look after your little brother?"

"He'll go with us."

"With you?" Lydia squeaked.

Pepper shrugged. "He'll have to stay put in the kitchen."

"What kind of life will he have if you have him . . . ? What kind of life?" Lydia straightened. "Do you even know what you're about to do?"

The girl sauntered toward her with a smirk. "Likely more than you know. I know what Mother did, and I've seen the way men look at me. If I don't work with Madam Careless—who'll put me up, pay for my dresses, and watch Robbie—then I'll be . . . I'll be taken anyway." Pepper's voice cracked, and finally something other than defiance shot from her eyes. "So might as well get paid."

"Pepper, you don't want to do this." Nicholas shifted Robbie to his other side and tried to reach for her, but she sidestepped. "Think about Angel."

She looked at her little sister for a second, and then bit her lip. "I . . . Madam Careless said she can't let no nine-year-old sit around the kitchen, that she had to work too, that . . . that she'd be real careful with her."

He hugged the boy even tighter, wishing it was Angel. "Pepper, you're a smart, good girl. You know better—"

"No I'm not!" Pepper whipped around and faced him. "I'm the daughter of a harlot." The girl swore and threw a paint jar across the room. Brilliant blue color exploded on the whitewashed wall.

Lydia blanched.

Please, Lord, don't let her faint. He already had his arms full. "Pepper, why don't you come home with me?"

"Why?" She curled her lip. "So you don't have to pay the madam?"

"No." Nicholas snatched her wrist and tugged her closer to look into her very dry, very angry eyes. "How many times have you seen me around this neighborhood?"

"A few."

"And have I acted like any of the men who visited your mother?"

"No. But—"

"Do you know why I come here?"

She tried to tug away, but when she couldn't free herself, she shrugged. "You gave Mother medicine once. Freckles Kate said you paid her fines so she could go home and nurse her baby instead of staying in jail. But Rosie Jo says you only do nice things because you want them to do things other men don't dare ask for."

Lydia put a hand to her throat and looked positively green.

That stung. All kinds of rumors floated around about him, and he usually laughed them off, but that one made him want to vomit. "Did I ever ask your mother for anything?" he asked hoarsely.

Pepper shrugged, not quite meeting his gaze. "Not that I know of."

"Would a decent lady like Lydia be out visiting with me if she thought that was why I was helping?"

Pepper turned to look at Lydia. "Why *are* you here?"

"Uh, Nick's showing me who needs help."

"And do you trust him?"

Lydia turned to look at him. "I trust he'd never do anything to harm you."

Pepper whirled back toward him, her eyes dangerously narrowed. "And what will we do at your place, mister?"

"We'll talk about it, you and me. I won't make you do anything you don't want to do. And, Pepper"—he snagged her hand and pressed it against Robbie's back—"you know you don't want to take your brother and sister to Madam Careless's parlor house. Do you want his role models to be the men who will treat you the same way Aces and the rest of them treated your mother?"

She huffed, but reached up to smooth the curl behind her brother's ear. "No, but I don't think I have a choice."

"And what about Angel? Do you want to take that frightened little girl in the corner and force her to become the stone she'll have to be to survive the kind of life your mother did? Don't you want to protect her from that?"

"Of course I do, but what decent person's going to hire me? I don't know how to do nothing but what Mother'd done. She told me I was too old not to be working anyway."

He'd known Thick Lips Annie hadn't been the best of mothers, but she'd kept her girls from working this long. What had changed? "I promise I can find you better work. Let me help you—at least for Angel's and Robbie's sakes. Do you know Queenie? Perhaps—"

Pepper lost her scowl. "You work with Queenie?"

"I do."

She stood still for a moment, then smoothed the hair away from Robbie's eyes. "All right, we can try it. But if I don't like anything at all, we're leaving."

The air left his lungs.

Thank you, Jesus.

18

Lydia sorely wanted to slide down the coach's bench seat and sleep all the way home. What she wouldn't give to erase from her memory the images of two little girls painted like common women and a boy so thin he looked like a skeleton. But she'd seen their eyes brighten after Nicholas mentioned Queenie and later shine with tears when they were all seated at the reformed woman's table in front of bowls of a nondescript stew.

"Are you all right?" Nicholas's soft voice wafted from the far side of the carriage.

"No." She put her hand to her throbbing forehead.

"Thank you." His voice was whisper soft, sincere.

"For what?" She'd fought him all afternoon and still wasn't sure about the way he'd forced her to come. But she was glad she'd been there to help the children escape such a horrific life.

He'd been right. She needed to see how the poor and destitute lived—all types of poor and destitute.

His hand rubbed the worn cushion seat beside him. "I wouldn't have convinced Pepper of my honorable intentions if you hadn't been there."

"You'd have eventually hit on Queenie's name. That turned the girl faster than having my support."

"But you telling her that you trusted me—"

She held up a hand. "I only said I trusted you wouldn't do anything to harm us."

He stared at her as their wagon rattled over a few potholes. "And what's that supposed to mean?"

She swallowed and turned away from his intense hazel eyes. "You might care for these people who need you, but do you have any love for those who disagree with you?"

He sputtered and leaned forward, closer. "Are you saying that just because I think your quilting project's ridiculous, I somehow hate you?"

"I'm saying it because of how you're going about 'helping.' Have you ever considered you may be harming people with your high-handedness? Truth be told, you seem to enjoy making me as uncomfortable as possible. If I'd refused to go to Annie's, you said you'd no longer fulfill my wishes. But these people would still need that help whether I came or not. You're preaching God's love for the least of these, but only if it's done your way."

He shook his head vehemently. "Would you have come with me today if I'd told you where we were going?"

She leaned her head on her hand, staring out the window at the buildings passing by. "No. But don't you see? Those children . . ." Lydia rubbed her temples. "They needed help, true. But the rules of etiquette—the rules that warn me against having anything to do with women of ill repute because of how they might lead me astray—the wisdom of such restrictions is demonstrated by those children and by what they were about to do. That Pepper would hand over her little sister to . . . to . . ."

"But you and the ladies in your moral society are grown women." He scooted to the front of his seat. "You're mature enough to see the wrong of it. Pepper hasn't been instructed any better."

She swallowed against the warmth behind her eyes at the very thought of what Pepper had almost done to herself and her sister. "God says we aren't supposed to have anything to do with corrupt people for a reason."

"In the church, Lydia, corrupt people in the church. How can we bring the Good News to the world if we stay away from sinners? Rather we're supposed to avoid those who claim to be Christian yet blatantly sin and refuse to repent. If we cloistered ourselves away from those who sin and sin frequently, those who need Christ, then we'd never leave the church's four walls. And even there we can't get away from those who sin."

His eyes burned into her own. "Lydia." He waved his hand. "They're all under judgment out there. How will they come under grace if no one tells them they can have it?"

She rubbed at her temples again. She couldn't argue that, but he wasn't completely in the right either. "Yet you separate yourself from the church. That's definitely not what the Bible teaches."

He broke eye contact and fidgeted, his seat creaking. "Most Christians I know would make places like the red-light district worse, since holier-than-thous expect those people to clean themselves up before being allowed to hear of God's love. If sinners could stop sinning without help, why do they need a Savior? Christians still mess up, yet we expect prostitutes, drunks, and ensnared men to stop sinning all on their own? If Thick Lips Annie cleaned herself up, would you dine with her? Would the church invite her to Bible study? Who's going to hire her? You?"

She chewed her fingernail and studied his shadowy figure. She couldn't work with him anymore. He made her feel incapable of doing anything good unless he thought it up for her. The Littles and her father already found her wanting. Why keep another person in her life who disparaged her unless she meekly complied with everything he said?

Sebastian wanted to use her to gain voters. Father wanted to use her to secure his future. Nicholas wanted to use her to further his agenda.

They were all much the same, though Nicholas's maneuverings did end up benefiting more than just himself. "You thought you knew what I'd do without asking, so you strong-armed me into doing as you wished. Then you're angered when I dare offer up a counterpoint to your methods. You wave off the moral society's attempts to help reform the lost because you don't like how we do it. Why not try to behave civilly and talk to us like we're rational creatures?"

The coach slowed in front of her house and turned down the alleyway. She braced herself for the stop. "I don't agree with everything you do, which seems to be something you can't handle." She'd been giddy over how much money she'd get to help him distribute, but it was clear now she had no say at all. What was the point of continuing? "I'm sure you see that our continuing to work together is not a good idea."

The carriage stopped, and they sat in cold silence.

When she couldn't take it anymore, she nodded toward Nicholas as she slid toward the exit. "Good day."

Nicholas opened the door for her. "I'll send you word when the library books arrive. Hopefully it'll be no more than two weeks. We can meet then to discuss how to proceed with the library."

She tripped down the stairs.

When she got her footing, she looked back up at Nicholas. "You still want me to work for you at the library? I thought declining to go on your escapades meant the deal was off."

He sighed. "You're right that needs don't disappear even if you do. And so, even if you no longer wish to be involved, I'll start the library, and the position is yours if you want it."

She'd just said working together would be untenable . . . but he'd not be at the library every hour, questioning her judgment, her morals, her heart.

He exited the coach and put out his hand as if he intended to touch her, but dropped it just shy of doing so. His hands clenched tightly at his sides. "If your future plans don't work out, I want you to have an income. A woman with means can stay out of trouble. Besides, you're perfect for the job."

Though the library position would fit her talents and interests nicely, working in his library would mean her future would be forever entangled with his. Did she have the fortitude to endure his high-handedness forever?

She clasped her hands together. "I'll think about it." She'd have to pray before committing.

But one thing she did know, she wouldn't sit at home and do nothing just because Nicholas wouldn't be dragging her around town anymore in his run-down vehicles. He wasn't the only one who could help those poor kids.

19

Lydia tromped into the police station, and an officer behind the front desk lifted his head for a second and nodded toward a line of chairs. "Have a seat. I'll be with you in a minute." Then he went back to writing.

Settling herself onto the hard chair, she willed herself not to think of Nicholas, not to replay anything they'd said to each other yesterday, because examining it now would only make her madder. But as the minutes ticked by . . .

What had he meant by saying the librarian job would keep her out of trouble? Was he referencing Queenie's statement that some women choose prostitution because they're penniless?

She straightened and scowled. How dare he believe she'd be so morally weak!

Those ladies had to have been morally weak from the beginning to choose to become some man's lover for monetary gain.

Monetary gain.

Sheets of burning ice enfolded her entire body.

Choosing to be with a man for monetary gain.

Her hands shook as the parallel popped into her brain.

No, she planned to marry. The institution of marriage itself made what she planned to do perfectly acceptable. For centuries, families married off their daughters to increase their wealth. Even people in the Bible married without love.

Planning her life around a job that could fall through at any time was what was foolish. She wasn't even sure she could work with Nicholas on a permanent basis. Her best bet was still marriage.

Blowing out a breath, she conjured up an image of herself in the wedding gown she planned to sew. A creamy blue dress to match her eyes, with black accents to highlight her hair—a gown she'd wear later to fancy town gatherings.

But instead of seeing herself in that gown on a campaign platform beside Sebastian, the image of her with Nicholas in the gardens behind his red-roofed white mansion popped up. And no matter how hard she tried to imagine Sebastian holding her hand, gazing down into her eyes lovingly, his brown eyes kept morphing into Nicholas's gold-flecked hazel ones. How would it feel to have him look at her with approval, the intensity of his gaze pinned on her not because he was finding fault, but because—

"Miss?"

She jumped at the officer's bellow. Placing a cool hand on her cheek, she hoped she wasn't as red as she felt. "I'm sorry?"

What was she thinking? She didn't like Nicholas. At all.

"I'm ready for you now."

She stood, though she'd rather have stepped outside for a minute to cool off. "I need to report some children in need of assistance."

"Your children?"

"Goodness, no." She took a seat in the chair in front of his desk. How to tell him about the children without giving away her whereabouts yesterday? She might not like Nicholas, but he was filling needs no one else did. He'd planned to go back to Queenie's to pick up Pepper and her siblings, but what if Pepper changed her mind about going with him? Queenie hadn't enough room for three children, let alone the resources to care for them for very long. But Lydia couldn't tell the officer Nicholas's intentions. She didn't want to ruin his work, even if he hadn't sworn her to secrecy. "They are the children of . . . uh . . . They came to my attention through some poor woman who . . . works for a family friend."

"Do you not attend a church that can assist them?"

She picked at her skirt. Nicholas didn't think the church would help, and it miffed her that he was likely right. "I think they need more assistance, within the law and all. They've been abandoned."

"I see." He pulled out his paper and picked up his pen.

"They were left in the care of a drunkard. They're so thin I doubt they've ever had enough to eat. The youngest is lethargic and doesn't speak, and the eldest girl seems to think her only hope of feeding her siblings is to . . ." She breathed out, hoping to cool the heat in her cheeks. ". . . is to find work at a house of ill repute."

One of his eyebrows shot up. "And where do these children live?"

"On Twelfth and Willow, I believe. They're currently at the house of a woman named Queenie, though I don't know for how long."

The man pursed his lips and leaned back in his chair. "How old is this girl?"

"Perhaps fourteen? I really don't know."

"And living in that section of town, I assume her mother is a sporting woman?"

Lydia swallowed and pulled at her high collar. "I don't know the woman, but I've heard that it's so, and that she's left them."

"Well, the children of a prostitute don't know much different." He shrugged. "The girl was bound to turn in that direction."

"But she intends to take her nine-year-old sister to work with her." She leaned forward and pointed at the pen he'd laid on the desk. "You need to do something about innocent children so neglected and hungry they're embarking on a very, very evil path. I know the town wants to remove the red-light district since it's in clear violation of the law, but to do that, you must stop the influx of people, mere children, entering this unsightly business."

"Ma'am, I know you mean well." He turned down the corners of his mouth with a poor attempt at sympathy. "But you being who you are, well, you don't understand these people. They're—"

"I understand that there is a little boy and two girls in need of police guidance and protection."

"But it's not in our—"

"I'm a friend of the Littles." She thumped the desk with her fist. "As you know, Sebastian Little is running his campaign on the platform of joining together to rid our state of this evil."

He shook his head, evidently unimpressed.

Wasn't Sebastian's father his boss, or at least his superior?

Yet he didn't pick up his pen.

She narrowed her eyes at him. "How would it look if I told the mayor his future daughter-in-law came to you for help but you did nothing?"

Though he seemed more interested in assessing her than starting his report, he dragged his writing utensil off the desk, flipped open a pad of paper, and sat back in his chair. "So you're the one marrying Sebastian?"

She forced herself not to shrug. It seemed the Littles' name had been the only thing that had gotten him to move. "We expect to marry, yes."

"All right." He started to write.

Though it seemed the admission had caused him to start doing his job, she almost wished she could take back the words. They weren't engaged yet, but admitting it would happen soon made her feel as if she were handing the officer the keys to lock her up in one of his cells.

She rattled off everything she knew about the children. "So you'll see to this?"

"I'll write down your concerns in the record book, and then we'll see to it when we can."

When they could? How could abandoned, starving children not be a priority? Looking at his indifferent face made her droop. It looked like the law wouldn't do much, but the church had to— despite what Nicholas said about them. Surely the children's story would stir the hearts of Christ followers. "Thank you, I suppose. I'll have the Littles check on your progress."

He shrugged. "Sure."

Walking out of the precinct, she turned in the direction of the parsonage.

The way Mrs. Little viewed the streetwalkers, she'd probably shoot down any suggestion for the moral society to help the children. And Mr. Little seemed to have little interest in her ideas.

But surely the pastor and his wife would help immediately once they heard. Didn't Nicholas say something about the Wiselys being good people? And she knew that was true.

Bernadette answered her knock with a weary smile, or maybe a grimace? "Come in, Lydia. I'm afraid Evelyn's not here."

She shrugged. "I'm actually here to see you."

"Oh? What brings you by?"

"Trouble."

Bernadette's expression lost all happy pretense and tightened into a look of pain. "I hope everything's all right at home."

Not exactly, but that was neither here nor there. "I'm not the one in trouble."

"I'm glad of that—not that I'm glad there's trouble." Rubbing at the spot above her temple, Bernadette sighed. "Well, come in and have tea."

Lydia reached out, feeling the tense muscles in the woman's arm. "Are you ill?"

"I don't feel my best, haven't for a while. I'm having terrible headaches that I can't shake, and they seem to be getting worse. But, please, come in."

"Why haven't you shared how you feel at prayer meetings?"

She sat down at the table and poured two cups of tea. No steam rose from the liquid. "It's hard to complain as a pastor's wife. I always feel as if I have to be this model of Christian womanhood." She dropped some sugar in her drink and swirled her tea hypnotically slow with a spoon.

"We all have weaknesses." Lydia sipped the lukewarm peppermint tea and set it back on its saucer. "Surely we'd extend grace to you if we expect it for ourselves."

"We'll find out soon enough." Bernadette looked through her at some distant spot.

Lydia frowned. Bernadette might have asked her to come in, but was that only because she believed she should as a pastor's wife? She certainly didn't look well. "Maybe I should leave."

"As long as you don't need something from me, you can keep me company for a bit—though I'm not exactly good company right now."

Lydia stared at her tea, which smelled slightly medicinal. "Um . . ." She had indeed come for something, but surely Bernadette would want to know about Pepper and her siblings. "I just learned about some children needing help. You're the most sacrificial woman I know, and your husband always praises your servant's heart."

"Yes." She didn't sound happy about the compliment.

"These children have been abandoned, and I figured you could help me find them some food, maybe a home . . ." She trailed off at the troubled look in Bernadette's eyes. Something more than just pain.

Bernadette tipped her head back to stare at the ceiling. "You're testing me right out of the gate, aren't you? And with one that's not so easy."

Lydia's eyes sought the same corner, though she knew she wouldn't see God there.

"I can't help you." Bernadette sighed and frowned. "You'll have to find someone else."

"You can't help starving children?" What hope had she if Bernadette wasn't willing to help? The pastor's wife had filled Lydia's belly countless times over the years after the older woman realized how often Lydia and her mother lived on one meal a day. "I can't believe there could be anything God could ask of you that would be more worthy."

"I didn't say helping needy children wasn't worthy. But you'll need to shoulder the task yourself. . . . I won't be volunteering for anything anymore."

"No more volunteering?" Lydia's mouth hung open. This woman had pushed them to serve. Her husband—the pastor himself—did less charity work than she. Bernadette was a model of virtuous activity. "Why would you quit everything? Are you that sick?"

"No, it's not that." She swallowed hard, then grabbed her teacup and gulped. "I know what people are going to think. But my husband supports me, so I'm not going to explain myself to anyone." The redness in her eyes bespoke sleeplessness, and her troubled gaze kept Lydia from prodding her anymore.

"But I feel like I should tell you." Bernadette reached over and squeezed her hand. "I've worked hard for the Lord the twenty years I've been at Walter's side. It's expected of you, if you marry a pastor, and I was determined to be a model pastor's wife." She let out a chuckle and winced. "But I was doing it all for me, all for Walter, all for the good opinion of the people looking to us as examples." She looked away, as if she couldn't bear to look at her. "But I did none of it for the Lord," she whispered.

"That's not true. He can take anything and use it for His good."

She nodded slowly. "He can, and I'm thankful he's used my last twenty years for something—He has indeed done some good things through me." She looked at her hands for a bit before grabbing her cup again.

"Then you're being too hard on yourself."

She set down her cup and faced her. "What would you think of me if I told you I've not read the Bible once in twenty years unless my husband instructed us to do so during a sermon?"

Lydia ran a hand along her temple, trying to form a response.

"Or that I only pray in Sunday school class when asked? That I encourage people to share their prayer requests, knowing I'll likely not pray for anyone because I forget to speak to God once I leave church?"

"Are you saying that you don't believe in God—"

"No, just that I'm a rather immature Christian."

Was she any better? She read a lot, but how often did she turn to a novel first? "Then what will you do?"

"I'm going to take this headache that comes on in the early afternoons as a reminder that I need God. Nothing has helped the pain for three months—tea, compresses, rest. I've spent the last two days reading the Bible until I fell asleep despite the pain. And that's all I'm going to do. I'm quitting teaching the girls on Sunday morning. I'm quitting the moral society. I'm quitting the knitting group . . . everything." She made a sorrowful face. "If I don't have anything inside to give, I have no business telling others how to live."

"But helping the poor—"

"Is a very good thing. But not for me. Not right now. Maybe Evelyn can help you when she gets home. She shames me with her dedication to the Lord."

Evelyn would certainly want to help, but she was a young woman under her parents' roof without resources to dip into or much sway with the elders, just like Lydia.

Lydia put her hand on Bernadette's hunched back and was about to ask if she could pray for her, but she didn't need permission to pray for her friend—she just should. *Lord, heal my friend. And heal me.*

She'd prayed very little these last few months herself. Uncertain God would provide her with the security she wanted, she'd been too busy making sure she'd be taken care of *her* way after Mama's death.

And she'd just been thinking poorly of Bernadette because she wouldn't help with the children.

Thinking poorly of the police officer because he didn't see things her way.

Thinking poorly of Nicholas because his motives were different than hers.

Were any of them doing what God wanted them to do?

20

Henri leaned back in the leather chair as if he owned it, an amused expression on his face.

Nicholas scowled, then pivoted and paced back across his study. His friend had picked an inconvenient time to drop in unannounced. Nicholas needed to get to his weekly meeting with the mill's supervisor, but his lawyer was evidently running late with the paperwork he needed to sign for a later meeting with his company manager, Mr. Renfroe.

Not that Henri ever made a habit of asking when would be a good time to visit before he showed up.

Henri broke the silence. "You're acting as if you're debating over asking some woman to court."

Nicholas stopped to glare at his friend, who was rolling a pen between his fingers.

Henri's mouth twitched, and the pen stilled. "You are!"

"I am not." He stiffened and went back to pacing. "Don't be ridiculous. Who would I court?"

"That pretty little lady with the pale blue eyes."

Nicholas scrunched up his face as if he never thought about her. "Lydia?"

Henri's smile grew wider.

Blast. "Uh, I mean . . . Miss King."

Henri tapped the pen's tip on the desk blotter decisively. "It's about time you thought about marrying again."

A lecture was not what he needed right now. "No, it isn't."

"I saw your face, Nick. You're attracted."

He needed to get his jabbering friend off this tangent. "And when, pray tell, Bachelor Beauchamp, will you settle down yourself . . . for the first time?"

Henri leaned back in his chair and walked the pen through his fingers. "I've no need to settle down. You, however, are wound tighter than a grandfather clock. A woman would do you some good."

"If you must know, I'm taking Miss King to see the library after lunch today." He stopped at the window and surveyed the new coach waiting near the carriage house in the peachy morning light. "I'm not sure she's going to like it."

"And since when do you care what people like?" Henri looked up at the ceiling, tapped his chin, then clapped his hands. "Oh, I know, it's when you're not thinking about courting them."

Nicholas tried the evil glare again. "Shouldn't you be getting to work by now?"

Henri only rolled his eyes. "I thought you said she liked books. So what's not to like about a library?"

"It's not the typical library, and she's already disappointed in me."

"And since when have you ever let someone's disappointment bother you?" Henri grabbed the newspaper off the side table and flicked it open with a dramatic clearing of his throat.

So he'd seen this morning's article already? Likely why he'd come over then.

Henri turned directly to page five and started reading. "'Little Rosa fined sixteen dollars for public indecency with a man aged five and twenty in plain view of the train station off Eleventh. She's a strumpet of the worst kind, leaving a husband of two years behind to dally in the red-light districts of Baxter before moving to Teaville.'"

"And of course the upstanding male dallying with her isn't named," Nicholas muttered.

Henri paused to look at him before continuing. "'Evidently not everyone believes these lewd women should pay for their sins. Our illustrious Mr. Lowe approached the marshal at her arraignment and requested the fines be dropped if any of these frail ladies renounced their profession and chose honest labor—which he could provide if necessary. Obviously, Mr. Lowe hasn't enough money sitting atop the hill south of town, so he plans to exploit these women as well. What sweat shop is he setting up for these women? The myriad fines obtained from the alley cats and johns at least end up in our city coffers, but he'd rather take advantage—'"

"Stop. I've read it twice already."

Henri dropped the paper into his lap. "I have to say, I'm actually impressed you did something this public. Please tell me this isn't the end of your little adventures. I do so enjoy running around with you behind the bigwigs' backs, putting kinks in their plans on occasion."

Nicholas sat down and stared at his hands clasped between his knees. He couldn't keep the charade up. Lydia was right. A lone wolf could only do so much. And though God could do mighty things through a willing individual, there were so many deeds of darkness to expose, so many sinners in need of rescue.

And he hadn't asked the church for help since moving here, certain that this town's Christians would be just like those in his old neighborhood in St. Louis. They'd refused to comfort him or his wife in her final days because they were too good to be associated with Gracie or him any longer.

Not even pleading for a modicum of mercy on his wife's behalf had moved them.

And that's why he'd left Missouri. After the story of how Gracie died had made its rounds, they'd never treated him the same. Never listened.

Effie walked by the open doorway, humming.

Nicholas bolted from his seat, crossed the room, and shut the door before Henri got a good look at her.

"Did a bee sting you?" Henri looked at him as if he were crazy.

"Uh, no." He looked about for an excuse as if one were just lying around. "Felt a draft."

"All right." Henri drawled as if talking to someone slow in the head.

Would Henri buy his explanation for the women and three children under his roof? He'd finally convinced Pepper to come to the mansion last night. She likely didn't trust him a whit more than before, but the light in her eyes when he'd mentioned his cook indicated Queenie's steady diet of beans had at least pushed the girl into giving his place a chance. Hopefully she'd see how well Angel and Robbie fared in his home and would settle in. If he let the church know what he was about, he'd have to tell them everything, but why not start by informing Henri?

No, he had to tell the maids first. They still didn't know he was aware they were ex-prostitutes, since Caroline and Roxanna had acted as if they were sneaking them in under his nose.

His maids would bear the brunt of exposure more than he.

"She's good for you."

"What?" He laid a hand on the door. At least Henri hadn't recognized Effie as she'd marched past.

"This Miss King. I've never seen you so unsure of your cocky self."

He turned slowly, his arms crossed. Who was this man calling cocky? Henri was the king of braggadocio.

"Not that you don't have the right to some good old-fashioned arrogance. A man of your age wouldn't have accomplished so much unless he believed in himself. But you're too blasted sure of everything and everybody."

"I don't know how my business skills and a very lucky discovery of natural gas make a woman who's with another man good for me."

Henri waved a hand about the room. "You have everything a man wants—money, prestige, servants."

Nicholas only shook his head. He didn't want to discuss this anymore anyway.

"Well, I must be off to work, as you said." Henri threw the paper onto the table and took one last swig of his tea. "A man like you gets the woman he wants, Nicholas. Don't let some two-faced conniver have her."

"And you have evidence of his conniving?" Nicholas followed Henri to the hall tree. Hopefully he really did have something beyond the rumors he'd heard.

His friend grabbed his hat. "You and I both can read people—he's slimy."

"I don't like him, yes. But I don't like a lot of people." Nicholas sighed. "And I have no proof he's anything except full of himself, which you just accused me of being."

Henri smiled. "Still, you could win her if you wanted her. She's not engaged."

Nicholas watched his friend saunter toward his coach.

Henri was right. He could win Lydia away from Sebastian in any number of ways. The lawyer didn't deserve her.

But . . . he didn't either.

Henri was wrong about her being engaged though. She may not have Sebastian's ring on her finger, but *she* considered herself Sebastian's intended.

And he'd never, upon his life, steal a woman away from the man who'd won her.

21

Nicholas rubbed his arms as he strode up to his house as quickly as he could. His early morning meeting with his mill's supervisor had run late, and after that, it seemed he'd been putting out one fire after another. He pulled out his pocket watch. An entire hour and a half past when he'd had Mr. Black tell Lydia he'd meet her. She'd told Mr. Black she intended to arrive early to visit with Pepper, Angel, and Robbie, but what if she'd given up on waiting for him and left when the children had been summoned to lunch? His maids could have easily told her how often business kept him out later than he intended—and it wasn't as if he and Lydia had been on good terms the last time they'd been together.

He shivered against a gust of wind—the temperature had dropped at least twenty degrees from the time he'd awoken. Despite the cold, he was actually looking forward to putting on his threadbare coat, now that he'd had his maids wash it so as not to subject Lydia to its odor anymore.

As he crested the rise, his front door opened. A well-bundled Lydia stepped outside and scurried to meet him at the end of his portico. The smile she flashed him was tentative, and perhaps . . . ill-at-ease?

"Good afternoon, Nicholas." She rubbed her hands together

briskly as she picked up her pace to meet his. "I'd almost given up waiting on you, but Robbie kept me company."

He glanced back over his shoulder but saw no little silhouette in any of the windows. He'd not had much time for Robbie this past week. He'd been busy coordinating a merger and meeting with his lawyer several times over some bungled paperwork.

Lydia shivered beside him. "It's not a nice day for a stroll into town. Yesterday would have been so much better."

"True, but don't worry, we'll be riding." He'd sent Mr. Parker home about forty minutes ago to get the new library coach ready, and his horses were likely ready to get their blood pumping. "And the coach is equipped with plenty of lap furs."

She glanced toward his driver checking the horses and then surveyed the coach. "Do you have a different conveyance for every day of the week?"

Mr. Parker chuckled as he handed Nicholas his threadbare coat.

How many vehicles *did* he have? Not important.

"I ordered this coach made especially for you."

"For me?" She put a shaky hand to her chest. "Why would you buy me a coach?"

"Step inside and see." He twisted the brass handle on the enhanced coach and held out his hand. Despite her wearing gloves, her hands felt stiff and cold in his. He helped her inside and almost didn't let her go, wishing he could warm her fingers until he was certain they were no longer as cold as ice.

She slid onto the bench in the middle—the only seat available—and ogled the interior with wide eyes. "This is . . . incredible. But I don't understand."

He stepped inside and sat beside her. Too close, but he couldn't stand up the whole ride, either.

He'd only let himself travel with her today, no more than a few hours to endure the soft floral scent that enveloped her and made him want to—

Spinning away, he gestured at the interior as if she hadn't noticed already. "This is your traveling library."

Every inch of wall was fitted with bookshelves, the single window being the one in the doorway. The workmanship was rather ingenious. He'd given the wagon maker an idea, and the man had created a masterpiece.

Nicholas pulled the lap robes out from under the long bench seat, thankful he'd ordered them before he thought he'd actually need them, and handed one to Lydia.

He pointed to the shelves to his right. "These are school books."

The coach jerked forward, and the momentum slammed her against him. His fingers encircled her upper arms to steady her. How dainty she was. Despite imagining tucking her closer, he forced his fingers to unfurl and let go.

She colored nicely, the rosiness in her cheeks making her dark eyelashes and pale blues even more arresting.

He went back to pointing. "They're arranged by grade level from top to bottom. I ordered them for the children who might not be in school. I figured their mothers, or hopefully someone literate in the household, could help them read. They can keep them for the year."

He rotated slightly on the seat to face the back wall, his mind clearing a little without her skirts brushing against his knees. "These are newspapers, farming quarterlies, and ladies magazines. Behind you are the cookbooks, health guides, and sundry manuals on woodworking and whatever else I thought the men might be interested in to improve themselves. And over there on that shelf"—he indicated the one on her other side—"is literature."

She ran her hand along the single shelf of novels and pulled out the copy of *Roughing It*. "I suppose this shelf is for Theresa."

"I'm sure others will succumb to the magic of you talking about novels and want to read one or two."

"Magic?"

"When you were talking to Theresa last week, you were mesmerizing." His cheeks heated at his choice of words. He should shut up.

"That's silly."

Or perhaps she was more enchanting now, with her eyes wide

and her lower lip tucked between her teeth. What would she look like after being kissed really well?

He straightened and scooted away lest she hear the thumping in his chest. He needed to keep a steel trap on his mind or he'd get into trouble. Blast Henri for suggesting the nonsense that he could have any woman he wanted.

Lydia sighed and looked away, running her fingers along the small shelf of popular fiction again.

He'd thought having his heart race was bad enough, but the current dip in her brow and the sag in her shoulders made the beats turn sluggish. "You're disappointed."

He'd told Henri she'd find his library idea wanting.

"No, no. I . . . I didn't expect this. Yet, after the past several weeks of dealing with you, I should have . . . should've realized you'd not do things like I expected."

Yes, he prided himself on doing the unexpected, but this time . . . "Did I do better or worse?"

She gave a noncommittal shrug. "Different." But her tone said worse.

He slid a primer off its shelf and flipped it in his hands. He'd decided from the beginning not to consult her, wanting to do things his way simply for the sake of thwarting her preconceived ideas. Though as this day drew nearer, he'd hoped this would please her.

But even if he had consulted her, he probably still would have chosen to do things his way.

He'd never cared if anyone thought poorly of him before—not even Gracie. Which of course had done nothing good for his marriage. She'd abandoned him for another, and only returned when she had no other options. None whatsoever.

And he really shouldn't care what Lydia thought of him.

She placed a hand on his arm, the slender imprint of her fingers trailing down to his elbow. "I'm—"

"Look . . . " Nicholas grabbed her hand and squeezed. "I'm sorry I'm not fulfilling your wishes as you wanted." She'd be plenty pleased with what he had in store for her later, surely. But he'd hoped she'd be delighted with the traveling library. It was a great way to help so many who couldn't or wouldn't take advantage of a normal library.

"No, I was just about to say I shouldn't be disappointed. I don't deserve anything."

"Of course you do."

"No, I don't." She tugged her hand from his and shook her head. But then a slow smile lit her face. "But I got it anyway, and you obviously put a lot of thought into this." She let out a disparaging laugh and gestured at the coach's interior. "You're fulfilling my desire for the town to have a library, and providing for me. What better job could you have offered? I didn't even know I needed one." She looked up at him, her forehead all wrinkled up again.

Did she like it or not?

His fingers ached to smooth the furrows on her brow, but he knew better than to touch her right now, lest he forget himself and take the wayward wisp of hair dangling in front of her face and tuck it behind her ear, then let his fingers trail down the bit of her exposed neck to feel her pulse throbbing there. Was it heightened like his was, sitting this close to each other?

She closed her eyes. "It's not what I hoped for, but thank you. For everything."

He tore his gaze off her earlobe and blinked. Though he didn't give her what she wanted, she was still thankful? An honest-to-goodness grateful woman?

He tipped his head back and stared at the ceiling, his Adam's apple working. God help him. If she got one more thing right, he'd start pursuing another man's intended.

He tried to find another inch or two on the seat to scoot over. He really should've thought about how small this bench was before he'd hopped in here with her. "You're welcome, though I see now I should have consulted you."

She fidgeted beside him. "Perhaps, but even so, I don't deserve the consideration you've shown me. And through it, I've learned a few things . . . not exactly things I wanted to learn, but I'm glad

154

of it." She gave him a small smile and turned back to reading the titles around her.

In silence, they swayed with the coach's movements, each little bump bringing them within inches of each other.

As she perused the books, the smile slipped back onto her face, her lips wriggling occasionally whenever she found a title to her liking.

He should stop looking at her mouth, but since she seemed oblivious . . .

She suddenly turned to look at him, and her smile died.

He swallowed and shuttered his features. Though likely too late for her to miss where he'd been staring.

The wagon slowed and stopped. Nicholas slipped off the seat and opened the door before she could say anything. "We're only visiting the Blairs today."

She looked over his shoulder to the lowly hovel behind him, her smile growing bigger.

He let out a sharp exhale to keep from kissing her and wiping that smile right off. "I figured you and Theresa would like to talk about your new library."

He hopped outside and waited for her to descend. "I'd like you to take out the library coach twice a week. I doubt many will read fast enough to warrant visiting more often—except Theresa, of course."

Lydia remained on the middle of the seat, the copy of *Roughing It* in her hands, staring at the small shelf to her right. "Just a minute. I need to memorize the available titles since Theresa won't be able to look herself."

After a moment or two of his standing in a mud puddle, she took his offered hand, but he failed to keep her from mucking up her hem. She hadn't worn a work dress today. A lovely blue skirt with purple embroidery embellishing its hem fluttered under the edges of her navy cloak. Hopefully when Theresa saw the book in Lydia's hand, she wouldn't notice how her dress outshone his worn lumberyard uniform.

He linked his arm with Lydia's and tore his gaze away. Would it be wrong to tell a woman courted by another man that she looked lovely?

He had to get someone else out here before he said or did something foolish. "Hello, the house! Theresa? Errol?"

22

Beside her, Nicholas was oddly quiet.

Given that she'd already looked at the books lining the inside of the carriage three times over on their way back to town, she allowed herself to look at him.

He was completely entranced by the passing scenery in the coach's one small window, though there was nothing but brown grass and brown trees to look at.

He'd hardly talked at the Blairs'. Granted, Alec hadn't been there, but even so, Nicholas had said hardly a word all afternoon. She fidgeted beside him, the silence strangely uncomfortable.

Had he really found her mesmerizing when she talked about books? And that look on his face when she'd caught him staring . . .

She'd resisted the urge to peek at him while she told Theresa of the handful of novels in the library coach, but she couldn't help sensing him watching her—again—and more than he should have.

He'd played checkers with Errol but had lost every single time. And he didn't seem to be purposely throwing the games.

And though she'd tried to forget about him as she and Theresa dreamed up a list of books to order for the library, she felt his eyes on her every movement.

When she'd turn to catch him, he'd drop his gaze instantly.

But she'd caught one look that mirrored her father's expression back when Mama was well and he was in high spirits. The one that made her mother blush as he twirled her in his arms and whispered in her ear.

It was a good thing Theresa carried most of the conversation on her own. That look had so jumbled Lydia's thoughts that Theresa could've insisted Mr. Elton would have been a better husband for Emma than Mr. Knightley and Lydia would've hummed in affirmation.

The coach jolted, and Lydia blew out a breath.

All this afternoon's talk of Jane Austen heroes must have been what scrambled her brain. She'd not caught Nicholas looking at her like that again, even after he'd joined their conversation on what books they should buy. Maybe she'd imagined it.

She glanced down at the list of titles he'd helped them compile. So many books they wanted to read, but with the size of this coach and his desire to dedicate most of its space to the education of the poorest of the poor . . .

Though she wanted to be happy with this traveling library setup, she'd dreamed of a grand room filled to the brim with stacks of novels she wanted to read herself, heading up a ladies' reading club, sitting behind a desk, sneaking in a page or two of Twain or Libbey between attending to patrons.

She sighed and shook her head. After a day or two, she'd recover from that lost dream and be ready to start work in this odd mobile library in good spirits.

The rolling library stopped sooner than expected. They couldn't have returned to his mansion already.

Nicholas got out and waited. They weren't outside but rather inside a small carriage house. The large doors behind them didn't open onto Nicholas's expansive acreage but instead faced a building's brick wall across a wide alley.

Mr. Parker pulled the two giant doors closed, and the room dimmed.

She put her hand in Nicholas's and looked around as she alighted. "Where are we?"

"At the library." He pulled her to the side.

"But I thought the coach was the library." She passed in front of him and through an open door.

The room's chipped tile floor and high ceilings weren't exactly inviting, but the walls were lined with barely filled shelving. A large table and desk were thrown in the middle of the room, and a few rolled-up rugs drooped across the arm of a floral couch. Four crates and their lids littered the floor.

So she didn't have to settle for a tiny coach of books? Why did her heart hiccup as if she'd just received a gift and not a job? She couldn't help but gaze at Nicholas with a cheek-hurting grin, but he wasn't looking at her.

Probably a good thing, considering the way he'd stared at her earlier.

She blew out a calming breath. This building would have been small for a store, but for a library? The number of books she could put in this room . . . "It's enormous."

"Then we can fill it with lots of books." He rubbed his hands together, smiling just as widely as she had earlier.

Her heart fluttered again. Sebastian was never this giddy over something she loved.

Nicholas perched on the edge of the desk, just as he had on that day she'd barged into his lumber office at the beginning of October demanding thirty dollars and comparing him to Scrooge.

How much had he spent on her requests since then?

Much, much more than thirty dollars.

"This will be good for the town. I hadn't thought of starting a library until you wrote it down. I'd often lent my own books, but not everyone would feel comfortable asking me. You had a great idea, and I'm sure you'll make this a great outreach." He scooted farther back on the desk. He was acting more like a big brother than a boss, arms crossed, his heel thumping against the desk.

159

How had she ever compared him to the red-eyed, thin-lipped Scrooge?

He stopped his kicking, his smile fading. "I know you weren't thrilled about continuing to work with me last week, but I won't be involved much beyond paying bills. I've got plenty of business to get back to."

Why did his no longer being involved make her want to frown? "Are the books I requested in these boxes?"

He leaned back, pulled out a desk drawer, and fished out a familiar sheet of her stationery. "I had a quarter of your list in my personal library already." He pointed to a shelf filled with several small stacks of books. "I figure there'll be some in town who'll donate. You've said I need to involve others, so we'll wait to order the rest of these and the list we came up with at Theresa's until after we see what comes in. I did order manuals and books I thought the farming folk might like, though. I want everyone to have access to books that would interest them." His shoulders lifted with a deep breath and he looked straight at her, his eyes penetrating but gentle. "Which means I want Queenie to have access, and she'll borrow for the other ladies."

So last week was not the last time she would have to converse with prostitutes. What would her mother say to her taking this job if she knew that?

His mouth twitched. "I want you to reserve three, maybe four, hours for library maintenance or whatever you want to call it. Queenie can come in at those times if someone wants to borrow something so she doesn't make any patrons uncomfortable."

Lydia paced over to a brand-new shelf beside the front doors and looked out the window. They were eight blocks north of the corner of the red-light district, far enough away for no one to worry about its proximity but close enough to walk.

"I know it's a lot to ask, but I hope you'll tolerate Queenie. I'm not asking you to deal with the others. They know you shouldn't associate with them, but those who have extra time . . . If they don't occupy their minds, they fall into even more trouble. And perhaps something in this library will help one of them. Words are powerful things."

How could she deny anybody a book?

"Are you still interested in the job? Will you have a problem with Queenie borrowing the same books as your friends?"

She pressed her arms against her stomach; the uncertainty in his voice made her feel small and petty. "Red-light fines help pay for our schools, streets, and other municipal improvements, yes?" When she'd asked Sebastian why they allowed the women and gamblers to return to the streets instead of jailing repeat offenders, he'd said the fines were too lucrative to ignore.

"They do."

"Then if the town takes their money for our betterment, they can use our books for theirs."

Nicholas stepped closer, his breath ruffling her hair and tickling her ear. "I hadn't thought I could like you more."

She looked up at him. Did he see the gooseflesh pop up across the back of her neck at the grit in his voice?

He didn't back away. And he wasn't looking at the gooseflesh on her neck . . . not that looking at her neck would have made his gaze any less unsettling.

Parker walked in from the carriage house and cleared his throat.

She took a step back. They were employer and employee. Nothing more. She'd only imagined how his eyes had sparked—they were uncommonly piercing, after all, and the man did seem to analyze and pick apart everybody and everything.

"Shall I escort Miss King home?"

"No, I will. See you tomorrow morning, Parker."

His driver nodded and shoved his hat on his head before preceding them out the door. "Good night, then, Miss King." The man's grandfatherly gaze held a bit of warning.

But surely he wasn't afraid of Nicholas's harming her in any way. His intentions were always honorable. He'd given her a desk, a library, an income . . . He was looking out for her, as he did for so many others without the town knowing about it.

If Nicholas wasn't waiting, she might have started unpacking boxes, smelling new pages, deciding how to organize despite the waning afternoon light.

But he was waiting—and the thought of walking home with him pulled at her almost as much as those half-packed crates of books.

Or maybe more.

Not good.

When had she started wanting to spend time with him instead of avoiding him at all costs? "I don't want to be a bother. Well, no more than I already am. I appreciate your offer, but I can see myself home."

He smiled. "You're no trouble. During the winter, I expect you to close the library early so you don't walk home near dark. Drunkards might wander nearby." His smile disappeared. "Promise me you won't ever stay after hours if it's dark."

Her mother would have a conniption if she ignored such commonsense advice—it wasn't as if she couldn't come back the next day, and the next. A small, giddy huff escaped. What was Sebastian's book allowance compared to this? "No need to worry about that."

"Good." Nicholas gestured for her to go outside ahead of him, and she shuffled past.

On the sidewalk, she stopped and looked down at her skirt and then back at his faded uniform. "This is the first time we're . . . Should we walk through town together with you dressed as Nick? Your work clothes won't conceal your identity to anyone who knows you."

And if anyone saw them together, Sebastian would know within a day or two.

"Our secret adventures are over, and it will soon be common knowledge that I'm funding the library." He rubbed at his frayed cuff. "The only reason I still need the poor-worker disguise is to keep the trust of the truly needy, whose pride keeps them from taking what they need unless someone as bad off as they are does the giving."

She clasped her hands behind her back to thwart him from deciding to offer his arm. They might walk together, but they shouldn't look . . . together. "As long as you're doing what you think best."

"You've made me question my methods and motives a lot lately." His brow furrowed. And was he actually slumped a bit?

Though she might imagine he sounded like a repentant Mr. Darcy from *Pride and Prejudice* or Mr. Thornton from *North and South*, he wasn't really like either of those two characters. Darcy and Thornton had been so cold . . . but, well, so was Nicholas, or at least she'd thought him to be . . . once. Like the other two . . .

Did Nicholas think about her the way Darcy thought about Lizzy Bennet? Thornton about Margaret Hale? Or could a gruff man just be a gruff man?

But would a truly bad-tempered man look at her the way he had at the Blairs' today?

No, she was just being silly. She shook her head and let out a breath. She must not ruin things with Sebastian because of her overactive imagination. Besides, she'd agreed to be courted by him, and he'd done nothing worthy of being jilted—except maybe paling in comparison to her romantic notion of a mis-understood hero.

She tripped on an uneven brick in the sidewalk, and Nicholas's firm grip kept her upright. "I'm sorry, I wasn't minding my feet."

What a romantic fool she'd become—just like her father warned her would happen after reading too many novels.

She was neither Lizzy nor Margaret.

They were the quintessential women of independence, moti-vated by the ideal.

And she'd sell herself to marriage with Sebastian for worldly security.

Nicholas wouldn't want a woman who accepted the most con-venient solution to her problems, ignoring deeper issues like her motivations and distrust of God's provision.

He was only trying to be nicer after she'd harangued him the other day in the carriage. Surely that was it.

And she needed to stop thinking he felt anything for her before she began believing he did. "So how do you think Robbie, Angel, and Pepper are adjusting?" The children were more important to be ruminating on anyway.

"I'm not sure. I'm afraid Pepper will make good on her threat to leave one day. She puts up a fight anytime she's asked to scrub floors, wring laundry, or otherwise contribute. Angel's having a grand time, though—she thinks dusting is fun."

"But surely Pepper knows that sleeping in a closet at your place is far better than living at Madam Careless's—and I know you wouldn't put them in a closet."

He gave a little chuckle. "Sometimes Pepper's mouth makes me wish she were confined to a closet." He sighed. "She's hard. Very hard."

"What do you plan to do with them?"

He stuffed his hands in his pockets and kicked at a rock on the sidewalk. "They're definitely not ready for school, but it's not like I have a nanny. And I'm sure no nanny or tutor I've ever met would put up with Pepper's disrespect. The maids are trying their best, though."

"Do you think I could help in any way?"

He shook his head. "Thanks, but the maids are socially closer to them and likely have the best chance at reaching Pepper."

"What about Robbie? Has he talked any?"

"Unfortunately, he seems more withdrawn every day."

As they crossed the street by the Methodist church, a movement in the shadows made her heart jump. A dark form rose from the steps.

"I need help," a slurred female voice called. The figure stumbled but caught herself on the banister. The woman swayed forward, awash in the pale lavender and magenta light of sunset.

Lydia gasped.

The woman's eyes lit with recognition at the same time. She lifted an unsteady hand to point at her. "You."

Nicholas's hand clamped around Lydia's arm. A good thing too, or she might have bolted like a ninny.

No lady of the night should address a decent woman in town. Ever. And only during a crusade would Mrs. Little or any other moral woman dare to engage such a woman.

"This isn't your church, is it?" The streetwalker nodded over her shoulder at the stone stairs she'd just vacated.

Nicholas took a step closer to her. "We attend Freewill—"

"Good." She cut him off with a sneer. She eyed his clothing and took an unsteady step right of forward. "Her and that holier-than-thou group can go to—" The woman stumbled and cursed at the flask she dropped.

Lydia tugged on his sleeve, hoping he'd get the hint to put some space between them and move before things got worse.

And though Nicholas was a member of Freewill, he was definitely not of her group. He would actually attempt to help a streetwalker in the middle of town. Except this woman was not only drunk at the moment, but also incensed.

"This woman threw a bottle at me," Lydia whispered. "I think we'd better not engage her."

"Go on with you! Go home to your warm beds and families." The lady flung out her arm, winced, and dropped her flask again. "Pray God keeps you safe since *you* deserve it."

"No one deserves what God wants to give each and every one of us." Nicholas leaned over, picked her flask up, and surreptitiously dumped the contents. "I don't deserve the forgiveness He gave me for the blackest of my sins." He handed the shiny metal container back to the woman.

"What do you know of sin?" She spat. "You're lily white compared to me." She dragged her torpid gaze off Nicholas and lifted a weak, unsteady arm to point at Lydia. "And what about you? Done nothing wrong in your life, have you?" She narrowed her eyes, as if she could see into Lydia's soul. "Liar!"

Lydia's body turned leaden and cold.

Nicholas stepped between them, shielding her from the woman's accusations—accusations he might have thrown at Lydia himself if he weren't a gentleman.

"You said you needed help." Nicholas held out his arms, palms forward as if showing the woman he was unarmed. "What kind of help?"

Oh, couldn't he be sensible just once and walk past? The streetwalker probably wanted more liquor, and if she found out Nicholas had dumped what she had left, they could be in danger if she had a weapon.

But . . . if Nicholas didn't help, she'd be disappointed in the man who lived out his convictions no matter the repercussions.

Unlike her.

"My arm." The rabid expression in the thin woman's eyes dissolved and her face suddenly slacked. She pulled at her sleeve, the left one, which dangled in shreds and was darkened with a shiny stain. "Some john cut me."

Lydia gasped, feeling as if her shoulders had sunk all the way down into her toes. A bloody bandage peeked out from beneath the woman's ragged sleeve. The woman had been bleeding this whole time and she'd not noticed?

She would've walked right past this fire-breathing, bruised, and broken woman had it not been for Nicholas.

He eyed the woman's arm from where he stood. "Why didn't you go to Dr. Hiller?"

"Dr. Hiller?" Her eyes grew wider and a little less frightened. "You know Dr. Hiller?"

"Yes. Did you go to him?"

"He's busy with Busty Bess—pumping her stomach. I didn't want to wait."

Lydia's insides churned. Had Bess poisoned herself or been poisoned?

"I'll take you to Dr. Lindon, then."

Lydia snatched his sleeve. "You can't be seen escorting her uptown. What would happen to your reputation? Your business contacts?"

"She's stumbling all over the place and shouldn't walk alone. You could come with us if you're worried."

"I can't be seen with her either!" Her hands trembled. Had she not made that clear the other day? If she walked side by side with this woman, she'd be dragged down to the level of a streetwalker in the eyes of so many that she might as well give up any and all good society.

Nicholas looked down at her, his mouth a hard line.

Maybe not all of society.

She couldn't keep his gaze. She'd said Queenie could come borrow books from the library without any fuss—wasn't that enough?

The streetwalker lowered herself back onto the step, cradling her arm and muttering to herself.

"This lady needs a doctor, and she's too inebriated to understand directions. She might just lie down in an alley and bleed out overnight."

Why was she hesitating when what he said was true? She wasn't this hard-hearted toward her father when he was hurt, and he'd actually ill-used her.

Nicholas clasped her shoulders and bent to look in her eyes. "Look, if I'm seen with her, no one will care." He let out a breath, his hands tightening. "There are men of high social standing, supposedly of good morals, who frequent the red-light district, who don't bother with disguise, who've visited this woman in full view of others, and no one cares much. It's the woman's name, reputation, and life that's dragged through the mud, not the man's. So don't worry about me. It likely won't matter much if they assume the worst."

Frowning, she couldn't keep her eyes steady with his. He might be right. His life probably wouldn't be ruined by walking through town with a prostitute—but no one would believe he'd simply escorted her to the doctor either. And he didn't deserve that.

He reached out and anchored a finger or two in a strand of her hair and slipped it behind her ear. "However, I'd like you to come with us. It's almost dark, and I'd like to make sure you get home."

Of course he'd been worried about her safety instead of his reputation.

She looked at the last orange vestiges of sunlight reaching out from below the low-lying clouds. Then to the streets that hardly anyone occupied, considering the cold that had blown in this afternoon.

If she helped this woman for the right reason, being seen with her shouldn't matter. God knew what they were doing. She lifted her chin and sucked in a fortifying breath. "All right."

Nicholas nodded solemnly and went to help the lady up.

Though knowing God knew why and where they were escorting the prostitute, she'd still pray no one saw them.

23

Hobbling up Dr. Lindon's stairs, Nicholas clamped his arms around the waist of the lady of the night as she struggled to step up to the porch. He helped her over to the swing and breathed a sigh of relief once he released her. She'd been more intoxicated than he'd thought, and her unsteady weight and erratic pace had made for quite the trudge uptown.

He knocked on the door and then turned to give Lydia a reassuring smile. "I'll get her inside. The porch has a great view of the sunset while you wait." He tilted his head toward the horizon just visible past the granary, where the sun's fiery orange was encapsulated by a frosty light blue.

"Too cold to sit outside. Besides, I'll see if the doctor wants my help."

He pursed his lips. "Are you sure?"

She looked over at the prostitute slumped in the swing as she drew closer to him. "If a doctor isn't looked down upon for his clientele," she whispered, "then why should I be if he needs a nurse?"

"You don't have to."

The thumping of someone descending the stairs sounded behind the door.

"But she obviously needs help. . . . I just never thought that help was needed from me." She looked up at him with deep, wide eyes. "As you've said before, if no one else will help, then why not us?"

"Right. Us." He swallowed against his tight throat. He knew that *us* was simply a grammatical term for him and her, but his heart was both elated . . . and disappointed by the word.

Only a small sliver of time remained when *us* would mean the two of them doing anything together. Once she married Sebastian that *us* would fade into the past. As it should.

The bolt slid with a *thunk,* and Dr. Lindon swung the door open wide. "Mr. Lowe, what's wrong?"

"This lady . . ." He cringed at how little he knew of the woman on the swing. How would she believe he truly cared if he didn't even bother to learn a thing about her? He walked over, grabbed her hand, and tilted her lolled head up to look at him. "What's your name, miss?"

"Raspy Rachel."

"No, your real one."

"Still Rachel."

"All right, let's get you up and inside." He grabbed her under her good arm, slung his around her back, and steered her around to the door. "Rachel has a large laceration on her upper left arm. I've tied some cloth around it, but it needs stitches."

The doctor stepped aside, and they hobbled in.

"Follow me." He led them into a small room and grabbed a lamp.

"I can light those so you can get prepared," Lydia said as she stepped into the room.

The doctor turned, his eyebrow cocked. "Miss King?"

"Yes." She swallowed but held out her hands for the matches.

The doctor didn't move, just stared at Lydia's palms.

Nicholas cleared his throat. "I was escorting Miss King home from her job when we happened upon Rachel. Miss King didn't want to leave her to suffer just so she could get home on time."

Lydia paused for a second to frown at him before taking the doctor's matches.

He helped Rachel onto the padded table, and she moaned as she rolled toward the middle. Her ashen face was worrisome, but hopefully she'd look better once Lydia lit a few lamps. "Do you want her sitting up?"

"She's fine however." Dr. Lindon waved his hand back behind his shoulder as he gathered utensils on a tray.

Rachel rolled her head toward the doctor. "I need whiskey."

The doctor barely glanced at her. "I think you've had plenty."

"You'll be all right." Lydia finished lighting a third lamp and set it on the table beside the bed.

"Not without whiskey." Rachel's eyes widened when the doctor turned around holding a huge pair of scissors. "He gonna cut me?" She jerked back, wincing immediately.

Dr. Lindon harrumphed. "Just the bandage Mr. Lowe put on you. Perhaps your sleeve as well."

"Here." Lydia came around the table and took the hand of Rachel's uninjured arm. "You squeeze my hand as much as you need to."

Nicholas backed away, strangely feeling unneeded.

Rachel gave Lydia a look that bespoke distrust, but she didn't yank her hand from hers.

"So, Rachel." Lydia took a quick glance at the doctor before turning back to the patient. "Um, what . . . no . . ." She pulled her bottom lip in and scrunched her brows.

Nicholas pressed his lips together to keep from smiling. Lydia was clearly at a loss for talking points. But what could a lady and a prostitute converse about?

"So . . . where did you grow up?" Lydia gently turned Rachel's face away from the doctor and toward her.

Rachel didn't seem thrilled at being thwarted from watching the doctor's ministrations. "Louisiana."

"You still have family there?"

"Might."

The doctor swabbed something onto Rachel's arm, and she flinched and cursed.

Lydia didn't so much as narrow her eyes at the woman's use of profanity. "Squeeze my hand, remember?"

Rachel screeched with the doctor's first stab of the needle.

Dr. Lindon growled. "You have enough alcohol in you, this shouldn't hurt that much. If you can't hold still, I'll have Lowe hold you down."

"We don't need that to happen, right?" Lydia swiped the hair back from Rachel's eyes and looked straight at her. "Just grit your teeth and breathe," she commanded.

Seemed Lydia was a natural nurse.

She stared into Rachel's eyes. "Now, why don't you tell me how you ended up in Teaville?"

Even the doctor glanced up at Lydia with the same quizzical look Rachel wore.

Nicholas couldn't help his smile.

Rachel grunted as if trying to scare Lydia away.

But Lydia kept her gaze on the woman without a flinch. "Go on, tell me. It'll keep your mind off things."

With another jab of the needle, Rachel tensed. "James . . . He and I were together—been that way ever since we met catching frogs in the creek." She cringed with another needle poke. "I told him he'd done gotten me with child." She hissed again. "He was better than me though. Richer. High-society folk. He was about to take over some older man's business, a Mr. Sandoval." She winced again. "And the old coot wouldn't have looked too kindly on me being swollen with James's child." Rachel started a curse word but didn't finish it as she finally took Lydia's offer and squeezed the hand that hadn't left hers. "Sandoval's daughter was our age, and hang it if she weren't prettier than me."

"There." The doctor made a quick knot and clipped off his last stitch. "Won't be pretty, but it should heal as long as we keep it from infection."

Rachel opened her eyes to look at Lydia.

Lydia frowned. "I'm so sorry."

The prostitute closed her eyes and shrugged.

The lump in Nicholas's throat edged upward, and he swallowed against it. Simply taking Lydia to the red-light district hadn't made her the kind of woman who would allow a lady of the night to squeeze her hand so hard she left fingernail divots in Lydia's flesh.

But would she have ever willingly accompanied a soiled dove to the doctor if he hadn't taken her there first?

Nicholas moved over to the table to help Rachel sit up.

"Take her to the room across the hall." Dr. Lindon was washing his hands in a shallow basin. "I doubt I'll have more patients tonight, and I'm concerned about how much she's had to drink. I'd like to check on her in the morning."

"All right." At least that answered one of his dilemmas.

But the thought of granting Lydia's next wish niggled at him. How would Lydia take it? As well as she did the library coach?

He should've talked to her, given her time to see things as he did, as she claimed she would with time . . . but he'd already arranged everything. The date was set.

Rachel passed out after the first step, and he had to carry her across the hall.

Lydia ran in front of them to open the door, then turned down the blankets on the small cot in the corner.

"Thank you." He rolled Rachel onto the bed, and Lydia immediately started unbuttoning the woman's shoes, so he slipped out of the room.

Leaning his head against the door, he stared at the ceiling. He couldn't change his plans. He'd already given his word to the pastor. And Lydia would get over any disappointment he'd cause and buck up to the task just as she had with Rachel.

After settling with the doctor, Nicholas found Lydia outside, leaning against the porch railing, staring at the first pinpricks of stars in the beginnings of the night sky.

They'd better get going before they couldn't see enough to walk—they'd spent far too long at Dr. Lindon's. Hopefully Lydia wouldn't think about how he'd get back home. He looked around for the moon and located it to the east. At least it wasn't cloudy tonight. He stepped forward and lightly touched her arm.

She gave him a slight smile and slipped her arm around his.

Together.

Together, they could do plenty of good.

He shook away the thought and walked her down the steps. Just like he'd do for any lady at church.

Though he kept a brisk pace on the way to the King residence, he wasn't walking fast enough to stifle conversation, yet Lydia remained quiet, her brow furrowing occasionally, and sometimes she'd let out a frustrated sigh.

Clearly she was struggling to think through things.

And he was glad of it.

For if she easily gave in to others' wishes, beliefs, or goals, she wouldn't be the stalwart woman he was beginning to admire. She had convictions. And right or wrong, she didn't toss them aside lightly.

Maybe *us* wasn't such a dream after all. What if she began to believe in what he was doing? What if she wanted to help?

Her house appeared, and though the vestiges of the sun would disappear within minutes, he had to know. . . . "What are you thinking?"

"I was wondering how best to help women like Rachel."

He couldn't suppress the smile that bubbled up. Maybe they would be doing more together.

"You and Queenie both mentioned it was near impossible to leave prostitution, so I thought keeping a woman from entering the profession would be easier than taking one out."

"Prevention would be easier. An ounce of that is better than a pound of cure, as Franklin said."

"And if Rachel had known somewhere safe to go with her baby, maybe she would've chosen a different life."

How might Roxanna's life have been different if she'd known someone like Lydia would care about her predicament?

"So as a senator's wife, I was thinking I could encourage

Sebastian's colleagues to switch their focus from fining prostitutes to giving desperate women alternatives."

He swallowed and nodded. But her arm—which had felt so light and warm only seconds ago—suddenly felt like lead.

"Do you think I'd have a chance at spurring the state into creating an organization to help unwed mothers?"

He tried to focus on what she was saying, but the words *"as a senator's wife"* kept replaying in his mind. "Uh . . . I think most politicians would say that need was being met by the counties' poor farms."

"But that certainly is nowhere to raise a child. Surely we could do better. Something like a poor farm crossed with an orphanage."

"That sounds like an idea," he rasped.

And it was a good start. The kind of thinking he'd hoped for just weeks ago.

Though he'd hoped to groom someone to help him around here.

But of course, having someone who thought like him discussing these things with people of influence across the state might help his cause more. . . .

He stopped at the bottom of her steps and forced himself to let go of her arm. "I think you'll do a lot of good, Lydia."

She gave him a sheepish smile and shrugged. "Thank you."

What else was there to say that wouldn't betray the illogical path his brain had taken minutes ago? He lifted his hand slightly. "Good night."

"Good night." She turned up the stairs and disappeared inside.

Squeezing the balustrade, he stared at her door far longer than necessary. It wasn't her fault he'd allowed his emotions out of the padlocked sections of his heart.

She'd do a lot of good through Sebastian. Might even make the man see the light.

So hopefully granting her next wish would help her see the needs of a different group of people who were just as needy as those in the red-light district. If she'd champion them as well, maybe all this turmoil would be worth it.

24

The small group of women who'd shown up at the church on this extremely cold morning was quiet and grave as they sewed. A few minutes ago, Bernadette had walked in with her husband and asked for the group to forgive her for quitting, without a hint at the reason.

Even Mrs. Little—never at a loss for criticism—sewed in silence after Bernadette left hand in hand with the pastor.

So quiet was the basement, Lydia could hear her eyelids blinking.

She'd known Bernadette was going to stop volunteering, but these ladies hadn't. Perhaps some good news would help. Surely it would be all right to tell the women of Nicholas's intention to bolster church funds, even if they had yet to meet with Pastor Wisely. "I know Mrs. Wisely's leaving isn't happy news, but we do have something to rejoice over." She smiled at the ladies around the quilt. "Our needs for the quilt project should be fully funded by the end of the day."

Mrs. Little's head popped up first, and she narrowed her eyes.

Evelyn's face brightened, probably ready to latch onto anything to draw attention away from her mother's announcement. "So you finally got Mr. Lowe to cave?"

Lydia bobbed her head. Her heart warmed at the thought of

him. Her dreams the past few nights had been filled with him. And when she awoke each time . . . she'd let the dream play out in her imagination. She had never allowed herself to dream of a man as wealthy as Nicholas before. Even though Papa had said her pretty blue eyes could win over any man, she'd not bothered to believe him since her family and financial situation were much less attractive.

But Nicholas didn't seem to care what anyone thought about anything. If he took a fancy to a certain young lady . . .

She shook her head. What was she thinking? She had to push away such thoughts. If she dreamed about it too much, all she did was invite disappointment. He might be attracted, but he was too honorable to act on any interest he may have as long as she was tied to Sebastian.

But what if she no longer was?

She huffed and poked her needle back into the cloth. How many times must she remind herself of how reality worked? Fantasizing about stirring up the male interest Nicholas had displayed would only cause heartbreak. There were just too many differences to make them compatible, like their social standing and the size of their bank accounts.

Oh, if only half her life hadn't been spent getting lost in the happily-ever-afters of women of humble means who'd found love with princes among men.

She started another line of stitching. Time to return to what she knew could happen. Yesterday morning Mr. Black had informed her of today's scheduled appointment.

"Mr. Lowe agreed to make a donation to the church and plans to discuss which funds to put it into with Pastor Wisely. How much more is needed for the machines, Mrs. Little?"

Sebastian's mother sat in silence for a moment, but then dropped her needle and thread and scuttled over to the carved wooden box. "I've got twenty-three dollars and fifty cents. That should pay for one machine and some fabric to go along with what was donated. If we get at least ten more dollars, we could buy two machines, but fifteen would be better so we'd have plenty of fabric." She rubbed her chin and looked at the ceiling before turning her eyes toward Lydia with . . . admiration, maybe? "How much are you getting from him?"

"I don't know exactly, but it isn't a small amount." Maybe it wasn't wise to reveal too much to Mrs. Little. "I don't think so anyway."

"Well, get as much as possible. We don't need to limit ourselves to machines. We could buy material for some banners for Sebastian—for the slogans that fit the moral society's purpose, of course. Maybe hold a rally of some sort, bring in a real on-fire preacher to confront The Line's wickedness."

Lydia squirmed in her seat. "Mr. Lowe will want a say on what his donation is for, and I don't know if—"

"Those are just the first ideas off the top of my head, of course. But if you've wrangled something from him when we've never succeeded before, you can get more. He might not give again, so we should wring out what we can now."

Lydia shook her head. "I doubt—"

"Fifty would be good, a hundred better. We could put the extra in the coffer and decide what to do with it later."

"I—"

Evelyn squeezed Lydia's hand. "I knew you could do it."

Mrs. Robinson clapped her hands. "We could buy new music for our serenades."

"Or more literature to hand out." Mrs. Little smiled. "I saw some excellent tracts on the evils of staying open for business on the Sabbath."

"Or what about . . ."

Lydia worked to keep the smile on her face. She'd definitely cheered the room, but Nicholas wouldn't approve of half these ideas—she wasn't even sure he'd agree to put the original thirty dollars she'd asked for in the moral society's fund.

She'd only intended to prod him to cover the sewing machines. But then, would it hurt to ask for a little more? These women did other good things, like hand out turkeys at Thanksgiving and evangelize at the town's festivals.

In addition to the sewing machines, she'd hoped he'd supply the children's Sunday school fund so they could buy a set of Bibles and give a sizeable chunk to the building fund for the parsonage. But fifty dollars for the moral society wasn't too much more than thirty.

The ladies talked excitedly, their ideas growing into projects that would take hundreds of dollars, but Lydia held her tongue before she made things worse. She'd find out soon enough what she could get.

A fast quarter of an hour raced by with the ladies shocked out of their gloom.

"Would you like to have lunch with me at Reed's?" While all the ladies were cleaning up, Evelyn wrapped a muffler around her neck and pulled on the homemade mittens Lydia had made her last Christmas.

Christmas presents . . . Why hadn't she thought of Christmas presents for the children at Nicholas's? Had they ever received any?

She was in the middle of knitting a sweater for herself—a large, thick sweater—but if she unraveled it, surely she'd have enough to make Pepper, Angel, and Robbie each a set of mittens.

Lydia put her notions away in her basket. "I'm afraid I have other plans." Or rather, not enough money. "Maybe I could have you over for lunch after our next meeting?"

"I'll plan on it." Evelyn squeezed her shoulder. "And I'm so proud of you."

After Evelyn left with the others, Lydia made her way upstairs with a lilt in her step. Surely Nicholas would buy the children something, and with the mittens she hoped to make, they'd have a rather pleasant Christmas—maybe their first.

Moving through the church's silent hallways, the wood creaking loudly beneath her feet, she padded over to the entrance's double doors. The only carriage outside was the shabby one they'd used to visit Queenie and Annie's children. Why would he come to a meeting with the pastor in his disguised vehicle? Her rapid breath fogged up the pane.

He wouldn't.

And yet, he would.

She took a shaky breath. When Nicholas told her about his plans to bolster church funds with a donation, had he mentioned Pastor Wisely or Freewill Church by name?

He isn't planning to meet with Pastor Wisely at all! Please, God, no. What about the Bibles for the children's class, the blankets for the poor, and the fixes for the parsonage? Don't you want them taken care of?

She pressed her hands against the sudden ache in her temples.

I should have known better. If I'd have thought logically, instead of losing myself in romantic daydreams, I'd have realized he'd do the exact opposite of what I wanted.

But please, please let me be wrong.

But she was fairly certain she was wrong in another sense—wrong for having told those ladies Nicholas Lowe intended to help them in any shape or form.

Trembling with the mixture of cold and hot coursing through her limbs, she shoved her arms into her coat sleeves, smashed her hat into place, and forced herself outside and into the frosty air.

Mr. Parker jumped off his seat and pulled his hands from his pockets to open the door for her. "Good afternoon, Miss King."

So Nicholas wasn't getting out, and she was getting in. She shuddered in her coat, rubbing her arms, which did no good in warding off the frigid temperature.

She forced words to the driver past the lump in her throat. "I'm sorry I left you sitting out here so long in this weather."

"If the horses can stand it, so can I." Mr. Parker smiled and handed her into an empty coach.

Where was Nicholas so she could strangle him? Not that her hands were steady enough right now to be of much use.

She pulled a blanket over her knees, huddled next to the window, and watched the church disappear, blinking back disappointed tears.

What kind of lesson was Nicholas attempting to teach her today by thwarting her good intentions once again?

She didn't want him to try to teach her anything anymore! Maybe Freewill Church didn't support all of the same things he did, but they weren't financing criminals either.

He was too stiff-necked for anybody's good.

The last few days, she'd let her imagination run free, despite all the warnings she'd given herself, secretly hoping he'd woo her away from Sebastian. *Stupid, stupid, stupid.*

Why had she ever considered attaching herself to someone who didn't trust her with the details? Who wouldn't help her with the things she believed in?

At least Sebastian had never led her to believe one thing and then handed her another. He had straightforwardness down to an art. He was predictable. Boring.

She closed her eyes and let her body sway with the side-to-side movement of travel. But no matter how mad she tried to be at Nicholas for his high-handed ways, her heart still leapt toward the miniscule hope of capturing the love of a man with such passion for others, a man who sacrificed himself more than anyone she'd ever known. Someone who loved books as much as she did. Whose eyes looked at her as if he found her attractive rather than simply tolerable.

What kind of woman was she to remain attached to a man she didn't even like because she wasn't certain she had a chance with one she did?

The more she grew fond of the unpredictable Mr. Lowe, the more she disliked herself.

25

Nicholas nodded as he inspected the spot on the rise where Pastor Weaver planned to build a church. "Considering the watershed, I'd agree this would be the best spot." The sticks marking off the future foundation made a rather small rectangle. "But I hope you'll consider expanding the size."

The pastor's angular face warmed with the possibility despite the frigid air. Good thing the man couldn't see Lydia standing behind him. She mustered up a smile whenever the pastor turned around, but Nicholas felt the disappointment radiating from her.

She'd expected him to give the entire donation—her third wish—to their church, but he'd already set up this meeting with Pastor Weaver a month ago.

This time, he'd explained why he'd chosen to fulfill her wish this way beforehand. During the long ride into Oklahoma, he'd described the Indian mission and how badly they needed funding. Pastor Weaver did not want to take money from the government—which would dictate how he ran his mission.

She'd been quiet as he'd explained and had nodded in agreement occasionally.

Hadn't she?

Pastor Weaver held his hands up in front of him as if in prayer.

"I appreciate this, Mr. Lowe, more than you know. My mind insisted this building was too much to attempt, but I felt a peace and started with faith. And how quickly He provided." He looked up at the open sky, his face awash in gray afternoon light. "I am humbled. I shall never again doubt that the Lord can do miracles for my people."

Nicholas smiled at the man's gratefulness. But Lydia hadn't offered a single opinion during their discussion of the mission's needs. "Do you see anything we've overlooked, Miss King?"

She tore her gaze off the dirt. "I think it would be more appropriate to ask Pastor Weaver if you forgot anything."

The man's dark hair flopped as he shook his head vehemently. "I wouldn't question someone who has given me more than I deserve. He's met the needs I'd hoped for and more."

She colored a little and nodded.

"If you think of anything else I can help with, let me know." Nicholas stole a glance at Lydia. Her gloomy stance only made him rub his forehead to ease the pain building between his eyes. He'd been certain since the day at the library that she'd be disappointed, but he'd expected her to bounce back toward cheerfulness like she had before.

And he'd talked to her about it this time. Isn't that what she'd asked for when they'd argued in the red-light district?

Though the ride back to Kansas would likely be awkward, he was ready to leave Oklahoma behind. "I've given you enough to get started, and in a few weeks, I'll have my men bring down enough lumber for you to double the size of your building. If you need anything else before I return in March, write my secretary, Mr. Black."

Pastor Weaver stole his hand and shook it vigorously. "Bless you." He turned to Lydia, snapped up her hand, and kissed it. "Bless you both."

She gave him a slight nod.

"We'd best head back so Miss King can reach home before dark." He laced her limp arm through his while they said their farewells, then walked her toward the coach.

"I'm sorry you're upset," he said once they walked out of earshot.

She sighed. "No, you're not. Not really."

He hesitated. She pulled away.

"It's just—" She cut herself off with a frustrated wave of her hand. "I thought that you . . . perhaps thought well of me. But to know you really don't . . . that you would . . ." She huffed. "I thought I was beginning to like you more, that I . . . Well, you have plenty of good qualities I admire, but you insist on slapping me in the face with them. Sometimes I can't decide whether I hate you or . . ." She took off.

"Wait."

"Why?" She skirted a puddle, putting distance between them. "You don't even care what I think."

"Yes, I do."

She stopped to scowl at him. "You assumed I was a hypocrite before you bothered to learn anything about me. Do you realize you treat everyone in our church that way?" She took off again.

He charged after her. "You can't deny there are hypocrites in our church. If you need me to name a few—"

"No." She held up her hand. "I know plenty. Papa refuses to attend church because of them. Several treat us poorly because we can't afford to return their dinner invitations, and those who know that my father drinks, that he . . ." She huffed again. "But what about the Wiselys? They used to bring us lunch when Papa's earnings barely fed us twice a day. And the Renfroes have given me their girls' outgrown dresses since I was six." She spread out her pretty patterned black-and-white skirt, then gestured toward a hint of purple satin popping out of her nicely tailored coat's sleeves. "Do you think my parents can afford these clothes?"

He'd given little thought to her dresses, other than noticing that they looked nice on her. Though he had noticed one or two of her dresses had fuller sleeves than the current fashion dictated, he'd only thought her too practical to discard decent dresses just to keep up with the times. However, hand-me-downs would be another explanation for the puffy sleeves.

"The Renfroes even buy me new fabric every Christmas so I can make myself one gown like all the other girls'." She dropped her skirts, hiding her scuffed boots from view again. "But does Papa use the Wiselys and the Renfroes as excuses to stay *in* church? No." She took off again. "So if a whole lot of nice people can't keep you in church, then you can't use a whole lot of bad people to keep you out."

He pulled at his collar and hustled after her. "True, but—"

She glanced back at him for a second but kept striding toward the coach. "So by refusing to help your own congregation, you might punish the handful of Mrs. Littles, but you hurt the sweet Evelyn Wiselys too." She put her hands on her hips and slowed, catching her breath. "Our church could've used that money for some very necessary things. The pews need replacing, the heating system needs fixing, the—"

"Moral society needs sewing machines?"

She crossed her arms against her chest and stopped walking. "Yes. For the fifteenth time, there is nothing wrong with giving poor people blankets. I don't know why you seem to think there is."

"Because you're not thinking about the poor—not really." He ran his tongue along his teeth, slowing his speech so his tone would stay calm. "What would they do with your fancy needlework? They'd stuff it away in a chest if they had one, afraid to soil it. Whereas that same thirty dollars you wanted could buy almost sixty cheap wool blankets. You could help thirty or more families instead of six." He met Lydia's heated stare and braced himself—for what, he wasn't quite sure.

But instead of spitting fire at him, Lydia's posture wilted, and she hung her head, shaking it slightly. "Wool blankets would be cheaper and could help more people, yes, but I know how it feels to have 'good enough.' But to receive something beautiful . . . " She ran a hand down her sleeve, catching the bit of satin ribbon at the end. "The Renfroes' maids' castoffs would've sufficed, but they gave me fancy dresses I didn't 'need.' These pretty frocks took away the stigma of my poverty and let people above me judge me

185

for who I am." She looked up at him, her intense eyes making him squirm. "Or at least helped somewhat."

He really hadn't ever thought about how being poor felt—he'd only taken the price of their needs into account.

It had taken God swinging a spiritual two-by-four at him to realize he had to forgive and love the kinds of people who frequented the sporting section—why hadn't he realized his giving to the poor would have been enhanced by more love as well?

He knew Theresa and Alec would be grateful for extra wool blankets, but would a pretty quilt uplift their spirits? It might not have made much of a difference to him, but he was surrounded by nice things all the time.

Yet he'd nearly had to force Alec to take his scrap lumber to burn.

"Well . . ." Lydia sighed and then strode toward Parker, who'd jumped down from his sunny perch. The low-hanging gray clouds from this morning had rolled away, and the sunshine had ushered a bit of warmth into the November afternoon.

How could he make things better with Lydia? This was the last of her wishes and she'd wed Sebastian likely by the end of the year, so they wouldn't be spending much more time together.

He didn't want them to part ways with her thinking the worst of him. Though he wasn't nearly as good as he'd thought himself to be before she came along.

But to explain why he operated as he did, his character flaws, his mistrust of the church, he'd have to tell Lydia everything.

Did he trust her enough? Only Henri knew anything of his past, and he only knew about Roxie and that Nicholas and his wife hadn't gotten along.

After scraping his boots, Nicholas signaled to Mr. Parker that they were ready to go and hauled himself in with Lydia. "I'm sorry I've kept you in the dark so much."

She gave him a quick glance before she let her head roll back to look out the window.

He sucked in a breath and forced himself to start. "The only person in Teaville who knows much about me is Henri—so part of me is surprised the whole town doesn't know everything he knows." He attempted a lighthearted chuckle, but it fell flat. "But he is sworn to secrecy and somehow manages it despite talking all day long."

She made some noise as if only responding out of politeness, then closed her eyes.

"So . . . I should start by telling you about my wife." The last word tore from his throat and hung.

"Wife?" Her eyebrows perked up, but the wrinkles on her forehead seemed drawn in, as if she wrestled with a headache.

"She died almost eight years ago." He turned to look at the passing landscape Lydia had found so riveting. "When I told you I sympathized with how hard it must be to take care of your mother, knowing you're powerless to stop the illness, it's because I really do remember that feeling of helplessness."

"I'm sorry for your loss. How long was she in pain?"

"Too long."

"Consumption?"

He turned back to Lydia to see her reaction. "No. The pox."

Syphilis.

Her hand covered her mouth. "Your wife was a . . . she was a . . . So that's why you are determined to help . . ."

"No." Close, but he wouldn't let Lydia think so. "She left me for someone else, a man who was as unfaithful to her as she was to me." He rubbed his hands along his slacks as if he could wipe off the shame of his failure, which felt embedded in his skin and on display for everyone to see, much like the sores that had once ravaged Gracie's skin. "He picked up the pox from the cribhouses he frequented and passed it on to her."

"But why would you have nursed her back to health if she was with another man?"

Yes, why had he? How had God guilted him into helping, considering how hard his heart had been? "Her lover accused her of giving the pox to him, and so he abandoned her. Her case was rather severe and spread faster than most. Her face . . ." He refused to close his eyes, otherwise the image of Gracie's skin covered with large swollen sores—some disintegrating her nose, others crowding her right eye—would taunt him.

A beautiful woman destroyed.

All because he'd been stingy and stubborn.

He'd been working on the miserliness over these past several years, but evidently his stubbornness hadn't decreased significantly. "She had nowhere else to go but to me. The church ladies refused to help, and her family and Christian friends wouldn't visit her during those terrible last days. She begged me to bring her company to get her mind off the pain, but no one would come."

"How did you handle it?" Her voice was whisper soft, but he didn't dare to look at her. She might not sound too disgusted with him at the moment, but she'd yet to hear everything.

"Not well. I was torn up by her betrayal, and she was still angry with me. Since I was her only attendant, the sickroom was the farthest thing from a calm environment—we had never done well together." He cleared his throat, wishing he hadn't started this trip through his past, but he might as well continue. "She married me believing I'd provide for her. I married her because I'd been struck dumb by her pretty blue eyes and dark hair."

Lydia fingered a curl near her ear.

Yes, Lydia, she was as beautiful as you—but not as kind. "By the time we realized our expectations and dreams were diametrically opposed, we were already married. She refused to give me what I wanted, and I refused to give her what she wanted."

"What did she want?"

"I had a fair amount of money back then, enough to reinvest in businesses, anyway, but not enough to splurge with. She wanted a grand house: five bedrooms, a library, a house for the gardener, a Tiffany lamp hanging in the dining room, a ballroom where she could throw a party every spring and fall, a conservatory, a formal garden—"

"Your mansion."

He nodded and waited until the knot left his throat. "I told her I'd build it for her one day—when my businesses were more firmly established." His voice sounded rougher than it should have. "But she didn't find me worth the wait."

"I'm sorry, Nicholas."

"It's not your fault."

They bumped along for a little while, and he stared out the window. Though dinnertime was not for another hour, revealing some of his secrets had taken its toll, and he longed to put his head down and sleep without dreams. He looked over at Lydia and caught her staring at him.

He raised his brow when she didn't turn to look away.

"What . . ." Her cheek twitched. "What did *you* want—from Gracie, that is."

A rather bold, invasive question. But when hadn't Lydia been bold?

Her eyes slowly lowered, and she fiddled with her sleeve. "I apologize. Not my business."

"It's all right." He rubbed the edge of his right eye where a headache was forming. "I wanted her affection. But evidently I had to buy it . . . and I refused."

Lydia pressed her lips together, and that look of pity he'd feared crossed her face.

"Don't feel sorry for me. It was years ago."

"I had no right to ask, but thank you for telling me. I think I understand you a little better now. Like why my concern about what I was going to get from these wishes made you unhappy, my worry over—"

"You aren't Gracie. Don't compare yourself to her." His voice stopped working. He attempted to clear his throat, but it didn't help much. "I only learned to love the unlovable because God forced me to with Gracie. Having to forgive her was beyond difficult. And for some reason, I thought I could force you into seeing what I do now without going through all the pain. I'd hoped you'd be able to see the people behind the immorality without being dragged through it with them—see the needs of people you might not have considered. But since I'm only making you angry, I've failed."

"You're not a complete failure, Nicholas." Her mouth tensed into what looked like a slight smile, and her icy blues lost their frost. "Though you've acted in a rather high-handed way, I'm trying to think differently about who deserves help and how. But someone should ask you the same question you asked me weeks ago. Who else will help our congregation think differently, if you won't?"

"Someone else can help them—like you."

"But not like you could."

He rubbed a hand down his face. "I'm bound to irrevocably mess things up." Like he almost had with Lydia. He couldn't open himself up in front of just anyone, and if he hadn't just confessed what he did, would they be having this conversation?

"You need to find sympathy for our hypocrite brothers and sisters. You said you were once coldhearted and bitter toward the people you help now, but God figured out a way to teach you how to care for and forgive the unlovable through your ordeal with your wife."

"Something I never want to go through again."

"Then you best pray God helps you find sympathy for those hypocrites before God employs a similar tactic to change your attitude toward them."

26

Lydia handed her mother a cup of peppermint tea and poured herself another. The clock steadily ticked toward eleven, and she'd soon have to drag herself to the moral-society meeting. Over the past week she'd invented numerous explanations for mistaking Nicholas's intentions to fund the rest of their project, but none would likely appease Mrs. Little. If only time would slow—and not just because she didn't want to face Sebastian's mother.

Worrying about what she'd say to the moral society had stolen some of her sleep, but hearing Mama's rattling cough grow more frequent stole the rest.

Mama couldn't read, couldn't sleep, couldn't sew much since the coughing made her so tired. Dr. Lindon wasn't optimistic about her recovering this time.

Mama was miserable and had said she prayed for death to come. Lydia sniffed.

Mama's hand crept across the sofa searching for Lydia's. "It'll be all right."

"I'm not ready." Lydia snatched her hand and kissed the translucent skin. "Doctors are wrong sometimes."

"I don't think he is. But you'll still have your father here." When Lydia didn't respond, her mother sighed. "Which means your heavenly Father will have to take care of you." She patted her hand. "But you'll soon be Mrs. Little. I can't think of a better way for God to ease my worry over leaving you so young. I will miss the grandchildren. Tell them I loved them."

Tears blurred Lydia's vision, and her teacup clattered as she placed it on the saucer. "I will, Mama."

But would there be grandchildren? Should she tell Mama she had misgivings about becoming part of the Little family, or just keep that ache to herself?

She rubbed her eyes, already bleary and now threatening tears. What Nicholas had told her about his late wife had only added to her restless nights. Had his cautionary tale been a warning against marrying Sebastian? Had he given her a job hoping she would save herself from a similar mistake?

A month ago she hadn't cared a whit what he thought. Now his opinion mattered greatly.

Her mother's hand went limp atop hers. Lydia startled and pressed a hand to Mama's neck, thankful the weak beat and the subtle lifting of her chest proved she'd only fallen asleep.

The doctor said she could die any day. Would ending things with Sebastian hasten her mother's death? She had asked God to allow Mama to find her ease in death, but she couldn't bear being responsible for rushing her departure.

But what if Mama struggled along for longer than expected and Sebastian got around to officially proposing? How long should she keep Sebastian tied to her without intending to go through with an engagement?

She couldn't engage herself with no intent to fulfill her word. She had to decide . . . or should she put things off for Mama?

She blew out a breath and forced herself not to relive the dream she'd entertained last night—hoping Nicholas would swoop in, propose, and remove Mama's fears over her daughter being uncared for. Right now she must face reality, not pray for a fairy tale. She had to go to the moral society meeting and admit she'd not won Nicholas Lowe over, that after weeks of working for his donation, she was empty-handed.

And somehow, despite that, she still liked the man . . . more than liked the man, even if he was beyond stubborn.

After rearranging the afghan across her mother's chest, she slowly readied herself to leave for the meeting. She didn't want to arrive a second before she had to.

While buttoning her coat, she took one last look at Mama, making sure she saw movement beneath the covers. Then she let herself outside and gently tugged the door closed to keep from disturbing her sleep.

Lydia shuffled toward the church through the light snow that melted the second it hit the street. She shouldn't feel depressed over failing to gain a donation for the sewing machines, but her heart hung heavy, and no logical reasoning eased the downward tug.

The tepid air inside the church didn't warm her, and the sound of vibrant female voices curled up the stairs to strangle her. Would her news kill their jolly mood, or would she only cause an insignificant pause and receive a round of "*chin up*"s?

Hopefully her mother would last until next week, so there would be something to be thankful for on Thanksgiving. Lydia pushed against the door, but it jammed against a wad of brown paper on the floor.

"Oh, let me get that," Evelyn's voice called, and Lydia pulled the door back as Evelyn tugged the obstruction from beneath it.

"Come in and see the surprise." She waved Lydia inside.

A shiny new Burdick sewing machine with an intricate wrought-iron treadle and gleaming black-and-gold body stood in the center of the room. Nearby, Pastor Wisely wrestled with a crowbar and another large crate.

Lydia let out the breath she'd been holding. She'd fretted for nothing. Now no one would care that she hadn't obtained a single penny from Nicholas. She pulled off her gloves and sidled over to

Evelyn, who gleefully pulled out more brown paper from one of the three long crates on the floor.

"Blue again." Evelyn pulled out a bolt of rich navy cotton, and then smiled down at Lydia. "The colors are rather plain, but we can spiff them up with the patterned fabric already donated."

Lydia pulled out another bolt of the same material. "I thought Mrs. Little had only collected enough to order one sewing machine. How could these have arrived already?"

"Oh, but she didn't order them. She was just as surprised as I was when Daddy hauled them in."

Mrs. Little circled the second sewing machine Pastor Wisely had freed from its confines. She ran a hand along its shiny body, pressing the other hand against her heart.

Charlie crouched in front of the other one, fiddling with the wheel. "I get to run one of these, right? They got to be more fun than pricking my finger twenty times an hour."

Lydia smoothed the cotton fabric. Several bolts of navy, brown, and gray were piled next to the empty crates. No imagination, but fine quality material . . . and two Burdick sewing machines, delivered on the day she'd have to admit she hadn't succeeded. Her heart fluttered. "Was there a note?"

Evelyn shrugged. "Mrs. Little or Daddy might know."

Lydia walked over to where Mrs. Little sat testing out the treadle. "Evelyn says you didn't order these."

"No." Mrs. Little looked up, her brow wrinkled. "But I would've thought you'd know that. I suppose he decided to order them for us himself."

Unsure how to answer, Lydia noticed an invoice tacked on the machine's crate. *Customer name: Lowe.* Her heart jumped into her throat, and she felt for the chair beside her.

For them to have arrived today, he would likely have needed to order them the day they left the Indian mission or even before.

But she hadn't changed his mind, had she? He'd still maintained the quilts were ridiculous compared to wool blankets. And though she'd told him a beautiful item would be appreciated, she'd decided he'd been right. They should try to help as many people as possible. She'd even resolved to persuade the group to buy wool blankets instead of a machine.

She stared at the machines and the piles of fabric while Mrs. Little squabbled with Pastor Wisely over where she wanted the machines set up.

Nicholas hadn't bought these for the moral society—he'd bought them for her.

But according to him, he'd never bent his will for his late wife, Gracie.

Lydia tried hard to imagine Gracie as a woman who failed to love him despite his stubbornness and Nicholas as a man with a stone-hard heart—but she couldn't quite do it.

Settling around the quilting frame, the ladies joyfully attacked their almost-finished quilt. Mrs. Little kept vacillating on what pattern they should piece together next, and the conversation turned to how to spend the surplus money they'd collected since Lydia's donor had come through.

"I say we make campaign flyers for my son, detailing how he's the best candidate for freeing our towns from immorality."

"But our donors believed their money was going toward helping the poor stay warm this winter," Evelyn said without looking up from her sewing. "Perhaps we should spend it on some charitable venture along those same lines."

"That's a good idea, Evelyn." Lydia folded her hands in her lap and pressed them together. She didn't want to see the money Nicholas had saved them from spending go toward something he'd cringe at more than the quilt project. "Perhaps wool blankets for the ones who aren't receiving quilts this year?"

"We'll always have the poor to deal with. Isn't that in the Bible somewhere?" Mrs. Little shrugged and then looked at the ladies around the quilt. "We have a limited window of opportunity to persuade voters to stomp on the people bent on destroying our towns."

Lydia's heart kicked. Did she have the strength to say what

Nicholas would have her say? Could she make them see the world differently? Her mouth felt chalky and leaden, but she couldn't sit and say nothing. "Who's intent on destroying our towns, exactly?" She jabbed her needle into her block, trying to look as if the question wasn't meant to affront Mrs. Little's authority.

"What do you mean?" Mrs. Little stiffened. "It's rather obvious every brothel and saloon flouts our laws. We need more regulations, bigger fines."

"Is that what Sebastian wants to do? Regulate?"

Mrs. Jones, an elderly woman who rarely made the meetings, cleared her throat. "They're the playhouses of the devil. They should be eradicated, not regulated."

"But where will the people go when we've torn down their businesses?" Lydia could barely hear herself over the thumping in her ears.

Mrs. Jones's face grew hard.

Lydia forged on. "They, ah, the saloon owners would rebuild elsewhere and the ladies will follow, unless we . . ." She closed her eyes and willed her breath to support her. Would they kick her out for saying what she was about to say? "Unless we help the women, teach them a suitable trade, accept them into decent society—"

"Nonsense." Mrs. Little snapped. "The presence of those women in our homes, in our gatherings, would threaten the virtue of our own young women and entice our young men into unholy thoughts. Most of those women are criminals and drunkards. They're better off handled by the police."

Lydia licked her lips, then clamped them shut. She couldn't change their minds in an hour, and she wasn't certain she knew what she believed anymore. Both Mrs. Little and Nicholas made sense. But those two weren't her ultimate authority. She ought to petition God more fully, take more time in His Word to find out—like Bernadette was doing. Lydia knew the Scriptures Mrs. Little liked to recite, so she could look those up. The next time she saw Nicholas, she'd ask him what Scriptures bolstered his position, and then prayerfully read all those verses and pray God would help her sort things out.

Because if she was going to defend Nicholas's opinion in future meetings, she would be a lamb bleating among wolves. If she didn't have a strong Shepherd at her side, she'd be devoured before she could tuck her tail and run.

27

Lydia slowed as she watched Miss Georgia Renfroe follow Nicholas out of the Mining and Gas Company office.

The pretty blonde laughed at something Nicholas must have said, his smile charming and bright as he turned back to hold the door open for her.

Carrying a small briefcase, Mr. Renfroe, Georgia's father, came out of the office, shaking his finger at Nicholas before giving him a wink.

Lydia stopped a half block away. Maybe she shouldn't bother him today. He'd donated the machines anonymously, though the company had left the invoice on the box, so he likely didn't want to be thanked.

She pressed a hand against the upset in her middle. Her stomach shouldn't be curdling over the scene in front of her. Nicholas had every right to have a pretty woman on his arm.

And Georgia was certainly that, along with being tall and elegant. She was the only Renfroe daughter left unmarried, likely holding out for a man wealthy enough to keep her in the style her father had accustomed her to. He'd been plenty successful before Nicholas moved to town, but after Nicholas had bought out some of Mr. Renfroe's properties and hired him to oversee a few others, the Renfroes' wealth had only increased.

Georgia swiped a long blond curl the wind had blown into her eyes and tucked it behind her ear. She looked back at her father with a smile and caught sight of Lydia. She gave her a small wave.

Nicholas looked toward where Georgia was waving, and instantly his face turned serious.

Ever since she'd met him, their conversations were typically troublesome, argumentative, and stubborn—in other words, the essence of vinegar. He likely feared she'd butt in and ruin his afternoon with a woman who was making him laugh.

If anyone was as sweet as honey, it was Georgia.

Oh, why had she ever thought he'd fall for her, a contentious pauper? Of course he wouldn't. She'd been the opposite of endearing the whole time he'd been trying to make her into a better person. And if her looks and her love of books had been her only hope of snagging his interest, then Georgia would be just as likely to win him considering her gorgeous blond hair and the fact that she loaned Lydia her books after devouring them herself.

Nicholas raised his brows as if waiting for her to approach.

Why hadn't she pretended not to have seen them and turned down the alley?

Forcing herself forward, she tried not to look down at her long coat or the pretty blue skirt peeping out from under it. Georgia had given these to her only a month ago. She'd had to replace the coat buttons with cheaper ones after discovering how much the missing button would cost to replace. And since Georgia was almost as tall as Nicholas, she always had to shorten the skirts, which required cutting off almost all the beautiful ruffles and lace this time. Georgia would likely consider her alterations appalling.

She'd never felt awkward in front of Georgia before, but considering the gray wool walking suit the woman wore was embellished with the prettiest velvet stripes, her feathered hat was the smartest thing she'd ever seen, and that Nicholas now knew Georgia was gracious toward Lydia's family without him having to chastise her into being so . . . well, she rather wished she wasn't here to let him compare them side by side.

"Good evening, Ni . . . Mr. Lowe, Georgia. Mr. Renfroe." She cleared her throat and plunged on. "I just came by to thank Mr. Lowe for his generous gift to the moral society."

"Our *church's* moral society?" Georgia straightened, then turned to take Nicholas's elbow, barely having to tilt her head to look into his eyes. "Why, I don't believe I've heard you say anything positive about that group, so I hadn't bothered to think of joining them."

Lydia stared at Georgia's gloved hand wrapped so effortlessly and comfortably in the crook of his elbow.

He cleared his throat but didn't step away from Georgia. "Well, perhaps I've been a little too rough on them. Seems I can't always see past my own prejudices."

Lydia wrung her hands, trying to think of a way to leave without being rude. "Anyway, considering I know how much that cost you, I figured I should thank you in person."

"How much did you spend, Nicholas?" Mr. Renfroe perked up. "I didn't know they needed anything much."

Nicholas kept his eyes on hers. "Enough for two sewing machines and some cloth."

"Oh, not so much, then." Mr. Renfroe turned to Lydia and smiled. "Do you need more cloth? I think my wife has a bolt of discarded fabric in the wardrobe. She bought the wrong color or something. I'm sure she'd donate it if it fits your needs."

"As long as it's something that would work in a quilt."

Georgia smiled. "It's a cotton print—should be perfect."

"Thank you." She nodded at Nicholas to let him know she'd said all she needed to say. "I won't keep you."

"Miss King." Nicholas rubbed at the back of his neck. "Before you leave, I want you to know I put money into an account at Reed's for your moral-society ladies. The cloth I ordered was purposely plain and utilitarian, but after our last conversation, I figured something more beautiful might be appreciated. I wanted to tell you myself, and since you're here . . ."

A lump stuck in her throat, but she squeezed out a thank you.

"I'm sorry to interrupt." Mr. Renfroe snapped closed his timepiece. "But I do have a meeting with Mr. Cardmon at seven fifteen, so if we're going to have dinner and not rush, I'm afraid we better get moving."

"I hope you two—I mean, three—have a nice dinner." Lydia put on a bright smile, waved, and turned before she said anything more awkward.

Around the corner, she slowed and gritted her teeth against the ridiculous flopping inside her chest. She wasn't worth his romantic attention anyway.

Besides, he'd given her enough—a job that would give her plenty of opportunities to talk about books with people who cared.

But what if that position fell through, or didn't last?

Wrapping her arms tightly about herself, she hurried home to curl up in bed and whimper over how much of a goose she was for wanting to cry at the sight of another woman's arm tucked around Nicholas's.

After slogging down her street, she fumbled with her gate's little latch. The moisture pooling in her eyes and the mittens encasing her hands made it difficult.

Oh, mittens. She'd forgotten to ask Nicholas about her stopping over to give the children their presents. Well, they had a month before Christmas, but could she just show up at the mansion now that her wishes were over? What if he actually attended Christmas parties? The Renfroes were said to throw a rather grand party—not that her family had ever been invited, considering who her father was.

Once the gate mercifully let her in, she pulled up short at the sight of Sebastian sitting on her porch steps, tapping some papers against his knee.

"Lydia." His smile was warmer than normal as he grabbed the handrail to pull himself up. "I thought I might have to leave without seeing you."

She sniffed, thankful the cold weather could account for sniffles.

"I'm sorry." She pulled out a handkerchief. "Did I forget you were coming over?" Though if he had indeed been waiting long, she couldn't imagine he'd look so at ease right now.

"No, but I had good news to share before I went to Mother's dinner thing." He rolled his eyes.

At least she wasn't the only one who dreaded eating with her.

He held the papers out to her and smiled. "I was able to draw up a new mortgage for your parents. Reduced interest, and I cut out a few penalties and clauses your parents never should have agreed to."

Her hand shook as she took the papers. "How . . . how much do we owe you for this?" Hadn't Papa stormed out of the house this morning grumbling about somebody demanding he repay a three-dollar loan immediately? This surely would cost more than that.

"Nothing, I did it on my own. The banker owed me a favor." He shrugged. "Thought it would ease things in the long run after we marry." He looked toward the house and lowered his voice. "I'm sorry, but I'd rather not have to take your father in after your mother . . ."

Neither did she. "I understand."

He stooped over and snatched a book off the steps. "And I brought you this."

A pale blue ribbon fluttered out from between the pages of a dark green book with a man silhouetted against a windowpane. *The Return of Sherlock Holmes.*

She took the book with a shaky hand and ran her finger against the indented title. "This is the new collection, where he returns from the dead." She raised a brow. "But I thought you were against me reading."

He shook his head like he was chastising himself. "I've never been clever with women. Forgive me." He clasped his hands behind his back and puffed his chest. "I've never had a relationship last long. Women—let alone pretty ones—never seem to make it past a second dinner with me or they bow out after meeting my mother. And I wasn't sure I'd stand a chance with you despite . . . Well, I figured since you've stuck around, I should exert more effort to keep you, because I would like to." He put his hand in his pocket and produced a small black box.

Oh no, this was too fast. She put a hand against her mouth. Not too fast for him, surely. This was about the time they should be getting engaged, but she'd just started rethinking that.

He put out a hand as if to stop her from advancing, though she hadn't budged an inch. "Now, don't get too worried. I still want an engagement party, like we've discussed, throw a big to-do and have a reason to wine and dine a few campaign backers at the same time. However, I wanted to make sure my great-grandmother's ring was acceptable ahead of time. If not, I'll need to shop for another." He wiggled the lid off and held it out to her.

She glanced at the ring, a pretty white opal surrounded by diamonds. Her lungs decided to completely deflate. Her parents had never been able to afford even simple bands. He might as well buy her parents' house with the money that ring would bring. "It's fine." She cringed at calling an expensive heirloom just *fine*. "I mean, it's beyond lovely."

"Good." He closed the box and shoved it into his pocket. He stepped closer, and his hand came up hesitantly.

He tilted her chin back, and she had to look up at him instead of his tie tack, probably worth half their house, considering the three little diamonds embedded in the gold bar.

His smile was uncertain, and he seemed to be searching for something as his gaze roamed her face. "We have more in common than you know and will better together than you might think."

It was hard to swallow with her head tilted back, but she had to in order to speak. "Like what?"

"Being passed over." He dropped his hand and rubbed at his jaw. "I'm at the age people feel compelled to ask me if I'm going to 'settle down,' and I'm sure you've had people act like they're in fear for your life if you don't snag a husband soon."

"Some."

"I'd given up on ever having a satisfying answer for the

busybodies, but not anymore." He smiled, put his hand back up to cup her chin, and gave her a peck on the lips. His breath smelled of mint this time instead of beet soup, but she couldn't respond to his kiss when all she wanted to do was step away.

He pulled back, his smile not quite complete. "Are you still coming to dinner tomorrow?"

After a good cry, some tea, and yanking her dreams back down into the atmosphere, surely she could endure a Little family meal by then. It wasn't as if she'd have to decide on whether or not she'd accept that gorgeous ring right there at the table. "I'll be there."

28

At the mansion's front door, Lydia thumped the knocker a few times, then waited, watching her puffy white breath get blown away by the wind. For the past several days, she'd knitted until her hands ached, and her brain had ached as well. What was she to do? The heirloom ring Sebastian had shown her last week and his solicitousness toward her the day after at dinner had jumbled her resolve. No matter how many hours she'd let her mind wrestle with what to do about Sebastian and her feelings for Nicholas while her needles clacked, all she was certain of was uncertainty.

An unfamiliar maid's head peeked out the door as if unsure she'd heard a knock.

"Is Mr. Lowe at home? I hope I'm not interrupting his dinner."

The woman's big dark eyes seemed leery, and she started to back up into the house. "No, he went out."

Lydia glanced back behind her to where the maid seemed to be looking but saw nobody coming up the drive. Why would the maid be scared of her?

"That's all right." Lydia pulled a paper-wrapped present from her bag. She was just here to give the children their hats and mittens, since the weather seemed to be starting to stay cold and they could be of use. Her ridiculous longing to see Nicholas needed to be stuffed away until the desire dissipated anyway. Sebastian was more important than him . . . or he should be. "Do you mind if I come in? I'd like to give the children some early Christmas gifts."

The maid simply stared at the package and frowned.

Maybe this woman's mind wasn't all there. "The children Mr. Lowe brought home a few weeks ago: Pepper, Angel, and Robbie. May I see them?"

She shook her head as if that were the strangest question she'd ever been asked.

With the amount of money Nicholas had, couldn't he hire more mannerly servants? "Are they not here? Did Mr. Parker take them somewhere this evening?"

"No."

"Would the head housekeeper know where they are?"

"No, I mean they ran off. Good day." The woman slammed the door.

Ran off? When had that happened? Her throat closed up and her limbs turned heavy. Why would they run away? Even if they had to live in Nicholas's stables, they'd be better off with him than where they'd lived before.

She stuffed the present back into her bag and stared out to the west, where the red-light district sat hidden behind several factories and the train depot.

If they hadn't been happy living in a mansion, where would they go?

The police. Surely they could help. Pulling up her collar against the wind, she headed toward the precinct.

Minutes later, she entered police headquarters, full of men and noise and, thankfully, warmth. The officers were huddled together, half sitting on desks, the other half in chairs, talking and laughing. She searched for the face of the man who'd taken her report. When Officer Vincent felt her eyes on him, he looked up and straightened.

"Excuse me, officers."

The others looked up. Seeing her, they quieted and headed toward separate desks as if their boss had caught them shirking duty.

"What can I do for you, miss?"

She sniffed and rubbed her numb hands together as she walked toward him. "I came to see what had been done for the children."

"What children?"

"The children I reported as being abandoned a while back. They—" Hmm, was it wise to tell him how they'd run away from Nicholas's? That might cause the officer to focus on the wrong thing right now. "Their names are Pepper, Angel, and Robbie."

"Oh yes." He scratched his scruffy jaw, a lost look on his face. "I believe I wrote that in the record book."

"You did. I watched you do so."

"So then . . . ?" He looked puzzled.

"What do you mean 'so then'?" She stuck her hands on her hips. He didn't even have the good sense to look abashed. "Did you offer them new homes or ask around if anybody would be willing to house them? Did you at least check if they had food or tell them where they could get some? I . . . I think it might be a good idea if you go see how they're doing now. That neighborhood is not decent for children."

"You've been in that neighborhood?"

She had to be careful. Her reputation was still spotless, yet a careless word could tarnish it in an instant. "I don't think anyone has to go there to know that area of town is unsafe for children. That's why I'm concerned."

"And why are you concerned about them in particular?"

"That's the essence of true religion, is it not? To care for widows and orphans."

He shrugged and about-faced. "Not those kind of orphans," he muttered.

She stalked behind him, trying to resist walloping him from the back.

He marched over to the record book and flipped pages.

He ran his hand down columns of notes, then tapped an entry. "You reported that they were at Queenie's."

"Yes."

"Well, that was probably the best thing that could've happened to them."

She waited for him to go on, but he shut the book. "You mean to tell me all you did was write it down?"

"If they weren't causing mischief, there was no reason to investigate."

"I didn't ask you to investigate. I asked you to make sure they were all right. Do you not care whether or not—"

"It's not our job to care, ma'am." He jutted out his chin. "It's our job to keep order. If they weren't out of order, they aren't our business."

"Would you have said that if I had younger siblings missing?"

He shrugged. "Look, lady, we have limited resources and time."

She glanced around at the remaining officers, one working at a desk, one twirling a pair of handcuffs, and the rest chitchatting quietly over their coffee mugs. "You certainly look really busy today, officer."

He plopped down in his chair and crossed his arms. "If we have time, we'll get to it."

"The time to get to it is over."

He leaned back in his chair. "I'm sorry, miss. I don't know what else to tell you."

Her stomach turned with his indifference. He should've told her the truth the first day she came in, that they didn't bother protecting prostitutes' children. "I won't bother you again."

"If *you* need us, miss, don't let this keep you from looking to us for help."

She clenched her fists and spun on her heels. She had to leave before she yelled at every man in the room. Hadn't Nicholas told her he didn't trust anyone in this town to help? And she'd not believed him.

She hadn't bothered the church with the children's predicament because they'd likely have been more worried about her visiting that part of town than the children having to live there, but the police were paid to work with those people.

Wrapping her arms about herself, she rushed back through the cold streets she'd just traversed, her eyes on the large red roof of Nicholas's mansion on the top of the town's southeast hill.

Her heart pumped warm and frantic despite the claws of winter invading her coat. Did Nicholas have any idea where the children were?

29

Lydia hurried back from the police precinct toward Nicholas's carriage house, which was hidden in his tree-filled side yard. Someone had to know something about the missing children. Hopefully Mr. Parker had returned Mr. Lowe from wherever they'd been today.

The late afternoon light, already dismal and gray, forced her eyes to adjust to the shadowed interior when she stepped inside the carriage house.

A sudden jingling sounded loud in the far corner. "Miss King?" Mr. Parker's shadow moved to meet her. "Is something wrong?"

"No. I mean, yes. Well, I came to see Mr. Lowe, and—"

"Sorry, miss, but he's not here."

"So you didn't take him out?" Hadn't that been what the maid said?

"I dropped him off earlier this afternoon."

"Then are you getting ready to pick him up?" Would it be wrong to ask him to take her home after he retrieved Nicholas? Then she could ask him about the children. Waiting until tomorrow would only send her imagination into a gallop.

Mr. Parker walked toward her, looping a harness in his hands. "No, I was headed home."

She blew out a breath. "Well then, do you know where the children are?"

His mustache drooped. "I'm sorry, miss, but they left sometime last night."

"Yes, the maid said they ran away. But where would they go?"

He winced. "I don't know anything for certain."

"You think they'd go somewhere like Madam Careless's?" But why would they do that?

He shrugged. "People tend to want to be where they're most comfortable."

"Comfortable!"

"I mean, where they feel they belong."

She looked down at the paper-wrapped hats and mittens in her bag.

Of course Nicholas cared and likely had done what he could, but with how busy he was, and considering Pepper's mistrust of men, and if that maid's coldness was any indication of how she'd handled the children . . .

She should have visited the children more often. Maybe they wouldn't have run away if they felt someone else truly cared, that someone besides Nicholas thought they belonged here.

"May I delay your plans?" Lydia glanced at the tack he was preparing to put away, knowing she was probably asking him to undo his work. "I know it's terrible to ask when you're ready to leave, but would you take me to Thick Lips Annie's?"

The man stopped coiling the leather in his hands. "Now?"

She nodded. Hopefully she'd find the children at their old place. "The police never checked on them. Not once, and with how cold it's been and considering what Pepper had been planning to do . . ."

Mr. Parker ran a hand through hair that shone yellow-silver in the lamplight. "I don't know if that's a good idea."

"Do you think they might have returned to Queenie's?"

"I delivered her firewood this afternoon. Didn't see them."

"We should at least go ask about them." If he didn't open the carriage door for her, maybe she'd just plop herself inside and hope he'd get moving.

"Don't you think you ought to wait until tomorrow?"

She opened the door and climbed onto the crooked step. "That's just it. We shouldn't wait."

"In the morning, Mr. Lowe could—"

"I won't wait for someone else to do what we can do now." But she wouldn't be foolish enough to go alone.

He rubbed his brow. "One day won't hurt."

"People die in the space of a day—an hour, even." Madam Careless could ruin them in minutes. Lydia's hands grew slick on the handle.

"I'm sorry, miss, but I think it's unwise."

"That's why I need you. It would be imprudent to go alone." She looked him in the eyes, hoping he'd believe her next statement. "But I will, if necessary."

He stared at her, but she kept her chin firm.

"Mr. Lowe will fire me if I let you go alone." He let out a frustrated rush of air. "And he'll likely fire me for taking you." He pointed to the inside of the carriage and sighed. "Get in and wrap yourself in a blanket."

When he turned away, she bounced with triumph, then shut herself inside before he could change his mind.

Once Mr. Parker had the horse rehitched and out the door, she settled back against the cushion. Her brain nudged her to take Mr. Parker's advice, to go home and return tomorrow, but how could she get comfortable in her own bed with children in danger?

Since Mr. Parker was with her, she was surely safe.

When the carriage stopped blocks later, she didn't wait for Mr. Parker to open her door. The sun was too close to the horizon, and she wanted to be home before darkness descended.

She'd already knocked on the door of Annie's alleyway apartment by the time Mr. Parker made it to her side. But there was no answer. She jiggled the doorknob. Locked.

Mr. Parker just shook his head as if she were a crazy woman trying to coax a corpse to sit up in a coffin.

She passed him to look through the apartment's one dirty window. Cupping her hands against the pane, she peered into absolute blackness. "They wouldn't be asleep already." She wiped at the grime on her gloves. Oh why couldn't they have come back here? "Whose care did they say their mother left them under? A Dirty Emily?"

"Emma."

She rolled her tongue around her cotton mouth and pressed her trembling hands to her stomach. Was she really going to visit a working prostitute? "Do you know where she lives?"

He shook his head. "I agreed to drive you here, nowhere else."

"But I won't sleep if I don't know they're safe." She laid a hand against the thumping in her chest. "I can't go home without trying everything."

"I'm not taking you to Dirty Emma's."

"But you *do* know where I can find her."

He pressed his lips tight.

"Well, if you won't take me, I'll find her myself." A man passed near the entrance to the alleyway, and she hailed him. "Sir!"

Mr. Parker grabbed her and yanked her back.

When the man stopped, Mr. Parker waved his hand in dismissal. "Never mind. The lady's with me." He turned her around, his hands rough, his face livid. "This isn't downtown Teaville. Do you know what he likely thought you to be doing?"

Her face heated. She'd only meant to get directions. "He'd have surely seen I'm not . . ." She closed her eyes, her head a bit dizzy. All this squawking to Nicholas about keeping her reputation pristine, and she'd about lost it in a second of thoughtlessness. Could've lost even more than that if Mr. Parker hadn't stopped her.

He muttered a soft curse. "I shouldn't have brought you."

"You don't understand. I really feel like something is wrong—"

"There surely is something wrong. Just being in this alley proves we're off course. Let Mr. Lowe take care of it."

Of course, Nicholas, the savior of the world. Then why weren't the children already back at the mansion? "No, either tell me where to find Emma or I'll look myself."

"No you won't. I'll hoist you over my shoulder and throw you into the carriage if I have to."

"Then it would be best if you help me now. Because if you take me home, I'll come right back."

"You will not."

She held his gaze, trying to conceal her threat's emptiness. She couldn't return alone . . . but what if her hunch was right? What if those children needed her now? They'd already spent one night on their own, and heaven only knew where. Could she bluff Mr. Parker into believing she was that impetuous? She swallowed against tears but then decided to let them fall. They were tears of frustration, but he'd never realize that.

He sighed. "She's down the street in a little white shanty, but this is not the time to go visiting."

Lydia bit her lip and tried not to imagine why.

"If you stay in the carriage, I'll knock on her door. If she answers, I'll ask her what she knows of the children." He narrowed his eyes. "And then will you go home?"

She rubbed her clammy hands against each other. "Depends on her answer."

Mr. Parker hesitated before helping her inside. After shutting the door, he climbed onto the driver's platform, and she caught a whispered curse amid his grumbling before the sound of wheels against brick drowned him out. Stopping a few minutes later, the carriage rocked back and forth as he climbed down from his perch. "Stay inside," he whispered through the window as he passed.

She strained to hear his voice among the sounds of fighting pianos, laughter, and the general hubbub down the street. She heard a knock and prayed he wouldn't simply rush back and say he tried. A minute later, the whine of rusty hinges grated on her ears.

"Are you Dir—? Are you Emma?" Mr. Parker's voice held a bit of uncertainty.

"I am. You got three dollars?"

"I'm not here for . . ." He cleared his throat. "I need information."

"And I sell my time, no matter what you want it for."

Another grunted curse from Mr. Parker. "Here. I'm looking for Thick Lips Annie's children. Two girls and a boy. They were supposed to have lived with you once."

"Yeah, they came back, but they're gone again."

"Where?"

"I sent them to Madam Careless."

Lydia gasped and forced herself to keep her seat. How could that woman! Entrusted with children but sending them off to the devil.

Mr. Parker's footsteps dragged across the bricks. A few seconds later, he opened the door. "She says they're at Madam Careless's. I'm afraid that's the end of it. I'm sorry."

"What parlor house does she oversee?"

"The California."

Lydia closed her eyes and envisioned the street she'd walked down for her first serenade. A weathered wooden sign with the terribly drawn state of California had hung on one of those buildings. "That's only a block over that way, right?" She peered down the bit of sidewalk she could see.

He blocked her view of the street, his arms crossed against his chest. "We're not going."

"Then I'll go."

"You can't just walk in the front door."

"I suppose not." But then, the children surely wouldn't be out front. She laid her hand on her chest, the thumping of her heart palpable under her wool coat. Could she live with herself if she went home and lay down on her comfortable bed while those girls, those children, "entertained"? She pressed her shaky hand to her lips. Going home was not an option. "Mr. Parker?"

"No."

"I won't talk to anyone. I'll just go in and look."

He put his hand against the carriage and shook his head as he stared down at his feet. "If they've got little girls in there, they won't be in the parlor. They won't let you see them."

"And if these were your little girls?"

By the way he gritted his teeth, she knew he was holding in another curse. "All right." He left her to hop into the driver's seat.

After a short drive that seemed to take forever, he hopped back down and whispered through the coach's window. "I'll be right back."

After she could no longer hear him, she pulled the leather curtain aside and frowned at the windowless walls of the back alley. Of course he'd not park out front, but why weren't there any windows so she could see in? Though it wasn't as if the children would stand at a window all day calling for help.

But she certainly did hear something. She held her breath and cupped her ear. Crying?

Peeping her head out far enough to see in front of the horse, she located a heap of pink silk and brown curls leaning against a loose iron railing on the back of a stoop. Lydia held her breath.

The woman crossed her arms over her stomach and doubled forward. "Oh, God, help," she moaned as she let her head drop against the metal bars, her shoulders jerking with sobs.

Lydia swallowed. Pepper's hair had been much lighter and Angel was smaller, but this woman's frame didn't look like an adult's either.

The young lady looked up and stared across the shadowed alley as she swiped at the tears on her cheeks. Her hands left smudges across her face from whatever she'd used to blacken her lashes. With her fresh face and dainty neck, she couldn't be much older than Pepper. And definitely not old enough to be within a mile of this place! Not that any woman should be here.

And if she wanted God's help . . .

Lydia's heart raced with the thought of stepping outside of the coach, where she was comfortable, safe, and unknown.

She'd told Mr. Parker a day was too long to wait to find the children. What if this young lady disappeared inside before Mr. Parker returned?

Lydia creaked open the door and stepped down before her galloping heart could chase her back into the vehicle.

When the young lady caught sight of Lydia, her tears immediately ceased, and she stiffened.

Though it was harder to go forward than backward, Lydia walked across the cracked, uneven bricks. Slowly approaching, she crossed over trash and skirted frozen puddles. "I mean you no harm."

The girl tilted her head and assessed her with narrowed eyes.

"Are you all right?"

The girl's sneer made her feel all kinds of stupid.

Of course no one her age dressed like that in the red-light district was all right. "I mean. What can I do to help?"

"You want to help me?" Instead of sounding tough like Pepper, the girl's voice held uncertainty and . . . hope, perhaps?

"Yes, if I can."

"I'm past help." She sniffed. "Certainly from a lady like yourself." Her eyes narrowed again as she took in Lydia's clothing.

This girl's low-cut silk confection couldn't be providing her much warmth, especially since she was sitting on concrete and clinging to an iron banister.

Lydia tugged off her coat and held it out to her as she came closer.

"I can't take that."

"Sure you can."

She didn't reach for it, but yet, she didn't flee either.

Lydia took the last step to reach her and draped it around her shoulders.

The girl fingered the lapel now resting against her neck. "Why are you here?"

Lydia wrapped her arms against herself. She might not have needed the coat as badly as this girl, but giving it up for a good reason hadn't magically made the cold wind bearable. "I'm looking for some children I know." She forced herself to keep her teeth from chattering. "One's about your age."

If someone's expression could testify to a person's insanity, this young lady's countenance could have sent Lydia to an asylum. "You know people here?"

She shook her head, her frown as heavy as her heart. "Barely."

"And what do you want them for?"

"I was hoping to take them away from this place if I found them."

The girl stared at her intently, making Lydia squirm.

"I'm looking for a girl named Pepper, her sister, Angel, and a boy about this tall who doesn't speak."

The girl shook her head.

Lydia closed her eyes as disappointment washed over her. But maybe God could use her to help someone else. She took a deep breath and squatted beside the girl, who immediately backed up a step.

Lydia touched her lightly but firmly on her shoulder. "What's your name?"

The girl shook her head. "Don't matter."

"It does to me."

She swallowed hard and after a moment whispered, "Dainty Bit."

Hopefully she hadn't seen her wince at such an awful name. "I mean, what did your mother name you?"

She shrugged. "Sadie."

At a sound behind her, Lydia startled and looked over her shoulder. Her heart slowed upon seeing a cat climb out of a crate full of trash. But Mr. Parker would be back any moment . . . and who knew who else might see her if she stayed in the alley much longer. "Do you have family?"

She shook her head.

"Did you mean it when I overheard you ask God for help?"

She only blinked up at her as if she couldn't believe someone had actually listened.

Lydia turned to look over her shoulder again. "I can't stay much longer, but I know of a place you can go where you don't have to work. You can go to school and—"

"School?" The girl swallowed hard.

"Yes."

"I've always wanted to go to school." She clasped her knees and hugged her legs close.

The door behind Sadie opened and Lydia shot up.

A large woman with a dirty apron over her worn dress and arms as portly as ham hocks came out holding a scrap bucket. Her eyes grew hard at the sight of her. "What you doing here?" She glanced down at Sadie. "Get inside."

Lydia stepped between them and thrust out her hand. "Don't touch me or Sadie."

"Sadie?" A moment of confusion contorted her face.

"Yes, Sadie. I'm taking her somewhere safe. Somewhere she can go to school." She looked down hoping Sadie wasn't as hard as Pepper, who'd fight such forwardness. But the girl only bit her lip and turned to stare at the beat-up coach Lydia had abandoned a few minutes ago.

The hefty cook's hand upset the gray curls flattened under her white gauzy cap. "You're asking for trouble, miss. More trouble than you know."

Lydia stepped forward, trying to look as convincing as possible. "For the love of this child, pretend you saw nothing. Let her disappearance be discovered without your help." When the woman only blinked at her, she turned to the girl and helped her up, hoping Sadie wouldn't take the fact that she was trembling uncontrollably as a reason not to come with her.

After noting that the cook hadn't moved, Lydia nodded her head in dismissal and nearly tripped down the stairs with Sadie. With each step, her heart pounded harder until it sprinted along with her legs as they ran down the alley, hand in hand.

What if they were seen or the cook alerted someone before Mr. Parker returned?

Lydia glanced over her shoulder. The cook was gone. Gaining the coach, the door handle jammed under her slippery hands. How could she be sweating in this cold? Was she mad? Surely she was. But certainly God would frown on leaving this child behind no matter what.

"I don't know about this . . ." Sadie's eyes were round in her paling face. The light red outline of a few fingers decorated her white cheek. Her curls blew forward with a gust of wind, hiding the remnants of a slap.

Squeezing the handle tight, Lydia finally opened the door. "It'll be all right." Or at least it would be . . . could be . . . hopefully. "We won't let anyone know where you're going." She pushed her gently into the coach then took a step to haul herself in behind her.

Footsteps approached on the cobbled street.

Her body trembled harder. "God help us."

"For crying out loud, Miss King!" Mr. Parker yelped behind her. "You'd like to give an old man a heart attack. I told you to stay put."

"Not this time you didn't." She pulled her skirts inside and slammed the door shut. "Drive, Mr. Parker. Drive now!"

He came over to the door window and pulled at the curtain. "Now why are you . . ." His mouth worked, but no sound came out as he stared at Sadie huddled in the corner of the coach.

Lydia worked the curtain from his grip. "Take me to Nicholas right now. I'm in big trouble."

30

Nicholas rushed toward Queenie's shack. The yelling he'd heard for the past block certainly seemed to be coming from that direction.

What man had dared to go in there? It seemed to be an unspoken rule here that women seeking temporary refuge at Queenie's were given it.

Was Caroline in there still tending to her sick sister with some man going off his rails? If he dared to lay a hand on her . . .

He flung the door open to see a seething Henri throw his hands up in the air.

"You expect me to believe that!" His voice was breathless and dangerously low.

He'd never heard the man so filled with hate.

Caroline held out her arms in front of her sister like a protective shield. Moira was curled up on Queenie's extra cot, her face pale and sweaty.

In the midst of the chaos, Queenie was on her knees at the end of Moira's sick bed, eyes closed. "Dear Lord, let this man find peace despite—"

A guttural cry loosed from Henri's throat.

Well, that prayer certainly hadn't worked. Nicholas launched himself across the room just as his friend grabbed a lamp and brought it up over his head. "Cease this instant!" He wrestled to extricate the lamp from Henri's grip. "Breaking stuff will not fix whatever's the matter."

Henri only growled and tried to yank his arm out from under Nicholas's, then tried to escape his hold by sending an elbow into his gut.

He deflected another flailing limb before it could damage his internal organs. "Let's talk about this elsewhere."

Raining down curses with every jerky movement, Henri struggled against him.

Suddenly, Henri let go. "Fine."

Nicholas stumbled backward, a table's corner jabbing him in the ribs as he fell. "Ugh."

"I knew I recognized you." Henri, out of breath, pointed at Caroline, his scowl deepening.

"I'm sorry, Mr. Beauchamp, for not reintroducing myself."

"Well, no wonder. What with Moira being a trollop now!" He spat.

"Enough!" Nicholas scrambled onto his feet despite the pain in his side to push Henri toward the door.

But the thick man planted his feet as if he were an ancient rooted oak and turned his accusing finger toward Moira. "You said I wasn't good enough. But dozens of filthy men every night are?" His face turned as red as a tomato and he sweat profusely, as if he'd just run ten miles in the summer's heat.

"Let's go." Nicholas grabbed Henri's arms.

Henri shrugged out of his hold. "I can take myself out." He stomped to the door and yanked it open. "All women should rot!"

Nicholas cringed as the door slammed shut, but the hinges held. The nerves that had held his body in check while trying to keep his friend from strangling Moira burst. His hands started shaking.

"I'm sorry, Mr. Lowe." Caroline glided over to him, tears on her cheeks, though her voice was steady. "I should have told you the moment I saw him, but I hadn't thought they'd meet. And he didn't seem to recognize me. I've added weight and I'm no longer, well . . ." A look so heartrending crossed his housekeeper's face that her silent tears looked happy in comparison.

Moira, also known as Irish Mary, groaned from her cot as she turned to face them. "I'm sorry, Caroline."

Caroline wrapped her arms about her stomach and stumbled into the closest chair. "We did this to him."

"None of this is your fault. I chose this path. Even if I had loved—"

"Stop!" Caroline slashed her hand through the air, sneaking a glance at Nicholas before facing her sister. "Don't say any more. It's over. If you hadn't put me ahead of yourself . . . and then chosen this . . ." She slumped. "This . . ."

Moira struggled to push herself to the side of the cot and puked into a waiting bucket. Queenie rushed to assist her while Caroline wept.

The smell and the emotions in the tiny cabin were overwhelming. Nicholas opened the door to let in some cold, cleansing air while a sobbing Caroline moved to help Queenie tend her sick sister.

He was torn between making sure Caroline was all right and running after Henri before the man did something stupid. "Miss O'Conner, I—"

"Go." She turned to him, holding a wad of her sister's limp blond hair. "He'll need you."

"I'll check on you tomorrow morning, then." He rushed out before waiting for a reply.

Henri was a block away, heading toward the brightly lit streets, where he'd find a saloon to drink away his anger—or make it worse. Oh, if only he hadn't asked Henri to help him search for Pepper and her siblings this evening, things wouldn't have gotten so out of hand . . . and he didn't even really know why. "Henri!"

His friend stopped, and Nicholas jogged to catch up.

Henri didn't turn to face him. His fists were tightly clenched at his sides, and his stiffened back muscles strained at his coat's seams. "Don't ask, Nick."

"I won't, but don't go on a binge. It won't help."

"Nothing will help." He whirled and gestured toward Queenie's dilapidated shack. "Your playing Robin Hood to these people is a waste of time."

"No, it's not."

"I no longer want to be involved. It's been entertaining to sneak around, annoying people with your crazy schemes, gathering information for blackmail—but I'm through."

Nicholas felt the wind rush out of him. "That's why you've been helping me?" He staggered over to a nearby tree to keep himself upright. "Blackmail?"

Henri rolled his eyes. "Oh, don't look at me like that. Of course I'm happy to help people—that's just being a decent person—but you know I don't have any of your Jesus motivations to do this stuff. You're the only Christian I've had any respect for, but you're insane to think you're making any headway with these people." He rubbed his eyes and looked away.

Nicholas opened his mouth but then shut it. Here he'd been judging his fellow churchgoers against this man—a man he'd thought God was sovereignly using to do the work the church wouldn't—yet extortion was what had driven his friend to help? And he'd aided him.

"Nick, you're on your own."

He shook his head. He couldn't let his friend go without more of an explanation. "Tell me what that was back there."

"If I understood it myself, I wouldn't have exploded." Henri punched a tree next to him, then went into a rage as he yelped and cursed over his bloodied knuckles.

A coach flew around the street corner, its unlit lanterns swinging. The orange sun about to slip below the horizon illumined the coach just enough to recognize his own vehicle. "What in the world?" He stepped to the side of the road and, waving his arms, hailed Parker.

His driver pulled the horse to a sudden stop. "Boss, we have trouble." Normally as calm as the Kansas winds were blustery, Parker wiped his hands on his pants and looked over his shoulder.

Nicholas jogged to the coach and looked up. "Is it your wife? A maid?"

"No. Miss King."

"Lydia?" Nicholas clenched the driver's footboard. "What happened?"

"She's in the coach, and she's kidnapped a girl."

31

Nicholas thumped the top of the coach and Parker took off, leaving Henri behind.

"I'm sorry, Nicholas. I didn't set out to . . ." Lydia wrapped her arm around the quiet woman pressed against her. "Well, I was looking for Robbie and his sisters, but even if you think running off with Sadie was wrong, I'd do it again."

What could he say to that? He couldn't distinguish much about the girl beside Lydia, other than her dark eye makeup and a dress with a neckline that revealed entirely too much skin. He leaned back against his seat, rubbed his eyes, and slid his hands slowly down his face.

First Henri, now Lydia. His life was complicated enough on its own, but now he had to account for other people's actions.

He opened his eyes to look at the girl again, and when their eyes met, she pressed harder against Lydia. He tried a smile, but Sadie only pressed herself back against the seat. "I don't think we should discuss this further until we get to my place."

"But where should we take her for the night? I can't take her to my parents, and she won't want to go with you."

"My maids will take her. They'll understand what she's going through."

"How will they understand?"

He rubbed his fingers against his scalp and stared out the window. He wanted to trust her, even believed he could, but he'd trusted Henri. He cut a glance at Sadie, who'd yet to speak.

He'd hoped Lydia would grow sympathetic to those in the red-light district, but he'd never envisioned her embracing a young prostitute. He had no idea how she'd even gotten near one, and yet she was holding the painted lady close, the semblance of an overprotective mother in her expression and posture.

She'd taken the news of his late wife better than expected too. Perhaps she'd accept or even approve of his secrets.

"You've got the look on your face that means you're deciding whether or not to keep something from me."

He tried to make his face blank, but her acute perception reached into his chest and twisted. No one but his mother had ever been able to read him like that.

Though he'd been doing his best, Lydia made him want to be better. But could he do more? Could he make her believe in him enough to give up Sebastian? What did she want with that man anyway?

"Well, I don't know what *that* expression means, but it's a bit intimidating."

She should feel in danger. Very little was preventing him from breaching what little etiquette barriers were left—considering they were already alone together, after dark, with a child prostitute. The desire to cross over to her seat, pull her close, bury his face in her hair, and forget everything but the smell and feel of her tugged at his every muscle.

She cleared her throat and squirmed. He scooted to the opposite side of his seat, as far from her as possible, and opened the window sash.

"I closed them because I didn't want anyone to see inside."

Yes, they should talk about trivial things like sashes and weather. "It's dark now. We're driving fast enough no one will see inside."

"I'm sorry I've done nothing but cause you problems."

"No." He jammed his hands in his armpits and hazarded another look at her. "You're not a problem. You're the best thing that's ever happened to me." He pressed his lips together and looked away.

He'd meant to say that, but until he heard it aloud, he hadn't realized how intimate those words sounded.

He imagined her turning a lovely shade of pink in that dark corner.

"I don't think you really mean that."

"I stand by it." He quickly flashed through the happy events of his life. "It's true. But I'm certain I'll not prove to be the best thing that's ever happened to you."

"How could you not?" Her whisper was so soft, he wasn't sure he'd heard her correctly above the sound of wheels and hooves flying over the brick street.

Seconds ticked by. Maybe her question had only been his imagination.

He couldn't stand it any longer. "May I ask why you're marrying Sebastian?"

No response from across the coach but the rustling of skirts.

"Money?"

"Yes, but—"

"Please." He couldn't have felt any colder right now, not even if someone dumped a bucket of ice down his collar. "You don't have to justify yourself to me. I shouldn't have asked. It's none of my business."

And she didn't elaborate.

However, despite his words, he wanted her to. Wanted her to convince him that marrying for money could somehow be a worthy pursuit, something he could look past.

He jiggled his knee and bit down on his inner cheek to squelch further interrogation. One second she lit his heart on fire with feelings he hadn't had for years—the next she fired up the rage he felt whenever he encountered a woman willing to marry for money alone and possibly make her husband miserable for the rest of his days. Did these women not realize he could see what they were after? Even sweet Georgia Renfroe had set her cap on him because he had money rather than because she had a real interest in him.

He couldn't love either one of them. No matter how much he wanted to forge ahead with his feelings for Lydia, loving a woman who'd choose a man for his bank account was one mistake he'd never repeat.

Silence reigned for the rest of the trip. When Parker stopped inside the carriage house, Nicholas opened the door and stood back so the girl wouldn't have to get near him to exit. He beckoned for them to follow him to the basement's service entrance, and the two women flitted across the sandstone path behind him, a rustle of skirts and nervous breathing. The one deep-set window near the door of the maids' quarters was thankfully still alight. After he knocked, he could hear scuffling and hushed women's voices.

"Who's there?"

"Nicholas Lowe and Lydia King."

The curtain in the side window moved, indicating one of them checked to make certain. The bolts on the door slid open, and Josephine peeked out. She looked at all three of them twice, then turned her suspicious gaze back on the girl whose painted face was quite unsettling in the lamplight. "Come in."

They shuffled inside, and if he wasn't already uncomfortable entering their living quarters at night, seeing Josephine in her nightgown with her hair down made things worse. He cleared his throat and turned his attention back to a fully clothed Lydia, pretty despite her wrinkled gown.

But she was hugging the girl against her, and Sadie's clothing certainly didn't cover enough of her skin to keep a man's glance from turning toward unholy thoughts.

So he chose to look at the unadorned table in the corner. "Lydia's taken this girl from . . . ?"

"Um, maybe I shouldn't say." Lydia's voice trembled. "I couldn't leave Sadie where I found her, and when I mentioned she could go to school if she came with me, she chose to leave willingly."

He looked at Josephine and Effie, who'd just joined them, and could tell they were thinking the same thing. Lydia's promise was empty. Sadie wouldn't be able to go to school, not in Teaville, anyway.

"I didn't kidnap her like Mr. Parker said. You can't kidnap an orphan, can you?" Her unsteady voice sounded too loud in the cement-walled room. He forced himself not to shush her. He looked to the women, his eyes pleading with them to say something, take over. Right now, he wasn't sure being in the room with Sadie and the others was a good idea.

Effie sidestepped Josephine and held out her arms to Sadie. "Why don't you come choose one of my nightgowns and then take a warm bath? There's a beautiful copper tub in the laundry room, and I have some pretty-smelling bath salts."

The young lady looked to Lydia, and when she smiled encouragingly, Sadie followed Effie through the bolted door that led to the corridor and into the service area of the basement.

Lydia pressed her palms together against her chest and turned to Josephine. "Thank you so much. I know that . . . that what she is can't be easy for you to accept . . ."

"Lydia . . ." Nicholas shook his head slightly.

". . . and I hope you'll not treat her poorly because of what she is. She's so young she can't—"

"Lydia," he said sharper this time.

She blinked at him, confused.

He turned toward Josephine, whose expression bespoke suspicion. After the first prostitute's suicide and the second's return to The Line, he and Caroline had decided to let any future maids believe Caroline was sneaking them in under his nose. That way they'd believe he was ignorant of their former employment. If they returned to their former life, they'd have no informational power over him, and they'd not share with every out-of-luck girl that he had a soft spot that could be taken advantage of.

But it seemed like that season of his life was over. He sighed and met Josephine's wary gaze. "I left Caroline at Queenie's house with her sister."

Josephine blinked again, her face growing more certain.

"Yes." He blew out a breath. "I know everything."

She nodded and glanced at Lydia.

"She doesn't, but I think she should."

Josephine let her hands slide off her hips. "Well, it's not time to talk about it now. It's late."

"Seems like no one wants to talk about anything right now, when I sure wish someone would tell me what's going on." Lydia's voice shook with frustration.

He couldn't keep his secrets from her any longer, no matter the consequences. "I'll tell you what you need to know on the drive home."

"I want you to tell me everything. I thought you already *had* told me everything."

Would his keeping this a secret for so long make it less believable? He'd practiced what he'd say to Henri whenever he toyed with coming clean to him, and it had always sounded ridiculous. Maybe it was. But what good would come from keeping it from her any longer? "Yes, I'll tell you all."

32

Nicholas gripped the doorknob, ready to leave the maids' quarters and breathe in the frosty night air. The thought of telling Lydia everything was making his heart and lungs seize. If she didn't take things well . . .

Josephine pressed a hand to Lydia's arm. "I won't blame you if you don't want to come back to see Sadie after Mr. Lowe talks with you."

Lydia frowned. "I'll want to see Sadie again, no matter what he says."

Josephine's smile was sad and cynical.

Nicholas nodded at Josephine before she shut the door. He'd have to talk to her too. She'd be the most effective in helping Sadie adjust. Of all the maids who'd sought sanctuary under his roof, Josephine seemed the most level-headed.

Parker walked up the path, hat in his hands. "What are we going to do? Did the maids take her?"

"Yes." Nicholas trailed a hand through his hair. For three years he'd kept his secret, and in one night his carefully constructed walls were about to tumble. He'd considered telling Henri for the last several weeks, but he'd had no peace about it. After tonight, he could see why.

But Parker? His driver often clucked his tongue at him for venturing into the town's sporting section but had never refused to drive him there.

He'd never considered telling his driver he harbored ex-prostitutes, since he was more an employee than a friend, but he wanted to tell Lydia everything . . . or nothing at all. What if she didn't believe he had good intentions for the women under his roof? What if she assumed exactly what he feared people would assume?

He strode away, heading for the carriage. "Let's get Miss King home, before we damage her reputation. It's late, and her parents are probably worried."

Parker punched his smashed hat back open and followed. "Arriving home late isn't worse than kidnapping a child. And I aided her."

"Kidnapping?"

They both turned to find Lydia grabbing at her throat, her eyes wide. "Stop saying that. That's not what I did."

Parker's face was as grim as a rock. "That's what they'd call it."

Nicholas held out a hand to stop Parker from scaring Lydia any further. "Who knows you took the girl?"

"You, Mr. Parker, and . . ." Her voice stuttered, and she swayed. He reached out to steady her. "Go on."

"Some servant from The California. I'd guess she was the cook. She came out before we left, but I don't know her name, and she doesn't know mine."

"And Henri was with me when Parker came flying by." Nicholas shook her shoulder to make her look at him. "Think. Is there anyone else who might have seen you?"

She shook her head and grabbed a fistful of his sleeve. "Even if I did kidnap her, you can't let her go back. They can't force someone so young to work like that."

Parker hung his head, and Nicholas's mouth went dry. "I'm afraid the laws in that regard are easily dodged. But no, they shouldn't. Grown women shouldn't be forced either for that matter. According to the laws, none of them should be there at all."

Lydia looked on the verge of crying, so he grabbed both of her shoulders and rubbed as Mr. Parker rushed back to the carriage. "We'll do the best we can. If no one makes a ruckus about her disappearance, then there may be hope. But she won't be able to stay here forever."

"Do you think the maids will treat her unkindly?"

"No. I'm worried about her staying for the same reasons any prostitute who wants to reform can't stay where she's known."

"Because of us." Lydia's voice was so full of self-reprobation his heart hurt.

He chucked up her chin and smiled. A real, genuine, from-his-heart smile. "No, not *us*. You and me, we're the germ of hope. One day society will not condemn a man or woman for a past choice and instead discern and judge the heart." He pulled her hand into the crook of his arm. "Come, we can't tarry. We don't want to worry your parents so much they question why you're out late."

They'd only just settled into the coach, Parker thankfully driving with more care now, when Lydia scooted forward on her seat. "What did you mean when you told your maid you were going to tell me everything? Is it what I've done to Sadie? Have I made things worse for her?"

He stopped Lydia's hands from strangling her skirt and held them loosely. "If she's not caught, her life will be infinitely better— I hope."

"What if someone turns me in?"

"I don't know." He closed his eyes against the thought of Lydia arrested and tried, though surely that wouldn't happen. If Lydia's escapade came to light, he'd expect the madam to get off with a slap to the wrist and, after the attention waned, covertly given back her "property." "If Sadie's caught and returned to whoever dares claim her . . . Well, we won't let that happen, not only for her sake but ours."

"Please don't tell me you think I was wrong."

He gave her a crooked smile. "I've always said I'll follow God's law before man's, but that doesn't mean we aren't called to hardship for it."

234

"But surely the law, Sebastian could—"

"I don't know if Sebastian could do much." He wanted to tell her that if anyone circumvented the law, her intended was likely one of them. But he couldn't be sure what Sebastian Little would do in the case of such a young girl. "The labor laws passed this year say no one under sixteen can be employed in a dangerous or immoral vocation. But unless officials work hard to stop it, parents or guardians either get around the law by manipulating the wording or paying the fine. Even if we passed stricter laws, I doubt they'd stop sending their children to work. And the city benefits from the fines from the red-light district. They aren't too keen on losing the revenue."

"That's disgusting!" Lydia pulled her hands from his. "It's not like she's working in a coal mine or a factory or even a dance hall."

Did she realize what dancers often did? "No, she's working in an industry people avoid—at least the good people. Without you, she probably had no hope. She may still have no hope."

"Without God's help anyway. Right?"

"Right." He struggled to swallow against the despair that sometimes took over when he didn't see God's mercy on display and he couldn't fathom why.

Lydia scooted back in her seat and curled up into the corner like a child. He reached for her, but she was too far away to touch without moving to her side of the coach. Should he break decorum to comfort her?

Did he not refuse to follow society's dictates every day?

However, he gripped his seat and stayed. Sometimes society's dictates were for a very good reason.

"Was that all you were going to tell me, that I didn't really help Sadie?" Her emotionless voice was worse than if tears had clogged it.

"Of course you helped Sadie, but no, I thought I'd go ahead and confess all the terrible sins I've committed since I'm now in the presence of a bona fide kidnapper."

Even without seeing her, he could tell her glare was scorching.

235

Wrong time for teasing. "Sorry. I just . . ." He sighed and clasped his hands. "I'm afraid you'll think poorly of me once you know. Most people likely won't believe what I'm about to say, but you . . . I don't want your estimation of me to sink back to that first day I refused to buy those sewing machines."

"Thank you again for those." Her soft, admiring voice made it even harder for him to stay put.

"Um, yes." He placed a cool hand on his blazing-hot neck, glad for the darkness of the coach. He'd only realized the day she'd seen him with Miss Renfroe why he'd caved and bought those sewing machines for her and why he'd worried they wouldn't arrive on time. It was his first attempt to show her he loved her—but she'd never know that. "You're welcome." The words choked, but thankfully she wouldn't notice how uncomfortably he sat in the dark.

He'd convinced himself to never become smitten with another woman, and yet here he'd fallen for one he couldn't pursue.

"So what have you done that's so terrible? I already know you're involved in the seedy side of town, but I also know why. And you've already told me about your wife."

"Do you know why I'm certain my maids will be the best people to care for Sadie?"

"No."

"I know I keep asking for secrecy, but I need you to keep this confidential—and this time it's not just for my benefit. It affects the lives of others more than me."

"Can I trust you to keep my crime of kidnapping quiet?"

He smiled at the slight lilt in her voice. "Yes."

"Then why wouldn't I agree to keep another of your myriad secrets?"

Good. "What it boils down to is that I live in a bachelor's mansion with a handful of women of ill repute."

"Hmm, your maids?" She didn't sound flabbergasted.

"Yes. Except Caroline. I met her in a saloon pleading with her sister to leave, but Moira insisted she liked the work, even though she downs more liquor than the men around her. Caroline and I decided to work together to help the ones who did want to leave."

"And how is that a sin?"

"If I'd told you months ago that I had a house full of former prostitutes trying to reform themselves, would you have believed me?"

"Probably not."

"You might think I'm crazy to believe they can change, but I'm more afraid you'll doubt my honorable intentions. As I'm sure others would if they knew who my maids were."

Her hand bumped his knee, and he grabbed for it. She didn't pull away but rather squeezed. "I believe you, Nicholas."

She believed him.

He swallowed a few times, trying to reply, but couldn't. Not that he had words to say.

The carriage stopped, and he scooted forward. The moonlight lit the right side of her face, and if he squinted, she seemed to be looking at him in the same manner he was looking at her.

"I—"

He silenced her with a finger to her mouth. Her warm, soft lips against his skin drew him forward.

The door opened and Mr. Parker ducked his head inside. "We're here."

To cover for their nearness, he kept moving forward but slipped out the door with her hand still in his.

Lydia started to rise, but then hesitated. "What about the children? Where might they be? Mr. Parker searched The California but didn't catch a glimpse of them."

Mr. Parker nodded as Nicholas tugged her outside and said, "I was out looking for them too, and will continue, but you need to get inside. We'll stay parked awhile, in case you need us to assure your parents we're the ones who brought you home."

"All right." She stepped down but didn't immediately remove her hand from his. She stared up at him for a second, then dropped his hand and shot off down the sidewalk.

Parker hoisted himself back into his seat. "If I'd headed home before she found me, we'd not be in this mess."

Nicholas watched Lydia disappear into her house.

Though it might've been easier on everybody if Lydia hadn't taken Sadie, at least he knew her heart had changed toward the people he felt most compelled to help. . . . Too bad that was as much of her heart as he would get to know.

33

After a full day of work at the library and a slight headache from the newly painted walls, Lydia hurried home, the frosty air clearing her head but hastening her toward the warmth of home.

Cinnamon and sage spilled out of her home's front door, the smells still lingering after the Thanksgiving baking she'd done yesterday. She had a lot to be thankful for: her mother lived, and Mr. Parker had informed her this morning that Nicholas's contacts in the red-light district had heard nothing about a lady kidnapping a child prostitute.

Nicholas figured Madam Careless knew the odds were stacked against her winning the child back—if she'd ever found out what actually happened. Maybe the cook had kept her secret. But what if the madam was only biding time, finding a way around the law and planning revenge?

Please, Lord, wash the details from the mind of that cook so she can't pinpoint me, Mr. Parker, or Nicholas. Let it be your will that Sadie be saved from such an awful life. Let it be my Christmas wish.

She rubbed her hands vigorously, then pulled off her gloves and hung her coat in the closet. A shuffling in the kitchen and a clink caught her attention. "Papa, are you home?"

"Lydia?" The silky masculine tenor made the hair on her neck prickle.

Oh, why hadn't she kept quiet? Then she could've slipped out the door once she'd realized Sebastian was there. Though she had to face him sometime. Was he irritated or worried that she hadn't attended his mother's Thanksgiving luncheon yesterday? But telling him why wouldn't help matters at all.

"I didn't want to go because my feelings for you aren't nearly the same as my feelings for Nicholas, yet I can't tell you it's over because I'm afraid it will hurt my mother."

Sometimes honest answers should never be uttered.

Sebastian came through the parlor door with Mama on his arm. Her face was more alert than usual, but the worry lines were deeper, and her frown intense.

"Mama, are you all right?" Lydia fluttered over to the couch and arranged the pillows to cushion her mother's frail body.

"I'm concerned." Mama clamped onto Sebastian's arm as he helped her onto the sofa. She glanced at Sebastian, then her eyes wandered, looking anywhere except at her daughter as she arranged herself amid the pillows.

What had she done? Mama only struggled to make eye contact with someone she was disappointed in—she'd hardly bothered to look at Papa for years. But Mama rarely had difficulty looking at her.

Surely if she'd somehow heard about Sadie's abduction, she'd approve. The one time Papa had been drunk enough to suggest their daughter serve drinks in his favorite saloon, her parents had yelled at each other all night.

The rocking chair beside her creaked as Sebastian took a seat. Was he the reason for Mama's upset?

Lydia sat beside Mama, who kept her gaze on the afghan covering her legs.

"Are you concerned for Papa?" Most family men would be home

by now, but she'd thought Mama ceased worrying about his late nights and occasional disappearances years ago. If she hadn't, surely her health would've declined much faster.

"No." Mama picked at the French knots on her decorative pillow. "Sebastian came by to tell me how worried he is about you."

Lydia gave him an apologetic smile. "I'm sorry I couldn't come yesterday, but I couldn't leave Mama on Thanksgiving." She squeezed Mama's hand. "Just didn't feel right."

"I hear you've been quite busy setting up the library."

Something in his tone made her tilt her chin. "Yes."

"Seems you're able to leave your mother for that."

She shrugged, choosing to ignore his accusatory tone. "I wasn't there yesterday. Not every day's a holiday."

Her mother cleared her throat. "Sebastian says you've been to the precinct a few times this month. How come you didn't tell me about that?"

If he knew she'd been there, he also knew her reason. "I only reported a problem and returned to check on its progress. Nothing alarming." For Mama anyway. "I didn't want to upset you over something we have little control over." She shot a look at Sebastian, hoping her glare would quell any further interrogation from him.

"But it makes me wonder." Sebastian raised an eyebrow, clearly not averse to worrying Mama's nerves. "How do you know about the problems of a prostitute's children?"

She glanced at Mama, whose eyes were pinned to some knick-knack on the shelf. Lydia trapped her pillow's lace between her fingers, imagining it was the soft flesh under Sebastian's arm—where her father liked to pinch her when she refused to hold her tongue. "Some man who's helping with the library told me."

When Sebastian's eyebrow cocked, she scrambled for something to say before he said anything else. "Since we're talking about the library . . ." She put a hand on her mother's arm. "I hope you'll help me make a slipcover for the library's couch. Mr. Lowe purchased some beautiful red rugs, but the donated couch clashes terribly."

"I'm afraid we're so far behind with the mending, we've no time, unless . . ." Her mother sat up straighter and addressed Sebastian. "Do you think your mother would allow Lydia to use one of the new sewing machines?"

Did Mama think Mrs. Little decided who could or could not use the machines? She was the reason Mrs. Little even had those machines. "I'm sure I can use them."

"I don't see why not, since Lydia was the one who dragged them out of Mr. Lowe's pockets." Sebastian turned to face her again, his expression unpleasant. "And now that she's working for him, maybe she can get more. How exactly did you obtain the library position again?"

Sebastian's narrow-eyed glare made her stomach flip. No wonder Mama was concerned. What had Sebastian been telling her?

Lydia turned to Mama and tried to paste on an easy smile. "Remember months ago when I took that book off N . . . Mr. Lowe's desk to read while I waited for him?" At Mama's nod, she pressed on, hoping neither had noticed her stumble over Nicholas's name. "He let me borrow it, and naturally I started talking about books." She turned back to Sebastian. "He'd been thinking of starting a library for a while now, seems he just needed someone with a passion for books to be the librarian."

"So the most notorious miser in Teaville suddenly decides to become overly generous, leaves you credit at Reed's to spend how you will, and sets you up with a job." Sebastian's jaw worked. "A job you took without consulting me."

Her jaw tightened and her fists curled. How dare he use that suspicious tone in front of her mother? Mama didn't need to be worrying about anything but her health at the moment.

Lydia stood. "I think we should get ourselves tea." With a yank of her head to indicate Sebastian should follow, she swept out of the room and stomped toward the kitchen. His heavy footsteps followed.

She whirled on him once they cleared the door. "I cannot believe you'd bother my mother with these conjecture-laced accusations."

"What accusations?" His confused, innocent expression didn't fool her. He had a dangerous glint in his eye that made her want to step back, but she wouldn't.

"You're insinuating I've procured a job with Mr. Lowe in a questionable manner." She moved away, unable to stand the proximity, and started collecting the chipped teacups. "I can't believe you'd put such nonsense in my mother's head."

"I don't want you working at the library."

"And you have to bring that up in front of my mother, who clearly can't tolerate strain right now?" The saucer rattled on the tea platter, and she stopped its motion with a heavy hand. "You told me once that it would be a good idea for me to work in a library."

"I hadn't expected that to happen until years after we married."

"But the town needs one now—"

"It's more that you need one. Admit it. It would give you an excuse to bury your nose in a book at all times."

She dropped the tea kettle onto the stove and cringed at the *thunk*. "Reading books isn't a librarian's job. Though a library would mean I get to read more often, that would happen whether I worked there or not." Evidently buying her Sir Arthur Conan Doyle's newest collection hadn't meant that he'd decided reading for enjoyment could be worthwhile. "And I will work there, your permission or not."

He leaned against the counter, his arms crossed against his chest, his eyes tiny slits. "When we first discussed marriage, you seemed to realize I needed a good Christian wife to face the voters with. I do not need a secretive, bristly, rebellious one."

"And I need someone to help me care for my mother and then me after she passes. But bringing this subject up in front of her when she's obviously ill indicates you're not such a good choice for me either."

"Your reputation affects more than just me. If your mother found out you were doing something she'd be ashamed of—"

"Working as a librarian is nothing to be ashamed of." Lydia transferred sugar cubes from the bag to the bowl, trying not to crush them with her little tongs.

"I heard a strange story the other day." Sebastian shifted, leaning toward her slightly. "Heard someone talking about a properly dressed woman skulking about in an alley off Willow. Then Officer Vincent informs me you're awfully concerned about some abandoned children on Willow." He grabbed the spoon she clinked against the china. "The Line is a wicked place, Lydia. You best not go there unless you're with a whole lot of elderly women carrying hymnals, or with me." He leaned back. "Not that I ever go."

"And why don't you?"

His brow crinkled. "That's an odd question from a woman whose worldly woes are exacerbated by a father who frequents the area. Why would you want your future husband going to that part of town?"

"Of course I don't want you going to The Line for the reason my father does. What I mean is, if you're going to campaign against saloons and parlor houses, don't you think knowing what drives people to work there would help you figure out how to dismantle it? How else will you know how to help them?"

"You think you're qualified to give me campaigning advice?" He snatched a cut-out cookie she'd placed on the platter and bit off the gingerbread man's head. "I get enough of that from my mother."

Comparing her to his mother was the exact opposite of endearing. She forced herself not to turn and walk away. "Perhaps we need a different perspective on things. If we get to know their prob—"

"Let me give you some rather obvious campaigning advice you've overlooked." He leaned forward, his eyes narrowing. "If the woman I'm courting is traipsing around The Line—alone and stirring up trouble—that doesn't reflect well on me, no matter what she's doing. . . . Which is what, exactly?"

"If you claim being there cannot at all be advantageous to your campaign plans, I won't bother you with the details."

"Don't go there again." He threw his broken cookie back on the plate. "You will not disobey."

She swallowed and met his gaze. Sebastian couldn't be God's best for her—not if he was more concerned about his image than helping others. "I will not obey, for I have no reason to."

"If you want to marry me—"

"I don't, and I won't."

He shoved away from the counter. "I thought you were smart. You've got nothing to entice a man to wed you besides pretty eyes and a cumbersome intellect. And your father . . . If only you knew how little you have to recommend you. But I was willing to try, to keep the peace, to give you a life you had no chance of getting any other way. I think you need to talk to your parents before you make a decision. What you do affects them just as much as it affects us."

She stopped messing with the tea service to keep her trembling hands from betraying her by clinking china pieces together. "So are you saying I have no choice but to marry you?"

"You have a choice, but you're certainly making the wrong one."

"Do you really want to marry me?"

"I suppose I've fallen for you."

"Suppose?"

"Look." He flung out his hands. "This is an arrangement that's convenient for the both of us. I need a wife who'll make me look trustworthy in the eyes of voters, and you need support. Love is a transient thing. It'll come and go. We can work at making that happen, but it's not what's important."

How could she force herself to love someone if they couldn't agree on the things that mattered most? "What are you planning to do for those children Officer Vincent told you I was worried about?"

"Why does that matter?"

"It just does."

"You want me to be worried about some no-account woman's bastards?"

The tea kettle whistled, and Lydia welcomed the excuse to turn her back on him. Just a few weeks ago, those words might have made her cringe only because he'd said them so loudly. She would've even silently agreed with him that they weren't her concern.

How had Nicholas seen anything redeemable in her that day she'd first stepped into his office? Maybe she was being too hard on Sebastian. Could he not change like she had?

Nicholas thought she could help change people's minds. Wouldn't changing Sebastian's be one of the best ways to help these people? As a politician, he could do so much to help them if he had more compassion.

She moved the kettle from its burner and set it on a folded towel on the counter, but she couldn't bring herself to turn and face him. Even if she could change him, her heart didn't race and her skin didn't warm when she stood next to the mayor's son. Not the way they did when she merely anticipated Nicholas's presence. Reactions she shouldn't have while expecting to become engaged to another man.

She had little chance with Nicholas, and therefore those feelings meant nothing—nothing except she couldn't lead Sebastian along any longer, no matter how poorly her mother might react to her daughter giving up what little future security she had within reach. Besides, she had a job now, and knowing Nicholas, it'd be a secure one that would provide her with enough.

"You're right." She spoke to him without turning around. "Life is stacked against me in such a manner that marrying you is the smartest move I could make. But it looks like I'm going to do something foolish."

The silence extended long enough that the ticking of his timepiece sounded overly loud. "So you're wanting to end things?"

"Yes."

He grabbed her wrist and spun her around. She fought to keep from cowering in front of those gleaming angry eyes.

"I want you to tell your parents this is purely your decision."

She shrugged, hard-pressed to keep her gaze even with his. "I will." She'd made Papa mad plenty of times before—she could endure his anger again.

246

"And though your reputation no longer affects me, you still ought to stay out of the red-light district. It's for your own good."

"I agree. It's for my own good." She wrenched her hand out of his grip. "But that won't stop me from going. Not if I can help the people there who need it."

34

Lydia shivered on the church stairs. God surely wouldn't mind if she wasn't in church every time the doors were open, but if she skipped tonight's Sunday prayer service just to avoid Mrs. Little, she might start finding reasons to skip Sunday school and the moral-society meetings too. Sunday morning services weren't so bad—just this morning she had easily avoided Mrs. Little in the crowd of churchgoers.

Might as well face the woman now.

Would anyone other than the Littles know she'd ended her understanding with Sebastian? She hadn't yet found the nerve to tell Mama.

Forcing herself to take one step after another, she looked around for one of Nicholas's carriages in the line of vehicles outside the church, though she was certain he wouldn't be there. He only attended Sunday mornings as far as she knew. But if anyone would be proud of her for standing up for what she believed in despite the consequences, it would be him.

The buzz in the sanctuary was livelier than usual. When she pushed through the inner doors, almost everyone turned to look over their shoulders, and then the place fell silent. Holding onto the door handle, the urge to step back and run overwhelmed her.

Pastor Wisely stood on the bottom step of the auditorium's stage. "Would you mind coming in, Miss King?"

The carpet sunk under her feet like quicksand. When had he ever addressed a latecomer from the front?

"Lydia?" The pastor beckoned her forward.

She yanked her feet forward and slogged past the pews, fuller than usual. A few congregants ducked their heads when she looked at them. Shouldn't they already be singing? Had Sebastian retaliated and told them about her being in the red-light district? But what evidence did he have besides hearsay?

She shook her head and took a deep breath as she forged forward. Perhaps this hushed crowd had nothing to do with her. But then again, why had the pastor beckoned her to come up front?

Pastor Wisely cleared his throat, and his wife patted a spot between her and Evelyn for Lydia to sit. After she did, Evelyn snatched up her hand, squeezed, and didn't let go.

Pastor took a side glance at her and cleared his throat again. "Now that the young lady is present, I'll allow these questions to continue, but we need to watch our tone. We know nothing for certain."

Lydia's stomach plummeted like an anvil into the abyss.

Mrs. Little stood up in the pew to the left. "I have heard from a reliable source that Miss King doesn't deny skulking about The Line unchaperoned. Her behavior should concern us all."

"And why is that?" Lydia muttered under her breath. Evelyn squeezed her hand tighter.

"I don't think we should be discussing this in front of the children," Bernadette said, but the elder Mr. Taylor spoke over her.

"She represents us in this community, and we're supposed to admonish our members if they're out of line." He tapped the top of the pew in front of him.

Muttered affirmations fluttered about the sanctuary.

Lydia looked over her shoulder and counted. About fifteen of the most influential church members weren't looking at her very kindly, and the handful who ought to support her seemed to be cowering like rabbits in front of a pack of wolves.

Nicholas had told her this congregation was more concerned about themselves than the poor, but she hadn't believed him because there were good ones in the bunch. Yet Charlie and her husband, Harrison, weren't present. And though the Wiselys sat beside her, most of the faces surrounding her weren't encouraging.

"Why didn't they wait to ask me about this alone?" she whispered to Bernadette.

"You can speak now. You do have a good reason for being there, yes?"

Of course she did, but since she wasn't at liberty to explain how she'd started going there in the first place, would they believe her?

She couldn't out Nicholas to save herself from their ire. If his disguise was exposed, who'd help Sadie? Who'd keep searching for Annie's children? Where would the women who wanted to leave prostitution go?

She could handle being disgraced if Nicholas remained free to assist those who needed help more than she did.

Angry voices, barely audible, whirled among the swirling fat snowflakes starting to drift down from above. As he'd planned to sneak into brothels to look for Annie's children tonight, Nicholas had expected to hear drunken, riotous voices, but not in this part of town. He flipped down his wool coat's lapel, uncovering his ears so he could pinpoint the disturbance.

Snow burrowed under his collar, and he squinted against the wet flakes attacking his eyes. Light flickered behind the church's thin, tall windows. Lydia was probably in there. For the first time in a long time, he wanted to attend a Sunday night meeting, but he wouldn't give in to the impulse. He wouldn't attend church just to get a glimpse of Lydia.

He scuffled his way past the massive stone church, and the irritated voices grew louder. Maybe he should take a peek inside. He turned to jog up the stairs, then pulled on the heavy oaken doors. A blast of lukewarm air escaped, hitting his frozen face.

After stepping inside the little corridor that separated the sanctuary from the out-of-doors, he kept a hold on the brass handles and gently let the doors shut behind him. The voices definitely didn't sound like worshippers singing. He turned to pad up the balcony's staircase, the mutinous tones growing louder the higher he climbed.

Creeping into the darkened balcony, he sat in the blackest shadow and scanned the cavernous sanctuary awash in light from gas flames. Lydia, wrapped in a navy wool cloak, sat up front with some of the women from that meddlesome moral society surrounding her. Quite a few elders of the church—a few with wives and children—were scattered near the front.

"We're all concerned, and for good reason." Pastor Wisely paced in front of the front pew and patted his sweaty forehead with a handkerchief, though the church's interior wasn't much warmer than outside. "But we need to make sure we're thinking clearly and judging with care."

"It's clear, Reverend." Mr. Taylor stood with a Bible open in his hand. "1 Corinthians 5, 'Therefore put away from among yourselves that wicked person.' According to this passage, we're to judge those within the church and send them away if they aren't repentant."

Leaning forward ever so slightly, Nicholas observed the faces in the crowd. Though it was impossible to recognize everyone, other than the Wiselys and Mr. Hargrove, he didn't see many known for their level-headed thinking. This didn't bode well for whomever they were debating on casting out.

The pastor held out his hand and swept it across the room. "We should not quote the Bible to justify our actions, but rather follow it in full, letting every bit of it direct us."

Well said. But would they heed his advice? Mr. Taylor was one of several men in this church who had no right to enforce that verse. Why, right now, he could go down there and reveal several of Mr. Taylor's moral shortcomings, even one or two misdemeanors he'd gotten away with.

But he couldn't expose Mr. Taylor's secret life without exposing his own.

Mrs. Little stood. "Whether or not she remains in our church, she certainly can't remain in our moral society."

Which poor lady was at the mercy of these militaristic women? And why did Lydia remain among them rather than stand up and leave? Had she learned nothing in all her time with him?

"In my eighty-two years on this earth"—Mr. Hargrove huffed as he pushed himself up from his seat—"I've lost friends and business partners over things I didn't do. Even after I tried to clear up misunderstandings, the damage had already been done. I think we need to stop talking about her as if she weren't here and start asking her questions. But before I sit down, I want to remind us all that Christ supped with the prostitutes and the tax collectors."

Evelyn stood to her full height and scanned the room. "Mr. Hargrove is right. Christ didn't shun sinners, he helped them. Maybe we aren't—"

"There is a fine line between helping sinners and being corrupted by them." Mrs. Little stuck her hands on her hips and glared at Evelyn, who didn't retreat to her seat despite the cold glare she was getting. "The moral society, as a group, can help sinners see where they've gone astray, but cavorting with them is asking for trouble. There is safety in numbers. My son is very concerned about her reputation, as obviously he should be. He's even warned her not to go there, but she refuses to listen to reason."

The mumbling escalated, and Nicholas gripped the back of the pew in front of him. If Sebastian was the one concerned, then that had to mean—

"Is that true, Lydia?" Mrs. Little shook her head as if she were disappointed in a small child. "Can you not see the wisdom in staying away from that area of town?"

A hush fell over the sanctuary, but a low, dangerous rumble rolled in Nicholas's throat. He clenched the pew, forcing himself to remain seated. His churning stomach was urging him to go downstairs and spew out the secret lives of some of the men looking so smug below. But he couldn't, not without the congregation asking how he knew, not without revealing things about himself he'd made certain very few people knew.

What had he done to Lydia? If he hadn't decided to teach her a lesson, she'd not be here now, feeling the condemnation of a group of so-called Christ followers.

He'd been responsible for what happened to Gracie—he knew that—but he'd been forgiven for it. But unlike with his wife, he'd not been unfeeling or self-centered with Lydia.

He swallowed against the bile rising in his throat. Why would God allow his actions to destroy her when his motivations this time had been good?

Lydia fidgeted in her cloak, then raised her chin just like she did when he'd chastised her. "I failed to hear anything reasonable in Sebastian's warnings."

He winced. She should say nothing and let them believe however they wished, or leave before she riled them up. He stared at Pastor Wisely as if he could jolt the man into ending the meeting.

Mrs. Little marched up to the platform stairs. "She's been seen in the red-light district talking to prostitutes several times apart from our crusades."

And who saw her? Sebastian? Why wasn't he here now? Was he so wrapped up in his mother's skirts he'd allow her to accuse Lydia in front of an entire assembly without showing his face? Certainly it was some male, since the witness was not on trial alongside Lydia.

He barely suppressed a maniac-like growl. How he hated the double standard. If he dallied with prostitutes, no man in town would quit working with him. If Lydia simply talked to a lady of questionable character, she'd be shunned and raked over the coals by men and women alike.

He could save her if he spoke up, though defending her publicly was equivalent to throwing away everything he'd been working on for the last few years.

"A decent woman would never socialize with a harlot. The corrupt nature of a prostitute is vile and contagious." Mrs. Little raised her fist. "She destroys young men with disease and lies; she demolishes marriages and community morals. Any lady seen keeping company with fallen women can no longer be considered respectable."

He stood so fast his pew thumped against the wooden floor.

A thump in the balcony arrested Lydia's attention. She turned slightly in the pew to see a tall bundle of black standing in the upper-story shadows. She gripped her hands together, as if she could anchor her heart from flying from her chest.

He's here.

For a moment, she'd thought it'd be a fool's errand to defend herself, but she had to say something to stop Nicholas before he came down and told them anything.

Lydia shot up beside Evelyn and turned to face the crowd. "I am a decent woman, and I'm ashamed to be a part of a congregation that condemns me before asking what I was doing."

"So what were you doing, Miss King?" Mrs. Taylor asked, her husband scowling beside her.

"I'm helping those who need help, like the church ought to do. As a member of the moral society, I think it's right that I be worried about those entrapped in a life of sin. If they want to get out—"

"So you don't deny being in the red-light district?" Was Mrs. Little's scowl actually a smile?

"I've been there just as you have."

"Going with the ladies in the moral society on a serenade is not the same thing."

"Who's going to fault me for looking out for the needs of three abandoned children?" She looked around the room. Very few eyes met hers. "You can go to the police station and look in the record books. I informed them of a very urgent need on behalf of some innocent children, and nothing was done about it."

"There are reasons, Miss King, that the moral society does things the way we do. Going against us—"

"Now, Mrs. Little." Pastor Wisely held up his hand. "Miss King has been a conscientious member of your moral society. My wife and daughter have mentioned her good heart several times."

Lydia shook her head at the suggestion that her heart had had much good in it, but at least it had gotten better. "I wasn't going against anyone."

"Hearing that you were alone in that area of town with no chaperone makes me question whether we can believe anything you say." Mr. Taylor's accusation caused a few gasps.

Lydia's skin froze, and in turn, her whole body. How could she answer that? If he believed such a thing, what could she possibly say that would make him accept anything different after she'd already explained her purpose?

Bernadette stood up on her other side. "We have no reason to believe Lydia is lying. She's told us she attempted to do charity, and we should take her motivation at face value. If God is calling her to help these people—and the Bible backs up such a calling—who are we to stand against her?"

"Then why aren't you taking up her crusade and going to The Line after dark with her, if it's God's will?" Mrs. Taylor's tone sounded as skeptical as her husband's.

Bernadette rubbed her arms. "I know what God wants me to do, and at this time, that's not it."

Evelyn helped her mother sink back onto her spot on the pew as her father held up his hand. "Now, people, let's watch what we're saying, or I'm going to end tonight's service. Maybe I should do that anyway."

"Just because your wife isn't worried about doing the Lord's work anymore, doesn't mean we aren't." An arrogant male voice echoed in the sanctuary.

Lydia stalked down the aisle. "I have nothing but respect for Mrs. Wisely's decision to pursue God instead of works, and you should too. She's more concerned about her relationship being right with God than pleasing you. And now, the same goes for me. I want God to tell me, 'Well done, good and faithful servant,' and whether or not you'd tell me the same doesn't matter to me anymore. I don't want to belong to a group more concerned with banishing the immoral rather than eradicating immorality. Christ didn't sit in the synagogue gossiping with his apostles on how bad the world was. No, He went out and changed it for the better, one person at a time, like Mr. Hargrove said."

She stopped in the middle of the aisle and spun in a slow circle. "Maybe I'm not going about it the best way, and maybe I can't make a real difference, but I know that sitting on my backside lamenting the existence of eight blocks of sin in the middle of our town won't do the people there who need Christ any good." She glanced up to where she thought she could see Nicholas standing in the shadows. "Not long ago, my motivations were terrible, but God has given me some wise examples to follow, and I intend to."

She looked back at Bernadette, who was focused on her lap, but Evelyn gave her an encouraging nod.

"Why are we willing to help some and not others? When I was forced to plumb the depths of my heart, what I found wasn't pretty, but I can change. I want to change. It may not be comfortable, it may not be safe, but I'll seek God's favor over man's. Won't you?"

Some woman's sniffles and the shuffling of feet filled the silence as Lydia waited for anyone to answer. She spun toward Pastor Wisely, who was holding his hand across his chin, a sad droopy set to his eyes.

She turned to Mrs. Little. "I can no longer support your son's political ambitions if all he wants to do is regulate immorality. What he needs is a plan to change the hearts of people who frequent sordid places. Otherwise, his slogans and campaigning are a waste of time." *Like this meeting.*

She shook her head. Their hearts wouldn't change instantly—hers hadn't. "I don't expect to change your minds tonight, because it certainly took me a while to see how my heart wasn't right. But please think about it. Don't shove away what I've said."

Mr. Hargrove smiled and winked at her, but mostly everyone else stared at their laps or scowled.

"I'll leave now. But please, the next time you hear things about me that worry you, ask me first."

She stalked out to the foyer and hovered a moment near the balcony staircase as the murmuring behind her grew. She climbed the stairs to peep into the balcony but saw no one. Had Nicholas left or had she only imagined the shadow of a man?

If he believed she'd just done the right thing, wouldn't he have stayed to steady her as she walked out on legs made of gelatin?

Well, whether or not Nicholas had been here, she hoped she'd made God proud, because He was likely all she'd have left to cling to as her world fell apart.

35

The snow picked up as Nicholas raced the flakes home. It was too late to look for the children now.

After Lydia had left the church, he'd stayed in the shadows to see how the congregation would react to her speech. However, Pastor Wisely had quickly dismissed everyone, trapping Nicholas upstairs until the crowd dispersed.

While they'd slowly made their way out, he'd pondered why he'd stayed in the shadows instead of coming to Lydia's defense.

At the top of the rise, his mansion's lamps flickered in the first-story windows, beckoning him like a sailor headed to shore. Except home wasn't where he'd find a stable beach, but rather turbulent waves of second-guessing everything he was doing.

He was the reason Lydia had been accosted tonight, yet she'd fearlessly admitted to her part in their escapades despite the hardships that would bring.

Whereas he'd hidden his mission to avoid the condemnation of his brothers and sisters in Christ.

Publicly declaring what he was about would make everything so much harder. And yet, he and Caroline alone couldn't help all the women and children desiring to be free of the red-light district's clutches.

Perhaps Lydia had been right. If they were given the chance, more people might be willing to help than he'd thought. Mr. Hargrove and the Wiselys had come to her defense tonight. Several more had filed out more slowly than the vocal naysayers, muttering their concern over how the congregation was treating Lydia and the people in the red-light district.

After thumping up the porch stairs, Nicholas tapped the mucky snow off his boots and unlocked the door, letting the welcoming heat warm his face. It was probably a sin to warm such a large place for just himself and his servants, even if it was his own natural gas fields fueling his brand-new furnace.

"Mr. Lowe?"

He spun on his heel to face the night, his neck hairs prickling at the unfamiliar voice in the darkness. "Who's there?" The door clicked shut behind him, and he forced himself not to yank out his pocket knife—it was a woman's voice, after all. But none of his maids would've skulked outside in the blowing snow to talk to him.

A figure unfolded from where she'd sat on the portico's stone ledge.

He held up his hand. "Stay right there and tell me who you are."

The house lights made the snow resting on the woman's cloak glisten. "Well, I'm . . . I'm not sure whether . . . I mean, does it matter what my name is?"

"It matters since you're on my property uninvited."

"I've heard you take in people like me, uninvited even."

It was too cold for talking in circles. "Tell me plainly who you are."

Silence.

This woman had to have a compelling reason to see him if she'd waited in the snow. "If you tell me who you are, I'll let you inside."

She shuffled back.

Was she worried about propriety? "My cook and housekeeper should be in the house since I've yet to have dinner."

"I'm . . . ah, I'm . . ."

His ears hurt and his fingers were numb. "It's too cold for either of us to be out much longer."

"I used to be called Bessie. I've heard you take in prostitutes—not for favors, but to work. No one wants to hire me for a regular job, and no one wants me for favors anymore."

Why hadn't she approached Caroline instead of him? Despite the freezing wind, he felt beads of sweat above his brow. He wiped the moisture off with his woolen coat sleeve.

If this woman knew what kind of women lived beneath his roof—and believed he knew it as well . . .

He looked up at the moon barely glowing behind snow-laden clouds. *You're done with me doing things my way—aren't you?*

If he acknowledged this woman now, it was as good as going public. If she left and told others . . .

He wasn't ready; he'd just escaped revealing his mission back at church.

But he couldn't turn away a shivering, desperate woman just to keep his secrets.

He licked his lips and opened the door. "Come in."

She swept past him.

He closed the door and pulled off his boots to keep from tracking in snow. "Take off your cloak, if you'd like." He could smell thyme, pepper, and rosemary wafting out of the kitchen. "I'm about to have dinner, if you'd join me—"

"I couldn't eat with you." She shook her head, her hood pulled so far forward her face remained in shadow.

He shook off his hat before hanging it on a hook. What did it matter anymore? If he admitted to taking in prostitutes for work, he might as well eat with one. The town would know soon enough.

But how did this woman know already? Although Henri was no longer helping him—and seemingly never had for the right reasons—he didn't believe his friend would expose him. "Who told you to come to me?"

The woman's wool-ensconced arms were pressed tightly against her chest. "That Irish girl with Queenie. She said her sister has been trying to convince her to come here. Since you've taken in several other ladies, Mary said you might take me."

Caroline surely hadn't mentioned to anyone, even her sister, that he was involved with her taking in soiled doves. Had he said something to give himself away the night Henri had discovered Caroline's sister was a prostitute?

Though why bother refuting it now? He pointed to the lady's cape and gestured for her to take it off. "No need to hide. No one will mention seeing you here."

Her arm moved unsteadily to the crown of her head. She dragged down the hood. Her hair spilled over her shoulders, and her gaze locked onto his feet.

He shut his eyes to block out the familiar sores on her face. The pox that crept up from her neck and wandered over her left eye was something he was intimately familiar with.

The same swirl of revulsion that had coursed through him when he'd found Gracie covered with sores on his doorstep returned to wreak havoc with his gut.

He swallowed hard and forced himself to open his eyes.

Gracie's lesions had wounded her vanity on top of killing her slowly. He didn't want to cringe at the sight of Bessie and wound her more than she already was. "Have you seen a doctor?"

She shrugged. "Madam Careless's doctor made it pretty clear I'm hopeless. He's seen me twice, and it wasn't pleasant."

"You're not in the worst stage yet. Maybe Dr. Lindon can be of assistance."

"Maybe." She reached for the back of a nearby chair but stopped herself. The large sore on her hand looked painful. She tucked her hands back around her waist. "I know you probably don't want to take me in, but Madam Careless kicked me out. The only options I have are to move down into a cribhouse for work . . . or something worse." Her voice clamped off. "I've wanted to quit since the very first day, but I was just so desperate. And then it became impossible to leave." She sniffled and rubbed at her eyes with the back of her sleeve. "I never should've left my husband, but . . ."

Nicholas sucked in a breath, a sharp pain piercing his chest.

"But he—"

"Don't say any more, ma'am. It's not for me to judge." The old, familiar ache tightened his insides as if he were experiencing the same anguish Bessie's husband felt over her unfaithfulness.

But what good was his mansion and all the speeches he'd given Lydia if he turned Bessie away just because she reminded him of the pain his late wife caused him?

Even so, he couldn't look at her right now, so he slowly unwound his muffler and draped it on the coatrack, letting his hands travel down the length of it.

He would take her in, but he wouldn't be her best attendant, considering how the echo of Gracie's betrayal had slashed through him when Bessie admitted to adultery.

Knowing Grace had never loved him, he'd been too raw to offer much comfort to her before she died. The first and last time one of his wife's acquaintances had stopped by, the woman had plainly told Gracie she'd gotten what she deserved—and he'd nodded in agreement.

He hadn't bothered to have a doctor assess his wife since he'd practically reveled in what he saw as the vengeance of God on his behalf.

Only after the pox had taken over her brain and turned her into a miserable, raving lunatic did he regret his cruelty.

Unfortunately, he hadn't repented in time to apologize, and the doctor had been called too late to do much good.

But who would nurse Bessie since he couldn't? Caroline was spending much of her days at her sick sister's bedside. Would one of his maids be willing to help? Would they believe a doctor if he told them they wouldn't contract the disease by attending her? Effie would be the most likely maid willing to play nurse, for she seemed the most compassionate.

"Come." His voice petered out, so he cleared his throat to try again. "You can stay upstairs in the green room. Someone will attend you until your symptoms subside or you're cured. Then we can figure out what household duties you can take over."

Bessie sank onto the ornate mahogany table behind her and dissolved into tears.

He fished out his handkerchief and handed it to her. Even if he didn't feel like it, he'd give her what he hadn't given his wife—mercy and the hope of forgiveness. "I'll have Caroline show you to your room, and then you can come eat."

She nodded, still weeping, his handkerchief pressed against her mouth, as if that would stop her breaths from rattling. With any other woman sobbing so hard, he'd be inclined to put a hand on her shoulder to reassure her, but he couldn't.

He knew he was in no danger of contracting her disease, but it would take a while before he could offer her real comfort, to see her as Jesus saw her, not as an echo of his regrets. She'd see through anything less than true compassion, just as Gracie had.

And, in truth, Christ was this woman's only real hope of comfort.

He could certainly tell her about God, but what if a man wasn't the best person to tell her about forgiveness and hope?

Though doubting they'd be willing to come, he decided to ask the moral-society ladies to visit Bessie once she was ready for visitors.

They could decide whether to let God use them or not.

36

Lydia knocked on Nicholas's door a second time, then stepped back to take in the mansion. Standing in front of the grandest structure in Teaville always made her inner romantic sigh, but when it was decorated for Christmas . . . Surely no palace could be prettier. The ivy with red velvet bows spiraling around the portico's grand columns and draping the large wooden door, the candles flickering in the windows, and the cold wind blowing through her hair and numbing her nose made her wish she was in the Christmas spirit. But she couldn't be.

She'd thought she was saving Nicholas from being exposed at Sunday's evening service, but perhaps she'd done the opposite. Her father had come home the next night, drunk and rambling about how Lowe's mansion would make a great hotel, saloon, and dance hall, all in one—especially since he already had the women.

Her heart had frozen in her chest. She'd never, ever heard such a rumor before, and no matter how much she questioned her father, he couldn't tell her any more than that he'd only just heard about it from some chap.

If her father had wind of such a rumor, someone connected to Nicholas likely had too. Had Nicholas heard about what happened Sunday and believed she'd exposed him? Was that why she'd not seen him anywhere around town since she'd stood up to the congregation three days ago? Was he avoiding her?

He was a stickler for keeping his word. If he believed she'd broken hers, the cold shoulder was likely one of the nicer ways Nicholas would show his disapproval.

Her hands shook and her head ached, but not from cold. She'd not slept for two days worrying that he might scorn her, which was half crazy, considering she should be more upset over how the church had treated her. Yet here she stood on his porch instead of meeting with Pastor Wisely or trying to reconcile with Mrs. Little, and she was going to be ill if she didn't find out exactly where she stood with Nicholas.

The housekeeper with the steady eyes and firm jaw opened the door. Miss O'Conner's brow lifted slightly. "Miss King?"

"May I come in?" Her chattering teeth were reason enough to invite herself in, weren't they?

Miss O'Conner backed up, swinging the door wider. "Can I help you?"

She couldn't tell the woman she'd simply come to see what Nicholas thought of her. Especially if he narrowed his eyes and turned his back on her, causing her to melt into a puddle the housekeeper would have to sop up.

But she did have another reason for coming. She walked in and pulled off her gloves. "I came to check on Sadie."

A huge pine tree in the middle of the foyer, alight with what appeared to be hundreds of candles inside little glass lanterns, made her jaw drop. Lydia stepped into the hall, mesmerized by the brilliance.

"Let me help you off with your things." Miss O'Conner took her cloak and hung it on the hall tree draped haphazardly with dark winter accessories.

The smell of the popcorn garland warmed by the tiny fires mingled with the smell of crisp pine needles. Lydia fingered a long red velvet bow trailing down the tree. "It's beautiful."

"You'll need to tell Sadie that," Nicholas's voice rumbled nearby.

Lydia startled and turned to see him nonchalantly leaning against a doorjamb of the entrance to what appeared to be a music room.

"She worked hours to pop and string all that corn." His shoulder rested against the doorframe, his hands in his pockets, and his eyes on her as if she were more mesmerizing than his ten-foot, no, maybe twelve-foot tree. He definitely wasn't looking at her with narrowed eyes or a hardened jaw. So why were her insides fluttering so much?

Her heart beat so far up into her throat, she wasn't sure her tongue had room to produce sound. "Is she here?"

"She's helping Cook with dinner." He walked toward her and stopped close enough to touch her, yet didn't. Nor did he say a thing, just stared at her with eyes much softer than she'd anticipated.

She took a step back toward the tree and fingered one of the red glass balls tucked in between the boughs. "I always wanted glass ornaments for our tree." She tipped her head back, noting that he had far more than one box of glass bulbs dispersed throughout the branches. "And you have so many of them. I've never seen anything more beautiful."

"I have." His velvety smooth baritone made her shiver.

She swallowed and chanced to look at him. Candlelight flickered in his eyes, and he gave her half a smile.

He was right. She had too. No matter how many ornaments or candles Sadie could pack into a tree, it wouldn't make the tree more handsome than the man standing in front of her.

She turned back to the pine and tapped a little bell, producing a dull clack. "Well, yes, a man who lives in a three-story mansion with a garden the town women can't stop talking about in the summer and likely wall-to-wall bookshelves in his library is surrounded by beauty."

He laughed.

At least he didn't seem disappointed in her.

Actually, he seemed rather . . . *un*disappointed.

She moved away from the tree—the candles' heat was making her uncomfortably warm.

"I should've known you'd think the best part of the house would be the library—even though you've never seen it."

"Roses do pale in comparison to walls of books." She shrugged and smiled. "Are you out in your garden often?"

"No." He pulled a pinecone off the Christmas tree and tossed it carelessly in one hand. "But I'm sure you didn't come here to talk to me about my garden."

She pressed her hand against her fluttering heart. "No, but I think I have the answer I came for."

"Which was what?"

"To find out whether or not you were mad at me."

His eyes narrowed. "Did you do something I should be angry about?"

"No, but you hadn't come to see me." She could have clawed her tongue out. How forward, how silly. She pressed her hand to her cheek, but since it was gloved, it did nothing to cool her face. "I mean, I hadn't seen you lately, and I'd gotten used to seeing you." That wasn't much better. She clenched her teeth before she said anything more.

"I've been busy with work." He tucked the pinecone back into the tree and kept his gaze fixed upon it. "And I'm sure you've been occupied with the Littles as they try to suppress the damage you caused to their political goals with your words last Sunday."

So had he been there, or had he just heard about it? "No, I haven't helped them cover up what I said. I stand by every word."

He looked at her, head cocked. "Surely your speech strained your relationship with them. I doubt Sebastian appreciated you telling his mother you could no longer support his political ambitions."

"I no longer worry about what he thinks."

He moved his hand as if he would take hers but let it drop to his side. "If I learned anything in my short years of marriage, it's that you need to learn to compromise. If you and your spouse's goals conflict, the cement of a wedding ceremony will quickly feel the pull and break apart."

"I'm sure that's true. So next time, I'll set my cap for someone who believes the way that I do." She moved over to the window, where he couldn't see her eyes. He might notice she'd already set her cap, far higher than she ought. "Sebastian and I are no longer together, and I wanted to thank you for the library position once again. Though it doesn't calm my mother's fears for me after she's gone, it has mine. I'm thankful my salary will be enough for us to let a room—"

"Dinner is ready." Miss O'Conner's heels clacked on the wooden floor. "Should I put out another place setting?"

"Oh, no, I hadn't meant—"

Nicholas cut her off with a swipe of his hand. "Sadie'd love to see you."

"You let Sadie eat with you?"

"They're all eating with me now. Since your former intended paid me a visit this morning, there's no reason for them not to." He held out his arm, but she could tell his smile was a bit pained. "Join us?"

Her heart bucked in her chest. She believed Nicholas had no evil interest in the women, but to sup with them? Could she add more scandal to herself? "Whatever could Sebastian have wanted that would make you change your dinner arrangements?"

He jiggled his arm a bit. "I can tell you over dinner."

She glanced sideways at his inviting arm. What wouldn't she do to take that arm? Hadn't she already dressed in rags and reexamined her soul just to stay in his presence?

Hoping he wouldn't notice she trembled, she looped her arm around his.

One day she'd not be able to savor the feel of his arm against hers anymore. For only in fairy tales did princes marry paupers, and someday, a rich young lady would catch Nicholas's eye, discern his true character, and they'd be married faster than Lydia's father could lay out a royal flush.

Nicholas pulled out the chair beside Sadie for Lydia, then moved to the head of the table, close enough to monopolize Lydia's conversation if he desired. Caroline and Cook shuffled around the sideboard since they'd refused to join them for dinner, insisting someone had to serve.

Bessie was too ill to come down, but Josephine and Effie sat stiffly to his right. They'd fussed about eating with him too but caved when he'd used his lumberyard-boss voice.

He tried not to laugh at the world under his roof, where a lady sat across from a prostitute at a gentleman's table, but a chuckle escaped anyway. It wasn't a laughing matter, but surely, where had anything more strange occurred?

"We shouldn't be here," Josephine said out of the side of her mouth to Effie. Why did she bother whispering when everyone could hear?

He picked up the opened envelope at the side of his plate and flourished it. "Since I pay for you to be here, Miss Michaels, I will enjoy your company."

Effie hunched in her seat, whereas Josephine sat up straighter and gave him a look.

Oh, that sounded bad. He cleared his throat and rubbed his forehead. "I'm sorry. I just meant there's no reason for us not to enjoy dinner together now."

"Why's that?" Lydia's gaze fastened on the envelope he was tapping against the table. She'd likely seen Sebastian's name across the top.

"This." The letter had blindsided him this morning, but now he better understood why he'd received it. Which almost made him want to kiss the letter—about as much as he wanted to kiss the woman to his left.

And he could now, if he wanted to . . .

Lydia's eyebrows tilted in confusion, making her look more appealing than normal. He might just try to confuse the daylights out of her the next time he saw her to get another glimpse of that endearing expression.

He pulled his gaze off her and extracted the letter. His heart needed to slow down. She'd only just broken things off with Sebastian. He didn't even know if she liked him much, for he had practically ruined her life over the past two months.

And if she attached herself to him, he'd likely ruin what was left of it.

Besides, if she could turn from one man to another so quickly, could she be trusted not to do so later in life?

He slowly unfolded the pages and flattened them. He needed to stop thinking along those lines. The poison of past relationships shouldn't control any possible future ones.

Not that any woman would want to attach herself to him at the moment, not unless she found the center of scandal exhilarating.

"Sebastian delivered this to me today." He pushed the note toward Lydia so she could read it. "Seems I owe the city fines for running an illegal parlor house."

37

"What?" Lydia grabbed the letter from his hands. She'd thought her father had only been spreading rumors about Nicholas having prostitutes in his house. She'd not figured anyone in power would believe it to be true.

Her eyes widened at the amount of money the town expected Nicholas to pay. How had Sebastian come up with so many fines? Did he believe the court would enforce these?

Of course he did. Sebastian had no doubt cackled over every word of legal mumbo jumbo he'd penned. This reeked of jealousy.

The day she'd called things off, Sebastian had implied improper relations with Nicholas had gotten her the librarian job. Had he noticed her feelings for Nicholas and jumped to the wrong conclusions, or was he simply lashing out at the man who'd given her the means to leave him?

"He seems to think if Miss Nance"—he nodded toward Effie—"and Miss Michaels live here, they automatically make my place a house of prostitution." He leaned over and pointed at a line halfway down the page. "And he goes on to indicate that I'm required by law to pay numerous fines for keeping the women on my property. He indicates I shall continue to do so monthly until I throw them out. Also—"

"But this is ridiculous." Lydia shoved the pages away from her.

"Of course it is."

Beside her, Sadie, attired in a youthful blue-and-green winter frock, ate quietly, but the maids across from her only stared at their plates. Cook and Miss O'Conner made a clink or two in the kitchen, but the whole room seemed quieter than a grave.

If she'd never attached herself to Sebastian, these ladies wouldn't have been exposed. "But I don't understand why he'd do this. His slogan is 'making every Kansas county a moral county.' You're doing what he campaigns for—helping stop immorality by getting ladies out of there."

"It's just a slogan, Lydia. I didn't want to tell you before, but I don't think Sebastian's father truly wants to shut down the red-light district. The fines he collects from the saloons and brothels pay his bills, and he won't want to give that income up."

"Sebastian told me the city uses the fines, but his father surely wants the laws to be followed, and Mrs. Little wouldn't support a husband who profits from immorality. And why would he back his son's political campaigns if he didn't agree with him?"

"I only suspect." He turned to the ladies on his right. "Do you know anything about the Littles?"

Miss Nance suddenly became extremely interested in the roast beef on her plate, and the wisps of honey-blond curls that had escaped her cap hid her eyes. But Miss Michaels turned her sharp green eyes toward Nicholas. "I never bothered learning the men's names, not that they often used their real ones when . . . when"— she glanced over at Lydia and gave her an apologetic look—"when they visited. But I know many of them were men of high standing in the community. Councilmen, police officers—"

"I can't believe that." Lydia wrung her hands. "At least I don't want to. And I'm not sure we should be talking about this in front of Sadie."

The young lady beside her no longer looked like the worldly woman she'd rescued just over a week ago, who likely knew more about the ways of men and women than Lydia might ever know. But still . . .

Lydia turned back to Nicholas. "What are you going to do?"

"I'm going to make sure you eat something." He slid the biscuits closer to her. "Other than that, I'm unsure."

"We're leaving." Miss Michaels smashed her crumbled biscuit on her plate. "Other than Bessie, who's going back to her ma when she's well, there's only me and Effie and Sadie. We talked it over, and we won't be giving you any more trouble."

Nicholas shoved the plate of ham toward Lydia. "If the judge finds me guilty of this nonsense, I still have to pay fines whether you three are here or not. Leaving doesn't stop what's already in motion."

"But we can save you from future fines," Miss Nance whispered.

"I don't deserve them even if you are here. I'm not running a brothel." His fist hit the table.

Lydia's empty coffee cup clattered onto its side. She felt like hitting the table herself—or at least clobbering Sebastian the next time she saw him. "Are you sure leaving's wise?" It might save Nicholas from scandal, but surely scandal was a light consequence compared to what these women would face. And what if their testimony could clear Nicholas of Sebastian's accusations?

If she'd feared how she'd be treated by simply being nice to these women, then what treatment would they endure out in the world without Nicholas's protection?

Miss Michaels glanced at her shy friend. "I'm not going to lie, we're not sure it's a good idea. Finding work other than prostitution is going to be difficult." She scowled at her plate. "But it was hard enough here, hiding and acting like we don't exist, knowing no one would ever accept us. Knowing we'd never get to go out, do anything—"

"We'd have to go farther than we've ever been, and we'd have to lie," Miss Nance volunteered.

"There's bound to be trouble if our lies find us out." Miss Michaels huffed. "But what else is there to do? Who'd hire us if we told the truth? And I'm not sure lying is gonna keep people from seeing right through us. But we're going to try, for Sadie. Try to get her into a school . . ."

Sadie flashed a smile at Lydia, causing a lump to form in her throat. If only one or two things had gone differently that night, would this girl even have had a chance at school? According to Miss Michaels and Nicholas, she might not have much of one even now.

Oh, how had she ever believed her life had been miserable? Sure, her father had left a handprint on her face or bruises on her backside occasionally, and when her mother died, she'd have to fend for herself, but at least she had respectability.

When she'd decided to end things with Sebastian, all she'd had to say was *no* and that had finished it. Even if she couldn't have escaped the relationship, she'd only have had to endure tedious dinner conversations and perhaps a longing for a husband who'd love her better. But these ladies couldn't extricate themselves so easily—or perhaps at all.

"Sadie might be able to have a normal life since she hasn't, uh . . . worked long, and she's young." Miss Nance wiped her mouth on a napkin despite the fact nothing on her plate looked disturbed. "We'll try for her."

Nicholas cleared his throat. "Now, let's not do anything rash. We have time to think."

Miss Nance ducked her head, and Miss Michaels sighed before grasping her fork and moving noodles around her plate again.

But did they really have time? Or had Sebastian already ruined everything Nicholas had done to help these women?

Knowing what Sadie faced if they couldn't escape, what could she do to help?

Oh, Lord, if there is anything I can do, I'll do it. You allowed me to extricate myself from my mistakes. You've forgiven me all I've done and have blessed me with a job, though I am undeserving considering how I've looked down on people more desperate than myself. And I've ruined these ladies' hope to be secreted here because of my wishy-washy heart. Whatever I can do, even if it hurts me, it couldn't be worse than what they're facing.

274

38

They ate in silence, but the thoughts swirling around in Nicholas's head were anything but peaceful. Maybe he didn't need to worry about what to do anymore. It seemed God was changing everything.

He couldn't argue that his maids should stay, not with that letter under his plate. How had he believed he could continue keeping their secret? He'd changed few people's minds in the past handful of years. Having only Lydia and Caroline supporting him wasn't enough to fight the backlash the politicians would stir up.

And considering the over-the-top fines mentioned in the letter, it was clear Sebastian had grown attached to Lydia and believed it was somehow Nicholas's fault he'd lost his girl.

Nicholas looked over at her as she sliced her potatoes with a faraway look. When she'd broken things off with Sebastian, had she mentioned him in some way that made Sebastian think she might have feelings for him, or had the man simply not liked how he'd turned Lydia against his method of campaigning against immorality?

He'd hand over his entire fortune to know what she'd said.

She caught his gaze, and he schooled his features.

He rubbed a hand over his face and turned to the women whose immediate futures depended on him. "I'm afraid you may be right, Miss Michaels. I've prayed you'd be able to rejoin society here, but maybe that's not what you are supposed to do."

Effie shook her head at Josephine. "We'll never have friends, besides each other." She looked at Lydia and shrugged. "You wouldn't even be eating with us if it weren't for Mr. Lowe. And he only helps us because he's God's angel of mercy."

Before he could clear his mouth to refute that, Lydia spoke. "You're right, Miss Nance. I . . . I wouldn't be here except for Mr. Lowe. I didn't think we'd have anything to say to each other, but if we could find some common interests, perhaps we could become friends?"

He sat back in his chair. Friends? Had she really come that far?

"You mean that?" Effie sounded skeptical.

Nicholas gestured toward Josephine. "She reads."

"Only dime novels." Josephine shook her head. "I'm sure Miss King doesn't—"

"Have you read Libbey's *Daisy Brooks*?" Lydia clasped her hands in front of her like she was praying Josephine had read it. "The wayward child, the dead mother, the kidnapped babe, the beggar demanding the key—all stuffed into the first chapter? I finished that one within a day."

"No, but did you read her *Pretty Madcap Dorothy*?" Josephine's face brightened, but when Lydia shook her head, she went back to frowning.

"You should." Nicholas fiddled with his biscuit. "It's about a girl who loves books as much as you do, works in a book-binding factory, gets into all sorts of trouble."

They all turned to look at him, their eyebrows crazily cocked.

He shrugged. "Miss Michaels left it on the table one day, so I skimmed through it during breakfast. Mostly girlish nonsense." He wouldn't tell them he'd read the entire silly thing.

Lydia's grin wriggled adorably. If pointing out how dime novels were nothing but over-the-top dramatics would make her eyes light like that, he'd read all of Laura Jean Libbey's tomes.

"I appreciate you trying to find something to talk to us about, Miss King." Effie gave Lydia a soft smile. "But we can't stay here now that it's hurting Mr. Lowe."

"And we won't be accepting any money to be housed elsewhere." Josephine speared him with a glance. "So don't even try."

He cleared his throat and took another bite. What was it with these ladies being so set against accepting monetary help when they needed assistance of every kind? He'd just have to buy them stuff before they left, as he'd done with Roxie. "I won't argue, but if you reconsider, you can stay. I don't care about fines."

And maybe they could stay. Lydia had actually tried to befriend them. If she could change so much in two months, surely there was hope for others.

"Maybe it can work out for other doves, but not for us, not while there's an uproar." Josephine nodded slightly toward Sadie. "It ain't good for her to be here either." She placed her wadded-up napkin on her plate and stood. "I can't eat any more. Are you ready, Sadie?"

The girl frowned at her plate, the only empty one on the table. "Is there dessert?"

Nicholas laughed. "Don't worry, Miss Michaels. I'll send her down with Miss O'Conner as soon as she's finished."

When the three of them each had a slice of pecan pie, Lydia sipped at her coffee. "Won't this place seem empty without maids in it?" She shook her head. "I've never heard rumors that you've courted any woman in town, but now that you don't have the maids you could get . . ." Her voice trailed off, and she fidgeted. "Well, of course you'd still have to have maids, though . . ." She swirled a spoon in her coffee, as if mesmerized.

He'd never thought of looking for a wife again until lately, but that wasn't because he feared a wife wouldn't want maids of their background working at his mansion. But now that Lydia . . .

No, contemplating marriage now was unwise. She'd just broken off with Sebastian, and he'd only known her for two months.

He'd courted Gracie for five before he proposed, and he'd been wrong—so very wrong.

But his throbbing heart kept ramming his chest, and he couldn't pull in any air. He couldn't keep lying to himself.

God help him, he wanted another wife.

He glanced up at the ceiling. *Her, Lord. I want her.*

Admitting to God the desire of his heart took his breath away. Now that she wasn't with Sebastian, he had plenty of time to think things through in detail, make sure this was right.

No rush. They should just continue to get to know each other.

Sadie scraped the last bit of gooey filling off her dish. "May I be excused?"

Nicholas nodded, and the girl popped up and planted a kiss on Lydia's cheek before scurrying away with her dirty plate.

"Good night, dear." Lydia's hand flew to the precious spot. A warm stain of tears rimmed her eyes, but she blinked to keep them from falling.

How could she have ever thought that helping people in the red-light district was none of her concern? The spring in Sadie's step was because she'd had the courage to steal her away from a madam's clutches, and if she hadn't, would anybody have saved her?

And yet, she'd only done so because she knew Nicholas would help—the first thing she'd told Mr. Parker was to drive her to him.

Nicholas shoved away the pie slice he'd barely touched. "Since you're finished, how about I walk you home?"

She tried not to let her hands tremble as she dabbed at her mouth with a napkin. If he was worried about her safety, she could remind him he had a driver for this very purpose—and that it was rather cold for him to walk when he didn't need to. But a little cold never hurt anybody. "All right."

He pulled out her chair and preceded her into the hallway, where he retrieved their coats. When he helped her on with hers, she couldn't keep from wishing this could be an everyday occurrence—except for the going home part.

A strong gust of cold flooded the entryway when Nicholas

opened the door, causing the lights to flicker. She glanced back at the beautiful Christmas tree still aglow, and then they pulled up their collars, tugged down their hats, and with hands in pockets, forged off into the elements.

All right, maybe she should've reminded him he had a driver . . . but then she'd not have this time to talk to him—if she could do so with her chattering teeth.

There had to be something wrong in her head—or perhaps her heart—for choosing to walk in this weather just to steal a few extra minutes with him. Thankfully, by the time they made it down his small hill, her body felt warmer.

At the fenceless gate, Nicholas stopped to rehang a wreath before continuing to plod toward town.

Why had he asked her to walk if he wasn't going to talk?

She might as well fill the silence with some of the clamoring questions in her head. "Can I ask you something . . . personal?"

He shrugged. "As long as you don't mind if I choose not to answer."

"Fair enough." It took her a bit to summon up the courage to ask him something that would likely make him uncomfortable. "My question is . . . why did you build the mansion since Gracie wasn't around to enjoy it?"

He shuffled along for a while. "Guilt," he finally answered.

"You had to be drowning in it to spend so much."

"Yes." He glanced at her for a second before returning to watching his feet. "The pox is normally a slow killer, but not long after the doctor informed me of that, she died of complications, an apoplexy. I didn't figure out what a heel I was until after she died."

She chuckled. "I just can't imagine you as a heel."

"I bet it's difficult." He looked over at her, a ghost of a smile under his serious eyes. "Believe it or not, I've not always been sunshine and roses."

Definitely not sunshine and roses, more a light in the darkness with a hint of sandalwood.

"Since the day we married, Gracie told me she wanted a house

with a ballroom, a bowling alley, a conservatory, and all the rest."
He looked back over his shoulder.

She looked back too. The roofline of his mansion just slightly visible above a stand of trees.

"But I refused her." He trudged forward again, head down, as if he found the shine on his shoes engrossing. "I told her I couldn't afford to build it, which wasn't exactly true. I was simply more focused on stockpiling money than making her happy."

"Well, a mansion isn't exactly a reasonable request." Had his wife also asked for an elevator, the forced-air system, the Tiffany lamp, and the hand-painted Italian wallpaper? She'd heard the New York lamp maker traveled to Teaville to hang the lamp personally, and the Italian designer had actually crossed the ocean to paint the walls himself.

"No, but a pearl necklace, fashionable hats, a trip to the theater . . . I could have given her all of those when she asked for them."

"No woman actually needs those things." Lydia repositioned her well-worn scarf since the wind had broken through. She'd once dreamed about being that rich, but with a decent meal sometimes being difficult to obtain, she no longer cared about much more than essentials—and books.

"I had money enough, but I was too tightfisted. Would ten dollars every now and then have been a terrible price to pay to show her I loved her?" He clamped his arms tighter to his body. "But the real problem was I didn't love her. I loved money more than her, and after two years together, she knew it. She went off to find love with someone else."

Lydia's step faltered. He'd never loved his wife? What had Gracie possessed that he'd married her without love?

Lydia had nothing worth giving a man other than how she felt about him.

And after this mishap with Sebastian, she wouldn't marry unless love was exactly what her groom was looking for.

Nicholas's slumped posture and slow gait bespoke sadness

and self-loathing. Too bad he hadn't offered her his arm, or she would've given him a good squeeze.

His wife hadn't been a saint, though. He shouldn't beat himself up. "Gifts don't equal love."

"They did to her. And if I had really loved her, I would've compromised. But I'm not really known for that, now, am I." He flashed her a stiff grin, then shrugged. "When she returned, any affection I'd once had for her had evaporated since she'd left me for a lover—though I'd taken up with one myself."

Her step completely faltered this time. Things were going from bad to worse now.

"Making money was my mistress."

She blew out a breath and sped up before he realized she'd lagged behind.

"Once Gracie left me, I threw myself into wealth's arms with a vengeance—investing, concocting new business schemes, speculating. Not until she died did I realize I'd never loved my wife more than money. Though by then, my wealth had blossomed." He pulled a hand out to rake his hair but knocked off his hat instead. He bent to pick it up and smashed it back on, but he didn't continue walking, so she stopped beside him. "There are so many more people God ought to have given my wealth to."

Hadn't she herself been more worried about Sebastian's money than his love? Yet God had blessed her with a library job anyway—which she didn't deserve. "God knew what you'd end up spending your money on, so He believed you deserved to have it."

He smiled, but looked at her pointedly. "No one else thinks I spend my money wisely."

Lydia squirmed under his glare, wishing they were still walking. "You can't blame others for not knowing what you do in secret."

"But should they judge me?"

"No," she whispered, staring at an icy crack in the sidewalk.

"Don't think I'm being hard on you." He lifted her chin. "I know you don't take exception to my miserly ways anymore." He gave her a halfhearted smile and let his hand fall. "And you've shown me that nursing grudges doesn't change the behavior of those I resent."

"If I picked up a dictionary and looked up *miser*, I doubt the definition would apply to someone who builds a mansion."

"Only if I enjoy it alone."

She bit her lip and looked down. Would he hint at needing a family to fill it up? Take her hand and—

"So that's why I figured I'd use it for ministry." He started walking again.

Her cheeks heated. Silly girl. She'd told herself countless times her romantic notions about Nicholas were ridiculous, but she evidently couldn't help herself.

As if Nicholas would propose to a woman far below him in both station and wealth. Marrying Miss Renfroe would make far better sense than choosing her.

He stopped when he realized she wasn't beside him.

She rushed toward him. She needed to think practically, as he was. "Wouldn't a hotel or boardinghouse be better suited for taking in women?"

"I never meant to use it to house ex-prostitutes. I built it telling myself I'd sell it—give the profit to the church. Though, honestly, I just built it to make myself feel better. But after my cousin Roxanna came, I thought God was leading me to use it as I have been."

She frowned and mentally envisioned the people she'd seen around the mansion. "I haven't met Roxanna."

"She's no longer here."

"But she encouraged you to take in these women?"

"No, she'd shamed our family by going into prostitution, but all I'd been told was that she'd been disowned." He looked up at the sky as if he could see something behind its layers of wispy clouds illuminated by the waning sunlight. "When some john threatened her life, my family wouldn't help her. She had to leave South Carolina. But knowing life out west would be much harder in her field of work, she didn't want to take her son along. I'm the only one who lives beyond the Mississippi, and having heard

282

my wife dallied elsewhere, Roxie hoped I'd take her son as my heir. She didn't know I was already a widower."

"So you couldn't help her?" Considering how he'd taken Robbie into his arms and fought so hard to keep Pepper from taking Angel to a brothel, how could he have refused to take in a child?

"I did help, but not in the way she'd hoped. I asked them to live with me, and they did . . . for a while. I thought to save Roxie from her profession so she could keep her son." He sighed. "But it looks like I was wrong to believe I could change the world."

"So she went back to . . . ?"

He huffed, the white cloud of his breath obscuring his face for a second. "No, she became a mail-order bride instead."

"Really?" She knew some men out west were desperate, but if they were willing to marry a prostitute, wouldn't there be plenty to choose from out there? "Did the groom know she was a . . . Did he know her history?"

"Amazingly, yes, and I recently got another letter from her. Seems he wasn't lying about accepting her as she is. She seems truly happy. And he's even a religious man."

Why did he act so depressed when he'd just told her a story of hope? "Why do you sound so defeated?" She pulled her hand from her warm pocket and snagged him.

He stopped and frowned down at her hand clutching his arm.

She softened her grip. "Don't you see? If this religious man came to accept her, then you *can* change the world, one person at a time."

He drew away. "Larry didn't come to accept her because of anything I did. I've had three maids return to prostitution, two kill themselves, one who's currently dying, and now my remaining three are leaving, hoping to survive by pretending to be something they aren't. Roxanna was my only success—though it wasn't my idea for her to pursue personal advertisements. Actually, that makes my success rate zero." He tipped his head back to look at the overcast sky again. "I need to stick with lumber and gas."

Lydia wanted to smooth the curls hanging over the furrows on his brow, but considering he'd just drawn away from her, she put her hands back in her pockets. "Don't give up. Even if you don't succeed at everything, you've succeeded at something. Sadie could still be in a brothel right now, but instead she has a chance."

"Not much of one."

"It's still a chance she didn't have."

"And you were the one who rescued her, not me."

"If it weren't for you, I wouldn't have." A smile split her face. "You see? You've had one success—me."

He slowed, and then turned to look at her. "And what shall I do with you?"

Lydia's internal temperature shot up with the intent look in his eye. The nuance of his voice hinted at so much more than what he'd said, but it couldn't mean . . .

Her desires had to be coloring her interpretation. "I'd intended to join Se— " Her tongue turned to sludge at having to bring up Sebastian right now. "I'd planned on joining the Little's crusade against the red-light districts, but I'd much rather follow your plans for helping those people. I believe in what you're doing, even if it makes me uncomfortable sometimes."

"I appreciate that, but it looks like I won't need help anymore. My house will soon be empty."

"Will you sell it then?" If he sold his house, he'd likely not stay in Teaville.

Her heart plummeted into her stomach and a small groan escaped. She wanted him to stay—and yet, she'd be better off if he left and dashed all her romantic hopes before they got worse.

His expression lost its intensity, and he turned his face away from her. "I might if I can't think of another use for it that the city won't tax me to the heavens for."

She watched a buggy drive by on the quiet road. A child's head popped out of the oilcloth-covered window and promptly disappeared back inside.

What if . . . "What about children?"

His eyebrows raised.

"Like Sadie and Annie's three."

"What about them?"

"What if you turned your place into an orphanage?"

"The poor farm in Liberty takes orphans, doesn't it?"

"Maybe, but will those children receive the understanding there that we could give them here? What about evil-natured men who find out about an orphan with a past like Sadie's and think to adopt one . . . will the superintendent be careful to let children as hard as Pepper only go to loving homes? Your cousin came to you for this exact reason—to find a safe place for her son."

Despite her numb toes, Lydia nearly bounced at the rightness of the idea. "Surely giving these children a decent future would be easier than turning prostitutes back into ladies. If you provided them with schooling and proper care outside of the red-light district, even if no one adopted them, they'd have more of a chance at becoming respectable adults. Annie's children weren't even considered worth a policeman's concern."

His face was a study in concentration. "Maybe . . . but how can I just ignore the women?"

"We start by changing the townsfolk's hearts with the children, then work back toward the women. We'll start by getting the city to realize that fining you is ridiculous, and then—"

"Who'd help me with the children?" His eyes weren't shining like hers probably were. "There could be a great many."

"Well, I would, of course, but I can't be there every day. And surely Miss O'Conner?"

"I don't know. She's focused on the women, because of her sister." His voice descended in quick defeat, making her want to shake some hope into him.

She was surprised anything could dishearten him since he always seemed so sure of himself. "Present this matter to the church. They want to help, even if you don't like their methods. And yes, maybe you couldn't convince them to talk to a prostitute right now, but force them to grapple with the plight of the children—look how that got me." The memory of Sadie dressed like a sporting woman crumpled on that alleyway stoop made tears fog her eyes. "If I'd have known children were . . ." Her voice disappeared, her throat too tight to say anything more.

"We'd be taking on the biggest challenge of our lives." He exhaled, filling the air with a white puffy cloud. "How will I be able to keep up with my businesses and the children if I'm not able to gather enough volunteers? What if people's opinions never change and your reputation is shredded? And would your heart survive if the children you cared for chose to return to their previous lives? You need to count the risk."

She swallowed hard and dropped her gaze. "As long as you want my help, you'll have it."

39

Flipping to the next page clumsily with her gloved fingers, Lydia couldn't help but step lightly as she walked home. Not only was *A Little Princess* promising to be a good story, but she was getting to read a novel the same year it came out! Several crates of new books had been delivered this morning, making it difficult to make her rounds in the coach knowing they awaited her at the library.

And thankfully Nicholas hadn't told her she had to put books in rotation before reading them.

The sound of an arguing couple down the street only enhanced the tense descriptions going on in little Sara Crewe's schoolroom. The headmistress would surely turn out to be quite the villain.

But the closer Lydia got to her house, the less the pages' drama held her attention. And the more she was certain the argument disturbing the neighborhood was her parents'.

Since Mama's sickness, they'd fought so little—whether from Mama's weakness or Papa caring enough not to upset her, Lydia didn't know—but whatever had held them back had broken.

"I can't believe you'd do this to us!" Mama sounded ready to crack.

"How else could I get money for your medical bills?" Behind

the curtains, Papa's silhouette raised its hands and waved in frustration.

"You're blaming me for this?"

"Well, you're the one who encouraged Lydia to think so highly of herself. A woman with smarts only makes more work for a man. And Little was going to take her. Do you know what I had to do to get him to even entertain the notion?"

Lydia pressed closer to the front door, her heart in her throat. What had Papa done, and why did he have to do anything? Did he think no man would have her unless he intervened?

"I don't want to hear any more. You've told me enough." Mama's shaky voice killed Lydia's curiosity and shamed her for listening from outside. Mama wasn't fit to be fighting with anyone.

"Then fix it, or we're out on our backsides." A thump was followed by the brittle sound of rattling china and glass. He'd probably punched a wall. "Talk some sense into Lydia, or I'll beat it into her."

Lydia took her hand off the doorknob, her insides shaking. He hadn't laid a hand on her for quite a while. Why now?

What had Papa expected to gain from her understanding with Sebastian?

Heavy footfalls headed her direction, so she scurried down the stairs and to the side of the house just as Papa blew through the front door. He plowed down the footpath and crashed through the gate.

A block away, Papa turned down an alley toward downtown, and Lydia stepped out of the shadows.

Before forcing herself inside, she relaxed her face—like she used to do when she was little and Mama came to check if she'd slept through one of their many rows.

"I'm home, Mama." Her voice sounded a touch too bright.

No response. If she hadn't heard their spat, she'd have assumed Mama was sleeping, though if Mama had fallen asleep so quickly, Lydia had more to worry about than Papa's rant.

"Mama?" Again no answer. She quit unbuttoning her coat and headed for the cramped parlor.

Her mother lay limp against the worn sofa's arm, her hands buried in her hair as if she needed to keep her skull from exploding.

Lydia peeled off a glove and pressed her hand against Mama's forehead. Clammy but not hot. "Do you have a headache? Have you taken your medicine?"

Mama shook her head but quit with a groan. "Medicine won't help."

"Then let's get you to bed." Lydia snaked her arm under Mama's.

Despite being no match for Lydia, she attempted to push away. "How could you?" Mama's hurt whisper sliced through her.

Did Mama believe Papa—that she'd done something wrong? He'd always blamed her for their troubles, most likely because she confronted him more often than was wise.

"Did I forget to help you with something? I didn't mean to be gone so long."

Her mother's pained eyelids parted, but only halfway. "Your father risked a lot to get Sebastian to court you, and you broke it off without asking us."

Lydia wanted to grab her mother's hand, to comfort where there was obviously pain, but she feared Mama would yank herself free. "I couldn't love him, Mama."

"What is this about love?" Mama's face scrunched as if she smelled something foul. "It only leads to foolish decisions."

Her throat clogged at her mother's dismissal of the one thing she now wanted.

"I told you Sebastian would take care of you. And now we have nowhere to go."

"Papa lost the house?"

Mama nodded. "Missed a loan payment. The bank sent him a letter."

But Sebastian had said he'd fixed it so this wouldn't happen. Had she hurt him so badly he used all his lawyer know-how to undo what he'd done just weeks ago?

Mama picked up a customer's shirtwaist and yanked at a seam, despite clearly being in no condition to work. "You need to get Sebastian to take you back. He could fix this."

Lydia's mouth turned dry. She rarely disobeyed her mother, and after the doctor had declared death imminent, she hadn't done so once. "I can't." Nicholas's face swam before her mind's eye. "I won't."

She might not ever be worthy of Nicholas, but she wouldn't do anything that would shut her out of his presence forever.

When she was ready to give up dreaming of a knight condescending to love a scullery maid, she'd search for a man to wed that she felt something for. But she wasn't ready to chuck away her daydream yet—not for Sebastian.

Mama struggled to sit up. "How could you do this to me? I'll not last a week on the street." She wheezed and searched for a handkerchief.

Considering her breathing, Mama might not last a week even if she had a handful of servants attending her, the best medicine money could buy, and the comfort of having her daughter under Sebastian's roof.

Lydia pressed a hand to her mother's back as she hacked into a stained linen. She then braced Mama's shoulders as the coughs escalated until her mother almost passed out. "Breathe, Mama."

When her coughing fit ended, her skin looked grayer. Mama leaned her head back and closed her eyes. "Make amends with Sebastian. It's the only way."

"He won't take me b—"

"Beg, then." The tense lines in her face relaxed only enough to look stiff. "His father's calling in his debts. At least buy your father some time and try."

"I'm sure Mr. Lowe could help." She cringed after saying that aloud. He'd think her father the kind of charity case that didn't merit aid. And she'd loathe seeing any of Nicholas's money in Papa's hands.

Mama shook her head. "Mr. Lowe gives nothing to no one."

"He gave me a job." Recalling the librarian position lifted the gloom. "And some sewing machines to the moral society." If only she could reveal the other things he did.

"No one's ever said he isn't a fair employer. But I can't do anything worth pay anymore." She gestured to the pile of garments beside her. "Mrs. Carpenter has been too gracious already. I should've finished these five days ago."

Lydia glanced at the overflowing basket, and then at her full basket waiting on the other side of the rocking chair. She'd have to stay up late and get them both caught up.

She rubbed Mama's arm. "But even if Papa loses this house, I can afford to get us a small room in a boardinghouse. I bet Mr. Lowe would allow us to rent the library's second floor for a while. At some point he intends to expand enough to use both floors, but now it's only used for storage."

"Is there a kitchen?"

"No, but we'd manage."

"Your father would never consent to living there."

"Then Papa can sleep on the street."

Mama's eyes flew open. "Hold your tongue."

With effort, she did. Mama looked like death as it was. Lydia lowered her voice and rubbed Mama's shoulder. "I'm sure God will make a way if—"

"He did, and you threw it back."

The pain of her words was as palpable as that of a slap. Mama hadn't a fever to blame those stinging words on. "Don't panic, Mama."

"Please go back to Sebastian." Mama's eyes turned glassy and wet. "Your father says he'd take you back. I need to know you're taken care of."

"But Mr. Lowe—"

"Won't help your father, even if he would help you." The tears in Mama's eyes spilled over onto her cheeks.

Lydia licked her lips. She wanted to say she couldn't care less about what happened to Papa since he'd never cared for her, but Mama still cared about Papa.

"If Jacob no longer has this house, no longer has me, or you, he'll . . . he'll . . ."

Lydia grabbed her mother's shaky hands and clamped them tight. Neither one of them needed to voice what might happen to him. None of the possibilities were pleasant, but Lydia was having a hard time caring. All she wanted was for her mother's last days to be peaceful, and right now, he was responsible for that not happening.

Well, along with her leaving Sebastian, but Papa wasn't making things any better.

"He's your father, Lydia."

"I don't wish him ill." She took a deep breath. "But I just don't think I can help him. His debts are his own."

"Sebastian can help us, but you have to apologize. If he'll take you back, then I won't have to worry about anything."

Lydia stared at the translucent skin on Mama's hands as she rubbed them. It seemed her mother wasn't going to be swayed from this train of thought, and considering her rapid breathing, she needed to stop fighting her—needed to do something to calm her. "I'll talk to him."

Maybe she could convince Sebastian to intervene and gain them time to make a payment, get his father to give them more time to pay whatever needed to be repaid, or . . . something that might calm Mama's fears.

Just as long as whatever that something was didn't lead to the altar.

40

Lydia climbed the stairs to Sebastian's second-story office, the sound of hushed male voices mumbling behind the door. At the top, she raised her hand to knock but stopped at the mention of her name. She held her breath, then heard her name again.

Looking behind her and seeing no one on the street at the bottom of the covered stairwell, she hesitated. She really shouldn't eavesdrop twice in one day.

Hang it all, she'd know better how to approach Sebastian for assistance if she knew where she stood.

As quietly as she could, she leaned toward the door, wincing when a board beneath her creaked. The men's conversation continued without hesitation, though, so she pressed her ear against the door and held her breath.

" . . . don't see why I should care."

Sebastian replied, "If she keeps going, someone will tell her."

"It's not like half the men in this town don't already know. If Lydia finds out and tells those moral-society ladies, who cares? Your ma'll discredit her, easy. I've got plenty of men who'll vouch for seeing her alone after dark with Lowe."

"Lowe." Sebastian's growl sent shivers snaking up her spine. "If he didn't have ties to Beauchamp, I'd expose them both. I can't believe the holier-than-thou stuff Ma said she spouted off at church, considering how she's—" Something thumped and cut off his words. "I don't know why Beauchamp insists on taking up for him. He's obnoxious, self-righteous—"

"Money buys people."

"He might own half the city—and Beauchamp's loyalty too, evidently—but half of Teaville's men and the women—well, prostitutes anyway—answer to you."

Lydia leaned against the door to steady herself. Had she heard correctly? Sebastian's father was financing prostitutes? Were the Littles campaigning one thing but doing another?

"Since you dragged me into this, you'd think you could get me the one thing I wanted." Sebastian huffed. "Well, I suppose I can get another girl, though likely not nearly as attractive."

The door fell away, and she stumbled inside onto her hands and knees.

Mr. Little frowned down at her. "I thought I heard something." He yanked her up by her shoulder, his tight grip digging into her muscle.

"I'm sorry." Her quickened heartbeat and erratic breathing made her words raspy. "I just came here to talk to—"

"Cut the lies." Mayor Little hauled her toward a brown leather chair near Sebastian's desk. "You'll answer for every one of them."

"I really am here to talk to Sebastian. My mother's upset." She tried to pull away from the mayor, but his grip was firm, too firm. She refused to let the pain mar her face. She looked at Sebastian, who'd remained seated, his shoulders slumped.

The expression on his face wasn't anger, like his father's, but pity.

For some reason, that made her heart drop even lower.

The mayor shoved her into the chair. "You make it a habit to lie against a door before you knock on it?"

"No." Her face heated, giving her away. "I mean, I did hear my name. . . ."

"This"—Mayor Little poked his cigar stub at her—"is why you don't court a woman with more than a grade-school education.

Thinks she can pull something over on you." He stabbed his cigar in a tray, bending it like a caterpillar. "Get rid of her."

"It's not like I'd kill her for you." Sebastian glowered, and she lost her breath along with the ability to sit up straight.

Kill? She crimped her eyes shut. *Oh, God, help!* Her fingernails dug into her armrests. "I didn't hear anything important."

"Saying that only means you did." The mayor glowered at her.

She pressed her trembling lips together to keep from saying anything else—her overactive heartbeat was beating her brains into a pulp.

Sebastian only stared at her, his hands steepled against his chin.

"You won't get elected if you let pity sway you, son. She's heard too much and has Lowe's ear." He glanced at her with narrowed eyes before turning back to his son. "There's a first time for everything."

Sebastian's jaw worked with indecision.

Surely he wasn't actually considering killing her. Surely she couldn't have been so stupid to have almost married someone who'd contemplate such a thing.

This had to be an act to intimidate her.

And by the way her heart was racing, it was working.

"She'll marry me now." Sebastian sat back and took a deep breath. "She has no choice."

She found her backbone and straightened. "I certainly do have a choice."

The mayor yanked her up by her upper arm and pulled her against him, his moist breath hot against her ear. "If I were you, I'd not argue with my son. He's weak enough to give your lying self the chance to continue breathing." He shoved her back into the chair.

Her head snapped against the headrest, and she grit her teeth to keep from crying out.

"I don't even know why you want her."

"She's a lot of things I don't want, but I need a morally upright woman. And what other one do we have any hold over?"

"Her respectability flies out the window the second anyone else realizes Lowe's been bedding her."

"What! We're . . . I'm . . ." Flames engulfed her face. "Don't talk about Nicholas like that. We're not . . . not . . ."

"She's too innocent to even say it." Sebastian huffed. "That was all conjecture on my part anyway."

The mayor sat down on the edge of the desk and stared at her as if he could tell whether she'd been involved in an indiscretion just by looking at her.

Since she couldn't sit still with her heart beating fitfully, who knows what he thought he saw.

"I still want a wife." Sebastian nervously rubbed his hands together. "And now I won't have to simper. I can plainly tell her what's expected and what will happen if she doesn't comply."

"Fine, if that's how you want to keep her quiet." The mayor grabbed his fancy cane and went to grab his hat off a rack. "You've proven you can handle others well enough, so I'll trust you to take care of things later if it doesn't work."

He gave Sebastian a halfhearted wave and pointed at her with his cane. "You'd best comply unless you want your mother to pay for your foolishness. And believe me, I can make her pay." He left with a slam, his footsteps thumping down the exterior stairs.

She hugged herself, trying to keep from trembling. "I don't understand how you think I'd be willing to marry you now that—"

"Stop." He put up his hand. "I'm going to make this simple. Believe me, I tormented myself plenty before I realized it's better just to go along. If you don't marry me, my father can have your mother out on the street tomorrow, your father in a jail cell, your job taken away—"

"He can't take my job."

"Oh, can't he?" He shook his head as if she were a bedraggled kitten, mewling pitifully. "All he has to do is have the commissioners rezone 142 Maple Street to shut the library down."

"Then, Mr. Lowe could move the library. Rezoning twice would make your machinations obvious—people would see right through it."

"It would only be obvious that I was lashing out in pain over my broken heart." He slapped a dramatic hand to his chest.

"I'll . . . I'll tell people what you're doing."

He crossed his arms. "Come on, Lydia. I know you're smart. Let's say it is possible to convince my father you're no threat, you wouldn't be stupid enough to talk. Who'd believe you over him?"

She took some time to breathe evenly to settle her heart.

He sighed and shook his head. "If you utter one peep about what he's doing, he'll come down on you like a tornado."

"But people would see what he was doing."

He raised a brow, his mouth askew. "No, he'd arrange things to look like your family was getting what you deserved. You are, in fact, the child of an unfaithful, gambling man who—"

"Unfaithful?" Her voice quavered. Papa loved Mama—maybe not as deeply as a husband ought to, but he still loved her.

But then, what kind of man stole from his own daughter, was more concerned about having enough liquor to drink than whether his wife had medicine, spent nearly every night in the town's sporting section . . .

She groaned with a wave of nausea over her naïveté.

"I could prove it with one or two witnesses, if need be, and arrange another church-sanctioned meeting to get your father stricken from the church register."

He'd orchestrated the prayer meeting fiasco? Now she really was going to be sick. She pressed a hand against her throat until she felt she could talk. "Why trouble yourself with a church meeting? He never attends anyway."

"Because it would bother my mother too much to have such a man on the roll." He sighed with exaggeration, shaking his head.

Mrs. Little might be all hellfire and brimstone, but would she be that persnickety? "How can you two live with yourselves, knowing your mother fights against the very things you overlook, if not outright promote?"

He said nothing, but the hitch in his lip and the cant of his eyes seemed to—

She gasped. "She knows?"

His face didn't change. "More than knows. She's involved with the blackmailing as much as he is."

The air rushed out of her lungs and she slumped against her chair's hard back. "Is there anything about your family that isn't manufactured to win governmental positions?"

He turned to look out the tiny window, the lace shade out of place in a man's office. "Look, I don't actually like doing my parents' bidding, but—"

"Then why are you?" Surely she could talk some sense into him. "Why not expose them? I'll help. Surely—"

"Because they'll expose what I've done."

She wasn't sure she wanted to know what all that might encompass. "Then why not just refuse to do whatever it is that you do for them? Or leave if you must."

He laughed as if she'd truly said something amusing. "What would you have me do?" He ran his hands down his lanky torso and patted his slight paunch. "Muck stables? Mine coal?" He gestured toward the books lining his wall. "I spent years studying to practice law. I won't let my father ruin that in seconds."

"But surely menial labor is a better alternative to illegal activity."

He shrugged and leaned against the desk. "It's not worth it. He only requires the occasional forged contract from me anyway. Mostly I just make sure his business dealings are as favorable toward him as possible—nothing so terrible that I'd rather muck manure. Though since it would be nice to be as free as possible, that's where you come in."

"How's that?"

"I need a wife willing to campaign beside me, as I've told you before. A wife who'll keep my mother from finding it necessary to tag along."

"But how can you be so sure, if they're both blackmailing you into doing their bidding?"

He gave her the most charming smile she'd ever seen on him. "That's the beauty of my mother not liking you very much."

Well, from now on, she wouldn't bother hiding that the feeling was mutual. "But if you don't expose them, and you win your election, you'd be giving them leverage over a senator."

He shrugged. "It's not like I'd have veto power over the entire senate. I expect them to ask for a few favors, sure. But what senator doesn't hand out those?"

This was getting her nowhere. "Well, you might not stand up to criminals, but I'm certainly not going to marry one."

"Good, we're talking marriage again."

"We are not!"

"I'm not that bad, Lydia. Sure, I did a few stupid illegal things that gave my father power over me, but we'd do fine together. I never expected you to get involved. And I don't have to bother you much, depending on how many children you want."

She grabbed her throat to prevent the nausea from overwhelming her.

"But there's no reason to keep trying to convince you," he continued. "You've got no choice. *We've* got no choice. Both of our fathers have done us ill, except mine has real power."

She rubbed her arms. She knew how it felt to be trapped by a parent's choices, and she could certainly empathize, but—

"And you already do this sort of thing, you know."

"What sort of thing?"

"Cover for people."

Did he know about Sadie? Though that wasn't covering anything up for a criminal. "You're wrong, I've never once—"

"So you don't keep your father's misdeeds a secret?" He shook his head, his eyes alight, as if he found this amusing. "How many times have you asked the moral-society ladies to pray for your father's soul before tramping through the red-light district on a serenade?"

Her mouth went dry. She'd never told them about her father—only the Wiselys knew why they were as poor as they were.

"According to Mother, you haven't ever brought him up. And my father heard you'd warned your father of a scheduled serenade once so he could steer clear."

"That's not because he didn't need to hear what we were preaching, but because . . ."

Because she'd not wanted anyone to know about her connection to one of the very people they rallied against. She hadn't wanted to face the embarrassment, hadn't wanted his sins to ruin her life any more than they already did.

"I see you've now realized we're in a similar sort of predicament, you and I." He patted his desk and then stood to walk around it. "But don't worry, this will work. Neither one of us will face more negative consequences than we already have. In fact, you'll be far better off with me." He took her hand. "And Lydia, I'm not worse than death."

"I can't believe your father would murder me or my mother."

"Him? No. But do you think all the people my father blackmails have scruples? Marrying me will keep you in check, because my reputation will become your reputation. And just like you haven't slandered your father, you won't slander us."

"No . . ." She tugged her hand free of his. Was there a way out of this? She could turn them in, but what if no one listened? Would Mr. Little actually try to crush her and her family?

Of course he would.

Oh, God, I'm actually thinking I might have to marry him.

"And Father doesn't mind playing with people until they break." He rubbed his fingers against his chin. "He found it quite interesting one of Madam Careless's servants identified you as the lady who appeared on the back step of The California during business hours a while back. Seems you stole some property."

"Property!"

"And I'd bet he'd like to know how the town would react if he told them you visit brothels."

"He can tell anyone he wants to. No one's going to be upset that I saved a girl from that kind of life."

"No, of course not, but you'd have to prove it. You'd have to produce the girl. Are you willing to parade the little harlot around to save yourself?"

"But . . ." If she did that, she'd take away Sadie's only chance for a normal life. And even if she did somehow keep Sadie out of the clutches of the madam, after being exposed to the town, would Sadie trust Lydia or anyone else ever again?

Hadn't she recently told God she'd do anything to help Sadie have a chance at a better life? That nothing she faced could be worse than what that girl would go through if she couldn't escape?

Was her desire to help no deeper than mere words?

41

Nicholas sat on the edge of his chair in Pastor Wisely's office.

Seated to his right, the *Teaville Journal* editor, Mr. Greene, jiggled his left leg with impatience.

Stretching his fingers, Nicholas released a steady stream of air. He was pretty certain his pastor wouldn't think less of him after this meeting, but Mr. Greene might. Asking him to attend the meeting was a risk, but his support would influence an entirely different set of men than Pastor Wisely could. "I asked for this meeting to admit that I've been wrong and need forgiveness."

Pastor Wisely's eyebrow cocked, and Greene stilled his leg and snatched his pencil from behind his ear.

"I have many reasons for coming today, but I'll start with the ones that will most interest Mr. Greene. If it'll be in print, I want the details to be right."

Greene slipped a small tablet from his pocket.

"First, the reason I built a mansion in the middle of nowhere."

The pastor leaned forward as eagerly as the editor.

"It's in memory of my late wife. The city doesn't need to know her history, but she died hurting. It was the house of her dreams, so I built it, but I've struggled with figuring out what to do with it until now." He raised his eyes to heaven, hoping God would keep Greene from adding to his words.

"The Teaville Ladies Moral Society and others rally against the saloons downtown, but they don't truly know what's going on there. Of course they know the call of cards, booze, and women draw men from our town. And despite the fact that brothels are illegal, madams have enough women to fill their rooms."

Both men nodded. And of course they would. Painting the red-light district in a bad light was easy. Convincing anyone that the people there were worth saving was an entirely different matter.

He forced himself not to squirm. "However, the city only fines the women, though the men create the 'need' for their existence. The officials do nothing for streetwalkers besides throw them back into the district to fine again later. And that's not helping anything. They should be ministered to so they can leave their sordid lives behind. But polite society balks at getting involved." Which included the two men he was preaching at. Thankfully they seemed to be willing to hear him out.

"What those of us who find ourselves on the right side of the tracks don't understand is, there are countless children affected by everyone's poor choices—those of the men and women who make use of the red-light district, and those that refuse to offer real help. If we want to stop the spread of vice, we don't need more laws or fines, we need to help the women and children leave that world behind."

Nicholas paused until Greene's scribbling slowed.

"The city found out that my housekeeper and I have been sheltering some of the women who wanted to escape The Line. They have slapped me with fines because I've taken away the fines they could've collected from those women if they'd remained behind."

The pastor cleared his throat uncomfortably, but the editor squirmed in his seat with a smile on his face, probably heady with the thought of how many papers such a controversial statement would sell.

"But as much as I want to continue helping prostitutes reform, I think I should start with the children. They should have an easier time finding a place in polite society if aided. So I am turning my home into an orphanage specifically for the abandoned children of prostitutes and children who've been forced to work in brothels."

The pastor rubbed the back of his neck. "Surely there can't be that many children."

Nicholas tried not to look at the man as if he were stupid. "Given the nature of the business, I'd think many children would be expected."

"I just mean . . ." Pastor Wisely grimaced and pulled at his tie. "Well, I haven't seen many children."

His pastor wasn't a bad guy, but he was just as sheltered as Lydia once was. "How often do you visit that part of town?"

Wisely cringed. "Point taken. So are you wanting to only help little children, or those old enough to have been . . . put to work?"

"Both. If the older ones forced into the business want to escape, they'll find sanctuary with me."

Greene looked up. "Forced? Being the product of such liaisons, they're bound to—"

Nicholas gripped his chair's arms. He knew Greene was key to getting the town to accept his plans, so he couldn't rile him. "They are sinners who've been given extra opportunity to sin, yes. But they're also children, and what hope do they have if no one will help them? How can we condemn children who've grown up knowing nothing but that life if we are unwilling to help them find a better way?"

His mouth had grown dry, and he wished he'd taken the pastor's offer to get some coffee before they started. He'd opined about this before to a handful of people who agreed with him, but now his heart fluttered doing so in front of those who could damage his ministry if they chose to work against him.

Although he'd been impressed with Lydia's speech in front of those gathered for the Sunday prayer meeting, he was even more awed that she had taken that stand before an audience she hadn't handpicked, as he had. He turned to Mr. Greene, determined to say all he'd prepared to say. "Before you write poorly of those who frequent The Line in the editorials you and your wife print, do you talk to them about their side of the story?"

Greene jolted in his seat as if he'd discovered he had been sitting on a pin cushion.

Wisely cleared his throat. "But it wouldn't be a good idea for you to live alone with lots of young children, especially girls who've, uh, started working." The pastor's face turned pink.

"I figured our church would help, and I'd need them to. If a handful of upstanding citizens supported me, and Greene here kept from editorializing against it, then this town might stop treating a specific kind of sinner worse than another."

Greene licked his finger and flipped a page. "Getting an entire town to accept prostitutes, even unfortunate child prostitutes, is a mighty big order."

"That's why I'm starting here—you two have a powerful influence over the people I need to reach."

"You'll need more than just our voices."

"Then which men in this town do you think will be the most receptive to the idea? If I get a few to rally around me, maybe I'll have a chance. I can't move my mansion, so I need to earn this town's acceptance. God's been teaching me that I am only one man, and He isn't expecting me to be His hands to the poor and powerless by myself. So I'm going to hold an event to raise funds and trust God will provide men of influence to come alongside me." He looked over at Greene. "And I'll buy a full page advertisement for the party. It'll be the talk of the town."

"It definitely will be." Greene huffed. "What's the date?"

"Two Fridays from now." Nicholas pinned his gaze on Greene. "Can I count on both of you?"

Even if Wisely had qualms about helping, surely he wouldn't deny Nicholas's plan was right. But Greene wasn't a believer, as far as Nicholas knew, and though an upright man, he wasn't against stirring up controversy to boost his sales. But then again, money talked. "Did I mention I'm planning to advertise in the *Teaville Journal* exclusively if I feel my ministry is being covered objectively?"

Greene chuckled and flipped his notepad cover down. "Sold." He stood and held out his hand. "Include first rights to any other fascinating news of yours, and I'll make sure I get your take on things before I run anything. I can't guarantee I won't print something that paints you in a bad light, but if you talk to me first, I'll talk to you before news goes to print."

Nicholas shook Greene's hand and let him pass to leave the room. He was probably running straight for the *Journal*'s office to get the article in before the press ran tomorrow's paper.

"Oh, wait." Greene spun on his heel and stuck his hand in his chest pocket. "I received some information this morning that you were interested in." He handed Nicholas a folded piece of paper and marched back out.

Fingering the note, Nicholas shut the door behind him. Probably another dead end, but right now he had to be sure of Wisely. He turned to his pastor, who was quietly staring out the window. "What about you? Can I count on your help?"

"Where is this coming from, Nicholas? I've asked you a hundred times to get more involved with the church, and you've always refused."

"Let's just say, someone's shown me that I need to give our congregation a chance."

"And who would that be?"

"Lydia King."

"I saw you hiding in the balcony that night. But I would've thought that circus would've hardened your heart to the potential of my flock."

"Lydia, at one time, acted much like them. To be honest, at one time, so did I. But she stood by her new convictions despite being unjustly accused. She didn't back down."

He took a seat and looked at the ceiling. Confession was good for the soul supposedly, but trusting anyone came hard for him. But he had to start trusting people, and who could he trust if not

306

this man? "God started changing Lydia by using me, despite my high-handed ways. For years, I expected God to change the men and women of our congregation without my help—which He surely can—but most times He wants to use us."

He couldn't go on pretending he could judge hearts. He needed to let the Lord do His work, through him instead of despite him. "I've been very unwilling to be used in certain areas." He laced his fingers together and looked at the ground between his feet. "I can't obey God's command to be a part of the body of Christ if I insist on working alone."

"That took a lot for you to say."

"Yes, and I still don't fully believe it's possible in here." He tapped on his chest, then moved to tap his temple. "But I can't justify my own disobedience up here."

Pastor Wisely frowned. "I'm not sure your orphanage will get much support. Considering how specific you're being in what kind of children you'll be sheltering, you might not attract many adoptive parents."

"But you think we could muster up some support?"

"God can do anything." The pastor's frown turned into a huge smile. "He can even persuade a cynical loner to ask for help."

Nicholas gave in to his own smile. "I suppose that is quite the miracle. So why not believe God will do another? And speaking of miracles, do you still want me to become a deacon?"

"Indeed?" Wisely's brows hit his nonexistent hairline and he whistled. "Christmas *is* the season of miracles. Lord, forgive my unbelief."

"And I plan to stop picking and choosing what things to fund and trust God with my whole tithe to this church."

"Tithing, ministry, becoming a deacon. What spell has Lydia cast upon you?"

"No spell, sir."

"Sir?" A half smile appeared. "And you just stopped looking at me. She has a hold over you."

"She has no hold, she'd uh, . . ." He forced himself to look up, but he knew his expression wasn't as neutral as he intended. "She's no different than any of the other members I hope to win to my side."

"And here I thought you'd just learned to stop being stubborn. Don't dig in your heels against any feelings you have for her." He shook his finger at him as if he were a misbehaving dog. "She won't be free for you to win if you wait too long."

"Taking my time to consider things carefully isn't being stubborn. I'll not jump into marriage hastily again."

The pastor's face brightened.

Blast it. He'd brought up marriage all on his own.

But there were things he needed to be sure about. She'd only just become free from Sebastian, so his thoughts about her had only just become . . . entertainable. He needed time to be sure she wouldn't marry him for money. She'd freely admitted to engaging herself to Sebastian for that exact reason, so why would he be any different?

Pastor Wisely cleared his throat and Nicholas startled.

"Don't do it, my friend. Don't wait. She'll get away." He steepled his hands against his chin and shook his head. "I never thought I'd see the day Nicholas Lowe humbled himself, but today I did. A woman who can soften a man enough to make him vulnerable indicates a worthy woman—and a man in love."

"I can't be." His words ripped through him. "It's too soon. She's . . . she's too young."

Wisely laughed. "Now that's quite the excuse to offer me. Bernadette is thirteen years my junior." He stood. "When you find the woman you're meant to be with, don't hesitate. The Nicholas I know is not a coward. If you truly intend to tithe, then you've let go of a portion of your money—good. But don't keep a tether on your heart. The right woman will change you into the best man you've ever been."

But did God have to make all these changes in the space of a few months? Nicholas put on his cap and stood as well. "Thanks for the advice. But I'm sure God will give me more than a few days to figure things out."

42

Struggling up Nicholas's driveway, Lydia wrapped her arms tighter about herself, less because of the early morning frigid temperatures and more because of the churning inside of her. She'd gone home with a headache and lain upon her bed all night thinking through every possible way to escape the Littles' snare, but she couldn't think of a way out without sacrificing someone else's safety.

But Nicholas regularly sacrificed himself for people, people who meant even less to him than she did.

Or at least, she hoped she meant something to him by now. And if she were wed to Sebastian, she couldn't help with the orphanage. Surely he'd be willing to help her even if there was risk to himself.

No matter how much she wanted him to help for more heroic, romantic reasons, she couldn't let herself hope for that. She had enough disappointment to deal with at the moment.

His hulking white mansion loomed large against a pale blue sky, dawn's light reflecting in its windows. She prayed he'd not left for work yet. Lydia hurried toward the porch and knocked on the door.

Miss O'Conner answered with a smile. "Miss King. What can I do for you?"

Rubbing her arms, she looked past the housekeeper. "Is Mr. Lowe at home?"

She shook her head and pulled the door open wider. "I'm afraid not, but why don't you come in and warm up?"

"I can't." Well, she could stand to be warmer, but she couldn't stand to wait. "I need to find Mr. Lowe. Is he at the lumberyard, the gas office, the hotel?"

"I'm afraid I don't know where he is."

Her stomach squeezed as if not seeing him this very hour meant she'd end up at the altar with Sebastian. She had three days until the engagement party. His family couldn't very well drag her to the altar, but they could drag her name through the mud if she didn't figure out a way around them. Rather than simply evade them though, she hoped to get them behind bars. That way anyone mixed up with the Littles would be safe from further blackmailing. "Perhaps I will come in—if you don't mind me waiting for him to return." Lydia stepped inside and stretched her cold fingers in the warm air. "He does come home for lunch, yes?"

"I'm sorry, dear." She shut the door. "But I don't expect him back for days."

Her feet felt as if they'd sunk in cement. "What?"

Miss O'Conner simply shrugged and started for the dining room. "He had business and left last night. But you should still have some hot tea before you go. It's awful cold out there."

More awful than Miss O'Conner knew.

Lydia pressed a hand to the pain between her eyes.

He was gone.

"Do you know where he is?" Surely he wouldn't be gone that long. "When he plans to return?"

Miss O'Conner turned and frowned at how far Lydia was behind her. "I don't."

Lydia staggered over to sit on an uncomfortable-looking chair. Now what? Who else could save her?

"Are you all right, miss?" The housekeeper had come back and gripped her upper arm.

"No, I'm not." She needed Nicholas more than she needed anybody else. Who might know where he was if his housekeeper didn't?

His driver. She clamped onto Miss O'Conner's hand. "Where does Mr. Parker's wife live?" No wait, she had dementia. "Or rather, his daughters. Surely he told them where he was taking Mr. Lowe."

Scratching under her gauzy cap, Miss O'Conner shook her head. "I'm afraid he didn't take Mr. Parker. He left on the last train."

Could the train station tell her where he went? But what could she do if she found out? It wasn't as if she had money to buy a ticket or had time to track him down.

"What is it you need?" Miss O'Conner squatted beside her. "Mr. Lowe leaves me with some authority. Do you need a ride home? A few dollars? His doctor can see to your mother, if needed. Dr. Lindon can charge it to his account."

Lydia let out a pitiful groan. If only all she needed was money for a doctor's visit. "I'm afraid you can't help me."

What could a housekeeper and a part-time librarian do to bring down a mayor and a lawyer who seemed to have half the town under their thumbs? "I just need Nicholas."

In more ways than one.

But the only hope she'd had was his help, and now she didn't even have that. "I need to get him a message. As soon as he returns, could you give him a note? It's urgent." She looked around for paper. "Do you think he might send a telegram about his where-abouts?"

"He never has before." She stood and headed for a desk in a nearby room, and Lydia followed.

She doubted Nicholas would ever stoop to ask her to be more than a coworker and confidante, but what would he think of her if he saw the advertisement announcing her engagement before she told him what had happened?

He'd believe her to be the most spineless woman ever. "Give him my message as soon as he arrives, and please notify me the instant he returns. Or if he sends a wire."

"Are you in trouble? Did you snatch away another girl?"

That would have been far easier to deal with. "I wish that was my problem."

Miss O'Conner slid Nicholas's inkwell toward her and pulled a sheet of fancy stationery from the top right drawer.

Leaving off sensitive information, Lydia penned a quick note asking him to come see her immediately upon return.

Nicholas might trust Miss O'Conner, but with how Sebastian and his family seemed to have their thumbs pressed upon so many, she'd not take chances. Surely Nicholas would return within three days and come see her.

But what if he didn't? Her father wouldn't help her—the Littles already had him under their influence. Besides, he'd been pushing her in this direction for quite a while. And her mother was in no condition to deal with any of this.

Might Miss O'Conner know something that could help her without being told the particulars of the situation? "What do you know of the Littles?"

"Nothing much beyond the elder is the mayor, and the son has a law office above Central Bank."

Lydia held the woman's gaze. Miss O'Conner's eyes seemed free of deceit, but the Littles had hoodwinked her good. Could she trust herself not to be duped again?

Since Miss O'Conner didn't seem ruffled at her question, she decided to press for more, despite her jitters. "What about any connections to the red-light district? You've been there more than most. What do they say about them there? Mrs. Little organizes serenades, which I assume makes her and her family unpopular."

The housekeeper shrugged. "I only go there in hopes of persuading my sister to leave. Since Moira has refused so far, I nurse the sick or abused so I can stay close to her, hoping she'll change her mind some day." She rubbed at her temple, frown lines etching her face. "I'm thankful Mr. Lowe offered me this position, for I'm not sure how long I could've kept a job in Teaville, considering how I spend my mornings. He has no qualms about me going to the red-light district to tend to the ladies, but I've never been involved in any of his intrigues."

Oh, if only she hadn't gotten involved in such intrigues herself.

But then she'd have never known she was engaged to a criminal.

Though that might have been better than being forced to wed him knowing full well what kind of villainous family she was marrying into.

Lydia folded the short note and handed it to Miss O'Conner. "I'd be grateful if you handed this to him as soon as he steps into the house."

Taking the note, the housekeeper scanned Lydia's face with a worried cant to her eyebrows. "Are you certain I can't help?"

She pushed herself out of the seat and glanced around at the beautiful floor-to-ceiling bookcases with a frown. Her gut roiled so much, she couldn't even enjoy perusing the titles surrounding her. "Thank you, but no. I'm not even certain Nicholas can help."

Miss O'Conner followed her into the hallway and placed her note atop the mail on a silver tray. "You sure you shouldn't have some tea? You don't look well."

She certainly didn't feel well.

Oh, why hadn't Nicholas been here for her? "Is there anybody I could discuss Mr. Lowe's intrigues with?"

With a suddenly blank expression, the housekeeper turned to stare down the hallway toward the western windows. She shrugged a little. "Henri Beauchamp likely knows what Mr. Lowe's about, since he used to go around with him."

"His friend the mill owner?" At Miss O'Conner's slight nod, Lydia bit her lip. Could she ask a man she didn't know for help? "Would Nicholas trust Mr. Beauchamp with his life?"

"I would've said yes." The housekeeper fidgeted. "But now that they're not speaking to each other . . ."

Lydia dropped her shoulders and blew out a breath. Too risky.

Maybe the maids knew something. They'd mentioned at dinner the other day that they didn't know the Littles' name, but surely they wouldn't keep any other knowledge to themselves since Sebastian was forcing them to leave by fining Nicholas.

She nodded good-bye to Miss O'Conner and forged back out into the cold. Despite walking briskly, she felt colder with each step. Even if the maids knew something, how could she and two former prostitutes take on the Littles? She needed someone with at least as much power as the mayor. Hadn't she heard of some prostitutes who held power through the information they gathered from clients? If a soiled dove had information about the Littles, it would certainly be the kind she needed. With hope, she strode to the basement entrance.

At Lydia's second knock, Miss Michaels opened the door a crack, but only wide enough to see half her face behind the chain, her hair still down in a braid. "Sadie's feeding the horses."

"I'm not here to see Sadie. I'm here to see if you could help me."

Miss Michaels's eyebrow rose.

"Please."

The woman shut the door and unfastened the chain lock. Without saying anything, she held open the door and swept her hand toward a small table with two chairs. An open newspaper covered its top.

Miss Nance sat at the far end, dressed for the day; her attention was riveted on Lydia, her pencil hovering above a few circled ads.

"I'm sorry for intruding while you're getting ready for work."

"We don't work here anymore. We quit."

"We're looking for positions." Miss Nance sighed and placed the pencil against her lips. Her gaze dropped back to the advertisements spread out before her. "Though it might be hopeless."

Lydia frowned at the circled paragraphs. "You don't have to tell the employers what you did before working for Mr. Lowe. Surely knowing you obtained work at a mansion could get you many a job."

Miss Michaels's derisive sniff made her jump. "Of course we'd keep that information to ourselves. It's finding a position that won't force us into prostitution again that's difficult."

"I'm sure Mr. Lowe will let you stay here until you find one that pays well enough."

"It's not the money." The meek blond maid at the table tapped one of the advertisements above a circle she'd drawn. "It's difficult to know which one of these requests are legitimate."

"But why would anyone advertise if they didn't want help?"

Miss Michaels answered. "Oh, they want help all right. Help from women who have no one to turn to. Women who answer ads from across the country for low-paying jobs are just the kind to stuff into empty rooms. That's how Effie got pulled into this mess."

"Not pulled." Effie swallowed and colored. "Forced."

Lydia put a hand to her stomach.

"Effie thought she was answering an advertisement for a board-inghouse cook."

"It was an advertisement for a cook." She rubbed the back of her neck. "Just not for a boardinghouse, and they . . ." Her face took on a faraway look. "Well, after the first day, I couldn't leave. And even if I had been able to get away, I'd left home because I was burdening my cousin's family, and they definitely wouldn't have wanted me back after that."

"I'm so sorry." She put a hand on Effie's shoulder. The woman looked over at her hand, tears glistening on her bottom lashes.

"Yes, well"—Josephine stopped her pacing—"your being sorry doesn't help us any."

"Oh, hush, Jo," Effie whispered. "It's more than we've ever gotten from the likes of her."

Jo tossed her braid over her shoulder, tramped over to the other chair, and then plopped down and glared at Lydia. "You didn't come to hear our stories, so what do you want?"

"I'd like to know if you could give me the names of any ladies of the night who blackmail."

Jo's face scrunched up as if she were watching a bird fly upside down. "Whatever for?"

"I need to talk to someone who might have information on—"

"Oh, talking to them is not a good idea, miss." Effie's face looked frozen in shock.

It was better than any other idea she had. "I know it's not a good idea, but I need that kind of information."

Jo shook her head as if she'd just met the stupidest person in the world. "You'd be eaten alive . . . or worse."

After Effie's story, Lydia didn't doubt she might walk into something she couldn't get out of. "Well then, maybe you could talk to them for me, or come with me to—"

"We're hiding in the basement for a reason, Miss King. We're not walking anywhere near The Line, let alone visiting."

Effie wrung her hands. "The less we're seen, the better chance we have of getting Sadie away unrecognized."

"And what happens if we don't come back from whatever wild-goose chase you want to send us on?" Jo flung out her arms. "Are you going to take Sadie in?"

No, Sadie needed to get as far away from Teaville as possible.

Lydia tugged on the fallen lock of her hair she'd inadvertently curled around her finger. Considering her current predicament, these ladies had a better chance of escaping town than she did—which made her hopes for Sadie tumble even lower. "All right, I'll have to think of something else, then."

But what else could she do? Who else could she possibly talk to? *Oh, God, why'd you let Nicholas leave now?*

43

Lydia flattened herself against her parlor wall next to the front window and peeked behind the curtains without touching them. Officer Vincent was still two houses down, dressed in a sweater and chopping firewood. The day was warm for December, and he'd shucked his coat a half hour earlier. Despite the laborer's clothing he wore, she'd first noticed him after returning from Nicholas's the day Miss O'Conner had informed her he'd left town.

Since then, Lydia had spied the officer several times near that vacant house, and she'd only gotten away once without the officer noticing. She'd spent that afternoon trying to discover Nicholas's whereabouts and even ventured over to Queenie's without escort . . . only to find her gone too. Was she with Nicholas?

Why wasn't God helping her? Time was up! Since leaving the newspaper office with Sebastian two days ago, after giving them their information for an engagement announcement, she'd gathered nothing more than additional hearsay. Nothing to thwart the Littles.

"I can't marry Sebastian," she whispered against the glass. "I just can't."

"I know."

Mama's voice made her jump, and the curtain fluttered. Lydia pressed her hand against her throbbing heart as she watched out the window.

Officer Vincent didn't move. Hopefully he hadn't noticed.

She turned to Mama. "How long have you been standing there?"

"Not long." She pulled aside the curtains, and Lydia backed away from the window.

Mama leaned heavily on the windowsill and scowled in Officer Vincent's direction. "I see he's still there."

"Yes."

Stopping once to catch her breath, Mama shuffled her way back to her rocker. Gingerly, she lowered herself onto the chair. "Will you forgive me?"

Lydia walked over to the settee, picked the afghan off the floor, and put it across Mama's lap. "For what?"

"Panicking and pushing you into a marriage you don't want. Here I thought I'd learned how to trust the Lord, but the moment a problem I thought I could fix came along, I forgot to rely on Him."

"You've trusted Him throughout your illness. I don't know of anyone who could be braver facing such a bleak diagnosis."

"Seems I don't fear death anymore, though I still fret over tomorrow where you're concerned." She stopped rubbing the blanket between her fingers, looked up, and gave her daughter a sad smile. "I certainly haven't trusted God to care for you without telling Him how to do it."

Lydia clasped Mama's hand. "Then you won't fight me if I call things off again?"

If she could figure out some way to do so anyway.

"I'd be relieved." She turned to glare out the window despite the curtain blocking the way. "No man who puts his intended under surveillance will make a good husband."

"Oh, Mama, you don't know the half of it."

Mama tucked one of Lydia's loose curls behind her ear. "I know you're keeping something from me. Is it because you think you'll disappoint me?"

Lydia stood and paced. "There are things about him that I

318

know but can't prove. I can't marry a man like him, but he'll make things worse for us if I don't." She turned to face her mother. "If I don't marry him, your faith in God may be tested beyond its limits." What if the stress of a confrontation with the Littles caused Mama to die sooner?

"If it's not tested beyond its limits, then is it really faith?" Mama sighed and smoothed the purple-and-white ripple afghan across her knees. "I wasn't ready to trust Him a few days ago, but I am now. Why I thought ordering you to marry without love would solve our problems, I don't know. I know what a trial a bad marriage can be, but a bad marriage with no love?" Her voice grew thick, and she grabbed for her handkerchief.

Lydia crossed over to kneel in front of Mama. "He promised that if I married him, he'd make our life easier—but if he's underhanded now, how can I trust him to keep promises? I've been trying to figure a way out of this mess without any of us getting hurt, but I've run out of time. If only I could find some proof to accuse him before the engagement party tomorrow, I may be able to keep us safe from his threats without marrying him."

"What has he done?"

Would it matter if Mama knew? Her life was already at its end. She shouldn't tell her too much though. "His family says they're against the saloons, but they're not. They're profiting from them. And Sebastian also hinted that he partakes of the pleasures there—and I don't mean cards."

Her mother's hiss sounded as if she'd dropped cold water on Lydia's heated cheekbones. "I can't believe I was that wrong about him."

She cast her gaze to the ground. She wouldn't give Mama even the slightest hint that Sebastian had said Papa partook of those same pleasures. "You were only trying to do what was best for me."

Mama stared at the wall, blinking bloodshot eyes. "And how far off the mark I was."

How far off the mark both of them had been about so many things. But she couldn't change the past. "Could you help me

319

distract Officer Vincent? If you could manage it, I could slip out the back door and try to sneak into Sebastian's office and find something incriminating. That's the last thing I can think of. And then I'll need you to do lots of praying."

"If overtaxing myself and crumpling onto the porch floor will distract that officer and gain you time, then my death will have served a higher purpose."

Lydia smiled at Mama's weak but feisty expression—she was too stubborn to leave for heaven today. Still, she kissed her mother's temple and squeezed her tight. What would she do without her?

Lydia's knock on the small gray house's door interrupted the sound of children giggling, and a mother's sharp reprimand followed.

Her hands were sweaty, and she felt like throwing up. She scanned the area for a bush or a bucket just in case, and then glanced over her shoulder to make sure no officers tailed her. If only Nicholas had been home today, she'd not be attempting this alone. But all she'd been able to do at the mansion was leave him another note.

The door opened, and Lydia spun toward Mrs. Falstaff's flushed face.

"I'm sorry." Lydia put her hand to her swirling head, hoping she wouldn't throw up on the lady's shoes. "I was looking for Mr. Falstaff."

"We're in the middle of dinner."

"It will only take a minute. I have a quick favor to ask him on Sebastian Little's behalf."

The older lady sighed. "I'll get him." She walked away leaving the door wide open.

Lydia stepped across the threshold into the tiny little room with discarded mufflers and hats scattered across the floor.

Lord, I should be asking for forgiveness for the untruths I'm about to tell, but instead I'm going to ask for help. Oh, how I need help. She silently rehearsed the speech she'd come up with on the way over.

Sebastian's secretary came around the corner. "Miss King? My wife said you asked for me."

She blinked in an effort to relax her face. If he noticed how tense and unsure she was, he might see through her request. "I'm sorry to interrupt, but Sebastian thought this would be quickest. He wanted me to run to his office to get Mr. Hammersmith's file." She held out her hand and shrugged. "But he didn't have his key with him at dinner, so he sent me here."

"Hammersmith?"

She forced herself to keep from reaching up to tug at her tight collar. Wasn't that the client Sebastian had told her about last week? She should've listened better. "Yes." All she could do was hope she'd remembered the name correctly or that Mr. Falstaff believed he'd forgotten a client.

He looked toward the ceiling. "I can get the file for you after we finish eating."

"Oh no, he wanted it right away, and I don't want to take you away from family." She couldn't have timed this better—how could she have refused his escort if she'd come after he'd finished his meal?

A high-pitched toddler's scream rent the air, making her wince. The shrill noise was followed by a *thunk* and a woman's frustrated wail.

"It seems you're needed, and I promise to bring the key right back." She couldn't be gone long in case he decided to check on her after dinner. How long would it take to find something incriminating? *Oh, please let there be something!*

Mr. Falstaff turned to look over his shoulder as his wife aired her frustration over one of the children dumping water in his lap. "All right, give me a minute."

Gripping the doorjamb to keep herself from puddling onto the floor, Lydia waited until Mr. Falstaff returned and handed her a long black key. "Would you like us to return your key after our dinner meeting is over or have Sebastian give it to you Monday morning?"

"Whatever's easiest."

She could've kissed him! "He'll likely bring it to work Monday, then. Thank you." *And please, God, let them not see each other until then.* She stuffed the key inside her hidden pocket and headed out the door as nonchalantly as possible. Despite Mr. Falstaff giving her the weekend, she needed to move quickly.

The early evening was abnormally mild for December, so more people strolled past her on the sidewalks than she preferred. Forcing herself to smile and nod as people passed, she maneuvered toward the shadowed stairway leading up to the office above the bank where Sebastian practiced law.

Stopping in front of the barbershop to the left of the covered stairway between the two downtown buildings , she pretended to fix her hair using the window's reflection. When the street cleared, she slipped up the dark stairs.

"Lord, help me find something worthwhile quickly." Despite whispering, her voice echoed in the stairwell. As she made her way up, she looked behind her a couple times. At the door at the top, she paused, heart pounding in her throat. Was the office empty this time? After listening as long as she dared, she wedged the key into the lock.

The doorknob turned halfway, then halted. Her heart sunk. Did Mr. Falstaff give her the wrong key? Wiggling the key, she twisted and jiggled until her insides turned into mush. She rattled the doorknob one last time and almost fainted when she heard a soft click.

She rushed inside and leaned against the back of the door. Catching her breath, she waited to make sure she heard no footsteps on the stairs. The light of dusk would only give her minutes to look through files. Turning on the lamps or pushing aside the shades would increase her risk of getting caught.

God, send me to whatever I need right away.

Padding across the floor, she stopped in front of two filing cabinets. Sliding out the drawers as noiselessly as possible, she glanced through the tabs, but they were simply last names—nothing out of the ordinary. A pile of haphazard papers in the back of the bottom drawer caught her eye. She flipped through articles and loose papers until the bottom of the stack yielded a dark red ledger. There was no title or any kind of indication of its content. The pages were filled with random lists of names and numbers.

At the desk, she sat and flipped to the ledger's most recent page. The last date entered was yesterday's. She ran her fingers along the names, and one caught her eye. *D. Emma*. Had she ever met a woman who went by an initial? Men, yes, but not any women she knew of.

The D could stand for *Dirty*. And she knew of a Dirty Emma—she would've been appalled at knowing such information only weeks ago. She scanned for other initialed names. Almost all were surnames, two she recognized as men her father had muttered about owing. Then she hit on another woman's name—*I. Mary*. Surely Emma and Mary weren't last names.

Her hands smoothed the pages, the markings rubbing off onto her palms. Why did this book give her butterflies?

The last date was yesterday, and yet it was buried in a back drawer. She slammed it shut and hugged it close. Maybe.

Opening a desk drawer, she riffled through pens and ink and stamps and—

The door opened and a man's shadow blocked the dim afternoon light for a split second. Her vision grew dark and her blood pounded in her head, roaring in her ears. How had she forgotten to lock the door?

Could she slip down onto the floor beneath the desk without catching the intruder's eye, or had he seen her already? Considering her heart beat as loudly as a blacksmith's hammer against an anvil, hiding likely wouldn't help.

"Miss King?" Mr. Falstaff turned on the wall's gas light. "Could you not find the lanterns?"

She stood, hitting her thighs against the opened middle drawer, and hissed.

"Are you all right?" Sebastian's secretary walked over, looking pointedly at the open drawers.

"I'm all right, just a bit of a bumbler." Could he see the panic in her eyes?

He looked a second time at the ledger in front of her. "I thought you were after the Hammersmith file."

"I was . . . but I needed this too."

"What is it?" He rounded the desk.

There was no use in trying to hide the book. "I don't know, he said it was red, and yesterday's entry would be"—she glanced down at the open pages—"Peter Toliver, and it is. Now that I found the correct ledger, I'll get the Hammersmith folder."

He put his hand up in a signal to stop. She schooled her features. She'd fight to look innocent until the end.

"That's why I came. I put Hammersmith's files over there only yesterday." He pointed to a table stacked with books and folders. "Sebastian probably told you to look in the vertical file."

She nodded.

His gaze strayed back to the book under her trembling hands. "Would you mind if I take a look at the ledger for a minute?"

"Of course not." She wouldn't pick the book up and hand it to him lest her shaking hands give her away. She got out of his way and tried her best to sound carefree. "I'll just go get that Hammersmith file, then." The overeagerness in her voice grated on her ears.

He looked at her a little suspiciously, but he didn't say anything.

Trying not to watch him over her shoulder, she shuffled over to the table and found the Hammersmith file within seconds.

Mr. Falstaff had sat down and was running his finger down columns. He scratched his chin and flipped back a few pages.

"Do I need to wait?"

He spooked in his chair and then shut the book. "Mr. Little

asked you to bring him this?" The incredulity in his voice made her heart skip.

He didn't believe her.

"Yes," she squeaked. She could have kicked herself.

He handed it to her, and she tucked the volume under her arm and tried not to melt in relief. Whatever she had, it must be something important, considering how Mr. Falstaff seemed suspicious of her having it. But what was it exactly?

Mr. Falstaff's eyes were sharp and penetrating. He knew what the book was and was likely trying to figure out if she did. What if he was involved with Sebastian's family's misdeeds? It would be best to act the dense, put-upon sweetheart. "I'm so glad you came. It would've taken me forever to find the Hammersmith file without you, and Sebastian really seemed to want it before he finished his dinner meeting."

"Hammersmith," he repeated. His eyebrows met in the middle for a second before he stepped back for her to pass. "I'm sorry for holding you up."

"Your key." She fished it out of her pocket and handed it to him, careful not to touch him lest he feel her clammy hands.

"I believe I'll do a little tidying before I leave."

She let out a sharp exhale of relief. Most gentlemen would have offered to escort her back to Sebastian.

But Mr. Falstaff did seem quite ruffled.

Had he realized she was here without permission and would trail her to see where she went? Or was he staying behind to destroy evidence before turning her into the police for thievery?

She couldn't force a *good-bye* out of her mouth, and Mr. Falstaff did nothing but stare at her with unsteady eyes. Evidently he wasn't moving until she left.

Finally, she mustered up a nod of farewell and walked out the door.

She prayed Nicholas was home now. For what good would another note do if he didn't return soon?

She kept glancing over her shoulder to make sure Mr. Falstaff wasn't trailing her. But what if he was doing something far worse? What if he went to Sebastian?

She raced to the mansion, praying everything would be all right while uncertainty wrapped itself around her heart, squeezing until she was no longer certain prayers would help.

44

Leaning heavily against the doorjamb to help him balance the weight of a drowsy Robbie clinging to his neck, Nicholas knocked on the servant's entrance door again.

The flicker of a candle in the window caused him to sigh in relief. He glanced back at Angel, who refused to get close to him. "They're coming."

The girl had refused to go inside the mansion's front entrance for some reason, and since ice crystals were already taking over the windowpanes, having them sleep in the stable wasn't an option.

"Who is it?" Josephine's annoyed voice sounded behind the door.

If he wasn't mistaken, his maid was holding a candle in one hand and a club of some sort in the other. The thought made him smile, though he'd be sure to wipe it off before she opened the door. She'd clobber him if he looked at her wrong, he had no doubt.

"It's Nicholas, and I've got the children." Well, two of them anyway. He shook his head and swallowed against disappointment.

Two of them were better than none. But he couldn't erase the sound of Angel hanging over the train car's railing, crying for her sister.

How Pepper had remained standing defiantly among the depot's crowd listening to her sister's high-pitched, frantic pleading, he couldn't fathom.

What awaited her at the brothel she'd taken her siblings to? He'd offered her escape, and yet she believed she had to return.

But since she'd had the gall to ask him for money in exchange for her siblings, he'd decided getting the younger ones away was more important than staying to convince her she should and could leave.

The chain dropped and the door opened.

Josephine looked at the children and sighed while rubbing her eyes. "Why aren't you putting them in the seamstress's room like last time? There's only three cots down here."

He'd ignore his cranky maid's ungratefulness, considering it was after eleven. "The girl didn't want to go inside the empty house with only me."

Effie scuttled out from one of the back rooms, yawning, but within seconds she sported a soft smile amid her cloud of blond hair. "What girl?"

He turned slightly and tipped his head outside toward the shadows, grateful to see Angel's silhouette. He didn't want to go traipsing through the trees calling for a runaway at this hour. "Angel."

"Oh, Annie's girl. Come here, darling." Effie held out a hand and made her smile even wider. "Just us girls down here—no one comes visiting."

Angel stepped forward, but her head was held at a suspicious angle as she tried to see into the darkness.

"There's a girl about your sister's age with us now, but she's asleep. No one else. You can look around if you want."

Once Angel finally took a hesitant step inside, Nicholas blew out a breath that turned straightaway into a yawn.

"Give me this one." Josephine held out her hands as if awaiting a crate of groceries or a basket of laundry.

The boy tightened his grip.

If only he'd fallen back asleep after they'd tumbled out of the coach. "Maybe I should bring him in." He jiggled his shoulder against the boy's chin. "Would you like me to tuck you into bed?"

Robbie nodded but clung even tighter.

Josephine let her hands fall with exaggeration. "Guess I have to make up a bed anyway. On the floor, I suppose."

"That'll be all right. As long as it's in the same room with your sister, yes?"

Again the boy nodded, so Nicholas stepped inside and headed for the chair next to the table with the candle. He had to get off his feet before he fell over with exhaustion. The boy didn't weigh much, but Robbie hadn't let him put him down for hours.

Effie came out of the back room and grabbed some linens from a small trunk. She came over to smooth Robbie's curls. "Just give us a minute and then you can sleep." Her gaze suddenly shifted to the table and she frowned.

Beside the candle lay a newspaper. His name at the top. "Oh." He shifted the boy to his other shoulder. "I see my story's out."

"You might not want to read that until morning, not if you want a good night's sleep anyway." She put her hand on it and pulled the paper away.

He stopped her. "Oh, I know I was intentionally jabbing the hornets' nest. But the question is if my trust in Greene is well placed or whether he's embellished." He pulled the paper toward him. Might as well read it while his maids got things ready for Robbie and Angel. Otherwise they'd have to drag his snoozing carcass upstairs if he sat inactive for long. "How have the towns-folk reacted, do you know?"

She reluctantly let go, shaking her head.

He smiled at the huge title above the fold. This orphanage idea would be the buzz of the town. He already had his first tenants, so hopefully this article would bring about some volunteers. Surely

Caroline could watch the children until then, though she had plenty of housekeeping chores—

Lydia's name atop the small right-hand column caught his attention.

SEBASTIAN LITTLE CELEBRATES
ENGAGEMENT TO LYDIA KING

He looked for the date, though it had to be one of last week's papers, considering his article was featured.

But the type blurred no matter how much he blinked.

"Yeah, that's what I thought you'd do." Effie made a sad clicking noise. "I thought for sure she felt what you felt for her."

He blinked up and frowned at his maid. "What I felt for her?"

"You might think you're gruff and beyond needing human company, but with Miss King around, you were more relaxed than I've ever seen you."

"No, I wasn't. She frustrated me out of my wits half the time."

She found her smile again. "Yeah, that too." Her frown returned, and she squeezed his shoulder. "I'm sorry."

She moved off with her handful of sheets, and his eyes couldn't resist returning to the big block letters that had made the beat of his heart disappear.

With some more blinking, and breathing slowly and steadily, he was able to get the words back into focus. A very ordinary engagement announcement. A list of their achievements, a list of their family, and a glowing political endorsement to cap it off. But then:

Miss King is a lucky young lady to be chosen to enter the Little family, a fairy tale come true.

A fairy tale? Did the newspaper's editor mean to insinuate Lydia had found true love or was shucking rags for riches?

Tripe straight from silly dime novels.

Money wouldn't give her a happily-ever-after—it certainly

330

hadn't for Gracie. Lydia might be banking on Sebastian's money to keep her mother alive and them off the street, but that's all it would do—if it lasted.

And to think, he'd meditated on Pastor Wisely's words the whole trip out to Dodge City and back and had decided the man was right. He'd returned home determined not to hesitate, but to pursue the woman he loved.

And in love he was. He'd come to grips with it and had been more excited to return to Teaville than ever before.

But love couldn't fix this. No . . . he'd not fallen in love—he'd fallen into folly, just as he had with Gracie.

But this time, God saved him from pairing himself up with another woman who'd toss him away if he didn't spend enough. He picked up the newspaper and lobbed it toward the wastebasket near the door.

He should be grateful.

Should be relieved.

But now all he wanted to do was find some more things to throw.

A soft snore sounded near his ear. The boy had finally gone back to sleep.

But he'd not be snoring anytime soon. Effie was right. He'd not be sleeping well tonight, if at all.

Josephine appeared in front of him again, her hands pulling Robbie out of his hold. "Caroline has been waiting up for you every night since you left. So find her and then send her down with more blankets, if you would."

"Waiting up?" Since when did his housekeeper ever wait up for him?

Josephine rearranged the boy none too gently in her arms, but thankfully Robbie slept right through the jostling. "She's been in a fuss, worrying over you for days now. Make sure you find out what she wants before you turn in. I think it has something to do with that lady who's been here so often lately."

So Caroline was waiting up to tell him about Lydia? He didn't need to hear what he already knew.

Effie walked out of the shadows, hands clasped in front of her. "Though if you don't feel up to it, Mr. Lowe, I'm sure her news will keep till morning."

Josephine huffed and shrugged. "Suit yourself, but by the way she's been acting, I wouldn't." She turned and walked Robbie off into the room where his sister had disappeared earlier.

"I'll say a prayer for you."

He looked down at Effie's hand lightly clasped about his arm and tried to respond to her, but after finding his throat and facial muscles unresponsive, he attempted to give her what he hoped she saw as a grateful nod. Had she ever mentioned God or prayer before? She'd listened to him politely when he'd spoken of his faith, but never had he seemed to convince her that God cared. However, he couldn't come up with a response, so he got up to head back outside.

"You could use the servant's corridor if you—"

He slammed the door shut on Effie's voice and stumbled into the darkness.

The frosty air did nothing to clear his brain or soothe the ache that burned from his heart up into the back of his throat.

Lydia . . .

He trudged up the sidewalk but slipped on a patch of ice. He crashed down on one knee before he caught himself with his hands. The coldness of the bricks seeped into his palms, and he let it spread up into his heart.

With a grunt he shoved himself up to stand, found his footing on the untrustworthy ground, then forced himself to step forward with more wariness than before.

As he would need to do every day from now on—with any woman who dared cross his path again.

The mansion's windows were dark, vacuous pits in his three-story sepulcher. Unfortunately, he'd not find restful sleep within its walls as the bodies in the tombs several blocks west did—not for weeks or months most likely.

Inside, the heat was set too low for him to remove his coat. "Caroline!"

His yell echoed up the entry stairwell and filled the dark, empty foyer.

While turning on the gas lamps, he called again. After no answer, he attempted to unknot his laces but finally had to yank off his stubborn shoes.

Elbows on his knees, holding his shoes in his hands, he stared at the mail across from him, gritting his teeth in hopes of keeping his thoughts blank.

After a bit, he called out Caroline's name again, but the roughness in his throat shuttered his voice to barely a whisper. His housekeeper wouldn't have heard him even if she'd been sitting beside him.

He chucked his shoes across the hall and closed his eyes.

Did he want to cry or do something else?

What he really should do was go upstairs, crawl into bed, and let sleep erase the hurt caused by loosening the chains he'd so wisely kept tightened about his heart until recently.

If only he'd not looked at the newspaper as Effie had advised. He'd have had one last night of blissful, ignorant sleep.

Was the engagement announcement the reason Caroline was anxious enough to make Josephine think he needed to talk to his housekeeper before going to bed? Or had the article he'd had Greene print hurt her or her sister?

Since she wasn't home, he'd likely find her wherever Moira was.

With the loss of Lydia's help—for surely Sebastian wouldn't let her volunteer in his orphanage in light of all the fines he'd jealously piled on him—he'd need help with the children.

He couldn't afford to lose Caroline, and it wasn't like he'd be going to sleep anytime soon.

With a groan, he got up to retrieve his shoes.

However, getting the knots out of his laces still proved difficult—about as difficult as keeping the moisture from his eyes, the hurt from constricting his chest, and the dry ache from overwhelming more than just his throat.

45

"You know," Henri said as he hiccupped and swayed, weighing Nicholas down until he was sure they'd both topple to the ground, "I never thought she was that pretty anyway, and I never really . . ." Henri's speech slurred into something unrecognizable.

Nicholas really didn't need a drunk friend to take care of—though becoming a drunken fool himself sounded perversely more appealing than it ever had. He had as many heartaches and problems he'd like to drown out as Henri. Maybe more.

He yanked on his best friend to get him to stand straighter. The heavier man was killing his neck. "Just keep walking. One more rise to climb, and then I'll get you settled in the green room."

Henri looked up and narrowed his eyes as if he hadn't noticed the massive mansion as they'd struggled up the driveway over the last several minutes. "Why are we at your house?"

"Because I'm not about to haul your sorry hide across the rest of town."

"Send me home with your driver."

"It's two in the morning. Everyone with a brain is asleep."

"Not everyone." He pointed at the house.

Every room in the lower level of the mansion was lit. He'd found Henri while he'd been looking for Caroline and had spent over an hour convincing his friend to leave his whiskey behind. His housekeeper must have returned while he was gone, but why would she have turned on all the lights? And he really needed to tell her to stop going out so late. Sometimes she helped a woman in great pain or in labor in the red-light district into the wee hours, but walking through that section of town in the dark was asking for trouble.

He was tempted to drop Henri and let the drunk man crawl his way up to the porch so he could run to the house to check if there was a problem, but he couldn't leave him out in the cold. "Come on. Faster."

"I'll get there when I get there."

Ignoring the man's inebriated protest, Nicholas half dragged Henri the remaining distance and dropped him at the door. He fished for his key.

Henri slid down the wall. "Hey, just because I'm no fun doesn't mean you should leave me outside."

"You can crawl in by yourself once I get the door open." Where was his key? He checked his coat pocket a second time.

"It's not nice of you to leave me. It's not a good night to do that." He mumbled a curse. "If Moira hadn't left me for a bunch of johns, I wouldn't even be here. It's all her fault."

Well, being left for a bunch of johns was probably worse than being left for someone willing to buy a woman unlimited fripperies. But then, what reason for being abandoned wouldn't hurt?

Nicholas slapped his breast pocket, relieved to feel the key's outline under his hand. "My brain is as befuddled as yours." Women. Always women to blame.

He frowned at his friend still sitting on the porch. "And Moira didn't leave you. She'd need to have accepted you first to be able to reject you."

"And why wouldn't she have me?"

They'd talked circles around this topic on the way home. "How am I supposed to know? You haven't accepted any of my theories." When, after the fiasco at Queenie's, he'd asked Caroline about what had gone wrong with Henri and her sister years ago, she'd stuttered an excuse about floors needing to be dusted and dishes needing mopped.

And it wasn't like he understood women himself. How could Lydia have missed his regard when everyone else seemed to have seen it?

He had more money than Sebastian, plenty to tempt her or any other woman wanting to get her sticky fingers on some misfortunate man's wallet.

Snarling, he forced his key into the keyhole. One day he'd probably thank God for saving him from the likes of Lydia King, but at the moment, all he felt was hurt.

The door flew open before he even turned the knob.

Caroline's shadow blocked the light, and she held out some envelopes. "I didn't open these because it's not my right, but you need to read these now. Effie came up and told me you came in earlier, but you didn't even touch your mail."

"I had better things to do than sift through mail." He didn't care a whit for anything right now anyway. It was two in the morning, for pity's sake. All he wanted was to shove his friend into one room and disappear into his own. Then he'd scowl at the ceiling for the rest of the night—er, morning.

She forced the envelopes into his hand, but the moonlight was too dim to make out anything. They should all be asleep, not reading mail.

"Let's get Henri inside before he freezes."

Henri grunted. "Maybe I want to freeze. Then my heart could be as cold as Moira's. That . . ." He mumbled off a few unpleasant monikers for a woman he claimed he still loved.

Nicholas would have kicked him if he thought it would've done any good. He shot Caroline the most apologetic look he could muster up at the moment. Though she knew what her sister had become, she shouldn't have to hear Moira degraded so.

She stared at the crumpled heap on the porch that was Henri and hugged herself. "I'll go get him coffee."

"All I need is sleep," Henri grumbled.

If only Nicholas would be getting some himself.

Caroline turned for the stairs. "I'll go ready a room."

"Henri doesn't deserve your kindness. Besides, you should be in your own." He needed to get his friend in and the door closed before he let all the warm air escape. "I can open the vents in the red room for him."

"No, I'll take care of Mr. Beauchamp while you read those letters."

"I have to at least get him up to the room first." Nicholas draped Henri's arm across his neck and heaved him up by planting his shoulder in the man's chest.

"Hey, I can get up myself, cause I feel . . ."

And then retching noises followed by an acidic smell wafted up from behind Nicholas's back. He cringed. Holding his breath, he slid the man off his shoulder. "Fine, get upstairs on your own." He thrust his handkerchief at Henri and pointed inside as if he were sending a scolded puppy outside.

"I'll do that." The man took a wide circular step to the left, then stumbled to the right, smashing into Caroline, who thrust out her arms to keep him at bay. "And I can open my own vents. I know where they are." He straggled over to the stair rail and grabbed on with both hands, grumbling curses as he began a laborious ascent.

Nicholas shucked his coat and left it out on the porch.

Caroline stared at the mess, her face slightly discolored.

"I'll clean it up." He shut the door. "You should already be asleep."

"No." She pointed at the letters again. "You need to read those. They're from Miss King, and I didn't like how she was acting when she wrote them. She wouldn't tell me what she wanted any of the times she came by."

She was likely writing him some sorry excuse for why she couldn't be involved in his orphanage anymore. "I don't see how waiting a few hours will make a difference."

"Please."

He chucked the notes back atop the mail pile. "And it's not like I can do anything now." Except fume some more while lying awake in the dark trying not to think about her.

"She came right after you left and has been back twice since. She clearly needs help."

"Which would be her fiancé's job now."

"Read them, Nicholas."

He huffed and retrieved them. As he ripped off the first one's flap, he looked up toward where the boards were creaking in the hallway above. "I'll read them if you make sure Henri gets to the right room."

She shook her head. "He doesn't want my help." Her voice turned rough, making Nicholas cock his head. Was she more emotionally involved in the spat between Henri and her sister than he'd thought?

He stared at her until she turned pink. When had she ever refused a request? Sure, her position in his employ wasn't normal—she was more a coworker than a servant, but even in the off hours, she'd played the part.

He forced his muscles to relax and his jaw to unclench. The lateness of the hour and his mess of emotions weren't her fault. "I'm sorry. You don't have to deal with my poorly behaving friend if you don't want to. Are you sure you can't tell me why your sister refused him? If I could enlighten him, he might be less apt to—"

"You're right, it's late." She breezed past him. "Read the letters." And with that, the basement door slammed behind her.

He lifted his head toward the ceiling. "What did you do to annoy them both so much?"

Shaking his head, he slid his shoes off his feet and unfolded the top letter, lest he have to listen to Caroline lecture him in the morning. Why hadn't Lydia just told his housekeeper what she wanted so he'd not have to deal with this?

He skimmed through a note about Lydia needing to see him.

Well, he didn't want to see her. Not right away if he could help it. Maybe he could find himself a reason to take an urgent business trip.

338

The next envelope contained another of his fancy sheets of stationery filled with disastrous penmanship, much unlike a woman's. Lydia's handwriting wasn't that poor. Was she so upset she couldn't write straight? He squinted, trying to decipher the script:

Sebastian and his family are profiting off the red-light district from both sides. And I need your help to somehow prove it. He's intending to ruin my family if I speak up. He's threatened me, and considering what he and his father said, I bet they'd hurt you too if they knew I was telling you. I told him I'd marry him to buy myself time, but I don't even know if that will help. I'm hoping you might steer me in the right direction, but I can't anger them until I have something that will keep them away from me and my mother and everyone else I hold dear.

His throat worked and bobbed. A bout of lightheadedness took over, and he clasped the arm of his chair.

She wasn't engaged. Well, she was, but not because she wanted to be.

He blew out a breath and shook himself. Not that it meant she had feelings for him, but at least he was back to where he started after he'd gotten off the stage with the children.

The weight that had clamped around his lungs fell off. He could pursue her, though she needed to be rescued first. He ripped open the third letter.

I think I found proof they aren't the upstanding individuals they want the community to believe them to be. But I'm not sure. I want you to look and tell me if I'm right. I need you to be back! If you make it home, please stop by the house before noon Sunday. The engagement party is at four. I'm not even sure this will turn out to be as incriminating as I think it is. If you don't want to risk being involved, I'll understand. Just burn these letters. But

I hope this ledger I found is enough to get him in trouble so they can't do anything more to anybody. I can't marry him. I just can't.

I guess you'll find out what happens if you haven't arrived in time.

I just hope I don't make things worse.

Nicholas read the note three times, then growled at the time on the clock. If he read this right, whether he stopped by her house in a handful of hours or not, she was going to accuse a rather influential family of things he only knew by hearsay.

Hearsay and a suspicious ledger weren't enough to make the Littles squirm. He needed to find more substantial evidence.

He flew up the stairs to his room, grabbed his thinner wool coat since he couldn't fathom putting the other back on, then ran downstairs and out the door, leaving all the house lights ablaze.

46

"It's time to go." Lydia's mother stood by the front door, leaning on her cane.

Lydia pulled aside the front room window's curtain. The carriage outside was Sebastian's, not Nicholas's. Though she'd looked a minute ago and about every minute before that, Lydia couldn't help but hope Mr. Parker was just around the corner, bringing Nicholas to catch them before they left.

But the street was empty except for Sebastian's carriage and a stray dog nosing through some trash.

She dropped the curtain and stared at the ledger on the table, its contents her only hope now. She'd marked all the names she believed might belong to prostitutes, and last night, she'd asked her father for the names of Teaville's saloon owners and found a few scattered throughout the book. The entries were certainly transactions between them and Sebastian, but what kind?

They were so vaguely written he could claim they were legal fees. Could this sorry piece of evidence and what she'd overheard be enough to convince anybody the Littles were working the system?

If she accused Sebastian and he lied well enough that no one believed her, all his promised wrath might fall quickly upon her and her family.

Miss O'Conner had knocked on her door sometime around nine o'clock this morning, informing her Nicholas had returned and wanted a list of names from the ledger. His housekeeper had had no idea what Nicholas's plans were and had left within minutes with a short list.

But what could those two possibly do to save her anyway? And why hadn't he come to see her himself? Her head pounded. "How I wish I could get out of my own engagement party with an excuse of a headache."

But Miss O'Conner had said Nicholas planned to meet her at the engagement party, and so she'd go.

"If you don't want to go, Mama, I'll understand." She rubbed her temples.

"I won't let you go alone." She nodded her head toward the ledger and looked over her shoulder. "Are you going to say anything? Your father won't like it."

"He'll more than not *like* it. If he knew what I planned to say, he'd tie me up and plead my headache excuse himself."

The back bedroom door opened, and her father hustled out, the knot on his tie horrendously done. No wonder he'd taken so long.

"Do you want me to redo your tie, Papa?"

He shot her a glance that would have scared an egg into cracking itself.

Fine. She pursed her lips. He could look off-kilter if he wanted. If she ended up having the guts to accuse the Littles, no one would remember how his tie looked anyway. She snatched up the ledger and shoved it into her large knitted bag.

"You do what God wants you to do." Mama squeezed her hand shoulder.

Papa scowled. "God says honor your parents. You do what's best for the family."

What he meant was *"You'll do what's best for me,"* but Lydia let it slide. What use would it be to argue with him now?

She led the way out the door and glanced down the street to

the south, one last futile attempt at hope. But there was only one vehicle waiting for her this gray Sunday afternoon.

What if the information in the ledger was worthless? What if the Littles really did use the people they blackmailed to hurt the uncooperative? She put a hand to her head and followed her parents, despite the overwhelming desire to run inside and hide in her room.

Papa nodded at the driver and helped Mama inside. Though they were traveling to an engagement party, the silent ride would've been more appropriate for a funeral procession. Her father's constant throat clearing, and her mother's painful inhales at every jostle, only made Lydia's nerves jump even more.

What would God have her do? She hadn't sensed an answer, though she'd prayed plenty—mostly for Him to send Nicholas to her, but God's answer to that had been no.

She'd wanted Nicholas to save her . . .

Not God.

Oh, Lord, I've got my eyes on the wrong person. You know how I feel about Nicholas. How I despised him at first, then doubted his motives and ruffled at his pretentiousness. How I fought against having any admiration for him whatsoever. Then how I tried to deny how terrible I looked in comparison. And how I love him . . .

She pulled aside the buggy's curtain a little, hoping the cold air would freeze her hot eyes and warm cheeks.

She loved him. How stupid of her. She'd been awed that Sebastian would stoop to marry her—and now she knew why he had. But Nicholas would never be desperate enough to look her way. Sure, he might have developed some concern for her over the last ten weeks as she'd grown into someone he could respect, but why must her heart leap so audaciously toward a man like Nicholas?

Those romance novels had gotten her into trouble, just as Papa always said they would.

And how the plot had thickened. She certainly had gotten herself into a scrape worthy of any dime novel. If only she could turn ahead several pages to see how she would get out of this . . . or find out if she'd only dig herself in deeper with the wrong move.

But the Littles should have to answer for their wickedness. Couldn't you have provided me with more evidence or helped me figure out an easier way . . . ?

She closed her eyes tight and her heart plummeted.

She'd twice attached herself to a man she didn't love because she didn't trust God to save her. She couldn't let fear that He would not help her the way she wanted Him to keep her from doing what was right.

She'd only followed Him when the path He set before her was inviting and cheery, ignoring His commands if obeying looked like a hardship.

What kind of faith was that? Did she believe God would watch over her even in the midst of terrible situations or not? Life was not pleasant for Paul, the disciples, and countless Old Testament folks, but that didn't mean God hated them.

She was making God in her own image, a heavenly benefactor who approved her decision making and delivered accordingly. Her preferred god gave her what she dreamed of: miraculous healing for her mother, a loving, easy father, excuses for ignoring people she wanted to ignore, the man she loved. And that god wasn't delivering . . .

The driver stopped outside of Lowe's Hotel, where Sebastian had wanted to hold the party, most likely to throw her infatuation with Nicholas in her face.

Lydia forced herself to accept the driver's hand to help her out. Her father steadied her mother, and the trio walked in silence toward the hotel. She laced her arm through Mama's, pretending she was only supporting her rather than anchoring herself into going forward.

After entering the dining hall ensconced in white gauzy fabric, silver bells, and candles, Lydia scanned the room of happy, smiling faces, buzzing with small talk. Nicholas wasn't anywhere in the crowd.

She had to trust God to help her without Nicholas.

"Ah, the woman of the hour!" Clinking of glass and utensils followed Sebastian's pronouncement as he traversed the room. His smiling face and ruddy complexion would fool everyone in the room into believing he was enamored with her. Most likely alcohol-enhanced punch and the pretentious hors d'oeuvres made him glow.

She let Papa take Mama to find a seat and grabbed Sebastian's elbow. "Can I have a word with you?" A jolt of pity for confronting him in front of everybody hit her, but she shook it off. She shouldn't care about humiliating a man trying to blackmail her—especially since this party was nothing but show. But she could at least try to avoid a scene, for her mother's sake.

He remained planted in the middle of the floor and took a sip of his punch, staring at her over the brim.

"Now, Sebastian. Somewhere else."

"Speech. Speech." A male voice behind her called.

Would that she could melt into a puddle on the floor. "No," she rumbled, giving Sebastian an intent look. Turning, she faced the crowd and waved for silence. "If you would excuse us for a moment."

Sebastian leaned down and spoke through gritted teeth. "If you do something to ruin my career, I promise I'll have no remorse over what Father will do to you later."

Papa's smoky smell filled the air beside her. "Honey, this is not the time to second-guess anything. Let's not upset the Littles."

"Please." She pulled away from her father's grip on her shoulder. "It would be wrong to go through with something that—"

"Ladies and gentleman." Papa snagged a punch cup off a nearby waiter's tray and held it high. "I'm so pleased to have you here for my daughter's engagement to this fine gentleman. I'm proud to be connected to the upstanding Little family."

"Upstanding?" Her incredulous tone was drowned out by a volley of agreements, well wishes, and the clinking of glass.

Sebastian pulled her toward the front table, where they were supposed to sit together.

She tried to get out of his bruising hold. Frustration over being bullied welled up in hot tears. "I can't."

"Don't." Sebastian's eyes were fiercer than his command. His smile, tight and scary.

"I'm sorry, everyone, but there's been a mistake." She escaped from Sebastian's sweaty clasp.

Mama gave her a weak nod from her chair, but Papa stood ramrod straight in the suddenly silent room, his hands locked into fists.

"I . . . I can't. I shouldn't have agreed to this."

"Excuse us for a moment. The lady's gotten a case of cold feet." Sebastian wrapped his arm around her in a comforting gesture, but his nails bit into her shoulder. "We'll work this out and be back before the first course."

"No, we won't." She'd wanted to speak to him alone earlier, but the dark look in his eyes made her think better of going with him now. "I can't wed a man who's only marrying me to shut me up."

A glass shattered on the floor at Mrs. Little's feet. Her face was fiercer than an enraged bull's.

"I wouldn't continue with this nonsense if I were you." Sebastian put a hand on top of her head and patted her as if she were loony. "Let's get you something to drink."

He yanked her arm so hard her shoulder smarted. She turned toward her parents and frowned at the look in Mama's eyes. "I'm sorry, Mama, I've made it worse."

Mama's frail arm, draped in a delicate shawl, shivered its way up into the air. "Hold on, Mr. Little." Her voice was rough with the attempt to hold a coughing fit at bay. "Lydia has some accusations I'd like cleared up before you proceed to manhandle her to the altar."

When Mama gave in to a bout of coughs, whispers danced around the room, which suddenly looked less crowded.

"Accusations?" Sebastian let her go and crossed his arms. A wide, wide smile cracked his lips, like he knew he'd already won. "You think anyone here is going to believe wild accusations?"

She closed her eyes, shutting out the faces surrounding her. None of them were her friends. Everyone in this room was probably being blackmailed or was in on Sebastian's underhanded dealings. Why hadn't she thought of that sooner? What other kinds of friends would he have?

Even if the ledger contained irrefutable proof, she couldn't hurt him in front of handpicked guests. If Nicholas didn't arrive in time, who'd bother to stand with her besides her feeble mother? She likely stood in a den of liars, cheats, and people as scared of the Littles as she was.

And what if Nicholas wasn't here because he'd realized there was no way to get her out of her predicament?

Should she pretend her mother's weakened state had made her delusional and beg for everyone to continue celebrating? Or should she tell the plain truth, knowing it would do no good, and trust God to love her when she ended up in the gutter?

47

Nicholas slid through his hotel's kitchen doors and into the silent banquet room. He almost knocked into one of his servers holding a tray of chicken-salad appetizers.

"Let me go." Lydia's voice, a mixture of stubbornness and pleading, sounded from the center of the room.

Nicholas pushed through the stilled crowd and stopped just behind a group of older women.

Lydia yanked her sleeve from a livid Sebastian's grip.

Nicholas let out a rush of air. He'd thought he'd be too late, but he appeared to be right on time.

"What's your mother talking about?" Sebastian's brow wriggled on his forehead as if he were confused, but the man's stance, with wide legs and tilted chin, indicated he felt in control. "I can't think of a thing you could accuse me of." He shook his head. "And I'm hurt you'd do this to me now, in front of our friends and my associates."

"I tried to get you to speak to me somewhere else," Lydia said.

"Why?" Sebastian's jaw worked. "I've got nothing to hide. You might as well share with them whatever it is you think I'm doing."

Despite the energy coursing through Nicholas, which had kept him running throughout the morning and afternoon with no sleep,

348

he couldn't help a face-splitting yawn but shook it off. He didn't want to miss watching Sebastian lose his smirk the moment she pulled out that ledger.

Lydia shook her head. "I'm not going to accuse you of any-thing."

She wasn't? Had she changed her mind? The weight of sleep de-privation smothered his lungs, and his vision swirled. He'd worked for hours to come to her defense. He'd only just finished convinc-ing Mr. Falstaff fifteen minutes ago to come with him. Sebastian's secretary was too pivotal for him to have walked away until he'd done everything he could to convince the man they could defeat the Littles.

"I don't have enough evidence to make any definitive accusa-tions, but I can tell these people what I've heard and let them decide, if you'd like."

Nicholas blew out his breath and let his body relax. Hearsay wouldn't be good enough, but that was all right; he was prepared.

"You're offering gossip as evidence?" Sebastian snorted.

A few other dissenting voices filled the still air, along with a smattering of tense laughter.

"It's not gossip when it came from your own lips."

"Then go ahead and clear your mind, my dear. As I've said, I've nothing to hide."

Lydia's face paled, but she threw back her shoulders. Nicholas could envision a sling and five stones in those tiny hands of hers. How he loved her tenacity.

She tore her eyes from Sebastian's and slowly turned; very few people met her gaze. "I overheard him and the mayor discussing their business practices. It seems that, though Sebastian is cam-paigning to get rid of saloons and prostitution, he actually has money invested in those endeavors. They make a profit by both damning the red-light district and taking advantage of it."

Sebastian's mouth hung slightly agape and he let his shoulders sag. "I can't believe you'd think that of me." The man swallowed with obvious exaggeration.

The lawyer should've gone into theater.

"I wouldn't have if I hadn't heard it with my own ears."

"Everyone has seen how passionately my family fights against vice. I promised you I'd try for better child-labor laws, and with my mother's serenades and my father working tirelessly to—"

"All shams, including your mother's serenades. She's in on it too."

Nicholas rubbed a hand against his chin as gasps and murmurs rose around him.

"I'm ashamed I ever marched behind her."

He'd assumed the biddy was as ignorant of her family's dealings, as she was of the uselessness of her evangelizing methods. But maybe this made more sense—if she truly didn't care about sinners, then her methods were for show and presented no danger to the Littles' profits.

He stepped out from behind the cluster of women he'd used as a blind and headed toward them. Why was Lydia withholding the ledger? "Do you have anything with you to back up your statements, Miss King?"

Lydia closed her eyes and her face relaxed, and then she slumped.

He caught her elbow lest she topple to the floor. "Are you all right?"

Her mouth moved, but he couldn't hear what she said with all the shuffling of feet and the buzz of surprise flitting about the room.

Sebastian yanked her away from him and then jabbed him in the chest with his long, knobby fingers. "I don't recall asking you to get involved. This is between me and Lydia."

Nicholas refused to push back, but he closed up the space between them. "Not when you force her to speak in front of all your *friends*." He glanced around the crowd, seeing a few men in attendance he hadn't been able to find earlier that morning.

"Everyone knows you have it in for me, Lowe. You have it in for anyone who tries to do anything that hurts your pocketbook. *You're* the devil profiting from the red-light district. And don't try denying it—five blocks from your home wasn't close enough to its pleasures, so you hid a handful of painted ladies in that mansion of yours to fire up more than your multitude of fireplaces."

Nicholas clenched his fists but worked up a sly smile. "Seems one of us is lying."

Sebastian did nothing more than shift an eyebrow.

"Lydia, didn't you have some proof other than an overheard conversation?"

"Yes." She clutched her bag and took a step closer. "I made some educated guesses with the evidence I collected."

"What do you have?" Sebastian grabbed for her bag, but she stepped out of reach.

The second she pulled out a dark red book, Sebastian's eyes glinted and the curl of his lip turned nasty. Nicholas worked hard not to grunt with victory. Whether or not she understood what was in the book, she had the right thing in her hand. The list of names she'd given Caroline had certainly helped narrow his search today.

"How did you get that?" His hand moved to his forehead and pushed back at his receding hairline. "I've not given you permission to rifle through my client's confidential files."

"You're right, I obtained it without permission, but—"

"You broke into my office and stole confidential information." He lifted his hand off the top of his head. "And we're supposed to believe *you're* the upright individual?"

She held up the ledger. "The entries are cryptic, but it seems Sebastian is keeping a tally of money passing hands between him and several prostitutes and saloon owners."

"I'm a lawyer. I don't choose my clients."

"Then why are you trying to hide their names? These records are vague and sparse. And some of it seems to have interest tacked on, like you're getting money back on a loan. Lawyers aren't in the business of giving out loans." She opened the ledger and ran her hand down a column. "And here you wrote 'jewelry and perfume.'"

"Prostitutes don't always have ready cash," he spoke through gritted teeth.

"But it's next to Reed's name—like you purchased it from Reed's."

He flung out his hands. "This is all conjecture—I could've sold it to him."

"Reed's isn't a pawnshop."

"Or I could've returned it."

"Why are you coming up with possibilities, Sebastian?" Nicholas took the book from her shaky arms. "Why don't you explain what the entries in this ledger actually are?"

Sebastian's jaw was so tight his neck muscles bunched. "I have no reason to explain my paperwork to you."

He reached for his ledger, but Nicholas held it away.

Mayor Little came out of the crowd, nonchalantly wiping his spectacles. "It seems to me Miss King no longer wishes to be engaged to my son, and instead of behaving like a lady and ending things privately, she's trying to justify stringing my son along by making him look like a criminal."

"I . . . I didn't string . . ." Lydia's face turned red.

"When did you decide you didn't want to marry my son, then?" Mayor Little's lips twitched.

"A few days ago."

"So . . . since the beginning, you've loved my son, and you've just now decided you don't?"

"N-no." She played with the buttons below her neckline.

"Hold on." Nicholas edged between them. "You, sir, are dodgy, along with your son. Let's not turn the attention away from what Lydia's brought up about your—"

"You're the problem, Lowe." The hot air from the mayor's bellow hit him in the face. "You've stolen my son's fiancée out from under him—of course you'd stick up for her. Good riddance." He clapped his son on the shoulder. "Let's call off this gathering before any more mudslinging happens. I'm frankly tired of that in politics. I don't want to have to deal with any more of this on a day that was supposed to be happy. Mr. Lowe has obviously tainted Lydia's weak mind with suspicions he wishes were true so he can dodge the legal fees he's incurred for running a brothel."

Nicholas was done having the mayor steer them off topic. He held up a hand to stay the few who were trying to slink out. "Let's review. We have what Lydia's overheard."

"She can say she overheard anything she wants." Sebastian shook his head. "Even if that is what I said—and it isn't—it's not worthy evidence."

"And a ledger"

"Stolen property."

"And a roomful of witnesses."

"Witnesses to unsubstantiated accusations?" Sebastian chuckled. "Did you forget which one of us is a lawyer? I'd advise you to forget any ambitions you have to pass the bar. You'd be wasting your money if you think any of this proves I've committed a crime."

Nicholas opened the ledger and turned it toward Lydia. "Where are the prostitute names you found in here?"

She flipped a page and pointed to the middle of a column. "Well, D. Emma I think stands for Dirty Emma. I know her."

The room swelled with a collective gasp.

Lydia sent them a wicked glance. "For those of you who missed the interrogation I received at church a while back, Dirty Emma was in charge of the abandoned children I was trying to find homes for. So I figured these other lady names with initials—since I know no ladies who go by initials—were also prostitutes. There's an I. Mary, an L. Liz, and an S. Annie."

Nicholas nodded. "I know an Irish Mary and Dirty Emma."

Sebastian scratched his head and gestured about the room. "Funny how two people who intimately know prostitutes are accusing me of wrongdoing because I've helped them with their legal matters."

"Well, let's just see if Emma and Mary can shed some light on why they're in this book." Nicholas gestured toward the small window in the swinging kitchen door.

Caroline's sister, Moira, who'd called herself Irish Mary since moving to Teaville, swaggered out in a dark pink silk, feathers flouncing in her hair. The dark circles under her eyes left behind by her sickness made her scowl look even fiercer.

Dirty Emma, true to her name, traipsed out in a dress that had seen better days. Her hair fell in greasy ringlets, and he'd bet the hand tucked into the folds of her full skirt held a silver flask.

The ladies in the room seemed to move en masse a step or two in the opposite direction.

All but Lydia. She took a few steps forward. "Emma? Mary?" They both nodded.

"What kind of business have you with—"

"This is ridiculous. Who's going to take the word of a prostitute for anything?" The mayor blubbered. "They're the dregs of society—given to drink and tomfoolery and hissy fits. They've both spent time in jail this past year—multiple times, if I'm not mistaken. Where's Officer Vincent?"

Moira put her hands on her hips. "The mayor's only afraid I'll tell you why his son visits me." She sashayed a little ways down the room, looking the men up and down. "Same reason why Mr. Custer here and Mr. Jones—"

A red-faced Mrs. Jones slapped Moira across the cheek. "You . . . lying . . ." The string of words Mrs. Jones put together caused her husband to blush more than he had when Moira stopped in front of them.

Dirty Emma chuckled. "I'll tell you why I'm in that book. Little busts me out of the clinker if I make myself available for free to some of his clients." She grabbed a goblet of punch off an abandoned serving tray and drained it.

"As my father said, they're nothing." Sebastian still had his hands on his hips, but he seemed to be shaking.

Nicholas beckoned toward the kitchen again, and three men and a woman stepped out. "I've got the owners of the Pink Lady, the Red Hot Robin, the Charlatan, and the Dutch Tulip here. Two will testify that you fund some of their enterprises or provide them legal services in exchange for those they provide, and two of them say you help cover up the fact that they run a brothel without bothering to disguise it as anything but, even though you're rather intent on fining me for doing so."

"Again, I'm the mayor's son, an upstanding citizen of Teaville, a lawyer—these men and women are scum. Their testimony against mine—"

"Then perhaps I can provide you with testimonies from your peers." Nicholas waved his hand one last time. Mr. Falstaff led out a small group of men that included one police officer and a county commissioner.

Nicholas looked around the room, trying to catch the eyes of a few men who'd refused to join him this morning and a few he hadn't yet talked to, who he hoped might be malleable depending on the direction of the wind. "Anyone else want to bolster our case? It's the best time to get out from under the Littles—do it now, or it'll never be done. They'll bear down harder if they aren't defeated now."

About five other men crossed the room, cutting a wide path around where Sebastian and his father stood fuming.

Mayor Little gestured toward Judge Greenbriar. "Sir, what make you of this?"

"Frankly, I'm appalled. Seems to be rather extreme lengths to break off an engagement. Even if the accusations against Sebastian of dallying with prostitutes are true, there's nothing out of the ordinary about that."

Nicholas raised both his hands. "Perhaps we should ask Circuit Judge Williams if he heard anything worth trying that you didn't." Because of Greenbriar's well-known friendship with the Littles, he'd spent the wee hours this morning racing to the next county to make sure there would be another judge in this room.

The tiny, well-dressed fellow who'd been standing near the entrance moved out into the crowd. "From the few men I talked to this afternoon combined with this display, I'd say there's some likely cases of extortion and obstruction of the law that need to be heard. Maybe after hearing the testimony of these others—"

"How could you two!" Mrs. Little swaggered forward.

"What?" Mayor Little barked.

"I cannot believe my own son would undermine the work I do. To think, you've had me raising money for your campaigns—"

"Mother," Sebastian snarled, "you've forgotten that Lydia's accused you too. Don't anger me or I'll expose everything you've done to make the saloons pay for your—"

"I told you marrying her was a bad idea." His mother glared up at him. "But no, a pretty face was all you wanted. Not your mother, who's slaved for years to get you where you are."

Mayor Little shoved his way between them. "Yes, Rebecca. If only we'd followed your plans . . ."

Nicholas pulled Lydia over to her mother and nodded at the officers he'd brought along to help. Since Lydia's father had disappeared, he assisted Mrs. King from her chair, and then, with Lydia on his other arm, they marched out as the crowd's racket buried the Littles' shouting match.

48

Lydia couldn't control her trembling, and the crisp December air wasn't helping. Accusing Sebastian and his family had turned her insides to jelly. Even Nicholas's presence—though very welcome—hadn't kept the involuntary tremors from escalating.

His arm tightened around hers. "You should buy yourself a thicker coat."

Yes, that was what she was worried about now—coats. "I'll burrow under a quilt once we get home." And hide there for a year.

Nicholas stopped suddenly, and Mama, still attached to his other arm, stumbled forward.

"I'm so sorry, Mrs. King." He steadied Mama and repositioned her thick shawl.

She waved her hand. "Don't apologize. I'm still standing."

"I didn't mean to stop so suddenly, but I realized your daughter can't go directly home—she needs to go to my place. My lawyer wants to talk to the witnesses. I've got to go back in and gather up everyone I can. Then I'll meet you at the mansion. We'll have to move quickly, because the Littles and Judge Greenbriar will surely start working to stop us once they get out of the hotel. And I'm afraid they'll do anything to save themselves."

Was their threat on her life still a possibility? Lydia shuddered even more. Would she ever be safe at home? Would Mama? She looked back over her shoulder. "Where's Papa? He should escort Mama home."

Nicholas cleared his throat. "He's probably helping put out fires."

"He's not helping put out anyone's fires other than his own." Mama huffed, then shifted her weight, leaning heavily on Nicholas's arm.

"I'll have Mr. Parker take you home, Mrs. King, freeing your hired carriage to take Lydia to—"

"It was Sebastian's hired carriage." Despite the weight on her heart, Lydia surrendered to a small chuckle. "I doubt he'd be thrilled to pay my way to your place. Though I'd like to see his face if someone handed him such a bill."

Nicholas only smiled a little. "As funny as that'd be, he'd only forward it to you, and I don't want you dealing with him more than necessary." When his own vehicle turned the corner, he stepped closer to the curb. "So I'll hire you another."

She frowned. She wasn't a charity case—not yet anyway. And did he not want her to ride with him?

Of course, rescuing her was enough. He'd helped her escape Sebastian, just as she'd prayed.

I'm so sorry I haven't even thanked you. You got me out of my predicament, and yet here I am wanting more. Forgive me and thank you.

"You've done plenty for us," Lydia said, trying to smile though her dissatisfied heart rebelled. "We can pay for the coach."

Nicholas eyed her. "When a rich man offers to pay, you should say, 'Thank you, sir.'"

"Sir?"

His face remained serious, except for the tilt of an eyebrow. "Unless there's something else you'd rather call me?" The lightness of his voice made her hair prickle on her arms, heightening the effects of the goose flesh caused by the cold wind seeping into her coat.

Surely he wasn't flirting with her. "Thank you, Mr. Lowe."

His eyebrow lost its elevation, and his lips almost formed a childish pout.

Had he wanted her to use his Christian name in front of her mother? They had called each other by their first names while whisking about town for the last two months, but it was against all propriety. And the sound of his name on her lips would likely clue Mama into her feelings for him. Worrying about her spinster daughter's enemies was enough for her dying mother to fret about. Lydia didn't want Mama also pitying her for loving someone out of her reach.

Nicholas closed his eyes, shaking his head a little.

Mr. Parker set his brake and jumped down.

"Will you be all right at home alone?" Lydia resituated Mama's slipping shawl.

"I'll be fine." She patted her daughter's arm. "You tell them everything you know, no matter how long it takes. I doubt I'll die tonight."

Lydia kissed her before Mr. Parker helped her into Nicholas's fanciest coach. Lydia waved good-bye to Mama while Nicholas hailed one of his hotel employees.

A young man in a fancy black suit and yellow-cord frogs jogged toward them.

"Run to the livery and procure a carriage or whatever's available, as long as it's covered."

The young man changed direction midstep just as the thin, high clouds above them decided to loose miniscule bits of ice.

Nicholas raked his hand through his hair, displacing the little white crystals decorating his wavy locks. Was it that long ago in his lumberyard office that she'd been tempted to brush the sawdust from his hair despite being incensed he'd refused to listen to her request for a donation?

He cleared his throat and stared off down the brick street, which was quickly being covered with shimmering icy slivers. "I wish all this could have happened less publicly, for your family's sake."

She shrugged. Nothing could be done about it now. She

tightened the collar about her neck to ward off the chill, not only from the weather but also from the awkwardness between them. Hopefully she was the only one who felt it. If she hadn't realized she was in love with him on the carriage ride to the hotel, she'd feel nothing but overwhelming gratefulness for his rescue. "Thank you for coming when you did. If you hadn't shown up . . ." But maybe she was still in trouble. What if Sebastian wiggled out of this?

Nicholas kept his hands firmly in his pockets. "If you were brave enough to accuse Sebastian in public, the least I could do was gather support for your case. I should've done more in the past to stop the Littles, but I figured I didn't have enough evidence—and I hadn't the motivation to find any. Besides, no one seemed to care. Many still don't, or are too cowed to admit what they know."

"I was more foolish than courageous."

"There's often a fine line between those two." Nicholas stared off in the distance again and cleared his throat.

Before he could say anything else, a carriage turned the corner and stopped in front of them.

A young, acne-scarred man leapt down from his high seat. "Are you Mr. Lowe?"

"I am."

"Mighty chilly out here, isn't it?" The driver opened the side door of his vehicle.

Lydia couldn't help but wish he'd kept right on driving. How many more times would she be alone with Nicholas before life separated them completely?

Nicholas took her hand to help her in. "I'd say it's more than chilly, considering the lady's fingers are like ice." He dropped her hand before she could step in and stuck his head into the interior. "I hope you have lap robes in here."

Without his fingers around hers, they really did feel cold.

After the driver helped him pull out a few robes from under the seats, Nicholas paid him. "I have business to attend to before I can leave. So take her to my place and escort her inside personally. If you've the time, my housekeeper should have coffee and pastries awaiting the crowd. Feel free to have some before you return to work."

"Obliged." He pulled out change, but Nicholas held out his hand.

"Keep it, and take care to avoid the ruts."

The young man smiled at the large bill in his hand before stuffing it in his pocket. "Yes, sir."

Nicholas's eyes twinkled when he looked back at her. "See? When a rich man offers you something, you say, 'Yes, sir.'"

The driver held out his hand for hers with a flourish. "M'lady."

If she weren't so miserable, she'd have smiled at the man's courtier-like gesture and terrible English accent.

Nicholas stood back a little.

He wasn't going to help her into the carriage?

Whether one man helped her inside or another, there was nothing special about the gesture either man would have extended to a woman, be she thirteen or eighty. Though that knowledge somehow didn't keep her from wishing Nicholas had stepped forward.

She sniffed before taking the driver's offered hand and climbed in. Dragging the fur onto her lap in the empty coach, she tried to thwart the threatening tears by not allowing herself to blink. There was no reason to cry. She was better off alone than with Sebastian.

The coach rocked a bit as the driver climbed onto his seat.

But before he called to his team, Nicholas opened the door and popped his head in. "Don't leave my place until we've talked."

She swallowed, but her throat was too tight to do anything but nod. She wouldn't cry in front of him; she only had to hold off a few more minutes until he disappeared.

He looked at her far too intently. "It'll be all right, Lydia."

She'd begun to think Nicholas was right about most everything, but he certainly wasn't right about that.

Reaching over, he cupped the side of her head and rubbed his thumb against the corner of her eye, wiping away a traitorous tear. "I'll take care of everything."

And then he was gone.

She caught a glimpse of Nicholas out the window striding toward the hotel's front doors before her coach lurched forward.

The driver turned a corner, and she stuffed her cold hands under the lap robe, wishing herself as warm and happy as she should be after narrowly escaping a life filled with listening to a criminal's dissatisfaction with his apple cobbler.

She'd not make a good match for Nicholas anyhow, no matter how she wished it to be different. What could she bring to any kind of relationship that would help him be better than he already was? Her pretty blue eyes had been the only thing her father thought would capture a man, and Nicholas could have his pick of pretty blue eyes. Miss Renfroe's were more vivid than hers, anyway. Some days they looked a deep teal, others a rich blue. Much prettier than her glassy blue ones by miles.

Being in love with him didn't change the fact that he was out of her reach.

Lydia leaned her head against the upholstered interior and tried not to think of Nicholas being engaged to someone else one day. She had enough of a headache—no reason to aggravate it with tears that wouldn't change a thing.

49

Leading Mr. Morris from the office to his front door, Nicholas turned and gave his lawyer a weary smile. "Thank you for staying until the end. This took much longer than I anticipated."

The much shorter man shrugged on his coat. "That's just how it goes sometimes, but the more information we get while emotions run high, the better."

"And I'm sure after their arrest this afternoon, Roger and Sebastian will make this as messy as possible."

"If only they hadn't been allowed to post bail. Seems wrong that two people who've inflicted misery upon so many get to sleep comfortably in their own beds." Mr. Morris pulled his hat down farther to cover his ears.

Nicholas opened the door for his lawyer, who buried his hands into his coat pockets and scuffled out into the darkness toward his awaiting ride. Falling snow diffused the light of the lanterns on his vehicle.

"See you tomorrow." Nicholas waved, then slipped back into his warm house and headed toward the last place he'd seen Lydia.

But his music room was empty. Had someone given her a ride home while he'd been in the middle of a conversation? He ran a hand through his hair and sighed.

Keeping his attention on the men who'd gathered at the mansion after the confrontation with the Littles had proven arduous with her in his house. The only thing that had gotten him through the men's lengthy debate over how to get a conviction to stick to the Littles was Lydia sitting quietly in the corner, waiting for him. Or so he'd thought.

His housekeeper walked in and gathered a handful of dirty glasses off the end table.

"Who did Lydia leave with? Didn't I tell you I wanted her to stay?"

Caroline swiped her brow with the back of her sleeve and mumbled—no, more like muttered things he was probably glad he couldn't hear.

"I'm sorry, it's not your fault she left." He collected an armload of glassware from his weary friend. "And let me help you."

Why hadn't Lydia told him she was leaving? Or at least made eye contact and waved good-bye? Probably because she knew he would demand she stay—regardless of how late it was.

How had she left without him noticing?

He couldn't go over to her house in the middle of the night. Or could he?

No. Not appropriate.

He sighed and picked up another dirty glass. The least he could do was help clean up before turning in. Caroline had to be just as tired as he was since Sadie, Josephine, and Effie hadn't been here to help with the house and the serving of the guests. He turned to her. "Why don't you hire a maid tomorrow—a nonprostitute one."

"Better yet"—she snatched the glasses from his hand and plunked them back down onto the table—"we leave the mess for the morning, I commandeer your huge bathtub for an hour, and you go apologize to Lydia."

"I can hardly apologize so late at night." Though if it had been summer, he would have had plenty of daylight left. He frowned. "And what am I supposed to apologize for?" Hadn't he just saved her?

"You broke that woman's heart and then made her sit in your presence all evening without saying a word to her."

He straightened. "I didn't do anything to break her heart."

"She certainly didn't look happy." Caroline's eyes narrowed, as if she could discover whatever it was he'd done wrong inscribed across his face.

No, Lydia certainly hadn't looked happy, but surely that wasn't his fault.

"So are you going to stand there and frown at me or go ask her about it?" Caroline pointed to the windows behind him. "She's in the garden."

He turned to look out his picture window. It was pretty much a black square, considering there was nothing but the dark evening sky behind it, though occasional fat white flakes swirled like dandelion seeds until the windows stopped their spiraling descent. He couldn't see anything through the sporadic wet trails left on the glass. "But it's snowing." Their second snow that month. Unusual for December.

"Exactly." Caroline crossed her arms over her chest. "What woman sits in a dead garden at night in the snow unless you did something to her or she's beating herself up over something?"

"Gracie never beat herself up over anything." He put his hand against the window to block the gas lamp's reflection. He still couldn't see her. "Everything was always my fault."

"She's not Gracie."

He backed away from the frosty window. He couldn't let his feelings over his late wife's betrayal freeze the part of his heart he'd decided to let go of. "No, she's certainly isn't."

"Go out and tell her."

"That she's not Gracie?" A woman's train of thought made about as much sense as peanut butter on ham.

"No, that you love her."

He licked his lips. Should he tell her that? It was certainly true, though he'd tried not to. But she'd just broken up with another man quite publicly. Would it be insensitive for him to declare himself on the same day? Or worse, what if she didn't love him in return? "But how can I be sure she feels anything for me? More than for my money, that is."

"You're just scared because your emotions are involved this time. I'm telling you, Miss King's heart is written on her sleeve. Your excuse is as worthless as dust." She snatched up her dusting rag and shook it at him. "Unchain your heart and you'll see what Miss King feels."

He took a step back and licked his lips. He'd been trying to, but the locks on those chains were rusty.

"Stop whatever it is going on in that head of yours and use the feelings you keep so tightly bound in there. As for me, I'm exhausted."

Caroline hobbled out into the hallway, and he glanced at the flurries. Was Lydia truly sitting outside?

He downed the last of his water, yet his mouth still felt dry.

After gathering his coat and gloves, he stepped into his conservatory and turned the switch for the gas lanterns along the garden walk.

Lydia startled on the bench beneath his foliage-bare trellis.

The humid hothouse air left in a rush upon his opening the all-glass door. He wrapped his muffler around his neck and stuffed the ends into his coat, then marched down the steps to the beautiful woman covered in a halo of powdery snow.

When she stood, he waved for her to sit and took a seat beside her on the bench.

She scooted away.

He forced himself not to slide closer. It wouldn't do to smother her, but the knowledge that he could get closer, that he wasn't invading another man's territory, made it difficult to stay away. Especially since it would be warmer without the gap between them.

The hushed sound of fat snowflakes and stillness filled his ears.

He rolled his tongue between his lips, trying to unglue them. "I . . . I thought you'd left."

"You told me not to." She wrapped her arms around herself. Her coat wasn't thick enough to be out in this weather, even with the slight windbreak behind them. "What did you need?"

He needed her.

But he couldn't talk of love when she looked sad enough to attend a funeral. He slumped forward and stared at the dark, shadowy line of bushes surrounding the garden. Maybe he shouldn't attempt to talk too much about his feelings tonight. Surely she'd been through enough upheaval today. Besides, if she loved him, as Caroline suggested, why would she be outside, hiding in the cold? "I wanted to tell you I'm sorry things with Sebastian didn't turn out better for you."

"You have nothing to apologize for. I was never thrilled with him anyway."

So she wasn't pining over the loss of her ideal future? He relaxed against the bench and extended his legs. "And how would you wish for your life to go?"

"For one, I wish I didn't have to worry so much about money."

He tensed. "Yes, money. Whether you have too little or too much, it's always causing problems."

"It's not that I need it for myself, but I'm worried for Mama. The doctor hasn't changed his opinion, says it's only a matter of time." She shrugged and burrowed farther into her coat. "I know the money wouldn't cure her, but if Sebastian's father figures out a way to boot us from our house—which I'm sure he will as soon as he has a free second—I need to provide for her. No matter how hard I try not to be, I'm afraid."

"Is the librarian's salary not enough? I may be a little removed from a working man's salary, but I thought I figured well enough for a modest living."

"Yes, it's likely adequate." She sighed.

"Then that's not the real reason you're frowning?"

"No, the librarian position is perfect for me, and yet I'm not satisfied." She huffed as if she were mad at herself.

"You no longer want the job?" His heart paused for the briefest of moments. If the orphanage idea fell through, he'd barely see her if she quit.

"The job's fine. It's just that I'm the most selfish creature in the world." She slumped. "And Papa's right. All those books put crazy ideas in my head."

He was lost. Was she talking to herself or him? "What is this about books?"

She kicked at the gravel at her feet, making a fresh spot for the snow to cover. "I've read too many fairy tales, I'm afraid. I wanted God to send me a knight—like Perseus freeing Andromeda, or Saint George and Princess Sabra. But I didn't get one, and now I wish I didn't have to go back to my peasant-like life."

He couldn't help but smile at her turning a serious conversation into a literary allusion. "Instead, Sebastian turned out to be the monster holding you captive."

"Yes." She turned her head toward the faint horizon. "Except I never really thought he was a knight. I figured I'd finally matured enough to realize God didn't put me in a fairy tale and that I had to deal with real life . . ." She huffed and hung her head, but then she looked sideways at him for just a second.

A second long enough to see that precious heart on her sleeve, or rather in her eyes.

He scooted closer, and she scrunched tighter, as if she could create space by making herself smaller. "Fairy tales are entertaining, but what about after the story? When the knight marries the princess, do you think he actually makes a decent husband? Just because he wears expensive armor and rescues her doesn't mean he's a good man. He might slay as many innocent dragons as he does evil ones. The princess marries a man, not a saint. Well, unless he's Saint George." He grinned, but she didn't smile back.

"That doesn't make saving a damsel in distress any less honorable." Lydia pulled on the scarf around her neck but didn't look at him. "And if he stoops to marry his damsel, he's the one most likely to be disappointed. A pretty face doesn't guarantee she can do anything useful."

Ah, so they were more alike than he thought. She didn't believe she deserved him any more than he believed he did her. "So a poor maiden can't ever be worthy of a knight, not even a flawed one?"

"What could a commoner possibly do to make a knight happy?"

He picked up a stray piece of her hair, smoothed the tendril behind her ear, and then let his finger wander down to the small section of her exposed neck. "You help him figure out which dragons need to be vanquished and which can be redeemed and trained."

She finally looked at him for more than a moment, her eyes as dazzling as the sparkling flakes dancing in the moonlight. "Are we still talking about mythology?" Her voice shook.

"No." He smiled. "I never thought we were."

A gust of wind swept away the white cloud of their breath. Her chattering teeth pulled at his heartstrings.

He captured her icy hand. "We should go inside and sit by the fire."

"Please don't change the subject."

"All right." He pulled his coat off and tucked it behind her.

"I can't take your coat. You'll have nothing to keep you warm," she whispered, the wet snow upon her hair glittering like a crown.

With his hand cupping her face, he wiped a snowflake off her brow with his thumb. "And you can't think of another way to warm me up, damsel?"

"Don't tease me, Nicholas." Her voice was a breathless whisper.

He couldn't tell if she sniffed because of threatening tears or the cold, damp air.

He slid closer. "Oh, but I'm not teasing you."

Her eyes grew wide. "Don't come closer." Then her gaze dropped to his mouth. "I'll . . . I'll get myself in trouble."

He dipped his head until her warm breath tickled his chin. "Is this close enough for trouble?"

The low hum emitting from her throat made his pulse thrum, but she didn't move.

He raised an eyebrow. "I have to get closer? I don't remember damsels being so stubborn about leaping into a knight's arms."

She laid her dainty hand against his chest, and his heartbeat accelerated. She shook her head. "For once, I don't want to live in a fanciful story."

"Neither do I. I'd rather live with you. Every day of my life."

Her gaze flashed up to his, her eyes glistening. "You do realize I'm not worthy of you?"

"What? Did you forget to tally up how many mistakes I've made? You've certainly not missed how harsh I am on others, myself, and you. Though I do have one knightly quality—I'll pledge my fealty unto death."

"And why am I worth that sacrifice?" Her voice caught.

"Because when you're excited, I'm in awe of your passion. I may not feel the same, but your honest emotions capture me. They make me want to feel like you do. I might choose to attack problems with strategy and logic, but your empathy could keep me from destroying something precious." He ached to take her hands, but she'd buried them in his coat. "And I've become a much better man because I've met you."

"I'll let you down."

The snow stopped, and he looked up at the hulk of a house that tied him to a woman who had never stirred the feelings swirling inside of him right now. Though these new feelings made him feel more vulnerable than Gracie had ever made him feel, he no longer wanted to tamp them down. Hadn't he said earlier today there was a fine line between being foolish and courageous?

He'd been foolish with Gracie. Courage was what he needed, even if that put his pride at risk. "You'll only let me down if you tell me *no*."

"No to what?"

"Loving me, wholeheartedly, devotedly, passionately. With every fiber of your being as only you can do."

With a finger, he pulled her chin toward him, her eyes as open and vulnerable as she'd made his heart. He swiped his thumb along her lower lip. "I love you, Lydia. You can have both my heart and pocketbook if you want them."

"Truly?"

"Yes." What did it all matter now anyway? His desire to keep a tight rein on his money had only driven Gracie away, and he'd been hard-hearted enough to let her leave. But his heart was no longer stone, though it was still tense, waiting for a blow. "But I'm not certain how you feel."

"The same," she whispered. "Though you could throw your pocketbook in the fireplace, for all I care." She huffed. "To think, I thought I needed such a thing. But if you say you'll take care of my mother, even without a penny to your name, I believe you could." She brought one hand out from beneath his coat and ran it slowly up his sleeve and onto his shoulder. "Aren't you cold?"

Everywhere but where her hand lay. "Yes."

"Maybe I should do something to remedy that." Her voice wavered. "Like you said."

He captured her hand and kissed her palm. "Please."

Her fingers caressed his temple as she brushed back the hair at his forehead. The shimmer in her eyes had nothing to do with the light of the flickering gas lamps.

His gaze traveled to her lips, pale and glistening in the lamplight. "Show me how much you love me, my fair Lydia."

"I'll try every day you let me." She closed the space between them, her lips brushing against his as soft and light as the snow-flakes floating around them.

When her fingers wove into his hair, he moved his lips against hers in an effort to give her the tender fairy-tale first kiss she'd probably dreamed of.

However, there was no sleeping beauty needing to be awakened, but rather the shaky faith of a disillusioned knight.

She pulled back, but he drew her closer, kissing her once, twice—but when she broke away again, his lungs lost all air as her mouth traveled slowly along his jawline.

"I love you, Nicholas," she whispered into his ear.

And with each brush of Lydia's lips, each subtle caress, the enchanted briars entangling his heart slipped off one by one. The moment her mouth came back to his, he couldn't contain himself any longer, and for the next minute or two, he let her know exactly what kind of man's heart lay beneath the brambles and chains she'd broken through.

Never in a hundred years had he believed someone could rouse the love that his past had cursed into lying dormant.

But then, true love's kiss was a wondrous thing.

Epilogue

"Hold it there, boys!" Lydia held out her hand, but Albert smacked the ball out of Harold's grip anyway. The ball knocked the vase of daylilies off the table. Water and glittering glass exploded against the tile floor.

The twin nine-year-old urchins froze.

Lydia closed her eyes and pulled in a deep, long breath. They hadn't done that on purpose.

Not like the toad Harold had slipped into Robbie's shirt earlier, or the pill bugs she'd found in the oatmeal yesterday, or the fishing line strung low and taut at the bottom of her bedroom door that Nicholas had tripped over this morning.

"We're sorry, Mrs. Lowe." Albert's lower lip scrunched up.

"Yeah," his brother said as he straightened and narrowed his eyes.

Albert's penitent face was most likely sincere, but Harold . . . the challenge in his stance was all too evident. He knew she wouldn't try to send him to his room again after the last time.

Although Harold was ten feet away, she cupped a hand over her protruding abdomen. Yesterday, he'd stumbled upon the secret

373

of delaying punishment—he'd punched her square on her belly, sending muscle spasms across her torso and lower back.

Lydia blew out a breath but refused to sink into the armchair. She couldn't appear powerless—if both boys turned on her, she'd have to move out of the mansion before Nicholas found someone to take over. How many more months would God make them wait? "Albert, find Miss O'Conner and tell her what happened. Harold, pick up the flowers and throw them outside. Be careful of the glass."

Albert left directly, but Harold stood his ground.

She glared right back. "Mr. Lowe's coming home for lunch. You don't want me to tell him you disobeyed, especially since you've been told countless times not to play ball in the house."

Harold sniffed and threw back his shoulders, but thankfully bent to pick up the flowers.

After he finished, she sank into the chair cushions and rubbed her tight stomach as she watched him march outside with the lilies. He passed his older sister making daisy chains in the yard with the newest orphan—a beautiful little girl who wouldn't talk, wouldn't let anyone touch her, and wouldn't sleep anywhere but the floor.

As much as Lydia wished she and Nicholas could stay at the mansion to ease open the tightly clamped shell around the newest toddler's heart, she had to worry about her own child now. And some of the children who came through the orphanage, like Harold, arrived out of control, lashing out at the other children. Raising her own child would be hard enough without the weighty baggage these cast-off children brought with them.

And if a newborn stealing her sleep would exhaust her even more than she already was, she wouldn't have the energy to do the orphans much good anyway.

Lydia jumped as hands clamped onto her shoulders but quickly closed her eyes when the scent of Nicholas's sandalwood soap registered. His thumbs rubbed in circles against the tightness in her neck at the base of her skull.

She hung her head and let out a sigh. "That feels wonderful."

"Rough morning?"

"Harold." That one word summed it up.

"He hasn't threatened you again, has he?" His hands stilled on her neck. "Maybe I should find him another home until the new couple takes over."

"No, he didn't, but the look in his eye . . ." *Wait*. She turned faster than she should have and grimaced at the muscle she pulled in her side. "New couple? You mean someone's finally volunteered?"

"Yes." His lazy smile told her he wasn't smiling about someone taking over, but rather that somehow he still found her beautiful despite her puffy ankles and the strange light splotches spreading across her forehead.

She put a hand to her face as if she could hide the darkening freckles from his view, though he said doing so only made him want to kiss them all the more. "I thought we were going to interview all the prospects together. How can we be sure they'll love them—all of them—considering some are . . . a handful."

"That's why I came home early—they'll be here any minute." He leaned over and kissed her neck before coming around to the front of her chair. "You can tell me what you think when they get here." He got down on his knees, wrapped his arms around her middle, and rested his head on her belly as he did whenever he came home from work these days. His fingers searched across her abdomen, so she positioned his hand over the little appendage that was the most active at the moment.

"I'd hoped you'd stay for a little while. I could use a nap."

He hummed against her side. "But if I let you nap, you'll sleep until dinner."

The scurrying in her tummy moved to the left, where Nicholas's rumbling voice vibrated against her skin.

"I think he knows your voice."

Nicholas pressed his lips against an elbow or a knee to talk against her stomach. "Hello, princess."

Lydia tensed against a kick. "Prince."

"We'll see." Nicholas murmured silly sentences against her stomach until her insides were nearly bruised.

She slipped a hand in between Nicholas's lips and the battering ram inside her. "Oh, stop, love. He's going to bruise me from the inside out."

The door chimes trilled. Nicholas gave her hand a quick kiss, then groaned as he pushed himself up. "I'm too old to be on the floor."

"You get no sympathy from me." She held out her hands for him to help her up, but once she was on her feet, he pulled her against him and nuzzled below her ear in the way he knew made her shiver.

She felt the heat rush up to meet his lips against her neck. "Caroline could usher the guests in any minute."

"They won't mind." He trailed some more kisses along her neck. "Too much."

She pushed him away and smacked him with a light hand. He caught it, kissed it, then escorted her into the entry.

Bernadette and Pastor Wisely stood arm in arm by the fireplace.

"Bernadette?" Lydia looked to Nicholas to see if this was the couple he meant. "Are you here to . . ."

The older woman swept over and kissed her on the cheek. "You look radiant."

"If *radiant* is the new word for *tired*, I'll admit to it."

"Well, then, I think it's time we stepped in and helped."

Nicholas beamed, looking less stressed than he had in weeks. He held out his hand. "Meet our new house parents."

"Really?" Lydia squeezed Bernadette's hand and looked her square in the eye. "I don't want you to compromise your convictions just because we're having trouble finding someone."

"I thank you for being one of the few who's been gracious to me as I've struggled, but I'm ready to do more than just help around the church now. Besides, Evelyn wants to do this as well."

"Evelyn?" She frowned, but then saw the pastor's daughter in the foyer talking with Robbie. She'd squatted down beside him to talk to him. "Is she going to live here too?"

Bernadette nodded, a slight frown on her face.

Lydia couldn't help but frown along with her. So Mr. Patterson hadn't interested her? Lydia doubted any man could deserve a woman as sweet as Evelyn, but she'd hoped the new druggist would have caught her fancy, especially since he was at least four inches taller than Evelyn, and she'd certainly seemed to have caught his eye.

When would Evelyn have the time to find a husband if she worked here? "But this isn't a small project, it's a dawn-to-dusk project."

"I've never been against doing something huge but rather doing things just because they were expected, or for any reason that wasn't for the Lord. God has given me this desire, and so He'll provide . . . as long as I don't abandon Him. I know He won't abandon me."

"But your congregation?" She looked at Pastor Wisely. "Some of them have never accepted what we're doing. Are you planning to quit the ministry?"

"This *is* ministry, no matter what anyone says, but no, I still intend to pastor." He reached for his wife's hand. "I've watched Bernadette during the time she's been questioned and even shunned for following her convictions, and yet she's grown in her faith in the Lord—into a woman I couldn't be more proud of. If I lose a congregant or two, well, the Lord will have to deal with them."

"But I don't think we'll lose that many." Bernadette smiled at her and Nicholas. "The change in opinion and hearts you two have started in this community, even within us"—she nodded toward Pastor Wisely—"is not insignificant."

"And we'll still be around to help." Nicholas's hand squeezed her shoulder in reassurance.

Lydia looked up at her husband. They would still be around?

Was it wrong to crave time alone with her new family without the drama that went on here?

Heat pressed against the back of her eyes, an all-too-common reaction to disappointments and worries lately.

Nicholas pressed his lips against her ear. "It'll be all right."

Evelyn walked over with a huge smile on her face. "Robbie is an entirely different boy than the mute, downhearted child we used to know."

Lydia looked out the windows and smiled at a glimpse of him running past the windows. A year ago, Robbie's first words were nothing more than a request for juice, but knowing he'd finally felt comfortable enough to use his voice . . . even Nicholas had been moved to tears.

Pastor Wisely rubbed his hands together. "Well, don't let us keep you. I know you've got plans."

"Plans?" Lydia looked to Nicholas. "Please tell me our plans involve a nap."

"I'm sure you can sneak one in." Nicholas put his arm around her waist and then shook the pastor's hand. "We are blessed to know we're leaving these children in the hands of a family we can trust."

"I only hope they don't wear us old people out before you're ready to return, especially if Evelyn leaves us any time soon." The pastor cleared his throat and raised an eyebrow. "Now, exactly how many children were you two planning to have?"

Lydia put a hand to her hot cheek, but before she could reply, Nicholas shuffled her out the door and into the awaiting carriage.

The scruff of Nicholas's beard scraped Lydia's temple as she nuzzled closer. She groaned. Every inch of her body reminded her how she never could get comfortable anymore, though her muscles complained more than usual at the moment. She yawned, keeping her eyes tightly shut, but the scent of sandalwood, horses, roses, and Nicholas wouldn't let her go back to sleep.

Wait, horses?

In her bedroom?

The white of Nicholas's work shirt and the shadows of the carriage interior were definitely not the green duvet and lacy curtains she'd expected when she opened her eyes. She blinked and tried to sit up. "How long have I been asleep?" Where was he taking her again?

"About an hour." He squeezed her against him, rubbing her arm.

"It took us an hour to get here?" Oh, if only her brain wasn't so fuzzy.

"No, about ten minutes. But I liked holding you—and it was quiet." He sighed. "Haven't had much quiet since we've been married, have we?"

She stretched and winced at the agony screaming in her lower back. "How long until the Wiselys take over? According to Dr. Lindon, we've got two months before we'll have a baby stealing whatever peace and quiet we find."

"Very soon."

She rubbed at her eyes, trying to force herself awake. "Maybe no one will bother us if we move into the basement, set ourselves up in the room beside the pump room. No one goes in there."

"How about a different house entirely?" He opened the door and waited for her with open arms. "Want to see it?"

"House?" She stepped down from the carriage and blinked against the sun. "You didn't ask me about buying a house."

"I wanted it to be a surprise."

"What if I don't like it?"

He rolled his eyes. "Then I'll buy you another one."

She shook her head. She was still adjusting to having the means to do such an unnecessary thing. "I'm sure I'll love whatever you've found for us. You're too detailed to not have thought it through."

"I love that you trust me."

"Because you deserve it." She kissed him lightly on the lips, then looked around the construction site she'd seen many times in the past year. The massive unfinished stone-and-brick structure with floor-to-ceiling windows along the front sat amid a newly sodded lawn. "We're going to live in the new library? Did you include an apartment that I missed?"

"No, but I figured a short walk from our new house to a building full of bookshelves would make you happy."

She squeezed his arm, purposely keeping her eyes off the lovely two-story Queen Anne complete with a three-story turret and wraparound porch she'd envied as it had slowly taken shape over several months. "Short walk to which house?"

"The one you haven't been able to keep your eyes off of lately."

She wiped away a tear. He'd been building it for her this entire time without even a word? She gave him a peck on the cheek before he led her across the road. "I don't suppose you put an elevator in there, because lately I've been really fond of the elevator."

"Sorry, but that would be a little more ostentatious than I'd be comfortable with in a normal-sized home." He helped her up the wide porch stairs and fished a key out of his pocket. "I did redraw the library's plans to include an elevator though. If we can ever get Theresa out of bed and into that wheelchair we gave her, she can choose books for herself from either level of the library."

"She'll feel terrible not using an elevator you put in for her." Lydia kissed his cheek. "An excellent, sneaky plan." Over the past year and a half she and Nicholas had visited Theresa and Alec many times. Nicholas had been relieved that their friendship survived after he'd come clean about who he was, but the couple resisted handouts more now than ever.

Nicholas's mischievous grin—the one she now recognized he'd given her back when she'd handed him those fated three wishes—made her sigh. How had she ended up with such a handsome man?

"What are you thinking?"

"Nothing your ego needs to hear."

"Hmmm, I love you too." He gave her a quick peck on the cheek before opening the door.

He pulled her inside and turned a switch. The lamps along the wall lit. "No fancy Tiffany gasoliers or Italian marble or hand-painted walls, but then, this house was built for you."

She sighed as she took in the white wallpaper patterned with pink roses framed by glossy walnut trim and the plush blue carpets on the hardwood floors in the empty rooms off the small entryway. "It's beautiful. I hope I remember how to keep house, though. The mansion staff has spoiled me."

"No need." He grabbed a letter off the solitary table next to one of the frosted windows that butted up against the front door. "This is from Sadie. Unfortunately, that fever Josephine had been struggling with in the last letter won out. Sadie asked if I might have work for her to do. Evidently she doesn't enjoy Montana's winters, so she willingly accepted a position as our housekeeper."

Lydia swiped at the tears in her eyes as she read the last lines of the note.

I can't think of a job I'd rather have than being able to care for Mrs. Lowe. Without her, I'd be nothing. Of course I accept. Thanks for taking a chance on me despite how young I am. I'll make you proud, Mr. Lowe.

She placed the note against her chest and sniffed. "Any day I think I couldn't be any happier with you, you do something like this."

"Oh, I'm not done yet." He took her hand and pulled her down the hallway.

"Did I forget my birthday or something? Why am I getting such special treatment?"

"It's not your birthday, just our anniversary."

"No it's not . . ." But it was, almost. "Nice try. Tomorrow's our anniversary." She wouldn't let on that her brain was too hazy to have remembered on her own. She took a deep breath, hoping to keep herself from crying over losing her mind with this pregnancy. She was all cried out . . . or should be! "There doesn't happen to be a bed upstairs already, is there?"

"Yes," he purred.

"Good." She cut her eyes toward him. "I'd like to finish my nap."

He playfully swatted her. "Not until you see the garden, sleeping beauty. It'll be too dark once you wake up again."

Their footsteps echoed through the house as they made their way to the back door. She caught a glimpse of the black-and-white-tiled kitchen before the overwhelming scent of flowers stole her attention. Nicholas held the door open, and she stepped out into a backyard surrounded by a wall of pink damask roses. A concrete bench sat in the middle of the yard, one solitary rose bush beside it. "It smells like Mama." She bit her lip to keep from crying—she probably wouldn't stop at all today if she started again.

"Fifty-one bushes—one for each year of your mother's life."

She gave in and let the tears fall as he led her to the concrete bench. "Are you trying to turn me into mush today?"

"Yes." He sat down beside her and kicked out his legs in front of him. "I'm hoping for another kiss."

"Another?"

"Do you recognize this bench?"

She ran her hand along the back and was about to make an excuse for her brain's lack of mental power, but then she remembered. She cuddled up into his side as if those cold December snowflakes were once again shimmying under her collar, her tears freezing on her face, and her heart galloping faster than any horse's hooves. "Our first kiss."

"I couldn't leave the bench behind." He tucked a strand of her hair behind her ear and let his fingers travel down her neck, his thumb riding against the length of her collarbone, his eyes glued to her lips. "And so, how much do you love me now, my fair Lydia?"

"More than then."

"Show me."

She wiped her tears and slid her arms around him.

That night in December, she'd proven she had a bit of her gambling father in her. She'd gone all in, kissing Nicholas with every ounce of desire she'd been trying to ignore. Only hours before that kiss, her life had fallen into shambles, and she'd figured if she were going to lose, she might as well lose big.

But she hadn't lost at all; she'd won a prize so great she was still counting her winnings.

Now, without any hesitation, she placed her lips against his and didn't stop showing him how much she loved him until he swooped her up and took her inside.

Author's Note

When researching how red-light districts and prostitution were dealt with back in the late 1800s and early 1900s, I found it sad how nearly hopeless it seemed for those women. It didn't matter how they got caught up in prostitution, the hope of getting out and being accepted back into good society was near nil.

Unfortunately many churches failed to offer much practical help, and the social mores of the day kept some churches from helping at all. One program that had some success—after which I patterned my hero's attempt to help his ex-prostitute maids—was one set up by the Roman Catholic Sisters of the Good Shepherd in St. Paul, Minnesota. Prostitutes wanting to leave their life behind could live in a religious community created specifically for them by these Sisters, yet it required them to be completely separated from society, denying them ordinary life and social experiences. Very few felt they could live that way until death, and some who tried—despite what awaited them outside of the Sisters' protection—returned to the world.

If interested in reading about that niche in history, *Daughters of Joy, Sisters of Misery* by Anne M. Butler was one of the books that gave me a ton of insight on the history of prostitution and, unfortunately, how the churches could have done better at that time.

Today, I'm very thankful for the churches I've had the privilege of being involved in, knowing how welcoming they are to people who've messed up, and messed up big. After reading about the churches that failed to extend the love of Christ to those who were in desperate need of it, I don't take my wonderful church family for granted!

Acknowledgments

Writing a book is such a monumental task, and I rely on so many people for help. Of course, all faults are my own, but I'd like to thank Naomi Rawlings and Glenn Haggerty for their excellent help in catching the big problems I start off with. Especially now that I seem to throw huge chunks at them to critique quickly. They are invaluable.

I'd like to thank Karen Riekeman and Andrea Strong for beta reading along with Cara Grandle, who came out of nowhere to lift me up.

I thank my mother-in-law and her quilting group for helping me get the quilting details right.

Thanks to my agent, Natasha Kern, for being willing to tell me the truth—though this time it had nothing to do with the book, but with the spiritual pit I found myself in while working on this story amid life's numerous curveballs.

I consider working with Raela Schoenherr and the Bethany House team a tremendous blessing that I don't take for granted. And with the absolutely gorgeous cover they commissioned for this book, how could I possibly forget how blessed I am!

The people who pay the most for my books are my husband and children. I'm so very blessed by the sacrifices they make so I can write. Their pride in my books warms my heart.

I really don't know why God has blessed me with these books, but I hope to glorify Him with my stories for as long as I am able.

Discussion Questions

1. In chapter five, Lydia desires meaningful conversation. In our present day, with distracting technologies, how have you successfully cultivated meaningful relationships? See Colossians 3:12–14. List things that hinder deeper bonding according to Proverbs 11:13, 18:2, and 1 Corinthians 3:3.

2. In chapter twelve, one scene involves a temperance serenade. Carrie "Mother" Nation was a well-known woman who toured Kansas in this time period serenading and protesting—even smashing bars with her hatchet in demonstrations later called "hatchetations"—in an effort to bring sinners to repentance. We cringe at the thought, but what are some present-day church practices that might make future generations cringe? Consider 1 Peter 3:15 and 1 Corinthians 9:19–23 and discuss biblical principles for evangelism and effective ways of changing people's minds.

3. In chapter fifteen, Lydia and Nick argue over protecting one's own reputation while doing the Lord's work. Who did you side with more and why? When does pursuing a good

reputation become detrimental? See 1 Corinthians 15:33, 1 Peter 2:12, and 1 Timothy 3:7–8. Then read Luke 6:6–11. How did Jesus respond to the Pharisees' legalism? How might this story apply?

4. In chapter seventeen, Nick thinks, "Why did it seem the only people driven to change things were those who'd been personally affected?" Do you find this to be true? How can we gain empathy for people in situations we've not encountered? See Romans 12:15–16, 1 John 3:17, and Galatians 6:1–2.

5. Jesus said, "Come to Me, all who are weary and heavy-laden, and I will give you rest" (Matthew 11:28 NASB). In chapter nineteen, Bernadette stops all her charitable volunteering to attend to her spiritual health. Do you agree or disagree with her chosen path? Ephesians 2:10 teaches that God gives an individualized set of "good works" for each believer. What happens when we take on more than God intended? How can we discern God's path daily? See Proverbs 3:5–6, 1 Corinthians 13:1–3, Romans 12:2, and Philippians 3:13–14.

6. In chapter forty-one, Nicholas says that "there are countless children affected by everyone's poor choices—those of the men and women who make use of the red-light district, and those who refuse to offer real help." Government laws do provide order, protection, necessary public works, moral direction, and provision for the needy. But consider 1 Thessalonians 4:11–12, James 1:27, and Deuteronomy 15:7–11, and discuss responsibilities the church has relegated to the government that God gave to believers. Why does this happen? Should anything be done about it?

7. In chapter forty-six, Lydia worries, "Those romance novels had gotten her into trouble, just as Papa always said they would." Some Christians say fiction isn't worth reading,

and yet Jesus used parables—clearly fiction—to drive home spiritual truth. See Matthew 22:1–14 and Luke 11:5–8. Has fiction imparted or strengthened spiritual truths in your life? Has it been detrimental? What principles do you apply when reading or choosing a type of fiction to read? See Psalm 101:3 and Philippians 4:8.

8. Also in chapter forty-six, Lydia suspects that she "was making God in her own image . . ." into an idol that would give her whatever she wanted. Jesus taught believers to pray to God, "Your kingdom come. Your will be done" (Matthew 6:10a NASB), yet He also commanded believers to ask with audacious faith (Matthew 21:22). Consider Psalm 37:4–6, Matthew 6:25–33, James 4:2–3, and 1 John 5:14–15. How do you hold audacious faith and submission together in your prayer life?

9. This book deals with a group of people shunned by the church and polite society of the time. Is there a group in your community that your church is not reaching well? Are some sins shrugged off while others are condemned? Consider Ezekiel 33:8, Matthew 18:15–17, Mark 2:17, Galatians 6:1, and James 5:19–20. How should we deal with sinners outside the church? Inside the church? Of all the book's characters, which one's approach is most similar to how you deal with unrepentant sinners? What can you do to improve your reach?

Much to her introverted self's delight, ACFW Carol Award winner **Melissa Jagears** hardly needs to leave home to be a homeschooling mother and novelist. She lives in Kansas with her husband and three children and can be found online at Facebook, Pinterest, Goodreads, and www.melissajagears.com.

Join Melissa's newsletter list for news about new releases, giveaways, bargains, and exclusive subscriber content on her webpage or at http://bit.ly/jagearsnewsletter.

Feel free to drop her a note at mjagears@gmail.com, or you can find her current mailing address and a list of her books at www.melissajagears.com.

More From Melissa Jagears

Visit melissajagears.com for a full list of her books.

After three failed attempts, Everett Cline is not happy when another mail-order bride steps off the train— a woman he neither invited nor expected. But is she the wife he's been waiting for?

A Bride for Keeps

When Eliza Cantrell arrives early to meet her absent groom, sparks fly between Eliza and her future husband's best friend. Could God have a different future in store for this mail-order bride?

A Bride in Store

Silas and Kate both harbor resentment over failed mail-order engagements. But for the sake of a motherless boy, can they move beyond past hurts— and overcome the secrets that have yet to come to light?

A Bride at Last